Don't Kiss the Bride

CARIAN COLE

dedication

To strangers who inspire stories in others without ever knowing the role they played

CHAPTER 1

JUDE

The screech of tires and Meat Loaf's *Two Out of Three Ain't Bad* blasting from tinny speakers pulls my attention from the blueprints I'm bent over. I frown at the silver '75 Corvette speeding into the high school parking lot next door.

It's one of my favorite songs, but not at seven a.m. on a Monday.

Until today, construction on this residential, two-story house has been quiet. No traffic buzzing by. No people milling around. Zero distractions. Exactly the way I like it. But that's all gonna change now that summer break is over and kids are back in school. Rowdy and giggling teenagers have been traipsing past the job site for the last hour.

"Hot damn," my foreman Kyle mutters under his breath and lets out a long, low whistle.

"What?" I follow his gaze to the school parking lot as I roll up the blueprints and snap a rubber band around them.

A young girl steps out of the 'vette, pushing aviator sunglasses up on top of her mane of wavy, waist-length blonde hair. She nudges the driver's side door shut with a casual sway of her hip—a move that instantly makes my mouth go dry. The door hinges squeak from decades of rust, but she doesn't seem to notice.

I push my hair out of my face, mesmerized by the fringe of the moccasins sashaying around her jean-clad calves. A black tee with a red kiss mark stamped across it peeks out from under a matching suede jacket. She struts away from the car with the attitude of a movie star who just stepped out of a limo and not a rusty old sports car that's more than twice her age.

Did she fall into a time portal that sucked her out of the seventies and dropped her straight into today?

"The things I'd like to do to her..." Kyle says, licking his lips like she's about to be his last meal.

My gut burns with a twinge of disgust and guilt as I tear my eyes off the girl. "She's a teenager, man," I say, giving his shoulder a hard shove. "Get back to work. I'm not paying you to ogle chicks."

Laughing, he hitches up his tool belt and plants a hardhat on top of his head. "*Teen* my ass, Lucky. Girls sure as hell didn't look like that when we were in high school."

True. If they did, maybe I would have been more interested in sticking around. Instead, I dropped out six months before graduation to take a full-time job.

I glance at the darkening gray sky. "The clouds are rolling in. Let's get some shit done before we get rained out. We can't afford to lose any more time on this job."

"You got it, Jude." He leers at the girl one more time before getting back to work.

Grabbing my thermos of coffee, I scan my four-man crew and try to gauge our progress. We're two days behind thanks to the homeowners' asking for last-minute changes, but I think we can get back on track and move to the next job on schedule. Ending or starting a job late pisses off the customer, and I don't need any ranting one-star reviews about my company plastered on the internet.

"Hey, Skylar!" a female voice yells. "The eighties called. They want their clothes and car back!"

I screw the lid back on my thermos as I'm sucked into the teen drama unfolding a few yards away. Three girls are laughing as they follow Corvette-girl to the rear entrance of the school. She suddenly stops, spinning around to face them in a whirlwind of blonde hair and suede fringe. They step back, bumping into each other.

"Wow." She looks the girls up and down before zeroing in on the tallest and prettiest of the group. This one's gotta be the head mean girl, based on all the movies I've seen. "Too bad your daddy couldn't buy you some brain cells to go with that nose job, Paige. The car's from the seventies."

The girls glare at her, then simultaneously roll their eyes up to their eyebrows. She stays rooted to the sidewalk, forcing them to walk around her. A smirk tips the corner of her mouth.

As she turns to enter the school, she catches me watching her. Holding my gaze with her bright eyes, she flashes me a teasing smile, blows a pink bubble of gum at me, pops it, then disappears inside.

I quickly wipe the silly grin off my face with the back of my hand and refocus my attention on my job. Distractions aren't a luxury I can afford. *Especially feisty, cute ones with trouble stamped all over them.*

"You need anything before I head outta here?" Kyle asks, glancing over the blueprints that are spread out on a table in the middle of the framed-in addition. We've known each other since high school, and he's worked for me since I started the company ten years ago. He's always the last of my crew to leave.

"I'm good." I wipe my dusty hands on a rag and shove it into the back pocket of my jeans. "See ya tomorrow."

"I'll bring ya a bagel."

After he leaves, I do a quick sweep of the job site to make sure nothing's lying around, then toss my tools in the back of my pickup. The telltale sound of an engine struggling to turn over comes from the school parking lot and I'm not surprised to see the blonde girl banging her fists against the steering wheel of her Corvette.

Hopping in the front seat, I light up a smoke and throw the truck in reverse. My rearview mirror gives me a glimpse of the girl prying the hood of her car open.

Does she even know what she's looking for?

She leans into the engine and pokes around for a few seconds, then stands back and crosses her arms.

"Shit," I mutter, swinging my truck around. I can't just leave a teenaged girl in a parking lot with a dead engine. Dark storm clouds are creeping across the sky and a warm breeze is whipping through the trees. It's gonna pour any minute.

I pull my truck into the lot and park next to her. "Need some help?" I ask from my open window.

Her mouth opens and then immediately shuts when she's interrupted by two high school jocks approaching.

"Hey, Skylar! If you need a ride, I got one for you right here." The kid grabs his junk and laughs hysterically.

"That's a little small for me, Michael," she yells back. "I'd rather ride your dad and make you call me Mommy."

Ah. She's a little firecracker, full of spark—which can be good *and* bad.

The guys aren't laughing anymore. "Fuck you, whore."

When they see me jump out of my truck, they immediately start walking in the other direction.

"You shouldn't provoke those punks," I say.

Her eyebrows rise. "Seriously? I can take care of myself, dude."

"I can see that, Sparkles. What's wrong with your car?"

"Sparkles?" she repeats.

"Yeah. You gotta lot of spark. Like a firecracker."

Her eyes turn a brighter shade of turquoise and the corner of her mouth slowly lifts.

"My grandfather used to call me smartass, so I guess Sparkles is a step up."

I let out a laugh and walk around her to look under the hood of her car. "So, what happened?"

She shrugs. "I'm not sure. It was fine this morning, now it won't start."

"Get in and try to start it."

She does, but the engine still won't turn over.

"I think it's your fuel pump," I say when she steps back out of the car.

"Oh." She chews her lower lip and stares at the engine. "Can that be fixed?"

"Yeah. You'll have to get it towed to a mechanic."

"Shit."

"Might be hard to find parts for this car, though. What year is this? '75?"

"Yeah. It was a gift."

I gently close the hood and wipe my hands across my jeans. "Nice gift, but it's probably gonna start costing you money. It's an old car."

She looks up at the darkening sky and lets out a big sigh. "Just great," she says.

"Do you or your parents have a local mechanic you use?" I ask.

Tilting her head to the side, she blinks at me. "No, um… we don't. My mom doesn't drive."

"I use the guy over on North Main. He's good and he won't rip you off. If you want, I'll call a tow and have them bring it over there for you."

"Okay. Thanks." She looks down at the ground and then slowly back up at me. "Is a tow expensive?"

The worry in her eyes tugs at my heart. "It's only about five miles so it'll be cheap. Maybe twenty bucks."

Visible relief washes over her face as I pull out my phone and arrange for a tow truck to come. Holding her purse and her backpack, she stares at her car with a forlorn expression.

I wonder if she can't afford to get it fixed. The car's older than dirt, and her clothes, which come off as hippie chic, may have been bought at Goodwill to save money, not to make a fashion statement.

I shove my phone into my back pocket. "The tow truck should be here in about fifteen minutes."

She nods and smiles. "Thank you for doing that for me."

"No problem."

Fat raindrops begin to fall, splattering onto the asphalt around us. Her eyes go wide as thunder growls in the distance.

"Do you need a ride home? I can wait with you until the tow truck comes." There's no other high school kids lingering around, and I'm gonna feel bad just leaving her here alone.

Her gaze roves over the tattoos covering my arms and hands. Takes in my shoulder-length, shaggy hair. Doubt flickers in her eyes.

Am I a nice guy doing a good deed? Or an ink-covered, longhaired scumbag with a rap sheet a mile long?

Maybe I'm both.

"Um—"

"You saw me earlier working on that house." I nod over to the new construction. "And this is my business name on the truck. I'm not gonna do anything shady. Just tryin' to be nice."

Her chin juts out. "You think rapists and kidnappers walk around with signs on them? They have jobs. Sometimes wives and kids. They look more normal than you do."

"You've got a point." I shake my head and laugh. "Okay then, I'm going to head home before we get soaked. The tow truck will be here any minute—I'm sure he'll give you a lift home. Or you could call an Uber."

"Wait," she says as I grab my door handle. "I'm kinda low on cash this week." She takes a hesitant breath. Still unsure if she can trust me. "If you don't mind giving me a ride..."

Between an Uber driver, the tow guy, and a random stranger, she's decided I'm the lesser of the evils.

Hey, I'll consider it a compliment.

"Hop in, then." A raindrop the size of a quarter splashes onto my face. "We can wait in my truck 'til the tow guy gets here."

Once in my front seat, she puts her backpack between us on the seat, like she's creating a barrier for safety.

"I have a knife," she says matter-of-factly. "If you try anything, I'll stab you in the dick."

Laughing, I light up a smoke. "Easy, Sparkles. Not everyone's out to get you. I'm staying over here on my side." I take a drag off my cigarette, wondering if this kid is just paranoid or if she has some sort of baggage that's making her suspicious. "And you shouldn't tell people you have a weapon. If I was a bad guy, now I'm anticipating you fighting back with a knife, and my first move is going to be to get it away from you. You want to surprise me with it, not fuckin' announce it."

She sighs and stares out the window. "Thanks for the tip."

If I were with my sister, I'd say *that's what she said* and we'd laugh like idiots. I'd also tell her she shouldn't be bringing a weapon to school. But my little sister is gone, no longer here to laugh at my jokes or take my advice.

I clear my throat. "My name's Jude, by the way. My friends call me Lucky."

"Are you?" She turns to face me. "Lucky?"

The tone of her voice and the way she's pinning me with her eyes unnerves me a bit. I shake my head and exhale smoke out the window. "Not really. My last name is Lucketti. That's where it came from."

"I'm Skylar."

"Nice to meet you." I drop my cigarette into an almost-empty water bottle in my console. "You got a thing for the seventies? The 'vette, Meat Loaf, the fringe suede jacket and moccasins. It's all cool, I'm just curious."

"I don't know," she says softly, spinning a silver ring around her thumb. "I guess I've just always been drawn to older things. They have character and give me a sort of comfort. They've been forgotten and tossed aside." She takes a wistful breath. "I guess I want to love them. Remind them they still matter. Does that make sense? Or does it sound stupid?"

Her eyes stay on mine, waiting, hoping I don't laugh at her. She *wants* me to understand. And I do. Her words have just snuck into my soul.

"It's not stupid at all," I say as the tow truck pulls up next to us. "And it makes a ton of sense. More than you know."

Way more than she knows.

I *am* one of those forgotten, tossed-aside things.

CHAPTER 2

SKYLAR

Jude doesn't talk much after I give him directions to my house. He's obviously not one of those people who has to fill the silence with random, dumb conversation like *what's your favorite class?* or *we really needed this rain.*

Instead, he says, "You like Pink Floyd, Sparkles?" with a cigarette hanging out of his mouth.

"Hell, yeah. Who doesn't?"

Grinning, he flicks a tattooed finger over a button on the steering wheel and the familiar, haunting sound of *Dark Side of the Moon* surrounds us with its unique lull. I don't know how many hours I've laid in bed with incense cones lit on my nightstand, staring up at the ceiling listening to this album when I felt overwhelmed with life. It always calms and grounds me.

"Nothing better than musical therapy, huh?" Jude says, as if he's reading my mind.

I nod. "So true."

We sing the lyrics together, which should be awkward, but isn't.

"You can just drop me off here and I'll walk the rest of the way," I offer when we near the bent address sign at the top of my street.

Ignoring me, he makes a left onto the bumpy road.

"Don't be silly. I told you I'd drive you home, not dump you off on a corner in the rain." He shakes his head and glances at me. "Which house is it?"

I point to the right and gather up my backpack and purse. "Two houses down. The one with the camper."

He slowly pulls into the driveway and throws the truck in park.

"Anybody home?" His forehead creases as he takes in the dark house, noticing how the thick curtains covering the windows don't allow the slightest glimpse of light in or out. No visible blue glow from a television playing in the living room. Cobwebs cover the porch light, which hasn't had a bulb in it for years.

"My mom is home. She keeps it dark because she gets bad headaches." I recite the lie well. After all, I've been telling it successfully for years. "Thanks for helping me today and giving me a ride."

"Not a problem at all."

I hesitate before saying good-bye, wondering if I'll see him again. "Are you still gonna be working on that house? By the school?"

He nods. "Yeah, we've got a few more weeks left there."

"Cool. I'll probably see you around, then?"

"I'm sure you will."

I bite my lip to hide my smile. "Well, have a good one, Jude."

"You too, Skylar. Stay outta trouble."

"I'll try."

When he smiles, one side of his mouth lifts higher than the other. All of a sudden it hits me that I'm in a car alone with a super-hot, *much* older guy with ink-covered, tan muscles, hair to his shoulders, and eyes the color of slate. He's not pretty or polished, but he's got that whole rugged, sexy construction worker package. Tight white T-shirt, faded dusty jeans and worn brown work boots. *Attractive dirtiness.*

I jump out of his truck and slam the door, but he doesn't pull away. I realize he's trying to be all noble and gentlemanly and actually watch me get to my front door safely.

Sighing, I trek up the crumbling walkway to the house, then turn to wave at him with one hand on the handle of the rusty screen door. I force a smile that says, *Yes, I'm home safe. Nothing to worry about.*

If only that were true.

I feel kinda bad when he smiles and waves back before reversing into the street, because he seems like a nice guy. After waiting a few seconds to make sure he's no longer watching me, I go around to the rear of the house and past the old camper my dad lived in. I step onto the wooden crate leaning against the house, slide my bedroom window open, and climb inside.

Fluffle-Up-A-Gus, my cat, jumps off the bed and immediately sprints over to rub against my ankles, tail held high like a flag. I scoop her up and sink my face into her soft, mink-gray fur.

"I missed you today, Gus." She erupts into purrs and kneads her paws into my shoulder. "Did you miss me? Let's get you fed."

I gently put her down and fill her dish with crunchy food, then pour water into her bowl from a plastic bottle.

Yawning, I pull my clothes off and throw them into the hamper, then carefully squat over a large bucket behind the closet door. I wipe myself with a small square of toilet paper and place it in a plastic trash bag, then scoop the clumped urine from the cat litter in the bottom of the bucket, sifting it into the trash bag. I repeat the process with the cat's litter box on the other side of the closet, then tie the bag up to throw away tomorrow.

I begin my daily ritual of cleaning my face and body with baby wipes, then spray dry shampoo into my hair.

Finally, I pull on an oversized T-shirt and a pair of cotton shorts. Gus winds around my feet, seeking attention, which I love. Smiling down at her, I kneel in front of my small refrigerator to take out a bottle of water, two slices of bread, and a tub of butter. Worry about my car plagues me as I spread butter on the bread with a plastic knife. I chew absently, trying to calculate how many extra hours I'll have to work at the boutique to pay for whatever's wrong with it. There's only so many hours I can do part-time, so it could take me weeks to pay it off.

Seems I can never catch a break.

Before I can settle into bed to watch TV, I unlock the three deadbolts on my bedroom door and peer out into the dark hallway. A sour, musty stench immediately fills my nostrils. My stomach roils with nausea. I can hear the television and see the dim flashes of light coming from the living room at the end of the hall.

"Goodnight, Mom," I call out, my voice wavering.

I can't see her, but I'm sure she's still there—on the old, green couch. It's been months since I've attempted to venture out of my bedroom, but I know she's surrounded by piles upon piles of stuff, possibly reaching the ceiling by now. To get to any other room, or even the front door, I'd have to squeeze through narrow pathways and climb over stacks of boxes and junk covering the floor. The kitchen and bathroom are so filthy and crammed I stopped using them two years ago. Even the old camper is filled to the brim with old clothes, blankets, fake plants, holiday decorations—you name it. My hopes of moving into it when it was empty were dashed when she had it filled in less than a month after my dad left.

My mother is a hoarder.

I've been forced to take refuge in my bedroom, unable to use the bathroom and running water like a normal person. There's probably two hundred bottles of shampoo, conditioner, and liquid soap out there amongst the chaotic piles, but if I try to take any, my mom will have an epic fit. I have to keep my bedroom door locked at all times because it's valuable real estate in her eyes. A twelve-by-fourteen space for her to fill with thousands of dollar-store items, life-size animal statues, treadmills, or faux fur coats.

She never uses any of the things she buys. They just get added to the museum of her belongings. But in some whacked-out way, it all gives her a kind of satisfaction that I will literally never, ever, understand.

My father lived in the camper for almost four years, unable to deal with it all. Then one day he was gone, leaving me with a note of apology and the reality of fending for myself in the jungle of this house. He tried to talk to her many times over the years, to get her to seek help, but she refused. I've done the same, but she won't listen. She shuts down and clams up. Now, she barely speaks to me. How can she when we have to wade through mountains of garbage to physically be in the same space? Instead, I have to call or text her to communicate. I used to wonder if she cared about what this was doing to me. If she worried about me climbing through windows, using a bucket as a toilet, and hiding in my room with my cat.

There's no use in wondering, though, because I already know the answers.

I close my door and relock it with a sigh of relief. I've managed to create my own little safe world in here with Fluffle-Up-A-Gus. We have everything we need to survive. It's almost as if the nightmare on the other side of the door doesn't exist.

But it's also slowly starting to feel like *I* don't exist, either.

CHAPTER 3

SKYLAR

"When are you getting your car back?" Megan asks as we walk our third lap around the track. A light fog is lingering in the air, dampening my skin and frizzing my hair. I've had PE first period every year, and my senior year is no different. It sucks getting all sweaty and worked up first thing in the morning when I'm barely even awake, but the plus side is I get to take a hot shower afterward. It fixes my dilemma of not being able to shower at home, and doesn't spark any suspicion from my classmates. During the summer, I had the interesting and skeevy experience of having to drive to a truck stop to shower twice a week.

No one knows how bad my mother has gotten. Not even Megan, and she's been my best friend since fourth grade. After a while she just accepted that I was one of those people who never had friends over. We'd be crazy not to hang out at her house, anyway. They have a theater room and a pool.

I swat a gnat out of my face. "I'm not sure when I'm getting it back. The mechanic texted me this morning and said he'd let me know after he figures out what's wrong with it."

"Hopefully it won't take long. I can pick you up every

morning, but I won't be able to give you a ride after school because I have all sorts of shit scheduled basically every day."

The only extracurricular activity I have is a part-time job.

"That's okay. I can walk after school to the boutique or home. I'm going to ask Rebecca if I can work the weekend for some extra hours. Who knows how much this is going to cost me."

"You should've just gotten a used Hyundai. They come with warranties. The 'vette is cool, and it was free, but it's practically falling apart."

"A Hyundai is just a car. It doesn't have any character."

Or sentimental value.

The 'vette was my grandfather's. He bought it as a project car a few years ago, with the hopes of totally rebuilding it and giving it to me as a high school graduation gift. I'm sure it was, in a way, a plot to keep me from dropping out. I used to sit in it in his old garage, dreaming about when I could drive it. Unfortunately, life had other plans, and it was left to me in his will. Now his dream for the car has become mine. Until then, I'm proud to drive it as-is.

Mrs. Stephens, our gym teacher, shakes her head at us as we stroll by the bleachers she's perched on. "Ladies, you're supposed to *run* around the track."

"What's the point of running if no one's chasing us?" I reply, smiling innocently.

Unamused, she pushes her dark-rimmed glasses up the bridge of her nose. "At least walk faster. You're not out here to exercise your mouths."

Megan laughs as she ties her long, black hair up in a ponytail. "This humidity is gross," she says to me. "I don't want to exercise *any*thing."

"Same."

"Friday night we should—" She stops short. "*Whoa.* Holy biceps, Batman."

"Huh?" Confused, I follow the path of her eyes, which leads me directly to Jude, who's walking down the sidewalk toward the house he's been working on. A small plastic bag from the convenience store a block away swings from his hand.

"That's *him*," I say.

"Him who?" she demands with her eyes still riveted on him.

"The guy who gave me a ride home. Jude."

He turns, and a slow smile spreads across his face when he recognizes me. A pack of classmates sprints past us on the curve of the track, momentarily blocking him from our view.

"You guys are doing it wrong," he jokes after they pass.

"We're exercising our mouths," Megan replies, walking slower and forcing me to do the same so we stay in line with him.

Laughing, he turns his attention to me. "How's the car? Any news?"

"Not yet."

Mrs. Stephens blows her whistle at us. "Ladies, if you don't start moving, you're both getting detention. Mr. Lucketti, I'm sure you remember what that's like."

My cheeks heat with embarrassment. Did he actually go to school here when he was younger?

Jude flashes her a cocky grin. "C'mon, you know you miss me, Mrs. Stephens."

"Keep walking, Lucky." A hint of affection laces her voice.

"You didn't tell me he was hot," Megan says, after Jude has disappeared behind the new walls of the addition his crew is building. "How could you leave that part out?"

"I wasn't checking him out, Meg." That might be a lie. I may have checked him out a teeny bit. "He's like, in his thirties."

"True, but he's still a total snack."

"I didn't know he went here. Has Mrs. Stephens been working here her entire life?"

Megan shrugs. "Probably. I'll bet that whistle is the only thing she's ever blown."

I make a face at her. "Gross. I'd rather not visualize her blowing anything."

"I'd like to visualize blowing that guy. Did you see all those tattoos? Does he have a cute, younger brother?"

"Calm down. I just got a ride from him. I didn't interview him for his biography."

She glances over at the house, but Lucky is nowhere to be seen. "I hope guys are that good-looking when we're that age. I don't want to marry someone cute and then have him go all bald and doughy on me." She shudders dramatically.

I bump my shoulder into hers. "You're crazy. When you marry someone, you're supposed to love them no matter what. It's part of the vows."

"Let's make a promise to see how we feel when we're in our thirties and married with kids. We have to honestly confess to each other if we're still attracted to our husbands."

I know us and our friendship. We will definitely be having this conversation in fifteen years.

"Why are you even thinking about marriage and kids? We haven't even graduated high school yet."

She shrugs. "Isn't that the end goal? Big wedding, two kids, a nice house, successful career? My mom's already planning my wedding, and I'm not even dating anyone."

"That's not what I want." We head toward the doors to go inside. "I'm not ever getting married."

"Don't tell me you're still stuck on that living-in-an-RV-with-a-bunch-of-cats idea?"

Megan wants what her parents have. A big house on a cul-de-sac. A family. Lots of get-togethers. Successful careers. I don't blame her, because in her world, that's pretty close to perfect.

But my world is different.

"What's wrong with living in an RV? I can go anywhere. Live anywhere. I don't want to be trapped. In a place *or* with a person. I want to be free."

She raises her eyebrow. "Then someday your free ass better park that RV in my driveway to visit me."

"Damn right I will. And if you're not happy with your doughy husband we'll drive off in it like Thelma and Louise."

"Deal."

♡

The day drags. I'm bored and restless, watching the clock in every class, counting the minutes until three p.m. when I can head to work. I used to love coming to school every day. Up until around third grade, it was fun and exciting. I soaked up learning like a sponge and had lots of friends. I remember going to their birthday parties, wearing silly hats and singing. Eating cake. But right around fourth grade, things got worse at home. Or maybe I was just finally old enough to realize that things were always *wrong*. School became an escape.

I couldn't escape myself, though. Not the fears that skittered in my head or the sick feeling that clung inside my chest.

I slowly withdrew from all my friends and classmates, until Megan decided I was going to be her best friend. She was the new girl, seated in front of me in class. On her first day, she turned around and blurted out her entire life story to me in one huge, run-on, rambling sentence. She was very animated—hands flying, black hair bouncing, eyes widening one moment and rolling the next. I blinked and nodded at her for a full ten minutes while she talked, caught in her spell.

"You have really pretty eyes," she said when she finally took a breath.

From that moment forward, we were best friends.

Sometimes I wish I could talk her into my RV dream. I'm going to miss her when she goes off to college and starts a whole new life. We'd have a blast driving around the country together, listening to great music, taking hundreds of selfies in new places. Instead, we'll be communicating through text messages and video chat.

The three p.m. bell finally rings, and I walk the mile and a half through town to Belongings, the boutique I've worked at for almost a year. Belongings sells local handmade items like jewelry, clothes, house decor, candles, candies, dolls, and even makeup and soaps. Although the shop looks rather small from the outside, it's much bigger on the inside, broken up into four rooms. All the rooms are decorated as if it were someone's real house—photos on the walls, jewelry in jewelry boxes, coasters and mugs set on tables—giving the feel of walking through a house where you can buy the things you like. I love the coziness of the shop.

Rebecca, the owner, bakes cookies in the small kitchen in the back of the store, which used to be a tiny diner. Two years ago, she and her husband divorced. She's thirty-two and has no kids, so apparently after they split she thrust herself into learning how to bake to keep herself "too busy to rebound into a bad relationship" as she put it. Turns out, she has a talent for whipping up amazing desserts. She puts the cookies in cute little bags for the customers to take. Rebecca is always trying to get me to eat them, but I've never tried one. They do make the entire store smell delicious, though. Sometimes I think half the customers come in just for the cookies.

The bell on the door of the boutique clinks as I swing it open, and the blast of air-conditioned air is refreshing after walking in the stifling heat. "Hi, Rebecca," I call out. "Sorry I'm late today. I had to walk."

She looks up from behind a rotating display of crystal

necklaces, and tucks her shoulder-length black hair behind her ear. "That's okay. You know I don't stress over things like that. Is something wrong with your car?"

I plop my purse and backpack behind the register counter, and a wave of dizziness makes me clutch the edge of the display case. Kicking myself for not calling an Uber in this humidity, I unscrew the top off my water bottle and gulp until the feeling slowly subsides. "I had to have it towed last night." Thankfully, I wasn't scheduled to work yesterday since it was the first day of school. "Not sure what's wrong with it, it's still at the shop."

"I'm sorry to hear that. Don't worry about being a little late when you need to be. Seriously." Her gaze lingers on my face. "Do you feel alright? You look pale."

Nodding, I say, "I'm fine. It's just really humid out. I was going to ask if you had anything I can do over the weekend? I don't know how much this car thing is going to cost…" I trail off, embarrassed, and hoping she doesn't think I'm trying to guilt her into extra hours.

"Hmm." She looks around the store. Her eyes suddenly light up. "Actually, I think I *do* have something you can do for me that I don't have the time or the patience for. I need pictures of the store and the products to be put on social media. Apparently, I'm supposed to post at least a photo a day. That's all the rage now and I've totally slacked off on it because it's a huge time suck."

"That sounds like fun, actually. I follow a lot of people and products on Instagram. I've been trying to build my own following. I can check out other boutiques and get some ideas."

"That's exactly what I need. I don't know why I didn't think to ask you to do this earlier. How's the camera on your cell phone?"

My heart sinks a little when I pull my old phone out of my pocket. "Um, not good. My screen is cracked. I don't know if that will—"

She holds her hand up, smiling. "You know what? I've been thinking of getting a new phone. Mine is old, too. Tonight I'm going to stop at the mall and get two new iPhones. My sister says the camera is amazing. I'll give one to you."

"Oh, Rebecca. I can't let you do that. Do you know how expensive those are?"

She's nonplussed. "I can write it off for the business. It would be a big help to have you take this over. You can have access to the accounts, use those cool filters, and reply to any comments or questions people leave. It can be a new part of your job, if you're interested? I'll give you a raise."

A new phone, new responsibilities, *and* a raise? I feel like I just scratched off a million-dollar lottery ticket.

The urge to hug her is huge, but that'd probably be unprofessional and awkward since she's my boss, so I resist. "Oh," I say, fighting back happy tears. "Thank you. Of course I'm interested. I'll do a great job, I promise. I'll research hashtags. I'll do that cool color-coordinating thing that all the popular accounts do. Maybe we can do a giveaway with a box of your famous cookies." My brain is already spinning like a top with ideas.

"See? You're already way ahead of me. You can come in this weekend and start taking photos. Just keep track of your time for me."

Things finally seem to be looking up.

CHAPTER 4
JUDE

This past week felt like the never-ending week from hell. My plan was to cut out of work early today since it's Friday, but nope. Didn't happen. The homeowners caught me as I was leaving *three hours ago* and wanted to go over more details and minor add-ons. At least they're happy with the job so far. I think I would've jumped off the roof if they weren't.

As soon as I get in my truck, I pour some of my water onto a paper towel and wipe my face, neck, arms, and hands. The heat and humidity lately have been brutal, the dust sticking to me like a gritty second skin. All I want to do is get home, take a shower, and relax on the couch with Cassie and a good movie.

About three miles into town, I see a girl walking on the sidewalk, a backpack with a glittery skull printed on it dangling from her thin shoulders. Realizing its Skylar, I hesitate, debating if I should offer her a ride again. It's hot as balls out, but it's not raining, and it's not dark out yet.

A gnawing deep in my gut reminds me it wasn't dark or raining when my little sister disappeared.

Sighing, I pull my truck over a few feet ahead of her and open the passenger side window.

She approaches the window with a grin on her face. "You stalking me, Lucky?" she teases.

"You still don't have your wheels back?"

"Do you think I'd be walking in this hellish heat if I did?"

I reach across the car and open the door for her. "Hop in, Sparkles. I'll give ya a ride."

"Maybe you should work for Uber," she says after she climbs in. This time she puts her stuff on the floor between her feet, not between us.

Glancing in my mirror, I pull back out into traffic. "You're the only one I've been giving rides to. I might just end up being your personal chauffeur."

Laughing, she says, "I see no problem with that."

"Any word on the car?"

"You were right. It was the fuel pump. He's giving it a tune up, too, since it's there. I'm picking it up Monday when my friend can drive me over."

I nod. "Good deal. You going home now or someplace else?"

"Home, please."

"Mind if I go through the drive-through on the way? I'm starving."

"Not at all."

"It's almost seven. Where are you coming from?"

"I work part time at Belongings Boutique."

"Rebecca's store?"

She turns in her seat to face me. "You know her?"

"Sorta. We went to school together." We knew each other, but we weren't friends. She was part of the cool crowd, and I was part of the cooler crowd.

"I didn't know you went to my school back when you were young."

The way she says *when you were young* makes me feel old. I'm thirty-four, not seventy.

I nod. "It's a small town. I've lived here my entire life."

"Me too."

I pull into the lot of the burger place and merge into the drive-through line. "Do you have any brothers or sisters?"

She shakes her head. "No, just me. I have a cat, though. How 'bout you?"

"A sister." I can't bring myself to say *have* a sister or *had* a sister. "And a dog."

"What kind of dog?"

"A little brown-and-white fuzzy thing. A shit zoo, I think."

She laughs. "It's Shih tzu."

"Guzunheidt."

She smiles.

I pull up to the glowing menu and recite my usual into the speaker before turning to Skylar. "Do you want something? My treat."

Blinking, she stares past me at the menu. "Um. Just a bottle of water. And a hamburger with no hamburger or stuff on it."

"Very funny," I say, shaking my head. I order her water, then move up to the next window to pay before pulling into a parking spot.

"I don't like to eat while I'm driving," I explain as I take my food out and hand her water to her.

"Thanks," she says quietly, looking down at the bottle in her lap.

Taking a bite of my burger, I hold my cup of seasoned waffle fries out to her. "Want some?"

She shakes her head, still not looking up.

"What's wrong?" Nobody ever turns down waffle fries.

"Nothing."

"Spill it, Sparkles."

She takes a deep breath. "You didn't get my bun."

I swallow my food and stare at her. "What? I thought you were kidding. You seriously wanted just a plain hamburger bun? With nothing else?" *Why?*

"Yeah."

She's dead serious.

"Stay put," I say, putting my burger and its wrapper on the console.

She starts to say something, but I don't hear her because I've already jumped out of the truck and shut the door behind me. If she wants a damn hamburger bun, I'm getting her one. I trudge inside the restaurant, stand in line for ten minutes, and ignore the crazy look I get from the kid behind the counter when I order a plain hamburger roll with no burger, no cheese—nothing.

"I don't even know how to charge for this, so just take it," he says, handing me the bag.

I throw a dollar into the tip jar. "Thanks."

"Jude, oh my God, you didn't have to do that," Skylar says when I get back in the truck. "I feel bad…"

Handing her the bag, I say, "Don't. I offered to get you something to eat, and I fucked it up. Now I made it right."

Her face lights up with a shy smile that could probably stop traffic. "Thank you. For a badass-looking dude, you're actually pretty nice."

I almost choke on my fries. "You think I look badass?"

"A little, yeah. You're very colorful."

A deep laugh rumbles out of me. "Annnnd that's badass how, exactly?"

"Okay, that's a bad description. It's just all the ink." Her eyes scan over my arm and then back up to my face. "The muscles. The hair."

At least she's not petting me, like people do. They always want to touch my tats and my hair, and it creeps me the hell out.

"Why do you just want to eat bread? They have salads, chicken, fruit cups, milkshakes. I hope you didn't get that to be cheap. I can afford to get you a real meal."

Her shoulder lifts slightly. "This is just what I want."

"Okay... As long as you're happy."

Hey, who am I to judge? I used to mash up peanut butter and jelly in a bowl and eat it with a spoon—sans bread.

"I got a raise today," she blurts out as she picks the sesame seeds off her bun and puts them in the paper bag. "I'm kinda excited."

"Congrats. What do you do there?"

"Usually I work the register, rotate the displays, that sort of thing. But now, Rebecca wants me to manage the store's social media. She's buying me a new iPhone to take pictures of the products and post online."

Wow. Rebecca's little boutique must be doing well to be handing out brand-new iPhones to a part-time, teen employee. "That sounds like a helluva lot more fun than working a register."

"Right?" she practically squeals, excitement bursting into a big, dazzling smile. "I'm starting this weekend so I can pay for my car."

It's cute to see her so excited about her job. I used to sell dope back in high school to pay for stuff, but I'm not going to tell her that, so I just nod. That past should stay exactly where it is.

Stopping to eat and driving Skylar across town gets me home way later than I planned, and Cassie goes into a fit as soon as I walk through the front door. I'm sure she's been staring at the door for the past three hours, pacing the house, getting herself all worked up.

"Calm down, girl," I say as she runs circles around my feet, her furry tail wiggling. Bending down on my knee, I pet her head, and she does her little raspy bark and paw stomp, telling me off like she does.

Someone has to keep me in line. Might as well be a cute dog.

After I walk her in the yard, I head straight upstairs, pulling my shirt off as I go, with the dog on my heels.

"We'll watch a movie after I shower," I tell her, and she tilts her head at me in anticipation, because she knows the word *movie* means *sit on the couch*. That probably says an embarrassing amount about my life and social status.

I stand in the shower, breathing in the steam, until the hot water turns cold. My mind drifts back to dropping Skylar off at that creepy, dark house. As I was pulling away from her driveway, I glanced in my rearview mirror and caught her climbing through a window.

Can't help but wonder what that's all about.

My sister used to sneak in and out of windows, too. To meet boys. To party. Who knows what else?

When she went missing, we put posters up in a hundred-mile radius. I didn't work for a month—searching nonstop for her. Sixteen-year-old girls don't go missing in this small town. There was even a search party with special sniffing dogs and a helicopter. Two weeks later I received a text in the middle of the night:

Erin: Stop searching, Jude. I'm not missing. I left.

Me: Where the fuck are you? Come home.

Erin: Just stop. Okay?

Me: Tell me where you are. I'll come get you. I just want you to come home.

Erin: Please stop looking for me. I have to go.

I never heard from her again, and her cell number was deactivated shortly after. It's been ten years, and there were never any leads or sightings. The case went cold. The cops basically wrote her off as a runaway, especially after I showed them the messages. I've never known if I should believe it was her who sent those texts. That last line *I have to go* bugged me. We were close, and I can't believe that'd be the last thing she'd say to me. She'd either say something funny or say *love ya*. Was she being *forced* to go? Did someone kidnap her and send it from her phone to throw us off? She could be dead. Or sold to some psycho. My blood chills just thinking about it. Or, maybe she really did run away and is out there in the world living her version of her best life.

I hope she is.

Later, when I'm stretched out on the sofa with a bowl of popcorn and the dog curled up on my feet, my phone pings with a message:

Skylar: Just wanted to say hi, and thank you for the ride and dinner.

Me: A hamburgerless bun isn't dinner.

Skylar: Anything can be dinner 😉

Me: True.

Skylar: Here's me and my cat right now.

A photo comes through of her and a furry, gray cat sitting on the floor. Her hair is up in a huge, messy bun.

I snap a quick pic of me and Cassie and send it back.

Me: Here's me and my shit dog.

Skylar: LOL. She's cute.

Me: Have a good weekend. Enjoy your new job stuff.

Skylar: Thanks! Hope you get some rest.

Earlier I gave her my cell number in case she needed a ride to pick up her car. I wasn't expecting her to start sending me random messages. In hindsight, I probably shouldn't have given my number to her. I don't want to become a personal taxi driver or get crazy messages riddled with emojis night and day.

But I can't deny it's kinda nice to get a message from someone who isn't asking for something or bitching about something, and who was just thinking about me and wanted to say hi.

Nail, meet coffin.

CHAPTER 5

SKYLAR

Unsurprisingly, I've never had a new cell phone. The three I've had have been hand-me-downs from my mom, and always came to me sticky, dented, and cracked.

But this new iPhone from Rebecca has me giddy.

It's like a work of art. Nestled and glimmering in a sturdy, pristine white box. Perfect, shiny black screen and—oh my God—the prettiest lavender-purple finish.

I'm almost afraid to touch it. It's *that* beautiful.

"Skylar?"

I look up to meet Rebecca's questioning eyes, and I have no chill. I can't control myself. I throw my arms around her and hug her, not caring if it might be unprofessional. Thankfully, there are no customers browsing the shop right now.

"Rebecca, thank you so much. It's stunning."

Laughing, she hugs me back, then slowly pulls away. "It's just a phone. But I'm really happy you like it. I thought the purple suited you."

"Like it? I love it. It's the most amazing thing I've ever had. I promise I'll take care of it. And if you ever have to fire me, I'll give it back. I won't wreck it. I'll get a really good case for it."

"Skylar, it's yours. You don't ever have to give it back. I have no plans to fire you. I'm excited for you to get started on all this social media stuff. I'm curious to see if it brings in more sales."

"Me too." I press the power button on the phone. "As soon as I have it set up, I'm going to load the apps I read about last night, then I'll start taking photos."

She smiles. "Have fun. Don't worry about the register today. I always work up front on the weekends. A lot of regulars come in just to chitchat anyway."

She takes a few steps toward the front of the store, then pauses. "I made fresh cookies and blueberry muffins. You should grab one before the customers gobble them up."

Smiling, I nod. "Okay."

My stomach is growling from the scent of the bakery items, and I'm sure they're delicious, but I just can't eat any of them.

I spend the day taking pictures of the products in the shop. Most of the items are already placed in photo-ready positions—the sweaters are neatly folded on top of a shabby chic dresser, the candles sit on distressed wooden shelves, handmade teddy bears are cozy in cute wicker baskets. I arrange necklaces, bracelets, and rings on the wood floor, snake a purple ribbon around them, and use the features of the phone camera to subtly blur out the items in the background.

Glancing through the notes I took on How to Make Instagram Product-Photos Look Amazing, I bring the photos into the editing app, add the filter I've chosen to apply to all of the photos to make our brand look cohesive, and *wow*… My heart does a little jump. I don't think anyone will be able to tell an eighteen-year-old with zero photography experience took these. They actually look professional. I even have that cool bokeh light thing going on in the background of a few shots, and a tiny glint of sparkle on one of the gemstone necklaces.

"How's it going?" Rebecca asks when she finds me at the small table in the kitchen.

"Awesome. I'm just planning out a schedule so two pictures will be automatically posted a day, one in the morning and one later in the day. I'm going to post short videos in the stories section, like a little virtual tour of the store."

"Great idea!"

"Look at the pictures, let me know if you like them."

She takes the phone from my hand, and the expression on her face says it all. Her eyes widen, her mouth drops open, and then she breaks into a huge smile.

"Skylar… these are better than I could've imagined. This looks like we had a professional photo shoot done. I can't even tell you how excited I am about this."

I try not to smile *too* big. "Me too. Tomorrow I'm going to grab some of those fall and Halloween decorations you have out back and take some photos with those so we have them ready. I think we should put a cute little sign by the register, telling people to follow you online to see new items, sales, all that stuff."

She hands the phone back to me, her earrings swaying as she shakes her head a little. "Keep this up and you'll end up being my marketing guru."

"It's actually really fun and interesting. I can't wait to see which photos get the most likes."

"I'm glad. Enjoying your job is the absolute best. If there are any words of wisdom I can pass down, it's to make sure you enjoy what you do." I can't help the proud grin I give her as she heads to the register. "I'll be up front if you need me."

I dig into my purse for a honey lozenge and pop it into my

mouth. My throat has been burning lately. I hope I'm not getting a cold. The last thing I need is to get sick.

"Did you get laid in the back room or something?" Megan asks as I climb into the passenger side of her Audi.

"No, why?"

"Because you're smiling like you did."

Rolling my eyes, I pull my seatbelt strap across my chest and buckle it. Megan drives a bit erratically and I'm not about to take a flying header through the windshield.

"Look at this." I present my phone to her as if I just caught a unicorn. "Is this not the most amazing thing you've ever seen? I got to keep my old phone number, too."

Her brown eyes flash. "Holy shit! Lavender! Did you steal that?"

"No. Rebecca gave it to me to take pictures of the products and post online. Dude, I'm loving it. I had so much fun doing this today. The time flew by. It's going to be part of my job now. She's giving me a raise, too."

"How much is she giving you?"

I shrug. "I don't know. I didn't ask. I don't care."

She reverses out of the parking lot, and my head wrenches back into the headrest as she floors it onto the main road.

"I don't know how you haven't lost your license yet," I say, gripping the armrest.

She ignores me. "Sky, you can't just not care about a raise. You need to know these things."

"To be honest I'm just excited for the opportunity to do something I enjoy while learning *and* getting paid at the same time."

"How much you're getting paid should be the priority,

though. You might be doing the kind of work that deserves like, thirty bucks an hour."

"I doubt it. I'm a part-time employee with zero skills. Rebecca has always been more than fair with my pay and my holiday bonus. I trust her. Not to mention, this phone was legit expensive and she gave it to me to keep."

Megan side-eyes me. "I'm jelly over that, I must admit."

My body lurches forward as she brakes abruptly at a red light. "Oh, hey," she says, unfazed by the sudden stop. "I'm really sorry, but I can't give you a ride to pick up your car tomorrow. My mom texted me earlier and told me they're going out and I have to babysit Johnny. Like seriously, they have no regard for my social life at all. *None.* I'd bring him, but I don't like putting him in the car. He always screams bloody murder."

I rub the back of my neck. "That's okay. I have a backup plan. No worries."

"Are you sure? I feel really bad."

"Absolutely. Don't feel bad. If you want, I'll stop by your house to visit on my way home." Her little brother is adorable, so I don't mind hanging out with her when she has to babysit him. He always makes me laugh.

"Cool. Do you want to go to the diner? I could go for a salad and a strawberry shake right now."

The idea of onions and lettuce commingling with mushed-up strawberry milk has my gag reflex on overdrive. There's no way I can sit across from her and witness that kind of culinary cohabitation.

"I'd rather just go home. I'm not feeling too great, and I have to work again tomorrow. I want to go to bed early."

"You never feel good. Why don't you go to the doctor?"

"I think I'm getting a cold. Or it could be allergies."

On that note, I unzip my purse and hunt out another lozenge.

I'm going to have to buy more. I'm gobbling these things like candy.

"Take some vitamins," she says. "Maybe you should get one of those IV vitamin infusion things."

"What's that?"

"You get an IV from a nurse that's filled with all sorts of vitamins. It's supposed to boost your immunity and make you feel healthy and energized. My cousin gets it done when she travels or doesn't sleep enough."

I'm sure I can't afford that, even though it sounds interesting. I feel tired no matter how much I sleep.

"I'll keep that in mind if I don't start to feel better," I say.

"You know that kid Erik whose locker is like, two down from mine?"

My mind shuffles through her row of lockers and comes up blank.

"No."

"Yes, you do. He's always been super quiet, kinda nerdy, and skinny? He had glasses like Harry Potter?"

Nodding, I say, "Kind of." I have no idea who she's talking about.

"Well, he's got contacts now and I think he's been working out because he's not so skinny anymore. He's still nerdy, but in a sexy way. And his hair is a bit longer."

"Okay…"

"I think I'm going to ask him out."

I almost choke on my lozenge."What? *Why*?"

"Because he's cute and he's essentially new meat now that he's rebooted himself."

"Meg, just flirt with him and wait for him to ask you out. You're a total babe, you know he will if you show him some attention."

"It's the twenty-first century! I don't have to wait around for a guy to make the first move."

That's true. "Yeah, I guess you're right."

"I want to get to him before someone else does."

"Geez. He's not an X-box."

"I know. But if *I* noticed how cute he is, the others will, too."

The way she says *the others* makes it sound like there's a ship of female Vikings coming to claim all the cute boys.

When she pulls into my driveway and puts her car in park, I turn to look at her. I can see her mind spinning, conjuring up ways to snag unsuspecting Erik.

"I hate to break this to you, Meg, but he's probably still a virgin if he was nerdy and shy up until this year."

Her mouth scrunches up. "Ya think?"

"I think it's a good possibility."

"Hmm. That could suck." She taps her fingers on the steering wheel, her lips pursed crookedly in thought. "But it could be fun, too. I could rock his world."

"He'll probably fall madly in love with you if you're his first."

She frowns dramatically. "He better not. I want fun. Not some lovesick puppy drama."

"Just be nice to him. No breaking hearts."

A laugh bursts from her. "I'll try." Her smile fades as she stares at my house. "This place is getting sketchy. Doesn't anyone mow the lawn?"

The knot in my stomach twists. "We're looking for a new landscaper. The last guy quit." It's a lie. I'm the one who mows the lawn, but I've felt too weak lately to do it in this heat.

"I hope you find someone soon or the grass will be up to your knees. There could be snakes slithering around in there."

"There aren't any snakes." I grab my stuff. "Thanks for the ride. I'll see you tomorrow."

"Okay. Love ya, babe."

"Love ya, too," I reply before I slam the door.

I linger by the mailbox at the end of the driveway until she's gone. I don't want her seeing me crawling through the window. She'll abduct me and have me living in her guest room on an IV drip in less than twenty-four hours. As much as I'd be grateful for the care, I don't want anyone feeling sorry for me.

Later, after I've settled in bed to watch TV, I stare at my pretty new phone screen, debating on whether I should take Jude up on his offer for a ride. He's already gone out of his way for me twice, more than anyone besides Megan ever has. He refuses gas money, not that I can really afford to give it to him. I would, though. I don't expect freebies from strangers.

Walking to the shop in the morning shouldn't be bad since the temperature will be cooler, but later in the afternoon when I have to get my car it's expected to be ninety-five degrees with humidity, and I just don't think I can walk that far.

Finally, I shove pride and the risk of being *that annoying person* to the side and send Jude a message:

Me: Hi.

Fluffle-Up-A-Gus curls up against my side, purring loudly. I scratch her head as I eye my phone for a reply.

Jude: Hey you.

Me: I hate to ask, but if your offer to drive me to pick up my car still stands, I'd really appreciate it. My BFF has to babysit, so she can't take me.

A few seconds creep by before his answer lights up my screen.

Jude: Sure. What time?

Me: I'll be at Belongings. I can leave at 3.

Jude: K. I can do that.

Me: I'm really sorry to ask. It's just kinda hot to walk that far.

Sure, I could use Uber or Lyft, but that makes me nervous. We're told from the time we can understand words *not* to get into cars with strangers, yet here we all are, paying strangers to let us get in their cars. I just don't feel okay with it.

Jude: Don't worry about it. I don't have any plans tomorrow.
Not a big deal.

Me: Okay. Thank you 😊

Jude: C-ya then, Sparkles. ✷

My heart flutters a little over his nickname for me, just like it does every time he says it in person.

CHAPTER 6

SKYLAR

"Lucky. Wow, it's been a long time. Can I… um… help you find something special?" Rebecca's soft, curiosity-tinged voice floats to the back stockroom.

Shit. It figures he'd come while I wasn't out front. I switch off the light and walk out. He's standing there, looking totally out of place in this cozy shop, in a white tee, black baseball hat on backward, jeans so faded they're almost gray, and scuffed, untied work boots. Grinning around a lollipop stick hanging out of his mouth, he nods in my direction as I approach them. "Already found it. I'm here for her."

My boss studies him quizzically. "Excuse me?"

"He's giving me a ride to pick up my car at the mechanic's, Rebecca," I explain.

Surprise lifts her eyebrows. "Oh."

I can feel her eyes boring into me as I pick up my purse from behind the register. No doubt she's wondering how Jude and I know each other, but I'll have to explain another time if I want to catch the mechanic before he closes at 3:30.

"Are these free?" Jude holds up one of the small robin-egg-blue paper bags filled with cookies, squinting through the little cellophane window under the logo. "Those better not be raisins in there."

"Technically they're free, but they're for customers," Rebecca replies. "And they're chocolate chip."

He flashes a smirk, which I've quickly realized is his signature sexy trait. "Can I just buy the cookies?"

Rebecca shakes her head, but smiles. "Just take them."

"Thanks. How's Adam doing?"

She grimaces at the mention of her ex-husband. "I'm sure he's doing great considering the last time I saw him his secretary was on her knees under his desk."

"Ouch," Jude says. "Sorry to hear that. He always was an asshole."

"That's true. And so were you."

"Hey, I'm a *nice* asshole. There's a difference."

I narrow my gaze at him. "What's a nice asshole, exactly?"

"Him," Rebecca replies, wiping down the glass cabinet. We always joke that it breeds fingerprints. "Exactly him right in front of you."

I give Jude's arm a tug. "We better go, nice asshole. The mechanic said he was leaving at 3:30." I smile at Rebecca. "I'll see you tomorrow."

"Have a good night. Enjoy the cookies, Lucky."

He waves. "If I like them, I'll come back and buy something so I can get more."

We leave to the sound of Rebecca's laughter—a sound I don't hear often. I wonder if she had a crush on Jude when they were young. I thought I caught a hint of flirting from her. But now that I think about it, I've never seen her interact with a man in the store before. They would actually make a cute couple.

"Maybe you should ask her out to dinner," I say on the walk to Jude's truck.

He pulls a face of shock and disdain. "Who? Rebecca? Why?"

"'Cause she's lonely since she got divorced."

He opens the passenger side door for me and I hop in.

"I have a no-dating-divorced-women rule," he says when he's settled behind the wheel. "Especially lonely ones."

Turning to him, I put my sunglasses on. "What's wrong with divorced women?"

"In my experience, they're usually trying to get married again. Which is weird, 'cause you'd think they'd want to never go down that road again. I ain't looking for a wife and kids."

"How come?"

He shrugs. "The divorce rate is insane. And kids are out of control, especially teens." He glances over at me with his grin. "Present company excluded, of course. I put my parents through hell when I was younger. So did my sister." He takes a deep breath and stares at the red light we're stopped at. "I just don't want to invest my heart and soul into someone who could shred it all like a raptor, take half of my stuff, mess up my kids, and let God-knows-who into their lives on weekends and holidays. Fuck all that."

I nod at my new kindred spirit. "I feel the same way. Like, I don't mind dating someone, but I'd rather leave it as a free-will arrangement, like when you work for someone. You can quit anytime; they can fire you anytime. There're no promises, no legal ties, no two-week notice, no expectations. You're free to go when you want. No hard feelings."

"Yes. *Exactly* all of that, Sparkles. Couldn't have said it better myself. Your parents divorced?"

"Yup."

"Mine too. That's a hell I never want to experience again."

My parents' divorce was quiet and uneventful. Dad just left. There weren't any screaming fights or drama that I can remember. They didn't fight over custody, or furniture. I doubt either of them had an affair, even though they're both decent-looking people. I'm not sure if my father pays alimony or child support. As far as I know, they just signed the papers and that was it. Marriage over. The only evidence they were ever together is my existence, which wasn't magical enough to make them fight to get better. To make it work. To think—or even worry about —*me*.

Jude comes into the dingy office of the auto shop with me. I assumed he'd just drop me off in the parking lot and leave, but no, he walked me inside, waited while I shelled out five hundred and ten dollars in cash onto the dusty counter, then walked me to my car in the back lot. He eats the three chocolate chips cookies from the bag as we walk.

"These are delicious." He's practically drooling over the cookies. "How do you not eat these all day long?"

"I've never had one, to be honest," I admit as I wiggle my key into the driver's side door lock. The thin layer of dust that was on my car when it was towed is gone, and I wonder if the mechanic took it through a car wash.

Jude's gray eyes blink at me. "Are you kidding? How the hell can you resist these? They're all soft and buttery and gooey."

Because eggs. That's how.

"I'm just not big on sweets."

"Start it up," he says, leaning against the hood. "Let's make sure it starts before I take off."

The engine turns over with its familiar, yet comforting, deep rumble.

"Yay!" I exclaim, clapping my hands. "I missed my baby."

He comes around the open door and kneels next to me, peering inside at the cracked, red vinyl seats. "I've always loved 'vettes, especially the older ones like this. I wanted one wicked bad when I was your age."

"You should get one."

He runs his hand over the ripped armrest, and I'm sure he sees it like I do—not for the condition it's in now, but for how it'll look with some love.

"Maybe someday."

I stare at his tattooed hand caressing my car door. Sterling-silver rings wrap around two of his fingers. One with an onyx stone, the other a knot of twisted metal. They're tarnished and dinged up, not polished and perfect.

Like him.

Like me.

Licking my lips, I inhale a short, nervous breath. "Hey, do you want to go for a drive? I mean, *you* drive. My car. With me."

"Really?"

"Yeah. I don't have anywhere to be." Except to stop by Megan's, but I can do that later.

My breath pauses as he chews the inside of his cheek for a few seconds, until a big grin blooms on his face.

"Fuck it," he finally says, standing. "Why not? That's an offer I can't turn down."

Smiling, I tell him to get in as I climb over the console to the passenger side.

He's like a little kid behind the wheel. Grinning excitedly as he pushes the seat back and adjusts the rearview mirror.

"Listen to that purr," he says wistfully before he puts the car in gear and heads out to the main road.

The word *purr* coming out of his mouth is sensual, almost secretive, as if I wasn't supposed to hear it.

"That's not the stock radio, Sparkles," he says teasingly, touching the volume dial. "I'm a little disappointed."

I laugh. "Trust me, I am, too. But I just couldn't drive it without listening to my favorite music. RingPop put this in for me. He got me a deal since he works at a car stereo place. Don't worry, I saved the original."

"RingPop?"

"He used to live next door to me. We've been friends forever. When we were like seven years old he proposed to me with a ring pop candy."

Jude laughs. "Very cute."

"It gets worse. I started licking it and it came off and got stuck in my throat. I choked on it until I couldn't breathe. I legit thought I was gonna die. He kicked me in the stomach and I coughed it up."

"Holy shit. I guess that explains your aversion to sweets, then?"

Actually, that's not why. But I nod in agreement anyway.

"I've been calling him RingPop ever since. He moved to a different town last year, but we still hang out once in a while."

"I have a good choking story too," he says, pulling onto the highway.

"Let's hear it."

"When I was in high school, I was kissing this chick I was with, and I had a piece of gum in my mouth and she thought she was being sexy and sucked it out of my mouth. It went straight down her throat and she started gagging on it. Total mood killer."

"Ew! That's disgusting," I say, repulsed. I could've lived forever without hearing that. "I guess she must've liked you a lot if she wanted to chew your gum."

I can't imagine liking a guy enough to want anything from his mouth in my own.

"Eh, she had the personality of a light switch."

He shifts to a higher gear and moves to the fast lane, gunning the gas pedal. "This baby is fast," he says.

"The fastest I've gone with it is 105."

He throws me a surprised glance. "Look at you, little speed

demon. Be careful. You don't want to wrap your pretty face around a tree."

"I only went that fast once." Maybe twice.

Okay, like, five times.

"So, what's a girl like you doing with a car like this?" His tone is playful, but my answer is not. I still get emotional talking about my grandfather, and today is no different. Especially when I'm in the car he gifted me, telling someone the story of how he wanted me to have something beautiful, cool, and created with love. Something symbolic of hope, of shiny new beginnings.

"Your grandfather sounds like he was a good guy," Jude says after I tell him how my grandfather meant to give the car to me when I graduated.

"He was." I wipe the tear from my eye before it trickles down my cheek. "I miss him a lot. And my grandma."

"She's passed, too?"

I nod. "Yeah. Two years before him. She was diabetic."

"I'm sorry," he says softly. "I didn't mean to bum you out."

"You didn't. I always get melancholy when I think about them."

"Nothing wrong with that."

I lose track of time and direction as he drives. Almost everything fades away—except the wind rushing through the open windows and my favorite playlist keeping us company. And Jude's voice, singing along with the songs he has no idea are the closest to my heart.

"You've got a great voice." I don't try to mask my surprise.

"I only sound good in the shower and the car." He turns down a bumpy side road. "Put me on a stage and I suck."

"I doubt that."

He slows down and pulls into a gravelly parking lot, near a small playground.

"I just want to have a quick smoke," he says, reaching for the door handle. I laugh as he tries to hoist his tall body out of the low car. "Holy shit that thing's hard to get out of."

"I got used to it. Thankfully, I don't wear skirts." I peer around at the empty park. "I'm going to walk around for a few minutes."

I head straight to the swings. There used to be a swing in our backyard, hanging from a tree. When I was little, I'd swing for hours every day, believing I could soar straight into the sky and live in the clouds. One day, the rope snapped on one side, and I slammed to the ground. For at least half an hour I was sprawled out crying, thinking I was dying. When my parents didn't come to help me, I stood up and quietly limped inside, my butt and legs aching with every step. Looking back, I'm pretty sure I fractured my tailbone.

The swing is still there, hanging from the broken, frayed rope. An icon of the day I realized I was on my own.

Jude has sauntered across the park to sit on the end of the metal slide. He watches me with an amused smile that's incredibly hot.

"Come swing with me!"

He shakes his head and blows a cloud of smoke up into the air.

"C'mon, Lucky. No one will see you."

"I don't care who sees me."

"Then get over here. Don't be a poop."

Laughing, he puts out his cigarette and tosses it in a trashcan on his way to the swings.

"You're a pain in the ass, ya know," he says, squeezing his muscular body onto the one next to me.

I pump my legs harder, my hair flying like a flag behind me. "I know. Don't care."

When I look over, he's gliding through the air next to me,

smiling just as much as he was when he got behind the wheel of my 'vette.

I'm glad to see the bad boy has an inner child.

"Whoever can land the farthest away gets to drive home," he says mischievously.

"You're on!"

He goes first, vaulting himself off the swing and landing in the beach sand fifteen feet away, rolling into a dramatic somersault.

"I'm too old for this shit, Sparkles," he says, kneeling in the sand. "You and your car are killing my back."

"Prepare to lose!"

I hit the sand three feet farther than him with a thud, and fall, not in any way gracefully, onto my butt.

"I won!"

"Yeah but it really wasn't fair. You're much lighter."

"True. I'll let you drive back. Because I'm nice and I like you."

He stands, brushes sand off his jeans, and holds his hand out to me. When I grasp it, he effortlessly pulls me up, and I stumble into his chest.

"I like you, too."

His voice, the sudden closeness... I'm a little breathless. I've never been this close to a man before. A *boy*, yes. But not a muscular, inked-up, sandalwood-scented-aftershave-wearing grown man with hands the size of my head.

I should've let go of his hand as soon as I was on my feet, but I don't. I hold on to it for a few seconds, liking the warmth and the feel of his callused palm against mine.

After a few seconds, he gently squeezes my hand, then pulls his from mine. It's a tiny, affectionate gesture, that squeeze. But us girls know what it is. A hand hug.

CHAPTER 7

JUDE

The distinct sound of her car engine, and Elton John's *Tiny Dancer* on full blast, announces Skylar's arrival before I even see her pull into the school lot.

She glances casually at the house I'm working on as she gets out of her car, but she doesn't see me way up on the roof. I wonder if the car gave her trouble this morning, because school started over an hour ago.

The weather has changed overnight, and a cool breeze has chased away the humidity. That might explain the funky, aged-brown-leather aviator cap and goggles sitting on her head. Two long braids flow from beneath the weird adornment, which, somehow, actually looks cool on her.

"Hey, Lucky!" Kyle yells from below. "Come check out the flooring."

"Be right there."

On my way down the ladder, something catches my attention out of the corner of my eye. It takes me a few seconds to realize that what looks like a pile of clothes thrown on the sidewalk, is Skylar.

"What the—"

Tossing my hammer onto the ground, I sprint across the lawn and kneel down next to her on the sidewalk.

"Skylar?"

My blood goes cold when she doesn't stir. She's totally *out*.

Breathing, but out like a light.

"Hey…" I touch her cheek as my heart kicks up its rhythm. Her cute little hat has fallen off, and seeing it lying on the walkway next to her brings a lump to my throat. I nudge her arm. "Wake up, Sparkles."

Her head turns. Her booted feet twitch. Slowly, her eyes open. She stares through me for a few seconds with boggled eyes until her focus finally returns.

"Wh-what happened?" she slurs, blinking.

"I think you passed out."

I help her sit up, but she immediately sways and grabs on to my arm. "I don't feel too good."

She doesn't *look* too good, either. Her complexion is stark white. Dark circles shadow her eyes. Yesterday at the park she seemed so vibrant, but today is a totally different story.

"Did you take anything?" I ask.

"Take what?"

"I don't know. Pills?"

Scowling, she rubs the side of her head. "I don't do drugs, Jude."

"Did you hit your head?"

"Maybe. I feel really dizzy."

Her eyes close and her fingers grip my arm tighter, as if she's about to pass out again.

"I'm going to take you to the emergency room."

She shakes her head. "No… I can't go to the hospital."

"Yes, you can. And you are."

Kyle approaches with a hammer in his hand and looks from

me to Skylar, still sitting on the sidewalk. "I've been looking for you. What the hell's going on?"

"I think she passed out."

"What's wrong with her?"

"Not sure. I'm going to take her over to the ER. Can you take care of things while I'm gone?"

"Sure. Maybe you should call an ambulance?"

"No," Skylar mumbles.

"Screw that," I say. "It'll take forever to get here. I can get her there faster if I take her myself."

He nods. "Okay. Maybe you should call her parents, though."

"Good idea." I lean into Skylar's line of vision. "Let's call your mom and I'll drive you to the ER. She can meet us there."

Eyes closed, she shakes her head. "I'm eighteen. I don't need or want her there."

"But—"

"Please," she whispers. "She won't come anyway. Trust me."

Kyle and I exchange a look. One that says we shouldn't get involved. But I can't just leave her here or let her drive herself. She can't even stand up, let alone drive.

"Okay. Do you think you can walk to my truck?"

"I think so."

I help her stand, but her legs wobble like noodles.

"I'm going to carry you," I say, swooping her up into my arms before she can protest. "Dude, pick up her stuff for me," I say to Kyle.

He picks up the hat, goggles, and book bag and hands them to her. "Thank you," she says, leaning her head against my shoulder.

Ignoring Kyle's skeptical look, I say, "I'll be back soon. Just keep things moving here."

"Will do. Send me a text and lemme know what's going on."

I carry her to my truck, wondering what the hell I'm doing

with every step, and carefully settle her in the passenger seat. Awkwardly, I strap the seatbelt around her.

"You don't have to treat me like a baby," she says when I start up the truck.

"I'm not."

"Maybe I should go home…" she says, pressing her fingers into her temples. "Maybe I'm just tired. And I've had a bad sore throat. It could be the flu… or mono."

Shit.

"I haven't kissed anyone in a loooong time, though." She leans her head back against the seat and closes her eyes. "In case you were wondering, yes, I'm a social loser."

"I wasn't. And you're not. But I think it's best to get you checked out. You passed out on the freakin' sidewalk. You might've hit your head. You could have a concussion." Suddenly, I'm channeling my mother. "Should we call the school and tell them you're not going to be there?"

She waves her hand dismissively. "They won't even notice I'm not there. They never do."

The Monday-morning traffic sucks, forcing us to sit through every red light twice. Skylar becomes more alert during the drive, but she still looks eerily pale to me, especially with the sun glaring through the windows.

"Are you hungry?" I ask. "Did you eat this morning?"

"I never eat breakfast."

I catch myself before I completely turn into my mother and tell her that breakfast is the most important meal of the day.

I'm supposed to be cool. *Badass.* Her words, not mine.

By the time we get to the hospital, she tells me she's feeling a bit better and can get out of the truck and walk without stumbling. That doesn't stop me from walking her inside and waiting while she checks in.

"Thanks for driving me here," she says, as we take seats in

the waiting area far away from the other four people. "You can go. I'll be fine now. I don't want to mess up your whole day."

"How are you going to get home?"

Her mouth quirks to the side. "I'll text Megan later. I'm sure she'll give me a ride back to my car."

Rocking on my heels with my hands shoved in my front pockets, I stare around the room. Then at her, sitting in the faded-yellow plastic chair with her blue eyes wide with anxiety, rubbing her hand over the center of her chest. The printed ID bracelet seems huge circling her wrist. I never noticed how thin her wrists are.

"Skylar Timmons?" a nurse bellows from the double doors.

That was fast.

Skylar stands, smiling weakly. "Thanks, Jude."

How can I leave her here when she's looking all sickly, scared, and alone?

"I'll wait here for you, okay? It shouldn't take long." They'll probably just send her home with some antibiotics and tell her to rest for a few days.

Clearly, I underestimated what goes on beyond the doors of the emergency room.

Three hours later, I'm still in the waiting room, vacillating between annoyed as shit and worried as hell.

And why? I don't even know this girl. She's not friend or family to me. The universe just keeps trying to turn me into her personal driver.

I send Kyle a text telling him I'm still waiting. He replies that I should leave. I get a soda and potato chips out of the vending machine. I stare out the window. I eavesdrop on a young couple sitting a few seats over from me. She thinks she's pregnant and they don't want to tell anyone. Her family hates him. She was drunk last week and now she's worried she hurt the baby. He wonders (loudly) if she's drunk now. A woman across from me is coughing nonstop and is wearing two different socks.

Yeesh. I want to get out of here, but now I'm invested in the wait. Wouldn't she be out by now if she was okay?

"Jude Lucketti?"

I snap out of my daze. "That's me."

"You can come in and see your niece. She's asking for you."

My niece?

I follow the nurse through the metal doors and down the hall to a small, private exam room. Skylar is sitting up in the bed with a flimsy gray gown on that dwarfs her, hanging off her shoulder. I try not to look at the thin, black lace bra strap showing. An IV is dripping into a needle taped to the top of her hand.

It feels too intimate—me being in a hospital room with her. Vulnerable, pale, and barely dressed. Someone else should be standing here. A parent, friend, or boyfriend.

Not some guy she barely knows.

"The doctor will be back soon," the nurse informs us as she leaves.

"You're still here," Skylar says.

"I was worried about you. It's been over three hours."

"I'm so sorry. You should go back to work."

"I've been sitting out there for hours. I'm not gonna leave now. Did they figure out what's wrong with you? And don't start calling me Uncle Lucky, *niece*."

She laughs. "I was afraid they wouldn't let you in unless you were family."

Narrowing my eyes at her, I sit in another impossibly uncomfortable chair in the corner of the tight room. "You sure you're eighteen?"

"Yes, Jude. I'm pretty sure I know how old I am. I'm a senior and I turned eighteen four months ago. I was held back in school when I was younger because I was absent a lot."

"Okay. Just checking. So what's going on?" I scan the room. Her clothes are folded on a chair on the other side of the bed. "Are you getting discharged?"

Her gaze drops and she leans her chin on her hand. "Maybe tomorrow. They're admitting me."

"Why?"

"They want to run some more tests. An endoscopy, I think, and some other things. The doctor talks really fast, I didn't catch all of it."

"What do they think is wrong?"

"Just some stuff..."

"Just some stuff?" I repeat. "Sooo... *stuff* is your diagnosis?"

She tilts her head and gives me a look. "No, but do you really want to hear all this?"

"I wouldn't ask if I didn't." I push my hair out of my face. "You don't have to tell me, though. It's cool."

She takes a deep breath and pulls the thin, white blanket up. Her fingers fidget over the hem.

"I have an eating disorder. And some other problems. With my stomach, esophagus, and overall health." She lifts her gaze from the blanket to meet my eyes. "And mentally."

"Oh," I say softly, letting that sink in. Now the eating of the burgerless hamburger makes sense.

"I've known for a while," she adds. "I was diagnosed a few years ago. I've just been in denial, I guess. I've been afraid to go back to the doctor, and I couldn't afford to. It's been getting worse lately, though."

"Then it's good you're getting help now."

"Yeah." She doesn't sound convinced.

I struggle to say something to make her feel better, but I've got nothing that doesn't sound cheesy or preachy.

"Do you want me to call anyone for you? Or bring you anything?"

She shakes her head. "No, I'm good. You should probably go, though. I know you have to work and they're going to move me to a room soon."

Nodding, I stand and step toward her bed. "If you want, me and Kyle can drive your car to your house so it's not sitting in the school lot overnight. I'm sure you don't want it getting towed."

"You'd really do that for me?"

"Sure. We'll do it tonight."

"Thank you. You're a really good guy, Jude."

I touch her hand and give it a reassuring squeeze. "Feel better, okay, Sparkles? Send me a text and let me know how you're doing. I'm guessing you're gonna need a ride home?" I tease.

She lets out a little laugh. "It's like you *know* me."

As I walk outside, I realize I've blown half the work day sitting in a hospital with some girl I barely know when I'm on a construction deadline. Where the hell are her parents? She's cute and all, but I can't be some kind of transportational knight in shining armor for her, coming to her rescue every time she needs a ride. I'll take her car home for her, and then that's it. I have to disengage.

But when I get in my truck and see her aviator hat and goggles sitting on the passenger seat, I know she's not the kind of girl I'm going to be able to just shove out of my mind.

CHAPTER 8

SKYLAR

Our bodies give us lots of warnings. What we choose to do with those warnings is up to us, of course. My body—and my mind—have been throwing up red flags for years. Like most people, I ignored them. Brushed them off. Made excuses. My mom did the same, ignoring my *attention-seeking antics* since I was a little girl. Finally, my body said *screw you, Skylar*... and whammied me into the sidewalk right in front of Jude.

The diagnosis I was given a long time ago is mostly the same, it's just all gotten worse.

Acid reflux.

Ulcers.

GERD.

Dehydration.

Vitamin deficiency.

Anxiety.

Depression.

Exhaustion.

And last, but certainly not the least, and my favorite to say—ARFID. Avoidant/Restrictive Food Intake Disorder.

But I'll digest (no pun intended) all that later. Right now, I'm worried about Fluffle-Up-A-Gus. Home alone in my locked bedroom with an unacceptable-to-a-cat amount of kibble and water. Not only will Gus be disgruntled, but she will seriously run out of food and water by tomorrow morning.

If something happened to her, I wouldn't be able to deal with it. She's my snuggle buddy.

I haven't texted my mom about my whereabouts yet, but I know she can't get into my room to feed my cat. She'd never climb through my window, and I'm sure there's too much stuff between the living room and my bedroom door for her to scale over. My mom doesn't even like cats.

Which is good, I suppose, because if she did? She'd probably have a thousand crammed into our house.

That leaves me with asking Megan or possibly Jude to go to my house, through the window, to take care of Gus.

Even though Meg's my best friend, she's never seen my living situation. She'll be horrified. I know she wouldn't tell anyone at school, but what if it changed how she felt about me? I pee in a bucket of cat litter. I shower at school. That's a little hard to accept.

Jude will be horrified, too, but he doesn't seem like the judgmental type. And we don't have a relationship. What's the worst that could happen? He'll think I'm a mess and never give me a ride again? I can live with that.

Right?

But... Jude's an adult. If he got caught climbing through the bedroom window of an eighteen-year-old girl, he could get into trouble. I can just see him explaining to police that he was only trying to feed my cat. Nobody would believe that.

Megan, being a fellow teen, is the safer choice. If she got caught, it would most likely be brushed off as typical teenage girl behavior.

I send her a text:

Me: Hi!

Megan: OMG where are you? I've been looking for you and texting you all day.

Me: I'm in the hospital.

Megan: OMFG what? 😳

Me: I passed out right in the parking lot this morning.

Megan: Get out!

Me: I did! Jude saw me and drove me here. Sooo embarrassing. 😱

Megan: Jude with the muscles and tats?

Me: Yes. 😘

Megan: You lucky bitch! LOL Are you sick?

Me: I have bad acid reflux and dehydration.

Megan: That sucks!

Me: I'm going to be here until tomorrow.
Maybe until Wed. I was wondering if you can do me a really big favor?

Megan: Of course.

Me: I need you to give my cat food and water and get my phone charger.

Megan: No problemo!

Me: I have to kinda tell you something.

Megan: Ok.

Me: You have to climb through my bedroom window. If you're in front of my house, looking at the front door, it's on the right side of the house. There's a wooden crate under the window to stand on.

Megan: Um……. Why? 😨

Me: Please don't make me answer that now. I promise I will. I just can't now.

Megan: You're scaring me, but okay. Is your cat going to bite me? 🐈

Me: No! She's a sweetheart. Once you get in my room, there're jugs of food and water right there. You can't miss it. My phone charger is next to my bed. You have to leave from the window, too. Please don't open my bedroom door.

Megan: What about your mom? Won't she wonder what I'm doing?

Me: No. She probably won't even hear you and she won't see you.

Megan: This is highly suspect but I'm here for it.

Me: 😂 Make sure you shut the window when you go in, and then when you leave so the cat doesn't get out.

Megan: Will do. Should I go tonight?

Me: If you can. I really appreciate it.
Megan: I'll bring your charger to you tonight before visiting hours are over.

Me: You're the best. I love you. I promise I'll explain everything.

Megan: Don't worry about it. I gotta go. Feel better! xo

Maybe this won't be so bad. Megan might not even notice the buckets. I only have a dresser and a nightstand, and my mattress is on the floor, but my room looks mostly okay. It's not messy or dirty—just sparse. So, I may just have to explain why I use a window instead of the door.

I can handle that.

I type a text to my mother that I'm at the hospital for the night, but not to worry.

Not that she will.

The nurse comes in, and we debate what I'm going to have for dinner. She doesn't want to give me bread and water. She tries to sell me on chicken soup and Jell-o. I gag just thinking about it. We settle on tea with no milk and toast with butter on the side.

She also hands me a tiny cup with a pill in it.

"What's this?" I ask.

"An antacid. It's for heartburn."

I don't like to take pills unless I see them come directly from the bottle myself.

She eyes me with irritation as I take a photo of the pill with my phone before swallowing it. Later, I'll google the markings on it and confirm it is what she says it is.

Half an hour later I sip tea and nibble on toast while I watch a game show on the television. I still haven't heard from my mom, even though my message is showing as read on her end.

Thinking about her makes me think about how much this hospital visit is going to cost. I don't have insurance. Or money. My mother is not the type to help me pay bills.

When I messaged Rebecca earlier, she was concerned but told me not to worry and to come to work when I was ready. But being out of work means not getting paid.

Of course, this had to happen right when I was given cool new job responsibilities and a raise.

My goal of saving up for an RV is going up in flames.

At around six p.m., Megan drifts into my room carrying a big pink shopping bag on one arm and a huge Louis Vuitton tote bag on the other. She immediately hugs me, then sits on the edge of my bed, piling her bags on top of me.

"First of all, your cat is the cutest thing ever," she says. "Second, what the hell is up with all the locks on your door? I'm not feeling good about this, Sky. Is someone in that house hurting you?"

I shake my head so hard I'm pretty sure my brain rattles. "No, nothing like that."

"You have to tell me. I promise I won't judge you, or tell anyone. But I can't just ignore this sitch. You're my best friend." She takes a breath. "How are you feeling? You're looking a little like you've got the worst hangover of your life."

"That would be great if I actually had a hangover."

She touches the pink shopping bag. "I hope you don't mind,

but while I was in your room I grabbed some clothes for you, and the book that was on your nightstand in case you want to read."

"You're so sweet. Thank you."

"Your charger's in there, too. Now tell me what's up."

Her eyes widen as I tell her about my mother, and her mouth hangs open just as wide as I divulge some—but not all—details about the hoarding and how it's taken over the house.

"Oh my God, Skylar. I don't even know what to say. It's horrible and disgusting and I can't believe you never told me this."

"I really didn't want anyone to know, Meg. It's embarrassing."

"But I'm your friend! I thought you were just being a weirdo who didn't want me to see your toys and clothes. You can come to my house any time to shower or use the toilet. Fuck this shit. I don't want you to feel embarrassed at all. I love you and nothing could change that."

Leaning up, I put my arms around her and hug her. "I'm so lucky to have you."

"I'm just as lucky to have you," she says when I let her go. "You've put up with my 'tude for years." Suddenly, she grabs on to my hand with excitement. "I forgot to tell you! Guess what!?"

"What?"

"I'm seeing Erik tonight! We're going to the diner, so I can't stay here long. I have to go home and fix my face. We're meeting at eight."

Her face looks fine to me. Unlike my own face right now.

"Wow! Who asked who out?"

"I asked him."

"You did!" I laugh, but I admire her for going after what she wants. I'm not sure I'd ever have the confidence to ask a guy out.

"I did!"

"You have to text me after and tell me everything."

"Of course I will. I'll take a selfie of us together so you can see how cute he looks now."

"That'll give me something to look forward to."

She squints at me and fixes the gown around my shoulders. "I'm worried about you, though. Maybe I should postpone my date and stay here with you."

"I'm fine. I want you to go. I'm just going to read and sleep. It'll be nice to be able to sleep in an air-conditioned room instead of sweltering all night."

"Are you sure? I can have dinner with Erik tomorrow night."

I smile at her. "I want you to go have fun. I'm living vicariously through you, so you have to keep me entertained."

Sadness creeps up on me after she leaves. I watch the sun fade from the hospital window. I'd be leaving work right now if I hadn't fainted, heading home to snuggle Gus and research photography tips. Eating a hot dog roll for dinner and a cherry life saver for dessert.

I wish I were having dinner with a cute boy like Megan is. I wish my face looked flawless instead of pale and sick. I wish I could go to the diner and eat cheesy fries and drink a creamy vanilla shake. I wish my house was a clean and normal home. I wish my mom acted like a mom.

I wish someone other than Megan and Gus loved me and cared about me. On that depressing thought, I close my eyes and try to get some sleep.

CHAPTER 9

SKYLAR

The doctors kept me in the hospital for four grueling days. Even though I wasn't sweating all night like I do in my own room, I slept like shit, and worried about Gus constantly even though Megan snuck into my bedroom every night to take care of her. She texted me pictures while she was there so I could see that Gus was okay.

She also sent me pictures of her and Erik, who actually *is* super cute. She's seen him every night since they had their first diner date. Things seem to happen so easily and smoothly for Megan all the time, while I drive the struggle bus.

My mother texted me once to ask what was wrong. I typed out a huge explanation that took up my entire phone screen, and she never replied. That's *six inches* of tiny words. I don't know if she just doesn't care or if she feels guilty. Or maybe she got distracted by something on QVC. I guess it really doesn't matter since the end result is the same for me.

An hour ago Megan dropped me off at home and now I'm sitting on my bed with Gus in my lap, as I hold five written prescriptions I can't afford to fill, and a treatment plan I won't be able to commit to. I can't pay for weekly visits to a psychiatrist who specializes in eating disorders, anxiety, and depression.

I've never considered myself depressed, though. Sad and frustrated sometimes, but not depressed.

Either way, I won't be able to go to find out.

Two nights ago, I sent a text to Jude telling him how I was, and he responded with a *Great. Hope you continue to feel better.*

It seemed short, almost cold and formal. He didn't even call me Sparkles. I was hoping he would, because it always gives me a little burst of happiness, and it's been a while since I felt that way.

Maybe I *am* depressed.

Since I came home from the hospital on a Thursday afternoon, Rebecca convinced me over the phone to stay home until Monday morning and not go back to school or work yet. I have a doctor's note for school, so I'm not worried about issues there, but I am worried about missing so much of my paycheck. I pay the electric and cable bill at the house. Not because my mother can't afford to pay it, but because she forgets to. Lights and TV are two things I'm not willing to live without, so I'd rather pay myself to make sure I don't end up sitting in the dark.

I've spent my entire Friday cleaning my room and researching the ailments I was diagnosed with to see what I can do to feel better without expensive doctors and prescriptions.

At five p.m., my phone chirps with a text.

Jude: Hey.

I stare at the screen with surprise. He's never texted me on his own before.

Me: Hi.

Jude: How are you feeling?

There's a constant burn in my stomach. It feels like there's something stuck in my throat and chest. My ears hurt and my insides feel jittery. I'm exhausted and have brain fog.

Me: Much better, thanks.

Jude: Good. I have your hat and your book bag.

Oh, shit.

Me: I totally forgot about those.

Jude: I can swing by after work and bring them to you. I'm leaving in about ten minutes.

Me: You don't have to do that. You can give them to me Monday when I go to school.

Jude: I'd rather bring them to you tonight.

Geez. He really wants to give me my stuff back.

Me: Okay. You can just leave them on the front steps and I'll grab them later.

Jude: Can't I just hand them to you like a normal person?

No, Jude. I look awful with no makeup on and I haven't had a shower in days and I feel grimy. And I don't want you to see me crawling in and out of the window because opening the front door is a huge nope.

The chirp of the message app pulls my attention back to the screen.

Jude: Are you avoiding me?

Me: Of course not. I just don't feel well.

Jude: I thought you said you felt better?

Me: I meant I felt better than before, but still not great.

Jude: Got it. I guess I'll leave it on your front steps, then.

Me: You don't have to, but thank you.

Forty minutes later, my phone rings, and his number lights up my screen.

"Hello?" I say.

"It's me. I'm at your house."

Damn!

"You can just leave the stuff. You really didn't have to come all the way over here."

He clears his throat. "Actually, I did. I ran into your friend earlier. I asked her how you were, and she said she was worried about you. She said something like 'especially about you having to live in that house.'"

My heart leaps up into my throat. I can't believe Megan actually said that to him! She promised she wouldn't say anything to anyone.

"Really?" I say casually. "What else did she say?"

"That's all she said. But it was pretty obvious she's concerned about something."

"Megan is a drama queen. I'm fine."

"Skylar, come to the front door. Just let me see that you're okay."

I haven't seen the inside of the front door in years. I'm not even sure if my mother uses that door anymore. I think she uses the garage door to get in and out and to have her new treasures brought into the house, which still requires careful navigation through rows and piles, only with spider webs.

"I can't," I reply. "Why are you being so difficult?"

"Why are you?"

"I look awful."

He scoffs into the phone. "I don't give a shit what you look like. I care that you're okay."

"Don't I sound okay?"

"No, you sound like someone who's trying to get rid of me."

"You obviously can't take a hint."

"You can't bullshit a bullshitter, Sparkles. I'm gonna knock on the door in two seconds—"

"Don't!" I say quickly. "Please don't. Come to the window on the right side of the house."

"You mean the one I've seen you climbing through?"

I gulp. "Yes."

"Okay, I'm hanging up. I'll see you at the window, Rapunzel."

I throw on a white hoodie, pulling the hood over my rumpled hair. I straighten my wrinkled comforter. On the way to the window, I grab the can of air freshener and give the room a few quick sprays, then make sure my closet doors are shut.

"Be cool!" I whisper to Gus.

Before Jude has a chance to tap on the window, I shove it open and peer outside to find him standing beneath it. He's almost tall enough to see inside.

"Hi," I say.

"Hi again." He reaches up and hands me my book bag, hat,

and a small, brown stuffed teddy bear. "I got you a get-well bear."

"Oh." Further words escape me. I put my things on the floor beside me, but clutch the little bear against my chest. "Thank you."

"Can I come in?" he asks.

My stomach sinks like a bag of bricks. "In here?"

His gray eyes pin me with the impatience of a frustrated parent dealing with an unruly toddler. I can't blame him, I know I'm acting like an idiot.

"Fine," I answer with a sigh, backing away from the window so he can climb through it. I'm surprised he's able to maneuver his wide shoulders through. For a moment, I was afraid he'd get stuck.

I close the window behind him. He slowly circles the room as if he's expecting a serial killer to jump out from under the bed or from the closet.

"You look better," he says when his gaze lands on me.

"Thanks."

He slowly moves to my bedroom door and nods at the three deadbolts.

"What's this all about?"

"It's not as bad as you're probably thinking, Jude."

Crossing his arms, he leans back against the door, his frame almost completely covering it. He seems much bigger here in my small room. "Nothing good would require that many locks."

"Why do you care?" I reply defensively, not wanting to tell him the truth.

His eyes soften for a beat, but harden again when he takes a breath. "I'm not sure, to be honest. But now that I'm here and I see *this*," he cocks his head toward the locks, "I'm not just gonna ignore it."

Jude's obviously like a dog with a bone. He's not going to

forget this and leave, and I'm too tired to think up a believable, creative lie. Jude's too smart to buy a lame explanation, anyway.

"You can trust me," he says. "Haven't I proven that to you already?"

Still holding the stuffed bear like a security blanket, I nod and lower myself down to sit on the edge of my bed.

"Yes."

"I'm not into begging people to talk to me, Sparkles. I worked my ass off in the heat today. I'm tired. You look tired, too. Make this easy on both of us, okay?"

He slowly crosses the room and I stare at the tips of his scuffed boots when he stops in front of me.

"Can I sit next to you?"

"Yes."

He sits about a foot away from me, and Gus immediately starts rubbing her cheek down the length of his arm. I always thought she'd be leery around a guy since she's never been around one before.

"Cute cat," he says.

"It's kind of a long story," I begin. "I guess there's a few things going on. There's what's out *there*." I swing my gaze to the locked door. "And what's going on with me."

His large hand gently strokes the cat's back as he waits for me to continue. Gus purrs like a tiny furry locomotive in response.

"I'm not sure when it started, but my mom is a hoarder. I think she probably always was, but it wasn't this bad when I was younger. She's got stuff piled almost to the ceiling in every room of the house. You can't get from room to room without climbing over things or squeezing between. She stopped cleaning years ago. The kitchen and bathroom are filthy, and there's bugs and rotting food." I swallow hard. Jude's chin rises a little and a muscle in his stubbled jaw twitches. "I can't use the bathroom anymore, so I use cat litter in a big bucket and just throw it away every day. I know it's gross, but I didn't know what else to do."

He shoves his hand roughly through his hair, the corners of his eyes narrowing as he scans the room, finally noticing the small fridge in the corner.

"I keep some food and water in here, and I shower at school every day, after gym class, or at a truck stop. I haven't heard from my father since he left a few years ago. And my mom… she just sits out there. She does customer service phone calls from home for work. But it's like she's forgotten I'm here. She doesn't talk to me. I don't go out there anymore, so I never see her. I just send her text messages. Sometimes she replies. I have to keep the door locked so she can't get in and pile stuff in here. I use the window because I can't get to the door."

"What the ever-lovin' *fuck*," he growls when I finish.

Wincing, I say, "I've learned to live with it until I can hopefully move out."

He stands up abruptly and points to the door. "Open it," he says. "Open that door right now and let me see."

My heart pounds. This is my worst nightmare. I don't want him to see—or smell—the rest of the house. "Jude, I—"

"Open it. Now," he says, his chest heaving up and down.

I stand and move to the door. My hand shakes as I reach for the locks. "You can't say anything to my mom, Jude. She's sick. Please don't—"

"I'm not going to say anything. Just let me see what's on the other side of this door."

My mom is most likely too engrossed in the television to realize anyone is in the house.

The pain in my chest spreads up to my throat and collarbone as I slide the deadbolts and swing the door open. Jude recoils, his nose crinkling from the foul smell. I'm sure whatever friendship I've forged with him will be over by the time he leaves tonight. Nobody wants to be friends with someone living in such filth.

He lets out a low whistle as he ventures just a foot outside my door—as far as he can get unless he attempts to squeeze his body through the narrow path of piles that are taller than him. I grab his arm and pull him back inside my room, shutting the door quickly and relocking it.

"Happy now? You've seen the house of horrors."

"Do you know what kind of fire hazard that is? Not to mention, endangering a child—"

"I'm eighteen," I interject.

"You weren't a few months ago. This is *fucked up*." He paces the length of my room, glancing every few seconds at the bedroom door.

"Do you want to sit in the backyard and talk?" I offer after watching him for a few seconds. I'm sure he's probably really wanting a cigarette right now.

He nods rapidly. "Yeah, I need some air."

Even though I've climbed out the window myself hundreds of times, he holds his hands out to help me once he's on the ground. Chivalry isn't dead with this guy. Silently, we walk in the dark to the back of the house and sit on an old, rusty bistro set that's been here for years. Actually, *I* sit. Jude lights up a cigarette and stares up at the sky.

His concern for me is sweet, but unexpected. I'm not sure what to do with this kind of care from someone. Should I be grateful, or suspicious?

How do we ever know if we can truly trust someone?

"You really shouldn't be living like this, Skylar. It's unhealthy in about twenty fucking ways."

"I know that. But this is all I've got. My options are limited. I'm doing my best to save money so I can get the hell out of here. That's why I was so excited about doing more for

Rebecca. I'm hoping I can work for her full time after I graduate."

"Where's your father?" He asks this facing the tree with the broken swing, which somehow seems very fitting.

"He lived in that camper out front until he couldn't deal with it anymore."

He spins around to stare at me. "He left you here to live like this?"

My non-answer is answer enough.

He drops his cigarette on the ground, smashes it with his boot, then sits in the chair on the other side of the lopsided table.

"Tell me what happened in the hospital. Did you have more tests? You okay?

I finger a leaf stem that's stuck in the filigree edge of the table.

"Yes. I've had some health issues since I was young, but I've never been able to take the meds or see the doctor for follow-ups. I guess it's all gotten worse."

"Why haven't you been taking your meds?"

"We don't have health insurance and my mother never believed it was serious. I was held back because I was out of school so much when I was younger. If I didn't feel well, she just sent me to bed. She stopped taking me to the doctor."

"Un-fucking-real," he says, shaking his head.

"My mom's just..." I grapple for a nice word. "Not right in the head. I've learned not to rock the boat. I take care of myself."

"You shouldn't have to."

I yank the leaf out from its trap and fling it onto the ground. "I don't have a choice."

"You're right." He rubs his hand across the stubble on his chin. "Are you okay? You have meds now? You'll feel better?"

I wish.

"Not exactly. I can't afford the prescriptions or the weekly appointments they want me to go to."

"*Weekly?*"

All these questions have me on edge. I've never had to explain myself to anyone before. I'm used to being brushed off and ignored. Able to fade into the shadows and disappear.

I bring my knees up to my chest and rest my sneakers on the chair, wrapping my arms around my legs.

"I think I told you when we were at the hospital, I have an eating disorder," I say, letting my gaze finally meet his. Tiny lines etch the outer corners of his eyes. "It's called ARFID. It stands for Avoidant Restrictive Food Intake Disorder. Apparently, I've had it for a long time, but I was officially diagnosed with it last year. I saved up some money and took myself to a doctor. I couldn't afford to keep going."

"What is that? Like bulimia?"

"No, I don't make myself throw up. I just can't eat certain foods. I mean, I *can* eat them. I just... Mentally, I can't get myself to. If I try to, I gag. Or feel nauseous and get sick. They told me it's like a mental illness. I've connected certain foods to traumatic things that happened to me when I was young, so its like my brain is trying to protect me by not letting me eat those foods."

I'm glad it's dark out, with only the streetlight and the moon casting a glow over us. I don't want him to see my face. I don't want to see his face while I'm telling him—this guy I barely know, but *want* to know—every embarrassing detail about my personal life.

"I think it started when I was little because my mom kept expired food in the house. Like milk. Eggs. Chicken. Fruit. Pudding. I didn't know any better, so I ate it. Then I'd get sick. I guess my mind related certain foods with getting sick. Sometimes it's not even the exact food, but the same color of that food, or the texture." I exhale and try to gauge his silence. Is he just listening? Pitying me? Judging me? "I have digestion issues, too. Acid reflux. I get really bad heartburn. And sore throats and sinus pain. Sometimes I don't eat or drink enough because it makes me feel sick. But then not eating or drinking makes me feel sick, too. I guess I'm just a hot mess."

"You're not. Don't ever think that."

The deep sincerity of his voice reaches way down into my soul and calms me like a warm blanket. I can't help but revel in it for a few moments before I start to talk again.

"You're the only person I've ever told all of this to. Megan doesn't even know everything, and she's been my best friend for years."

"You were dealt a shitty hand."

"Maybe so, but I'm not going to let it play out the rest of my life. I'll find a way to get out of here and I'll figure out how to eat a damn hamburger."

He lets out a laugh and nods with admiration all over his face. "And that right there is why I call you Sparkles."

I'm not sure how he does it. Somehow, he makes me feel like every molecule in my body has learned how to smile.

I like it.

I like *him*.

CHAPTER 10

JUDE

The walls are pink. Not a light, nursery room pink, but a bold magenta kind of pink. I pulled the beige carpet up a few years ago and it damn near took me two weeks to finish. Not because it's hard to rip carpet up—I can do that in my sleep. But because the brighter, cleaner, plushy areas of the rug were reminders of where the bed and furniture once were.

Memories can be a bitch.

The hardwood floor I'm standing on now is much better. Not harboring any ghosts. But even though I refurnished it with brand new furniture, this is the only room that continues to feel like a pit of emptiness.

I hate pink with a passion, but I could never bring myself to repaint it.

And yet, I still feel like it's screaming at me. This fuckin' room and its hideously girly walls. It's saying *Hey! Look at me! I'm a nice, clean, pink room without a person!*

Like a bun without a burger.

Leaving the room, I close the door behind me. I've always kept the door closed, hoping that, maybe someday, I'd hear Erin in there. Blasting music, giggling on the phone with a friend, or yelling wise-cracks at me.

The mind tells us silly things to appease us.

A long time ago, this house was home to what I thought was a happy family. But laughter turned to yelling, which led to divorce. My dad moved out when I was seventeen and Erin was nine. I spent most of my time partying. I drank a lot, got high a lot, and got into trouble a lot. I moved out when I was eighteen. Five years later, my mom was battling cancer and I left my dingy apartment to move back in—with the promise of getting my shit together to take care of her and my sister.

My mom got better, but Erin turned into a bit of a wild child that our mother couldn't handle. Wanting to be the cool older brother, I became more of a friend, and I let my sister's antics slide.

Then she was gone.

My mother sank into grief, then met a man who swept her off her feet, as the saying goes. She wanted a new beginning. Away from this town, this house, and anything that reminded her of her past—including me. She signed the house over to me and left the next day, becoming the third person to disappear from my life.

If I'd been there for my sister like I should've been, maybe she wouldn't have disappeared. Our mother wouldn't have run away. I wouldn't feel guilty, worthless, and abandoned. Who knows, maybe I wouldn't have a fear of relationships and I'd be living in this three-bedroom, two-and-a-half bath house on two acres with a wife and kids, and my mom and sister would be coming over for Christmas dinner.

I jump on my motorcycle and ride to my favorite place in the mountains, trying to forget about the empty pink room, but the voice is still in my head, just like it has been for the past week. What started as a crazy idea has taken on a life of its own. The more it sits in my brain marinating, the less crazy it seems, and the more right it feels

I can make things better.

I haven't talked to Skylar since I saw her at her house a week ago. I've seen her walking to and from the school parking lot, and we've waved at each other. But that night, guilt stalked me all the way home from her house. It's been hanging around ever since. Watching me. Staying out of sight, but making its presence known.

Even the hot shower I took when I got home that night couldn't wash away the stench of rotting food—or whatever the hell that smell was—out of my nostrils. Sleep didn't banish the images of the deadbolts, the piles of trash, and the sadness and anxiety in Skylar's eyes.

It all felt so gross, hopeless, and wrong.

And ultimately, not in any way, shape, or form is any of it my problem or concern.

But just like when I discovered Cassie—a tiny, dirty puppy all alone at an empty job site—I can't get myself to walk away. I tried with the puppy. For three days I watched her stumbling around in the leaves. I ignored her whimpers and her huge, sad brown eyes, assuming she could take care of herself, or someone else would step in and help her. That didn't happen. Finally, I snatched her up to take her home for the night because it was chilly, and I was afraid she'd freeze.

One night, my ass.

That was four years ago.

I pull my phone out of my pocket and send Skylar a text.

Me: Hey, Sparkles.

Skylar: Hi Lucky. 🍀

Me: Are you at work today?

Skylar: Yes, I am. Are you the job police? 🙃😀

I laugh and type back:

Me: No. 😊 Can we go for a drive when you're done with work?

Skylar: You want to drive my car again, don't you? 🚗

Me: 😂 yeah. But I also want to talk to you.

A few seconds pass before she replies.

Skylar: Is it something bad?

Me: No.

Skylar: Okay. If you want to come to the shop at 3:30, we can go for a drive.

I wait in the parking lot, smoking and leaning against the hood of her car. I don't want Rebecca to think something's going on between me and Skylar, but I really want more of those gooey chocolate chip cookies.

Me: Any chance you can snag me some of those cookies? 😊

Skylar: LOL. Sure! I'll be out in five.😀

She comes out right on time, still looking a little pale, but more energized than the last time I saw her. Today she's wearing her fringe moccasins, jeans fashionably ripped from mid-thigh to her knee, and a fuzzy black sweater with little feathers that looks like a crow exploded on it.

This chick has the weirdest, coolest clothes I've ever seen.

She approaches me with a big smile and hands me her keys along with a little blue bag of cookies.

"I feel like you only want to see me for my car and cookies," she teases when we climb in.

"Maybe it's to see what bizarre outfit you're wearing."

"What? You don't like my clothes?" she challenges with a confident, sassy smirk.

I start the engine and let it idle for a few seconds. "Actually, I dig your clothes."

When we get out of town, I offer her one of the cookies before I start chowing down on them.

Her nose crinkles. "No, thanks."

"Have you ever tried one?"

"Cookies are on my no list."

"Good. More for me." I flash her a grin and bite into one. "Have you seen the doctor yet?"

She shakes her head. "No. I'm figuring it out."

I'm not ready to have this conversation until we're parked someplace quiet, so I divert back to food.

"Are you hungry? I'll take you to get something to eat."

"Jude." She turns to glare at me, pushing her long hair behind her ear. "Please don't try to feed me. I'm not a pigeon in the park."

"I know, I just—"

"Just *don't*. I don't want to be analyzed or pitied by you. Just be my friend, okay?"

I swallow my cookie. "Friends don't let friends starve."

"I'm not starving."

"You fainted on the sidewalk."

"I was tired, and it was hot as hell. That had nothing to do with my other problems. I've fainted at least once a year since I was little."

She says it like it's totally normal, which is disturbing, but I let it go. My plan today was to help her, not annoy her so much that she wants to jump out of the car to get away from me.

She tells me funny stories about weird customers as we drive. I didn't have a plan on where to go, but we end up back at the playground where we jumped off the swings.

"Don't tell me you want to try to beat me at the swing jump," she says as she pushes her rusty car door open. "You'll lose again."

"Nope, I just want to talk to you."

She side-eyes me on the walk over to a picnic table farthest away from the other five adults and their kids running around.

"Why do I feel nervous that you keep saying *talk* like it's something serious?"

"'Cuz it *is* serious."

We sit on the bench next to each other and watch a little girl dump a pail of sand over her head and then giggle wildly. Skylar turns to me, her forehead creased. Her tongue darts across her lips nervously.

"So, what's up, Lucky? You're not dying, are you?"

"Fuck no."

My palms are clammy. I'm losing my cool fast, realizing this idea of mine is in fact, a supremely fucked-up idea. She might freak out, call me dirty names, and run for her car. She might think I have some twisted ulterior motive for trying to help her.

"Jude?" she urges.

"I've been thinking about your situation," I say, rubbing my hands together. "And I think I can help you."

A frown curves her mouth. "Which situation? My house? My illness?"

"All of it."

She leans her elbow on the table, chin resting on her hand, her blue eyes squinting slightly with intrigue and apprehension.

I still can't believe the words that come out of my mouth next. Words I never thought I'd say, especially like this. "I was thinking we could get married."

I'm sure she's not breathing. She's gone totally stone still and silent, staring at me for what feels like forever. Finally, she blinks and snaps out of it. "We could do *what*?" She almost shrieks the word *what*. Two of the women by the sandbox glance over at us.

I clear my throat and avoid eye contact with the onlookers. "Get married. Just on paper," I add quickly, as if it could lessen the shock. "I can put you on my insurance so you could go to the doctor and get your meds. You could live in my house if you want. I have an extra, empty room. You'd have your own bathroom. No strings. Strictly roommates until you get on your feet."

"You want to marry me?" she says, utterly stupefied.

"No," I say. "I mean yeah, but only to help you. It won't be a *real* marriage. Once you graduate and can work full time and get your own insurance, we'll get a divorce. No big deal. But it'll fix this shitty mess you're in until then. You'll have a safe, clean place to live, and you can get the medical help you need."

She looks like she's gone into shock. Her complexion has visibly paled even more. She stares past me at the kids playing behind us. She's gotta be petrified sitting here next to a guy who, in her eyes, must be coming across as a creeper. And I've gotta be a straight-up lunatic for suggesting marriage to an eighteen-year-old girl.

Who's still in high school.

Way to go, Lucky. You've officially lost your mind.

Suddenly, I wish I could spontaneously combust into a cloud of smoke and disappear.

"What's in it for you?" Her voice wavers.

My brain goes blank. What *is* in it for me?

"Um..." I push my hand through my hair and pull my cigarettes out of my pocket. I'm not sure how to answer that, because while technically there's nothing in it for me on the surface, there is on a deeper, personal level.

Redemption. The chance to help someone when I couldn't, or didn't, so long ago when it was right under my nose. To hopefully not let another young woman get dragged down to a bad place when she has so much potential.

I snap open my zippo, light my Marlboro, then take a long drag.

"Just want to do something nice." I exhale smoke away from her. "That's all."

"But why? Why me?"

Shrugging, I say, "Why not? I think you deserve a break. You're a good person."

She brings her legs up and tucks her feet under her, still staring at me.

"What about Fluffle-Up-A-Gus?"

I choke on smoke and go into a sputtering fit. "What the fuck is fupagus?"

"My cat, Jude," she says, as if I should know. "Fluffle-Up-A-Gus."

"Bring it. The more the merrier."

"What about your dog? Is she cat friendly?"

"I guess we'll find out."

Her eyebrow quirks up. "Do you live alone?"

"Yes."

"In this town? I'd stay in my school?"

"Yes."

A few quiet moments pass, and I assume she's thinking of more questions. Her complexion is slowly coming back. A hesitant, shy smile eventually spreads across her face. "W-Would I change my last name?"

I hadn't even thought of that.

"Only if you want to. That's totally up to you."

She exhales a long, slow breath, and closes her eyes for a few moments before opening them. "This is just… whoa. My mind is kinda blown right now, Jude. Here I was thinking my biggest decision this year would be what to wear to the prom. Not *this*."

"I wasn't exactly planning this, either. But after I saw the way you're living, and knowing you can't see a doctor, and finding you laying on the sidewalk, it all just rattled me. I don't know why, but it did, and I want to *do* something."

I don't know how to explain something to her that I can't understand myself. All I know is that I woke up after that night at her house feeling like I *have* to do this for her. Like it's some kind of mission that's been assigned to me.

"You're serious about this? For real?" she says.

"Totally serious. I want to help you. Nothing more, I promise. I just need you to sign a prenup saying you're not entitled to half my stuff when we split. That's all I want in return."

"I'm fine with that. I don't want your stuff."

My heart is pounding and I'm not sure if it's because I'm worried about what I'm getting into, or something else.

"Do I get a ring?" she asks in a playful, almost hopeful tone.

"Diamond rings are for *real* proposals. But I guess we'll exchange wedding bands, just to make it official. We don't have to wear them, though."

"Okay."

"So… is that a yes?"

Her head tilts to the side. "Maybe… I think, yes."

"You think?" I repeat, laughing. "Shit, I'm glad this wasn't a real proposal. I'd be sitting here crushed right now."

She gives my shoulder a playful shove. "You would not. I want to think about it for a day or two, okay?"

"Hell, yeah. You should think about it for as long as you want."

"You should think about it, too."

"I've been thinking about it since the night I was at your house. No one should have to live like that. I've got a house. I've got health insurance. I don't have a wife or kids. There's no reason why I can't help you out."

"Won't it cost you money, though?"

"A little. It's not a big deal. Don't even worry about it."

"Won't it be weird that I'll be in high school and legally married?"

"Yeah… but you don't have to tell anyone. I'm sure as shit not going to advertise it. It's just an arrangement, nothing more. I wouldn't marry you for real."

Her head slowly drops, and her long hair falls over her face as she looks down at the ground. For several long moments she stays that way, her face hidden from me.

"You okay?" I ask.

She nods, and sniffles. "Yeah."

Her raspy whisper nearly strangles my heart.

Gently, I push her hair from her face.

I wasn't expecting to see tears. I resist the urge to wipe them away.

"Hey, what's wrong? I thought this would make you happy."

She brushes her face with her fingertips and smiles weakly. "It has. So much. I'm… overwhelmed." She looks up at me, her big blue eyes idling on mine. "No one's ever done anything so nice for me. Not ever."

Before I can say a word, she throws her arms around my shoulders, and her warm, damp cheek is pressing into my neck.

"Thank you," she says softly. "You're amazing."

"I'm not amazing, Sparkles. Just trying to be a good guy."

She hugs me tighter. "You are. You're the best ever."

I wasn't expecting tears and hugs.

I also wasn't expecting to put my arms around her and hug her back.

CHAPTER 11

SKYLAR

I've been in a haze since I saw Jude yesterday.

Marriage.

An *arranged* marriage.

To an older man I barely know, while I'm a senior in high school.

I've seen movies about this—marriages of convenience.

On-paper-only marriages.

In the movies, it usually turns out all cheesy romantic, with the couple falling in love and living happily ever after. That's not going to happen to us, though. My eyes are firmly on the prize—my dream RV and exploring the world with Gus.

I wish I could tell Megan about this and get some advice, but the fear of her telling me it's the stupidest thing she's ever heard is stopping me. Or she might tell Erik, and he might tell someone else, and soon the entire school would know.

As always, I'm on my own, except now I'm trying to make one of the biggest decisions of my life.

I sit on the floor with Gus, who listens intently with her bright-green eyes fixed on me.

"It could be a disaster," I say. "We'd be living in a house with a man we hardly know. He could be a psycho. He might lock us up in the basement and force me to have babies. Or he could starve us to death, and no one would ever even know we were dead. He'd just tell everyone we stole some of his money and ran away."

The cat's whiskers bend forward, and she paws at my arm, wanting to be petted.

"Or maybe he really is just a nice guy. We could live in a clean house and learn to eat good food. We could actually use the front door. And have a real bathroom. I could save money for our RV, and a year from now, we'd be living our best life." I slowly scratch the cat's head and rub her cheeks. "All we have to do is trust him. He's been nice so far, right? He hasn't done or said anything creepy. He goes to work every day. And he calls me Sparkles, Gus."

Sighing, I look around my sparse room. At the closet where me and my cat have litter boxes. At the door with the three deadbolts.

This isn't a home. It's a prison.

I'm eighteen now—a legal adult. Responsible for making my own life decisions—whether they're right or wrong.

Jude is offering me a way out, and I'd be an idiot to say no. Marrying him and accepting his help could change my entire future.

I remind myself it's not a real marriage. Not a real wedding. It's nothing but a piece of paper that'll get me out of this place and allow me to take care of myself the way I'm supposed to.

"You don't have to call him Daddy, Gus. It's not like that. I'm sure his dog will be nice to you. You might like having a furry friend to hang out with."

The cat curls up next to me, apparently satisfied with our conversation.

I pick up my cell phone and press Jude's number.

"Hey," he greets.

"Hi..." I twirl my hair nervously around my finger. "I've been thinking about your proposal."

"Let's call it an arrangement, okay?"

"Arrangement," I correct. "I was wondering if I could come over and see your house first?"

"Uh, sure. I should've offered that first. I wasn't thinking—"

"It's okay. I only just thought of it myself."

"I just finished working out. I need to take a shower, so come around four?"

"Sounds good."

"You can bring your friend if you want," he offers. "If it'll make you feel more comfortable."

"I think I'd rather come alone. But thank you."

"I'll text you my address."

Seconds later, the text comes through and I smile at the address. Winterberry Road. It sounds whimsical and safe.

"Wish me luck," I say to Gus after I've put on a little makeup, a Doors sweatshirt, jeans, and black high-top sneakers.

Using the GPS on my phone for directions, I drive across town to a rural area I'm unfamiliar with. Winterberry Road is a wooded, winding side road branching off an equally winding side road. The houses are set back from the road and spaced far apart—nothing like the boring cookie-cutter houses on my street that are practically on top of each other. Jude's mailbox is visible long before his house is, and I stare at it, making sure I have the right address before I pull into the long gravel driveway.

My heart starts to beat faster as I pull up to the house. I sip from my water bottle and open the window for fresh air, hoping to ground myself. I want to appear calm, mature, and levelheaded, even if I'm freaking out on the inside.

The two-story farmhouse-style house with wraparound

porch, flowerbeds, and garage isn't what I was expecting. It looks like a house a family would live in—not a single guy covered in tattoos. If his pickup wasn't in the driveway, I'd think I was at the wrong house.

Befuddled, I park my car in front of the garage, next to his truck. As I walk up the brick path to the porch, the only thought running through my mind is; I could live here. I could sit on that porch swing. Gus could stare out the window at all these trees and see lots of birds and chipmunks.

"You found it."

I jump at the sound of his voice. I was so lost in thought I didn't hear him open the front door, and now a little furry dog is wiggling happily at my feet.

"Hi... I didn't... She's so cute," I stammer, kneeling down to greet the adorable dog. She attempts to smother me with kisses. "Aren't you the cutest thing?" I coo, running my hands through her soft fur. Her face is barely visible behind the mop hanging over her eyes.

"Cassie, come on. Let's not maul her," he says. "Sorry, she gets excited. We don't get a lot of company. She'll calm down once you're not exciting anymore." He grins awkwardly. "I mean, I'm sure you're exciting, but you won't be anymore. To her. I mean, you just won't be new." He cringes at his own awkwardness and it makes him sexy as hell. "You get what I'm saying."

"I do." I smile and gesture to the yard with a flip of my hand. "It's pretty here."

"Come inside."

I follow him through the front door, and I'm relieved and surprised to see the inside is just as pretty and welcoming as the outside. A big kitchen opens up to a dining room. There's a cozy living room with a gray-brick fireplace. And so many windows! Everything is neat and clean—with the exception of some basic clutter on the kitchen counter. The only scent in the air is Jude's cologne. Or maybe it's his aftershave or that beard oil I keep seeing on social media. Either way, nothing smells like it's been forgotten and rotting.

"It's beautiful," I say. "I wasn't expecting it to be so nice."

"Why, 'cause I'm a single guy?"

"Yeah."

His shoulders lift. "I'm surprised, too. It was my parents' house, and I somehow inherited it. I've been slowly remodeling. This level is done, but I'm still working on the upstairs, and then I'll finish the basement."

"It's beautiful. Really."

"Lemme show you something I think your fupagus cat might like."

Laughing at his massacre of my cat's name, I follow him to the back of the house to a sunroom—all glass walls and ceiling—with tons of hanging plants and more perched on little tables.

"Wow!" I say. "This is so cool."

"Thanks. My mom was into plants. It took me a while to not kill them all, but now they're doing okay." He moves across the room. "I've got an aloe plant." He points to a row of little boxes. "And I'm growing some herbs over here. The legal kind, that is." That devilish grin. "Do you cook?" A hint of hope tinges his words.

"Me?" I guess he forgot I haven't been able to even get into the kitchen at home for a long time. Or the fact that I don't eat much. "No, but I've always wanted to."

"Well, if you want to experiment, I'll be your guinea pig. I'm usually too tired after work to cook anything decent. If you want to. And if you decide you want to live here."

His nervousness actually makes me feel better about this whole crazy situation. I think he feels just as awkward and unsure about it as I do, and that makes it feel more like we're in this together, on common ground.

"I'd love to try to cook. I promise not to poison you." I spin around the room happily. "Gus will love it in here."

"Want to see the upstairs?"

I nod excitedly and he leads the way.

"Like I said, it's still a work in progress up here." He nods toward the spackle on the wall of the hallway. "But the bedroom and bathroom you'd be using is upgraded, never been used. This is the bathroom." We stop in front of a white door and I take a quick peek inside. It takes some serious self-control for me not to squeal and jump up and down. A tile shower! A toilet! Double sinks! Everything is so clean—all white and light gray. And it all smells so fresh.

"Jude… this is awesome. I might live in that shower, just so ya know."

His eyes glimmer with pride, as they should. He's done a great job.

"As long as you keep it clean, I don't care. That's all I'd really ask for."

"I will. I promise," I say solemnly. I could never, ever wreck any of this. Not his trust or his pretty house.

"Right next door would be your bedroom. Sorry it's not attached."

Like that matters. There are a few feet between the doors, but it's totally clean, a safe-to-walk-through, unobstructed walking area. This is like heaven for me.

He opens the door to reveal a room that's very obviously a girl's room with its pink walls. It's devoid of any decor other than two white dressers, two night stands, and a full-size bed with a light-gray comforter.

"Um… did you paint this for me?" A shiver of unease slithers up my spine. Did he just assume I'd be moving in and paint it ultra-girly pink?

"No. God, no. I'd never willingly paint a room this color." He rubs his hand across his face. "This was my younger sister's room. I got rid of all her stuff and the old carpet, but she loved the color. I just couldn't paint over it. Everything is brand new—the bed, the sheets and comforter, the dressers. I hate empty rooms. I furnished it long before I met you."

I let out a quick breath of relief. "It's pretty," I say, not missing how his eyes shifted downward when he mentioned his sister. There's definitely something he's not saying. But that's okay. I'm not here to pry into this guy's personal life.

"You can repaint it if you want."

"No," I say, touching his arm. "I like it. It's a happy color. I could definitely use that."

The room is much bigger than mine at home, and the closet is bigger, too. The windows overlook the trees and flower gardens in the backyard. Soon the leaves will be vibrant reds, yellows, and oranges—the perfect New England view.

I walk around the room, lightly touching the furniture, then turn to him. He's standing in the doorway, leaning against the frame. His hair is still damp from his shower, some of it hanging over his eyes. The material of his black shirt is stretched over his arms and chest, which look pumped from working out earlier.

It's hard to ignore all the ink, muscles, and how masculine he is. It's a little intimidating. The only man I've ever lived with is my father, and he didn't have such a large, captivating presence. But I'm going to have to get used to it if I want to live here.

And I *do* want to live here, very much. I want to move in right now.

"Skylar?"

"Huh?"

Oops. I've been standing here staring at him like an idiot. I hope I wasn't making a dumb, dreamy face.

But his grin tells me yes, I was definitely making a face. "I asked if you want to go downstairs and talk about all this?"

My cheeks are suddenly warm, and my heart is fluttering with embarrassment. "Sounds good." Shoving my hands into the front pocket of my sweatshirt, I smile and duck past him through the doorway.

When we settle in his kitchen, I'm worried I'm being rude by saying no to his offer of something cold to drink. People don't realize how often they offer food and drink to each other and how hard it is for people like me to have to decline and fear insulting them. Food and drinks are social behaviors. Hopefully, with the doctor's help, I can learn to get normal with all this sort of thing.

"Can I interest you in some bread, at least?" he half-jokes. "I have wheat bread."

I shoot him a glance. "Jude. I'm fine. Please just sit down. You have to let go of the food stuff. I promise I'll go to the doctor, and I'll do my best to try to overcome my food and drink aversions. But you can't force me."

"I'm not trying to force you. I just feel bad."

"I know, and it's sweet and I appreciate it. But for the sake of both our sanities, let's not play the 'what can I get Skylar to eat or drink game.' You can eat and drink in front of me, it doesn't bother me."

"It bothers *me*. It feels rude."

"It's not," I assure him. "I can't live here if I feel like I'm under a microscope. I'm not used to it, and it'll freak me out."

He leans back in the wooden chair and nods. "You're right.

We need less stress if we're gonna live together, not more. Especially you. I'll be cool."

Oh my God. Am I really going to do this?

How can I not? If I stay at home, the house will get grosser. I can't afford the medications and the doctor visits, so I'll get sicker. I'm afraid of getting worse, and I don't know how bad it can get. What will happen to me? What if I get so sick that I can't work? I could wither away and die, locked away in my bedroom. It'll take months for my mom to realize I'm dead. Gus will die, too.

My heart pounds, my head swims, my skin breaks out in a thin sweat. Why is it suddenly so hot? I wish I could take my sweatshirt off but I only have a bra on underneath. There're so many windows, but none of them are open. I need air—

"You okay, Sparkles?"

I blink at Jude, who's suddenly blurry.

"Skylar?" His face finally comes into my vision, and he's narrowing his steel eyes at me. "You're white as a ghost again."

"I'm sorry… I feel dizzy."

"Shit." He pushes his chair back and goes to the sink, where he wets a clump of paper towels. "Put this on your forehead," he says. I do as he asks, pressing the cold towels to my face.

"Try to drink this." He twists the top off a bottle from the fridge and hands it to me. "It's basically orange-flavored water. It has electrolytes. There's nothing weird in it. Nothing that can go bad. I know I'm breaking our no-pushing-food-or-drinks deal, but I can't let you pass out in my damn kitchen."

"Okay," I whisper, giving in. I vaguely remember drinking drinks like this when I was younger. I don't like putting things in my mouth that are crayon colors, because I never thought that could be right or safe.

My fingers shake as I grip the bottle. Jude wouldn't give me anything bad. I watched him twist the top off. I heard the little snap of the seal. This is a new, unopened drink. There's a bathroom right down the hall if it makes me sick, and Jude's already proven he'll take me to a hospital if I were to get really sick.

I trust him.

Tentatively, I sip the cold, mildly sweet drink, and it's not horrible. I wait for something bad to happen—what, I don't know—but nothing does. It's actually very refreshing. I wish it was clear and not bright orange, but as long as I don't look at the color, I think I can drink it without freaking out.

"D-Do you have a dark mug you can pour it in? And a straw?" I ask.

Four seconds later, he's pouring the flavored water into a tall, black mug and pops a green straw in it.

I smile in thanks and continue to drink with my eyes closed. The sweetness is nice. The lightheadedness starts to subside. Nothing bad is happening. "I think I was starting to have an anxiety attack," I say. "I don't think it's the same as when I fainted last time."

"Anxiety attack?" he repeats, plopping into the chair across from me. "Why? Are you scared to be here?"

Scared. Excited. Worried. Hopeful.

I lower my gaze to the dog curled up on a little rug in front of the sink, a faded teddy bear toy next to her. She's content here. Loved.

"A little nervous. I think I'm scared about making the wrong decision." I remove the damp towels from my forehead and place them on the table in front of me. "I'm so tired of living in that house. And feeling sick all the time. I'm afraid of what will happen to me if I stay there."

"So am I," he agrees softly.

"I almost didn't start school this year," I admit. "I was just going to drop out and work full time, so I could hopefully make enough money to rent a room or apartment." I swallow more of the cold drink. "But I promised my grandfather I'd never drop out. I know it's silly, but even though he's gone, I'm afraid he'd know if I did it."

"It's not silly. You should stay in school. Even go to college. It's so fuckin' hard to get your shit together if you make bad choices when you're young. Sometimes you can't ever get out of the hole. Trust me, I've been there."

"I feel like I've got one foot in that hole already."

"That's why I'm trying to help you."

Twirling the straw in my drink, I study him across the table and try to figure out what his deal is. Why is he living here alone? Shouldn't a good-looking guy his age be married already? Why didn't he sell this big house and get something smaller? Why doesn't he want to repaint that pink room? And why, why, *why* does he want to help *me*?

I lick my lips nervously. "I still don't understand why you want to help me. I'm just a nobody."

He recoils from my comment. "You're not a nobody."

"But you don't even know me... Not really."

"So? People help each other every day without really knowing them, don't they?" He leans his elbows on the table, his intense gray eyes fixed on mine. "Doctors help patients. People carry your bags at the store. Some donate money to strangers. They stop to help if your car's stuck on the side of the road. There *are* good people in the world, Skylar. People who don't want anything in return except to know that they helped someone else. I've had a shitty past. I've done some shitty things. Maybe I just want a chance to do something good for once. Is that so bad?"

I swallow hard under his raw sincerity. I don't think anyone, ever, has been so deeply honest with me before. I still think there's an underlying reason for him wanting to help me, but any thoughts I had that it might be for a sketchy reason are fading fast.

"And that's all this is for you? Just a random good deed?"

He leans back in the chair again and pushes his sleeves up his arms. "Yeah. That's all." But his rough voice doesn't hide what his eyes are saying—this act of kindness means something more to him.

"Well, I guess I'm lucky, then, aren't I, Lucky?" I try to lighten the mood with a smile.

He flashes his cocky grin. "Maybe a little."

Taking a deep breath, I put the mug on the table and push it back a few inches. "So, if we do this... how does this work? What's next?"

A myriad of wedding scenes from movies flash through my mind.

"You sure you want to talk about it today? Do you want to wait until you're feeling better?"

"I feel okay. I think we should talk about it now, so I can make a decision."

He nods and his hair falls into his face, which he flicks backs with a quick, backward jerk of his head. "Okay. I guess first I'd have my lawyer draw up a contract saying that when we divorce, you aren't entitled to any of my assets or alimony. Not tryin' to be a dick, but I have to protect my business and my house."

"I totally understand."

"If you want something added to the contract, let me know."

"Like what?

"I dunno. Like I can't have half your stuff."

I snort. "What, half of my beat-up car and my cat?"

"Yeah. I tell ya what... Just so it's all fair, I'm going to have the contract say that neither one of us are entitled to each other's assets, or anything we purchase while married. All of our finances will stay separate. I'll pay whatever it is to add you to my insurance, but you're responsible for any copays or anything not covered by insurance."

"I'm good with that," I reply, inwardly hoping I can afford to pay what isn't covered. "What about rent?"

"I'm not gonna charge you rent, Skylar. I own the house."

"Well, I can't just live here for free. Even at home I pay some of the bills. I don't want a free ride, Jude."

He sighs and runs his hand through his hair. "Fair enough. How 'bout you do the shopping and pay for the groceries? I hate shopping so that'll be a big help for me." His gaze travels around the room. "And you can brush the dog."

"Can I water the plants and clean the house?"

"You're not a maid. I don't want or expect that."

"I *want* to do it."

"You can do it if you want to, but that's on you. I don't want anything from you."

"I know. It'll just make me feel good to do something. Otherwise, I'm going to feel guilty as shit. I won't go in your room or bathroom, though."

"Deal," he says. "Then I suppose we pick a date, get a marriage license, and we arrange for an officiant. There won't be any guests or witnesses, just us."

"Okay."

I was never the little girl who dreamed of a princess wedding and a flowing white gown, so I'm not surprised at how calm my voice sounds; as if this is a totally normal conversation and not the craziest thing my brain has ever had to process.

And that's saying a lot.

"Do you smoke? Drink?" he asks.

I'm taken aback by the random question. "I'm not old enough to drink."

"Oh." The corner of his mouth tugs down. "My bad. I forgot you're only eighteen."

"I wouldn't drink even if I *was* old enough. And I've never smoked."

"Obviously I'm a smoker, but I never smoke in the house. Once in a while I'll toss a beer back. I come home and crash on the couch with the dog every night. Just so you know I'm not throwing parties here. It's always quiet."

With his long hair, endless ink, and rugged, sexy looks, I never would've thought he'd be the quiet, domestic type. I pictured him hanging at bars or strip clubs.

I'm relieved to find out I was wrong.

"I'm quiet, too," I say. "So is Gus. We won't bother you. I'm not dating anyone. Me and Megan usually hang at her house. All I want to do is get better, get out of that house, graduate, and get my life on track. I don't party. I'm usually in bed by ten every night."

He winks at me and my heart does a strange, baby-goatish gallop. "No wonder you're not dating."

"Thanks. Jerk." I kick him playfully under the table.

"Just kidding," he says. "I didn't think you were into any of that stuff. You seem way too levelheaded."

"This is starting to feel like a really weird interview."

He lets out a laugh and throws his head back a little, exposing his neck tattoos. There's a small, green four-leaf clover just below his ear that I love. "I promise this is as awkward as it'll ever get. I'm not going to give you a hard time."

"I'm not going to drive you crazy or do dumb things," I promise. "You won't even know I'm here. I'll stay in my room."

"You don't have to stay in your room. You can hang wherever you want. It's a big house. You've been confined to one room for too long."

I slowly shake my head back and forth with disbelief. "I can't believe we're really going to do this. This is crazy, right?"

"It is. Not gonna lie. But it'll only be as crazy as we make it.

If we're cool about it, it'll be fine. Just two people living together, married on paper so you can see a doctor and get out of hell house. No big deal."

I let that sink in. *It's not a big deal.* "Okay. You're right."

"I do have one request," he says, clasping his hands together in front of him. I can't help but study the designs and letters tattooed on them. "This is a deal breaker."

"Uh oh." I narrow an eye at him. "What is it?"

"I need to meet your mother. I have to tell her myself what we're doing and why."

My stomach spins with anxiety. "Jude, no—"

"Skylar, I have to. It's the right thing to do. She's your mother."

"She won't even give a shit what I'm doing! She never has." I vaguely remember my mom being loving and attentive when I was very young, but those memories have faded very far into my mind's vault.

"Maybe, maybe not. Doesn't matter. You might be eighteen, but you're still her kid, and I can't just let you move in with me, and marry me, without sitting face-to-face with your mother."

I don't like this at all. I can't picture him sitting on the couch amongst all the garbage having a chitchat with my mother about marrying me. She totally dropped the parenting ball years ago. This face-to-face will be epically humiliating and awkward.

"What the hell, Jude?" I scowl. "Can't you call her? Do a video chat?" Even *I* don't remember the last time I actually had an in-person conversation with my mother. That's just the way it's been since the piles of stuff got too high for me to hike over.

He shakes his head. "No. I have to do this right."

"You said yourself it's not even a real marriage!"

"But it's a legal marriage. This isn't negotiable, Skylar."

We stare at each for a few minutes, and it's clear he's not going to back down. I feel like I'm drowning in his gray eyes, mesmerized by the silver flecks, and I have to look away. "Can I be there?"

"Of course."

If he thinks my mother is going to clutch her pearls and say, "Oh no… you cannot take my baby girl away!" he's nuts. If anything, she'll ask him for money.

"Fine. You win. Good luck squeezing those big shoulders into my house."

"You're funny." His grin widens. "If we think of anything else, we'll have it added to the prenup. I should have that ready this week, then we can move forward."

I stand and push my chair in. "I do have one rule of my own," I say, smiling up at him. "No kissing the bride at the ceremony."

He stands, too, and swaggers across the room to put my mug in the dishwasher. "That's a given. I can promise you, Sparkles, I'll never try to kiss you."

I ignore the tiny cinch of disappointment in my heart.

CHAPTER 12

JUDE

Skylar wasn't kidding.

Even with her warning, I'm shocked when she unlocks the front door of her house and we step inside.

There's a total mishmash of crap everywhere, piled from floor to ceiling. Some of it in boxes and bags, some of it just tossed loose. Clothes, luggage, canned goods, magazines, books, and blankets. Bottles of lotion and shampoo. Random decor just thrown anywhere. It's like a dollar store exploded and this woman decided to stick a couch and television on top of the mess.

"Mom," Skylar says loudly as we squeeze through narrow paths and climb over shorter piles. "We're here."

Apparently, she told her mother I'd be coming over, but didn't tell her why.

"Oh, good," her mother replies in a completely normal, upbeat voice that only makes her come off as a nut, given the fact that two people are literally climbing into her living room.

When we finally get to the far end of the room, there's a two-foot radius around the couch that's clear enough for us to stand in. Out of the corner of my eye, I see either a large roach or a small mouse scurry under the couch.

What the fuck.

All I want to do is pick Skylar up and carry her the hell out of this place.

"Mom, this is my friend, Jude," Skylar says awkwardly, swatting a fly away from her face. "Jude, this is my mother, Nicole."

Disgust coils up in me like a cobra when I realize the woman sitting on the green velour couch is only a few years older than me. She's not the older, had-a-daughter-late-in-life, hair-starting-to-gray woman my imagination conjured up.

It's obvious she was pretty once—an older version of her daughter, with long, blonde hair and blue eyes. But something, whether it be hard times, alcohol, drugs, or mental illness, has made her look rough and tired. Her hair and skin are dull, her nails way too long. On a small table next to her is a pail of sand that she's using as an ashtray. I spy two roaches in the pail. Not the bug kind, the joint kind.

"Sit..." Nicole motions to her right, pushing bags of Cheetos and pretzels off the couch and onto the floor.

Skylar grabs my arm before I can move. "No," she says. "We'll stand. We won't be here long."

Skylar's discomfort is palpable, and I don't blame her. This is like standing in the middle of a hazardous waste dump site.

I ignore her and sit on the couch next to her mother. I'm sure I sat in worse places when I was younger and partied in seedy motel rooms with strangers.

Crossing her arms, Skylar remains standing, her eyes dark with impatience, her lips mashed together. I'm pretty sure she's biting her tongue.

The old couch cushion caves under my weight, and the back of my head smacks into something hard. I turn to find myself face-to-face with a four-foot giraffe statue with its neck stretching over the back of the couch.

"What is this, exactly?" I ask, running my hand over its black felt nose.

"It's a giraffe," Nicole says.

"Why is it here, though?"

I need some kind of glimpse into this woman's rationale. Maybe she has a good reason for collecting all these things. Who knows—there could be a master plan brewing in her mind that Skylar isn't aware of.

Nicole gazes at the statue with so much admiration I feel like I'm spying on an intimate moment. "Because it's pretty, and it was only two hundred dollars, and I don't have any other giraffes," she replies.

Nope. There's no rationale here. At least not a logical one.

Nodding, I give the giraffe one more glance, and try to come up with the right words to tell this woman why I've asked her daughter to marry me, so I can get the hell out of here.

"Mom, we came here to tell you we're getting married, and I'm moving out," Skylar blurts out, beating me to it.

"Are you pregnant?" Nicole asks in an accusatory tone, her gaze zeroing in on her daughter's midsection.

"No," we both say at the same time.

"Then why are you getting married?" she says to Skylar, then turns to me. "To *you*?"

I nod. "Because—"

"How old are you?" Nicole interrupts.

"I'm thirty-four, but—"

"You're thirty-four?" Skylar squeaks with bulging eyes. "I didn't know you were that old."

"Hey, it's not *that* old," I say defensively. I've got a fuckin' six-pack under my shirt, not a dad bod.

"Well, I'm thirty-eight," her mother states, matter-of-factly. "You're old enough to be her father…"

Yeah, if I was dumb enough to get someone pregnant when I was sixteen. Which I wasn't.

I put my hands up. "Can we back it up for a sec?"

"It doesn't matter how old you are. It's not a real marriage, Mom," Skylar interjects.

"Yes," I correct. "It *is* a real, legal, marriage. But we're not together. I'm not sleeping with your kid."

Nicole presses her fingers to her temples and closes her eyes as if this conversation is giving her a headache. It's definitely giving me one. "This is very confusing," she says.

"I didn't want it to be," I reply. "We're only getting married so I can put her on my health insurance plan and give her a place to live. She's sick, and she needs to see a doctor. She needs therapy and medication."

My blood boils when Nicole rolls her eyes. I kid you not, she rolls her eyes, and leans back into the couch with a big, dramatic sigh. "This one's always been a whiner. Her stomach, her head, her throat. Her this, her that. She's been doing it since she was five years old."

"Because I'm sick, Mom. What the fuck?" Skylar's cheeks redden, and she smacks the giraffe's snout in anger. Its neck tweaks from the blow, and now it's staring at us dementedly with its glass eyes. "You're stuck in your crazy fantasy world and I'm getting out of it!"

"Okay, calm down." I reach for Skylar's hand but she pulls away with a scowl, almost tripping over a crockpot box that's in the middle of the floor.

"She doesn't even cook!" she yells, kicking the box with her sneakered foot. "I told you she wouldn't care, Jude. *Look* at her."

I *am* looking at her, and I'm getting more pissed off by the second at Nicole's detached indifference. She's just sitting there, flipping through a magazine, oblivious to her daughter's emotions. I can't tell if she's a bitch, or if there's something mentally wrong with her. Or both, which is a twisted mix.

Resting my forearms on my knees, I stare at Nicole, hoping she'll make eye contact with me, but she doesn't. "I just wanted you to know there's nothing going on between us. We're just friends. I want to help her, that's all. She'll have a safe place to live, and she'll see a doctor."

She makes a tsk noise with her tongue. "No man on the planet just wants to help a pretty young girl," she drawls. "I wasn't born yesterday."

"Stop it, Mom," Skylar seethes, shaking her head. "He's not like that."

Nicole tosses the magazine onto the floor. "I don't care what you do. This is my house and you better not take any of my things when you leave."

Skylar rolls her eyes, and I regret suggesting this meeting and putting her through this. "Jesus Christ, I don't want any of your shit. I'm trying to get *away* from it."

"And I'm not paying for a wedding," Nicole adds flippantly.

"There's not going to be a wedding," I assure her.

"Good. Don't expect me to come. It won't last a year."

I don't bother wasting my breath trying to explain that's the whole point—it's not meant to last.

"Can we please go?" Skylar asks, her eyes pleading. "The smell is making me sick."

"What smell?" Nicole asks, twitching her nose up into the air. "I don't smell anything."

I guess being nose blind really is a true phenomenon. How the hell can she not smell the putrid air in this house she's living in? I've only been in here for ten minutes and I'm tempted to snort bleach.

Standing, I clear my throat. "Nice meeting you," I say as

politely as I can. There's so much I want to say to this woman about how she's treating her daughter, but that'll only turn this meeting ugly, and I don't want to add to Skylar's stress. "I promise your daughter will be okay." *Whether you give a shit or not.* "If you need help cleaning this place out, I'm a contractor. Me and my crew could bring a dumpster over, help you get things cleaned up."

She glares at me with a sudden rage. "Why would I do that? I don't want to throw my things away."

"Okay," I answer. "You let us know if you change your mind."

"I won't," she hisses. "You can take *her*; but don't you even think about trying to take anything else."

The way she just basically gave her daughter away without a second thought makes me snap, and I can't hold back anymore. "Well, shit," I say. "I was just thinking about taking that fucking giraffe home to stick in my sunroom."

Nicole glares at me with a fiery wrath in her eyes. "Get out," she hisses.

Skylar grabs my wrist. "Let's go, Jude. Please."

We gulp fresh air when we get outside the house, attempting to clear our lungs from the sour stench. I wonder if that bitch is hiding the dead body of her husband in there. Maybe he didn't leave like Skylar thinks.

I smoke a cigarette while Skylar sits on the front steps, staring off at the sun setting behind the trees.

"I told you," she finally says, her voice resigned. "She doesn't give a flying fuck about me."

I put my foot up on the step next to her and lean down into

her line of vision. "I don't really think that's it," I say. "I think she's messed up in the head."

"Ya think?" she says sarcastically.

"I'm serious. I think she *does* care. She's just too messed up to show it or process it." I hate defending that sorry excuse for a mother, but I have to say *something* to make Skylar feel better about the way she's been treated.

"I don't even care anymore, Jude. My father tried with her; he really did. She stopped taking her meds, stopped going to the doctor. I tried after he left, too. It's just..." She shrugs helplessly. "It's just impossible. You can't help someone who doesn't want to be helped."

"You're right."

She tilts her head up and stares into my eyes with determination. "I *want* your help. I wish I didn't, but you see what I'm living with."

I exhale smoke through my nose and nod. She doesn't need me to say anything.

"I want to leave tonight," she says softly. Almost a whisper. "Can we do that? Can I move in with you tonight?"

Surprise speeds up my pulse. I wasn't planning on her moving in for a few weeks. I thought we'd both have more time to let it all sink in. They say you shouldn't make spur-of-the-moment decisions, 'cause that usually leads to a mess.

But, fuck it. I've never been known to avoid a mess.

I throw my cigarette down on the cracked walkway and stomp the embers out with my boot.

"How much stuff you got, Sparkles?" I ask.

A slow grin spreads across her face. "*Just* enough to fit in your truck."

CHAPTER 13

SKYLAR

I'm not sure if it's sad or convenient that all my belongings fit into the bed of Jude's pickup truck. And, as luck would have it, my mother had a brand-new cat carrier stored in the bathtub under a fiber-optic Christmas tree.

She let me take the carrier as a wedding gift.

I hugged her stiffly good-bye before I left, and it made my heart hurt. She didn't cling to me or get teary-eyed. A part of me wishes she had. No matter what, she *is* my mother, and I love her. Sadly, she's become someone I have no idea how to understand, and I can't allow her to hurt me anymore, whether it's intentional or not.

I followed Jude to his place in my Corvette with Gus meowing loudly from her carrier, seat-belted on the passenger side. The house faded in my rearview mirror like a blurry memory, and even though a ball of emotion welled up in my throat, I knew I'd never go back there.

Jude and I carried my stuff from the truck up his pretty oak stairs to the room with the raspberry-colored walls. I didn't have much—just my clothes, various stuffed animals, books, and toiletries. Back at my mom's house earlier, he patiently convinced me to leave the dorm fridge. Not just because it would've been a bitch to get it out of the house, but because I have to learn to use the refrigerator in the kitchen. Food shouldn't be hidden in my bedroom. Of course, the logical part of me *knows* that, but I panicked at first. I felt like I couldn't breathe at the thought of leaving it behind. The small fridge was a magic box that kept food safe for me.

I did it, though. I left it there, which is exactly where it belongs.

I unlocked the three deadbolts before we climbed out the window for the last time. I'm sure within a month, my room and furniture will be buried under an avalanche of my mother's nonsensical stuff. All traces of me will be obliterated.

I'm snapped out of my thoughts by two quick knocks on my new bedroom door.

"Come in," I say from where I'm sitting on the floor with my clothes spread out around me, folding them neatly to put into the dressers and closet.

Jude saunters in wearing gray sweatpants and a black tank top. I wasn't ready for his nighttime, chilling-at-home-look, but damn if he isn't just begging to be posted on Instagram right now with hashtag #graysweats.

"You need anything before bed?" he asks, towering over me.

My mouth goes dry, which is more than I can say for *other* parts of my body.

I can do this. I can live with a good-looking man without getting all doe-eyed and swoony. Not to mention, he's thirty-damn-four! Almost as old as my parents. Totally not sexy at all.

"I'm good." I quickly divert my eyes from all things *him* and put the sweater I just folded on top of my pile of panties, which has been on full display since he walked in. "Just putting my stuff away. I've never had so much room and so many drawers."

He smiles, but it's more of a sad smile than a happy one. "It's late, you don't have to do it all tonight."

"I'm not tired," I say. My brain is a hurricane of anxiety, fear, hope, and excitement. There's no way I'll be able to sleep unless I keep myself busy enough to calm down.

He lifts his chin to Gus curled up on the bed with her catnip mouse. "She looks like she's all settled in."

I smile. "I'm surprised. I thought she'd be freaked out and living under the bed for weeks."

"Tomorrow we can let her and Cassie meet. I think they'll be okay, though."

"I hope so." Until then, I'm keeping her in my room with the door closed.

He yawns and squeezes the back of his neck, cracking it to the side. "Okay, I'm heading to bed. See ya tomorrow."

"'Night," I say, but then stop him just as he reaches the door. "Wait… Jude?"

He turns back to me. "Mm?"

I run my tongue over the edge of my teeth. "Thank you. For everything you're doing for me." I feel like I should hug him, but then, I also feel like I shouldn't.

He winks at me and grins. "Sleep tight, Sparkles."

As soon as he closes the door behind him, I let out a long, calming breath. He really is a good guy. He didn't leer at me sitting here with a white tee on with no bra. He didn't make any sexual innuendos. Earlier he made sure to give me my own key. He's done nothing but make me feel like I'm staying at a friend's house.

But still, there's a faint gnaw of fear in my stomach. I could be making a horrible mistake. What if things go wrong and I have to move out? I won't be able to move back in with my mother once her avalanche of stuff takes over my room. Where would I go? Would I end up in an even worse situation than I was to begin with? I might have to live in my car or under a bridge.

Oh, God.

No, I silently tell myself as I put my clothes away. *I'll be okay.*

It's almost two a.m. when I finally turn out the light, crawl into bed, and tuck myself under the new, soft comforter. I press my face into the pillow, inhaling the clean scent. I don't even know what the scent *is*, other than it smells fresh. Comforting. Even though I love older, vintage things, being in this room full of new bedding and furniture is a welcome change. All I want to do is breathe and breathe and breathe, as if it can somehow get inside me and give me a new beginning.

Maybe, hopefully, this *is* a new beginning.

CHAPTER 14

SKYLAR

Three Weeks Later

Today's the big day.

In some alternate reality, this would be the happiest day of my life. I'd be stepping into a white gown. Knowing me, it'd be something bohemian, long and lacy, with hundreds of tiny buttons. I'd wear vintage leather boots. My father would be pacing outside, waiting to walk me down the aisle. My mother would be trying her hardest to calm my anxiety. Megan would be my maid of honor, and she'd be telling me how pretty I am and how lucky I am that Jude has a great body and hair. I'd be saying yes to the man of my dreams, and we'd be starting our happily ever after.

But the reality is I don't believe in weddings, Mister Right, or happily ever-afters. And no one is with me on this day except Jude.

The officiant, whose name is Carol, will be here within the hour. The ceremony will be next to the flower garden in the far corner of Jude's backyard, under an old arbor with vines snaking through it.

What does one wear to her wedding when it's not a real wedding?

I've been standing in front of my closet, chewing on my lip, for five minutes asking myself that question. I finally decide on a flirty, tutu-style white skirt, and a long-sleeved, black-lace body suit. I throw a vintage black-leather motorcycle jacket over it and pull pink Converse sneakers over my white-lace socks. I top it off with a little veil attached to a hair clip, and fan it out over the back of my hair. I smile at my reflection in the full-length mirror. The outfit is super cute. Especially the white skirt. I want to look at least *somewhat* bride-ish so the officiant believes we're really getting married. Jude and I talked about this last night—we can't let her know our vows to *have and to hold 'til death do us part* are pure bullshit.

If she knew this was a marriage of convenience, she might not marry us.

After I do my makeup and spritz on some perfume I got from Belongings, I go downstairs. I find Jude sitting in a wicker chair in the sunroom with Cassie and Gus who, like us, have become comfortable roommates. Happily coexisting in the same space and staying out of each other's way.

"Hi," I say. "Carol should be here soon."

"Yeah." He glances up from his phone, and his eyes slowly travel from my face, down the length of my body. My stomach flutters when his attention lingers on my long legs, and a faint grin of admiration tips his lips. That is, until his gaze lands on my feet, and he does a quick double take, his smile disappearing.

"Skylar, you can't wear pink sneakers."

I look down at my feet. "Why not?"

"Because they make you look young."

I cock my head and stare at him. They're only sneakers. It's not like I walked in the room with a rattle in my hand. "I *am* young."

"I know but we're getting married. We don't have to advertise your age to the justice of the peace."

I cross my arms defiantly. "Lots of people wear pink sneakers. And I'm not doing this if you're ashamed of me, Jude. Screw that."

He lets out a sigh and puts his phone on the small table next to him. "I'm not ashamed of you. But you look young for your age. People always assume the worst. I don't want anyone to think I've done something to you."

I'm not sure where this is coming from—who he thinks this "anyone" is, or what this "something" could be.

"Like what?" I ask. "Slipped me a roofie and dragged me into the backyard to marry you?"

"No, like groomed you or brainwashed you into having Stockholm syndrome or some kidnapping shit."

I frown at him and reach up to fluff my hair. "I don't even know what that is."

He shakes his head. "Never mind. Maybe go put some more adult shoes on just for the ceremony. She'll be the first person to see us together as a so-called couple and..."

Now I get it. He's worried how we look *together*. Other than living in the same house, we're never together. But I can see how we might look a little bit mismatched to some people. I personally don't care, but maybe *he* does.

"Okay," I say. "But I don't think different shoes are going to make me look older."

I go back up to my room and change into the only pair of shoes I have that I think will look adult enough to satisfy him—a pair of black, four-inch pumps. I've only worn them once, and that was to a Halloween party last year when I dressed up as cat woman. Megan convinced me the heels would be sexy.

But when I get back downstairs, Jude does another double take when he sees the change of shoes.

"What now?" I ask. "You're still making a face. I'm sure white heels would be better, but I don't have white. I—"

Putting his hand up, he stops me from launching into a rambling shoe discussion. "It's okay. Really. Black is fine. They're just..." He stares at the shoes. "*High.*"

I blink at him as he stands. "Um, that's why they're called high heels."

"They're fine." He smiles, but that little muscle in his jaw is twitching. And he's still looking at the shoes. Actually, I think he's looking at my calves. "Don't worry about it," he says. "You look great. I'm gonna go get dressed."

I plant myself in the chair he just got out of and look out over the backyard, which looks like an autumn painting. The leaves are changing now—all reds, yellows, and oranges scattered across the grass. Squirrels are skittering around among the acorns and twigs, providing amusement for Gus, who's got her eyes glued to them.

Living here is even nicer than I thought it would be when I moved in three weeks ago. It's quiet and peaceful. I sleep better here than I ever did at my mother's house. Maybe because I feel safer, less anxious. Sharing a house with Jude is comfortable—he's never made me feel nervous or unwelcome. He's quiet and independent. A bit broody. But he's also got a teasing, playful side. I find the mix appealing. I think, though, what I admire most about him is his consistency. He goes to work every morning, comes home and eats dinner, watches TV, then goes to bed. On weekends, he works on the house, or plays pool with a friend. We usually eat dinner and watch a movie together. Growing up, my father was in and out of the house like it had a revolving door. His hours were always different. Sometimes he worked nights, sometimes days. He went out often with his friends to bowl or grab a beer. Many nights he didn't come home. I never knew when I'd see him—sometimes weeks went by without seeing him. If he ever made plans with me, he usually forgot or had something come up at the last minute.

And then he moved into the camper, which was the beginning of the end.

I also greatly appreciate being able to sleep with my bedroom door open if I want to, and the luxury of coming and going through an actual front door. My days of window climbing are over.

I turn when I hear Jude come down the stairs and enter the room, and this time, it's my turn to do a double take.

His hair is tied in a man bun—the first time I've seen it that way. I've never been a fan of that style on men, but it looks damn good on him.

So does everything else.

Black on black on black.

A black button-down shirt has taken the place of his usual tee or sweatshirt. The top four buttons are unbuttoned, showing off a glimpse of the tattoo in the middle of his chest. Black jeans and black biker boots. A black leather bracelet with a thick metal clasp twists around his wrist. My heart jumps when I notice the fourth finger of his left hand doesn't have his sterling skull ring.

Sudden warmth races through my veins.

Soon, I'll be slipping a ring onto that finger.

He'll be slipping one onto mine.

This man standing in front of me will legally be my husband.

And I'll legally be his wife.

Tingles travel up my spine.

Words like *mine* and *his* float through my head. Words I shouldn't be thinking of, because they're a sham. Not real. But sometimes, they sneak in. I wonder what it would feel like to *be* someone else's special person. To have them be *mine*.

I quickly shake away the feeling of sadness washing over me. No way am I letting myself catch feelings for Jude. Or any other man, for that matter.

"She's here." He offers me his hand, and I let him pull me up. "Let's go get hitched, Sparkles."

I take a deep breath, teetering on the spiky heels with wobbly legs. "Okay," I say, smiling. "Let's do this."

He holds my hand as we greet the Justice of the Peace on the front porch and continues to do so as we walk with her to the backyard. I'm not sure if he's doing it to 'show' her we're a happy couple, or to comfort me.

He's the first boy (or man, in this case) to ever hold my hand, and I like it too much to care what his reason is.

Carol doesn't stall or give us time to contemplate. She's got us standing in front of each other under the vined arbor before I can even blink. She asks us to hold hands, and I try not to giggle with nerves, suddenly feeling a burst of childishness—as if this is a game of pretend dress-up. Like when RingPop proposed to me when we were little.

The *adult shoes* have put me just shy of eye level with Jude, but I force myself to look down at our hands, or at Carol with her mane of silver hair, as she reads the vows in her smooth, cheerful voice. Jude's eyes have some sort of magical power that suck me in and make me feel like I can't think straight. Staring into them while I tell the biggest lie of my life seems wrong. Major bad karma.

My hand shakes when I slip the silver band onto his finger, and so does his when he puts a thin, sparkly ring on mine.

I freeze as I stare at the ring on my finger. We didn't buy the rings together; we just agreed we'd buy each other's so we'd have them for the ceremony. Props, for lack of a more fitting term. I got his while shopping with Megan at the mall at one of those sterling silver jewelry stands.

But the ring he just put on my finger looks like real little diamonds set into the rose-gold band. A metal and style I once mentioned to him I *loved* when we were watching a movie together, and the main character was given one.

I didn't think he was paying attention.

Apparently, he was.

And now I feel like crying, and I have no idea why.

"I now pronounce you husband and wife. You may kiss your bride!" Carol exclaims happily, closing her little book of vows.

We made a deal there'd be no kissing the bride. We'd kiss on the cheek and hope Carol wouldn't notice or think we were weird. But when I move in to do so, one of my heels gets stuck in the damp grass, and I stumble into him. His hand grasps my waist to steady me, but I still miss his cheek, and my lips land directly on his mouth.

His grip on my waist tightens and he pulls me closer. His lips open to mine. Our eyes close. My hand has found its way to the back of his neck. Our mouths linger breathlessly when they shouldn't—warm, and damp— before we slowly, reluctantly, pull apart.

With just one kiss our deal has been shattered, our fate sealed.

CHAPTER 15

SKYLAR

"Congratulations!" Carol exclaims as Jude and I pull away from each other. "You make such a beautiful, sweet couple."

I tear my eyes away from his, which have morphed to the color of pewter. My lips don't feel like my own anymore after that kiss, and I'm not even sure I can get them to form intelligible words.

"Thanks," Jude replies, his voice totally steady and normal. "We appreciate you coming out here for us."

"I can take some photos, if you'd like?" Carol offers.

"We'd love that if you have time," I say, taking a few careful steps toward my phone, which I put on a large rock a few feet away.

I can't bring myself to look at Jude. Is he feeling all shaky-quakey inside like I am?

Probably not.

It's possible the way I'm feeling has nothing to do with the kiss at all. I could be having another anxiety attack. Or it might be because I didn't eat this morning.

"I always take photographs for my couples," Carol says with

a smile as she takes my phone from me. "Maybe stand in front of that big tree? It has lots of pretty red leaves on it."

Taking her cue, we stand in front of the tree like two twelve-year-olds afraid to get close to each other. The sudden awkwardness between us is thick enough to slice with a knife. I don't know whether to laugh or cry about it as Carol fiddles with my phone. Finally, Jude puts his arm around me, and we smile as the camera clicks.

"Beautiful!" she says. "Now, maybe turn to each other and kiss. It's so cute how shy you two are."

Oh God.

We turn to face each other. A hint of his familiar, sexy grin is curving the corner of his mouth, and it makes me *want* to kiss him. He gently pushes my hair back, then palms my cheek with his huge hand, his thumb under my chin, tipping my face up.

I put my hands on his chest and slide them up to his shoulders. As he bends toward me, I close my eyes and lift one of my feet up into that flirty flamingo pose we see in movies.

Our lips touch softly, until he tilts his mouth over mine, capturing my lips with his. A barely audible gasp escapes me and he inhales it with a slow, sensual suck of breath. His hand squeezes my cheek, and then he pulls away, slowly dragging his thumb across my jawline before he turns to Carol and walks off to speak to her.

Leaving me standing there.

That second kiss may have been short, but the way he touched my face and moved his thumb across my cheek with that damn smile and those riveting eyes has my heart pounding.

Even still. Minutes later.

I've been kissed before. By at least six guys. I made out with a few of them pretty hot and heavy at parties and at the movies, and even went all the way with two of them. On separate occasions, of course. It's been a year since I've dated, but holy shit, none of them made me feel like Jude did with two short kisses and a touch. No one has ever made my legs weak and my thighs tingle just by touching my cheek. I don't think any guy I fooled around with touched my face at all, now that I'm thinking about it. They were too busy trying to grope my boobs and my ass.

How did I not know what a cheek caress could feel like?

Is it an older guy thing?

Or a Jude thing?

"You comin', Sparkles?" he asks, turning to look back at me as he and Carol head toward the house.

I blink at him as he walks through the crunchy leaves. In front of him, Cassie and Gus are watching us from the sunroom of his beautiful house. I'm struck with an odd, wistful feeling. I want to hold this image in my heart forever.

"Yeah." I take my heels off and follow them barefoot to the front porch. We sign our marriage license, Jude hands Carol a check, and we hug her thank-you before she climbs into her Volkswagen Beetle and drives away.

It all happened so fast. I think the entire thing took less than thirty minutes, and now we're married.

Legally, anyway.

Wordlessly, we walk inside, and he goes directly upstairs. I linger in the kitchen with the pets until he comes back down a few minutes later wearing his usual black Tee and faded jeans.

"I'm heading out to play some pool," he says, barely looking at me as he heads straight for the front door. "See ya later."

"Okay," I say, but he's already out the door.

Feeling dazed, I go up to my room and flop on the bed with a sigh. Gus and Cassie join me, probably hoping I'll take a nap so they can cuddle up against my legs. I'm tempted to crawl under the blankets for the rest of the day. At least these fur babies will chase the loneliness away.

I feel sad and jilted, like the main character in a bad romance movie, and I'm not sure why. We never made plans for after the ceremony. I guess I thought we'd spend the day together afterward. But now, I realize that was stupid. We're just friends. The ceremony was just a formality. A legal necessity so Jude can add me to his insurance.

Nothing more.

And the kisses? The first one was a clumsy accident, and the second was just for the pictures because Carol *told* us to kiss.

The cheek touching… Well, that was probably some smooth move Jude puts on the ladies, and he only did it out of habit.

That's all.

♥ ♡ ♥ ♥

The sound of the front door wakes me, and I sit up in my dark room, confused about what day or time it is. The clock on my nightstand says 9:30 p.m.

Shit. I've been asleep for six hours.

Downstairs, Jude is moving around the kitchen making noise. Cassie jumps off the bed and runs out of the room, reminding me I forgot to feed her. Yawning, I slip a pair of yoga pants on under the T-shirt I napped in and quietly tread downstairs.

"Hey," he says, glancing at me from behind the open refrigerator door. "Were you sleeping?"

"Yeah… I fell asleep reading."

"Did you eat?" He pulls sliced cheese and butter out of the fridge. "I'm making a grilled cheese."

"I'm not hungry."

"You didn't eat breakfast or lunch, and I'm gonna guess you didn't eat dinner. You have to eat something."

"Lucky—"

"I'll make you toast."

"Alright," I say, leaning against the island. I'm not in the mood to eat, but he's right. I have to eat every day. I watch him cook his sandwich in a black frying pan, then put two slices of bread in the toaster for me. Everything Jude does with his hands looks easy and fluid, like a magic trick. I find myself watching his hands a lot since I moved in, fascinated by his tattoos and trying to decipher the designs.

When he hands me a plate with lightly buttered toast sprinkled with cinnamon, I notice his ring is gone.

His wedding ring. Not his other rings.

That was fast.

As he eats his sandwich across the island from me, I'm still looking at his hands, even though the quick removal of the ring is bothering me. I can't stop thinking about how he touched me earlier, the way he held my face still for his kiss. It felt so romantically possessive.

I need to stop thinking about it.

After I finish my toast, I open the oven and take out the small, foil-covered pan I hid there last night.

"I made these for you. Us," I say putting the pan in front of him. "I thought we'd have them earlier, but you left…" *Bolted, is more like it.*

He wipes his mouth with his napkin and looks at me quizzically. I pull the foil off to reveal ten chocolate chip cookies decorated with icing to look like a groom's tux, and a bride's dress.

"Rebecca helped me make and decorate them yesterday. It's part of my therapy, to bake something from scratch, and then eat it." I take a breath, still unsure if I can get myself to eat one. "I haven't tried one yet. I wanted to do it together."

"Skylar…" I wasn't expecting to hear the slight pitch of emotion in his deep voice. Or to see his eyes soften as he looks at the cookies. "I can't believe you made wedding cookies for us."

"They're the same kind you like from the shop, just with icing. I hope that doesn't ruin them for you."

"You kiddin'? Icing makes them even better." He takes one of the bride-decorated ones out of the pan. "I wish I'd known you'd done this, I would've stuck around."

"You'd stick around for cookies, but not to hang out with me after our wedding?" I tease.

"Of course, for cookies. You know these are my weakness. But hanging out with my new fake wife would've been the icing on the cake." He winks at me and takes a bite out of the bride cookie. "No pun intended."

"How is it?" Fake wife asks. That's me.

"Delicious. If you're gonna eat one, you better do it before I eat them all."

Gingerly, I take one of the groom cookies out and study it. Rebecca did everything step-by-step with me. Showing me all the fresh ingredients and explaining the purpose of each. Like Jude, she's been patient and understanding with my recovery steps.

She also had a small hissy fit when I told her I was marrying Jude. She rattled off a list a mile long of reasons why it was a very bad idea. All of them valid. I totally understand her feelings, especially since she's been through a nasty divorce.

"Do you want to talk it out?" Jude asks, taking his third cookie while I'm still staring at mine. "Is there something about it that's worrying you? The color? What's in it? A memory?"

I shake my head. "No. None of that. It's just new."

"Do you want to break it up into small pieces?" he suggests.

That works, sometimes. A cookie that's four inches in diameter is less intimidating if it's broken into bite-sized pieces.

"I'm going to try that," I reply, grateful that he knows all my little steps. We talk a lot after each of my therapy sessions, and he truly listens. I think he understands the importance of it all because he was in drug rehab for a short time when he was younger.

I break the cookie in half, then in quarters, then take those pieces and break them into smaller pieces. Picking one up, I put it in my mouth, let it rest on my tongue for a moment, then slowly chew it. It's a lot of different textures and flavors. The chocolate chips are sweet and soft amongst the crumbly parts. The icing slightly slippery. I don't choke or feel sick.

He raises his eyebrow at me, waiting for me to react. Sometimes I like new foods, other times, I spit them out.

"It's good," I say after I swallow it. "I'm not obsessed like you are, but it's not bad."

He laughs. "Obsessed is a strong word."

"Well, if it fits..." I smile.

I thought things would be weird after the kiss, but we're right back to how we were before... like it never happened. It's driving me crazy wondering if he *felt* anything kissing me. Some deep part of me hopes he did, because I did.

But what would that even mean?

It's not like we're going to fool around or date.

He watches me eat another piece with a crooked smile on his face. "I know what you're thinking about," he says.

"Oh, really? What am I thinking about?" I challenge, knowing he has no idea what's going through my mind.

He pins me with his eyes and cocks his head to the side. "The kiss."

My breath hitches. Keeping my gaze on his, I take a sip of water, wondering how he can tell.

"What makes you think that?" I throw back casually.

"Am I wrong?"

"Just answer."

Reaching back, he pulls the black rubber band from his hair, and shakes his head. His long hair whips around his face like something out of a rock music video.

"Because I was thinking about it, too."

"And?" I prod.

"And I shoulda let you wear the sneakers," he says, picking up our plates and taking them over to the sink.

"See?" I play into the teasing banter. "I put on the adult shoes and I ended up falling into your face."

He turns around and shoots me a grin. "Don't worry, babe. You ain't the first."

Damn him.

"I'm sure I'm not," I say playfully as I cover the last two cookies with foil. "But, I *am* the first wife to."

"You got a point."

"I'll make a note to not wear heels around you anymore."

He nods. "Good. I don't want any more accidental kisses."

"Ditto."

We stare at each other, the space between us charged with more chemistry than a science lab. His jaw muscle is twitching. My heart is fluttering.

So this is how it's going to be. We're going to joke our way out of it.

"The cookies were sweet. Thanks," he says, reaching his hand out to me.

My breath catches when I realize he's going to touch my cheek again... Pull my face into his for another kiss.

I close my eyes, waiting for it.

He ruffles my hair. "G'nite, Sparkles. Happy wedding day."

When I open my eyes, he's gone.

CHAPTER 16

JUDE

Happy wedding day?

Did I really just say that shit—after I ruffled her hair?

Dude, you just married her. She's not five years old.

Fuck me. Today went all kinds of sideways.

You couldn't pay me to kiss an eighteen-year-old girl. I'm not the type to lust after younger women.

Weddings are poison.

Marriage is a curse.

I've heard it before, and this proves it. Not twenty-four hours in, and we're doing things we *shouldn't* be doing.

But Skylar is like a magnet. All night, I felt pulled to come back home to be with her. I felt it when I kissed her, and I feel it now.

Fuck, I've felt it since the first time I saw her in the parking lot. I should've run then, instead of allowing myself to get closer and closer. Now, I'm legally married to her, and she's living in my house. I can't escape.

And let's not forget—I kissed her. *Twice.* After I promised her—and myself—that I'd never, ever, cross that line.

But nope. My dumb ass put my lips right on hers.

Never again.

I've never felt sparks from kissing a chick before, but *fuck*, I felt it with her and it's got me rattled.

A few minutes ago, I heard her running the water in the bathroom down the hall, and now I can hear *Dark Side of the Moon* drifting from her room. I'm worried. I didn't miss all the signs earlier in the kitchen. How she peeked up at me with her big, sparkling eyes. The way she kept glancing at my ring finger. The bride and groom cookies. Which were fuckin' amazing, by the way.

She's got a crush on me. And that's fine, and cute, and not totally unreciprocated. But innocent feelings can turn into heartbreak. That's the last thing we—*she*—needs. Her therapy is going great, and I'm not about to let anything, especially *me*, set her back.

I have a little gift for her, which I forgot to give her earlier because she distracted me with cookies. I kick off my boots and walk down the hall to her room. The door is open a few inches, the bedside lamp casting a dim, amber light. As I raise my hand to knock, I see her standing in front of her dresser, her back to me. She's staring at the wedding band on her finger, turning her hand so the gems glint under the light.

My heart hiccups.

The ring is the first piece of jewelry I've ever given a woman. I went to four jewelry stores trying to find one that looked like what I knew she wanted. Turns out, a rose-gold band with little almond-shaped diamonds isn't easy to find, or cheap.

The marriage might be fake, but the ring is real.

As I watch her, she slips the ring off and puts it into the top drawer of her dresser.

Good. We're on the same page about not wearing the rings.

Cassie barks when I knock on the door, and Skylar's shoulders jump with surprise.

"Hey," she says, when she turns. "What's up?"

"Can I come in?"

"Sure."

"I see my dog has moved in with you," I joke. Cassie is lying in a pink polka-dot cat bed in the corner while Fuptagus is sprawled out on a fleece blanket on the bed. A flameless candle is lit on the nightstand. She's hung curtains, and some cool framed vintage illustrations of cats wearing hats and sweaters on the walls. It's nice to see the room with her touch on it. It doesn't feel cold and empty anymore.

"I think she likes me," she says. "She keeps following me in here. I hope that's okay? I can close the door and keep her out if you want."

"No, it's cool. It's good she has company. She loves attention."

She pushes her long hair back, tucking it behind her ear before she looks up at me. "What's up? I hope you're not here for the honeymoon." Her right eyebrow quirks up at me.

I can't help but laugh. "Definitely not. I have something for you. It's just something little." I pull the one-dollar lottery scratch-off ticket out of my back pocket, and she takes it from me with her brows knitted together.

"Ooh. Thank you. I never win anything, though—"

"Me either. But it's more of a symbolic thing. I'm going to give you one every day until you move out. You're always saying how bad your luck is. You're not gonna win every day, but I bet a few times a month, you'll win at least a dollar. Think of it as a reminder there are always good days coming."

"Jude..." Her eyes glimmer under the dim light. "That's so sweet."

Uh oh. It was meant to be *fun*. Not sweet.

I shrug. "Nah. It's just something fun. And it's only a buck."

She nods, holding on to the ticket like it's made out of gold. "Okay. But if I win big someday, we have to split it."

"Alright. But only if it's more than fifty bucks."

"Deal," she says. "Do I have to scratch it in front of you?"

I refrain from throwing back a sarcastic comment at that one. "You can do it whenever you want."

"I promise I'll tell you if I win."

"I don't think you'll be getting rich off a scratch-off ticket."

"If I do, I'm buying an RV."

"An RV?" I repeat.

"Yeah, a mobile home."

"I know what an RV is. It's just a big jump from your 'vette."

She flashes me a silly smile. "I basically want to live in it. Just drive across the country, going anywhere I want to. I can stay as long as I want, then leave. I don't want to be stuck in one place."

"I hope you have better luck with it than your 'vette, otherwise you're gonna be stuck on the side of the road waiting for a tow truck."

"Very funny," she says. "I'd buy a nice one. With a good engine."

I envy her young, free spirit. It won't last, though. In a few years she'll be bogged down like everyone else with a job, a house, and a family.

"When I was younger, I had the same dreams about jumping on my motorcycle and just riding wherever the road took me and living in cheap motels," I tell her.

"Why didn't you?"

"Because I also like to eat. Nobody was gonna pay me to cruise around through the mountains."

She chews her lip thoughtfully. "That's why I'm going to have a job that I can do from anywhere."

Life should be so easy.

"So, are you okay?" I ask, leaning down to pet the dog. "After everything today?"

"Everything?"

I straighten and meet her inquiring gaze. "Yeah… getting legally married and all that."

I don't even know what I mean by *all that*.

"I'm okay with everything," she replies. "Are you?"

"I'm good."

She's watching me again, in that indescribable way that she does, and I feel like I should get out of her bedroom before I end up doing something stupid—like kissing her or ruffling her hair again.

"Well, I'm gonna hit the hay," I say. "Looks like I'll be sleeping alone since everyone's shacking up in here."

"Aw, do you want to sleep in here, too?" she asks, then her eyes widen, and she quickly says, "I'm kidding."

Laughing, I shake my head and edge toward the door. "On that note, I'm saying good night."

Once I'm back in my room, though, I gotta admit, it sucks being alone when there's a cuddle party happening down the hall.

CHAPTER 17

SKYLAR

"Do you feel different?" Megan asks. It's Sunday, the day after the ceremony, and we're sitting on my bed doing our nails with a gel kit she brought over.

"Why would I feel different?"

"Because you're *married*."

I roll my eyes. "It doesn't count. Nothing is different."

It is, though. I don't know how to explain it. Suddenly, I feel a bond with Jude. Like some invisible thread has stitched us together.

"*This* is different," she says. "I can finally come over to your house to hang out with you."

"True. I'm happy about that."

"Me too. Who woulda thought you'd be living in a nice house, married to a hot guy? This is your year. I think all the good things are finally happening to you."

I hope she's right.

"Jude and I are roommates, Meg. Stop saying married. And don't tell anyone at school. Not even Erik."

"I promised you I wouldn't. Don't worry."

I want to believe her, but Megan likes to talk, and I'm afraid she's going to slip up and tell someone, or everyone, about my situation. Those snotty bitches will never shut up about it if they find out.

"How are things going with Erik?" I ask.

It's cute how mentioning his name puts a big smile on her face.

"He's *so* sweet, Sky. I swear, I can't get enough of him. I almost didn't come over today because I wanted to hang out with him."

"Gee, thanks," I say, lining up the nail polish bottles.

"I didn't mean it like that. You know I love being with you. I'm here, aren't I? I'm just saying I really like being with him. He makes me laugh. He's not a dick, ya know? He really likes me. He takes me to dinner. He cares about me. He's a *real* boyfriend, not like those other idiots I dated where we just randomly hung out."

"I thought you said you just wanted something fun? Remember you said you didn't want him falling for you?"

"I did say that, didn't I?" She smiles slyly. "I guess I changed my mind."

"Meg... are you falling in love with him?"

Her cheeks turn pink, and it's adorable. "I think I might be."

"Oh my God," I say happily. "Have you said it? Has he?"

She shakes her head. "Not yet, but I'm pretty sure we're both feeling it."

"That's awesome. Last year you thought he was a nerd and now look."

"Right? Life is so bizarre."

Nodding, I slide my hand under the UV light, hoping it's safe. I'm a little leery of things Megan buys off the internet.

"We have to find you someone so we can double-date. Remember when we were little, we always wanted to grow up and double-date? Erik and I were talking about his friend Carson. He's a little odd, but he might be fun for you."

I crinkle my nose and shudder inside. "I'm not going to date someone named Carson."

"Why not? He's cute… in a strange way."

Great. Sounds like a winner.

"Because Carson is a last name," I reply. "It's not even a name, it's two things stuck together. Car and son."

She gives me a frustrated frown. "It's just his name, Skylar."

"I don't like it."

Letting out a sigh, she scrapes a file across her nail. "You're so weird. You focus on the strangest things."

"And your point?" I say, grinning.

"It's cute, but you're limiting your options. You can't be so picky about food and men. You'll be hungry and single forever."

"I'm not picky about food, Meg," I say defensively. "Men, yes. But not food. It's different."

Her shoulders slump. "I'm sorry, I didn't mean it like that. I know you can't help the food thing. You're getting better, though. I'm so proud of you for eating that cookie."

Earlier we ate the last two wedding cookies together before we came upstairs with the nail apparatus.

"I like my therapist. She's like talking to a friend instead of a doctor. I've only seen her a few times, but I already think she's helping me. We talk about everything, not just my eating disorder."

I'm not ready to tell Megan I'm taking an antidepressant. Just the word makes me uncomfortable. Anti*depressant*. I'm not depressed. I'm happy and I have goals. It's not like I'm holing up in the bedroom all day, refusing to leave, wishing I didn't exist.

"What does the therapist think about you getting married for insurance?"

Gawd. It sounds so bad when it's actually said like that. It makes me sound like I'm involved in an insurance scam, or like I'm using Jude.

"I didn't want to tell her at first, but the only way she can help me is if I'm honest about everything. I could tell she was shocked, but it's not her job to judge me. If it wasn't for Jude, I wouldn't be able to see her in the first place."

Because I'm not on Jude's plan yet, I've paid cash for the first few appointments. But if I had to be in therapy long-term without insurance, I'd be broke in a month and have to stop going.

"True," Megan says. "It's just a really weird situation."

"And that's why I only want people to know who *need* to know. I don't need people judging me."

"I got you, boo. No worries." She looks over at my hands. "I like your color better. Why did you let me do electric blue?"

I picked a pretty autumn, coral-ish color. She chose a fluorescent blue.

"Like you would've listened to me?" I tease.

She laughs. "You know me so well. I guess I'll deal with it. I'm too lazy to do it all over."

When we're done with our nails, we clean everything up and sit on my floor, gossiping about our favorite reality TV shows. I have to admit I've become addicted to the drama of them. Especially the relationship ones.

"Do you want to see the pictures from the ceremony?" I ask, after debating it in my head for at least ten minutes. We've just had a huge discussion about *Married at First Sight* and how awkward it must be to marry a stranger, so it seems fitting for me to show her.

"You have pictures, and you haven't shown me yet?" she says. "Are we even best friends?"

Laughing, I grab my cell phone and bring up the first photo

of Jude and me standing next to each other. I edited all the photos last night, and now they look really pretty and dreamy.

"Aw, look how cute you look!" Megan says. "That skirt is the bomb!"

"Thanks." I flip to the next photo, and she grabs the phone out of my hand, zooming the photos with her fingers.

"Wait… are you two *kissing*?"

"It was just a quick peck. The officiant asked us to. She doesn't know the deets, so we did it just to make sure we looked legit."

"Um, it looks *very* legit. And look at your sexy foot up in those heels, girl!"

"I'm never wearing those again. I almost broke my neck."

"That hand on your cheek, though. Dammmmm. Those tattoos. Fuckity fuck. My ovaries are exploding."

"Right?" I say, taking the phone back to look at them again for the fiftieth time. Carol caught us in some perfect moments over several photos. Jude and I staring into each other's eyes. Our lips touching. His thumb across my cheek.

Gah. We *do* look like real newlyweds. In that moment, I felt like one. Pictures can be so deceptive.

Damn that whole *kiss the bride* thing! It's opened up a pandora's box.

"You look stunning," Megan comments. "I'm not surprised he couldn't keep his hands off you."

"His hands were *not* on me."

"I'm going to try to talk Erik into getting some tattoos after graduation. That shit is sexy as hell."

Agreed. Jude has totally turned me on to tats. Like Megan, I'd love to date a guy who had a few.

"You think you'll still be together then?" I ask.

Her smile fades, and her eyes narrow at me. I wish I hadn't said that. "Why wouldn't we be?"

"You've never dated anyone longer than three months. I didn't think you wanted something serious?"

"I literally just told you a few minutes ago I love him."

"I know, I just didn't realize you meant *love* love. Like, long-term love."

"Duh. What other kind of love is there?"

Lots, actually. But, we're just high school girls. Do either of us know what *love* love really is?

CHAPTER 18

JUDE

"How was your ride? Swallow any bugs?" Skylar asks when she steps out of her car and walks up the driveway. I just got home myself after finally having a Saturday free to take off on my Harley for the day. She watches me as I open the garage door and push my motorcycle inside.

"It was good. No bugs flew into my mouth this time. How was work?"

"Busy," she replies. "I'm not used to working Saturdays."

I pull my T-shirt off and use it to wipe the sweat off my forehead and face. I catch the way her lips part slightly as her eyes zoom in on my chest, then flicker down to my abs. I'm just as guilty. My own gaze has been pulled like a magnet to her bare stomach, exposed by a thin, white blouse knotted just above her belly button—and the thin silver ring looping through the delicate flesh. The sun glints off a turquoise gem—the same color as her eyes—dangling from the belly button piercing.

Fuck. She could easily be a fashion model. Endless tousled blonde hair, long, tan legs, flat stomach, pink, pouty lips shiny with gloss, torn jeans, and cowboy boots. Those ocean eyes—

always a myriad of emotion—dazzling one minute, soulful the next. And damn, that fucking smile. My favorite curve.

I tear my eyes away when I remember this perfection is all wrapped up in an eighteen-year-old girl.

This chick will undo me.

"It was hot as shit out there today," I say, emptying my saddlebags.

She runs her fingers over the airbrushed wolf's head design on the gas tank, then slides them down over the worn seat. Her palm flattens over the leather as if she's caressing it. Unfamiliar jealousy burns through me, wishing that touch was for me.

"I've never been on a motorcycle before," she says wistfully. "Maybe someday I could go with you?"

The offer is tempting.

Too tempting.

Nope. I don't trust myself to be trapped between her thighs, with her hands wrapped around my waist for hours on end while we're way up in the mountains with nothing—and no one—around us but trees and blue skies.

This low-key, flirt-fueled heat simmering between us has me tweaked. It's been two weeks since the wedding-day kiss, and the memory of it still invades my thoughts when I'm alone at night.

Throwing my shirt over my shoulder, I wink at her. "You ain't tall enough to get on this ride, Sparkles."

A flirty smile plays on her lips. "You talking about the bike, or you? 'Cuz I think I can handle both."

Oof.

Laughing, I shake my head. "I guess I asked for that, didn't I?"

"You sure did."

"Did you eat?" I ask, quickly changing the subject. "I'm gonna take a shower and make a quick sandwich before I head out to meet Kyle."

She nods. "I had soup earlier with Rebecca."

"I'll be home late," I tell her as we step out of the garage. I yank the door shut behind us and lock it.

"I'll be binging *Outlander*, so I'll probably still be awake."

"More men in kilts?"

"You know it." She glances sideways at me. "Maybe you should wear one. You have nice legs."

"I don't think you could handle it."

She grins as we walk up to the house, and I unlock the front door, swinging it open to let her go in first.

We're greeted by Cassie and Gus with wagging tails and chirpy meows.

"Gus seems to be slowly turning into a dog," she says. "See how she runs to the door now when we come home?"

"It's even better when *I* come home—all three of you come running to see me."

She playfully punches my arm. "Shut up. It's not to see you, I just get excited about a front door that people can actually go in and out of."

"You lie like a rug."

"Want me to make your sandwich?" she calls after me as I head up the stairs.

"Do you really hafta ask?"

For someone who's afraid to eat a lot of food, she makes a mean grilled turkey and swiss on rye.

The Possum's Den is a small bar known for its decor of taxidermized critters, most notably, a cross-eyed possum perched on a shelf behind the bar that once was the owner's pet.

They also serve a killer cheese-stuffed burger on a toasted bun with a side of homemade balsamic ketchup.

I'd be eating that shit right now if I hadn't eaten that turkey sandwich Skylar made me.

"'Bout time you showed up." Kyle slaps my back after I wade through the crowd to our usual spot in the back.

"Better late than never, right?" I scan the room, which is unusually busy—even for a Saturday night. "Are they giving away free beer or something?"

He shrugs and tosses me a pool cue. "College kids celebrating some sport thing. The chicks are hot, though, and they'll be drunk soon."

Ever since Kyle's fiancée dumped him, he's been plowing through half the town's female population like a lawnmower.

While he racks the balls, I flag the bartender for a beer and chalk my cue stick.

"You go riding today?" Kyle asks.

Nodding, I lean over the table and break. "You should've come with me. Got a good hundred miles in. Probably the last chance I'll get this season."

"My clutch cable's still snapped."

I pull a sip of my beer and put it back on our table, glancing up to find a redhead watching my every move and making no effort to hide it. I take a quick visual inventory. Pretty smile. Twenty-something with makeup, thirty-something without. Short skirt. High heels. Waist-length, spirally red hair. Thin, gold chains draped over cleavage busting out of a tight V-neck blouse. Thick black eyeliner.

I might be game.

Snaring the eye contact, she comes over, cocktail in hand.

"I love your tattoos," she coos loudly, wrapping her hand around my bicep.

I watch her hand move over my arm, then lift my gaze to meet hers.

"What's your name, red?"

She cocks her head to the side and purses her lips around her straw, sucking bright-pink liquid from a goblet, before answering.

"I'm Jolie," she says.

"Hey, Lucky, your turn, man," Kyle yells.

The girl's brown eyes widen, and a teasing smile dances on her lips. "Your name is Lucky?"

I nod.

Her hand waltzes up my arm, beneath the sleeve of my T-shirt, dragging her long nails over my skin like a raptor.

She leans closer. Close enough that her breath tickles my ear. Her perfume permeates my senses, but it's not a scent I like. "Want to get lucky, Lucky? I know I do."

I let out a snicker and flash her a bored look. "C'mon, red. You're gonna have to do better than that."

Her smile twists into a disappointed frown as I slowly back away.

I make my way back to the pool table, throwing a look over my shoulder to find her still watching me even though she's mingled back in the fold with her friends.

Kyle stares at her as we continue our game, attempting to hijack her attention. He fails. Red only has eyes for me, it seems.

Picking up women has been a competitive sport for Kyle since we were in high school. I could give two shits which one of us wins the girl. It's not that important to me to get laid every weekend.

He, on the other hand, has to leave with a different woman every week.

When we finish up our game, Jolie and a blonde friend approach us and split like a wishbone—the blonde moving to Kyle and the redhead sidling up to me.

"You going to tell me your name now, handsome?" she asks.

I finish off my drink. "You already know my name."

She stares up at me with intoxicated eyes, leaning her hip against mine. "Something tells me that's a nickname."

"That's all you're gettin'."

Her fingers touch the ends of my hair. "Do you come here a lot?"

Jolie obviously isn't winning any points for original conversation.

"You tryin' to pick me up or put me to sleep?" I ask jokingly.

She giggles. "You're a hard one, aren't you?"

"I might be if you weren't boring me, darlin'."

To my left, Kyle has his tongue down the blonde's throat and his hand up her shirt. Jolie watches them kiss, then licks her own lips.

"Do you want to get out of here?" she offers. "There's a motel down the street."

There was once a time I spent so many nights at that motel I'm surprised my name's not on one of the doors instead of a number.

It's been a while. My hand could use a rest.

I'm just about to grab her waist and steer her to the back door when Skylar's smile flashes through my mind.

How her eyes sparkled when she handed me the turkey sandwich earlier—made exactly how I like it with a light layer of spicy mustard—even though the color and smell of it makes her gag.

I chew the inside of my cheek.

Jolie's hand slinks down to my wrist.

"C'mon," she whispers. "You can find out if my hair color's real."

I blow out a gusty sigh. "I'm gonna have to pass. I'm kinda involved with someone."

Her lips press against my cheek and she whispers, "I won't tell if you won't."

Scandalous indiscretion used to turn me on.

But now, it just feels dirty.

"I'll see ya around, red."

I don't look back this time when I walk away and head to the bar. Staring at the cross-eyed possum, I nurse a soda while I wait for Kyle to return from his rendezvous in the parking lot.

"What's wrong with you?" he asks when he comes back. "That redhead was smokin'. I would've taken her over the blonde."

We jostle through the crowd to a small, private table, passing Jolie and her friend who are now hitting on two other guys. She smiles at me and I just shake my head and laugh.

"Eh, I'm just not into her," I say when we sit down.

He throws back his Mind Eraser shot and grimaces. "How could you not be into her?"

I lean back in my chair and run my fingers over the condensation on my glass. "I gotta tell you something wild I did, man."

"Now you're talkin'"

"It's not a sex story, asshole."

"Oh." He coughs and straightens. "Sorry."

"I got married," I blurt out.

He stares at me, face frozen, then busts out laughing. "Good one, Lucky. That's not even fuckin' funny."

"I'm serious." I give him a deadpan look and he slowly stops laughing.

"Wait… come on." He blinks, waiting for me to admit I'm joking. "Are you *serious*?"

"I am."

"Back the fuck up. To *who*?"

I'll probably regret spilling my guts to Kyle in the morning, but he's my friend and I feel like I need to tell someone. He has his moments when he's not a total dick.

"No one you know," I lie, deciding not to tell him it's Skylar. He doesn't need to know that she's only eighteen.

"So, who is she?"

"Just a girl I met. But we're not together. I married her because she was in a bad situation."

"Holy shit, did she need a green card?"

"No, she lives here in town. She's got some health issues and needed insurance. She was living in a really shitty, unsafe situation, so I said… why the fuck not? I'll help her out."

He grabs the edge of the table. "Have you lost your mind, man? You fucking hate the idea of marriage."

"I know, but it's not real. It's just an arrangement. On paper."

He stares at me and chugs his beer. "I'm gonna need another shot."

"I think you had enough."

"Lemme get this straight. You married some chick just to give her health insurance. And now she's living in your house?"

I nod. "That's basically it."

"Is she ugly? She's gotta be ugly."

My jaw clenches. "No, she's hot. She's beautiful."

"Is she a ghetto rat?"

"No, dickhead."

"She better not be involved with a psycho. You don't want to get messed up in that shit, man."

"She's not dating anyone. She's just a nice, normal girl that life kept kicking."

"Is she at least letting you hit it?"

"I know this might be a hard concept for you, but I actually don't think with my dick 24/7."

He looks at me like I have ten heads.

"Did you have a wedding? You didn't even invite me? Shouldn't I have been your best man?"

"There wasn't a wedding. Just a private ceremony."

"This is so fucked up, dude."

I shrug. "I wanted to do something nice for someone. It feels good."

My seriousness sobers him up a little. "So how does that even work? Does she have her own room?"

"Hell yeah, she does. She's in Erin's old room."

"How long is this supposed to last? Forever?"

"Nah, maybe a year. Then we'll get a divorce and she'll move out. That's all. It's just a temporary thing."

His eyes blink rapidly with confusion. "I never would've expected this from you, man. My mind is blown." He makes an explosion sound.

"Yeah, mine too."

"Is that why you didn't hook up with that redheaded hottie? You feelin' some kind of misplaced marital guilt or some shit?"

Yes.

It doesn't make any sense. We're not really married. We're not even dating. I'm free to stick my dick in anything I want.

And yet, I don't want to.

I pause before I deny it. "I dunno. Maybe," I reply. "That chick was just into my tattoos."

"So? Who gives a fuck?"

My cell phone buzzes in my pocket and I pull it out to see a text message from Skylar. It's a picture of Cassie and Gus all snuggled up together on the couch.

Skylar: OMG look how cute they are. They love each other!

Smiling, I type back a quick reply.

Me: Very cute. How's the men in kilts?

Skylar: Sexy. How's pool? Did you get all the balls in the right holes? 😆😉

Me: LOL. I always do 😀

"Who's that?" Kyle asks, nodding toward my phone.

"It's her."

"The wife?"

Wife. It sounds so fuckin' strange.

"Yup."

His eyes narrow as I shove the phone back in my pocket. "You like her, don't you?"

"Of course I like her."

"No, I mean you're *into* her. I can tell. You never smile like that."

Shit. Is it really that obvious?

"I always fuckin' smile," I say defensively. "And she's just a friend."

"Can I meet her?"

"I don't think she's ready for you," I say. "Maybe someday."

Something brushes against my shoulder and I look up to see Jolie passing our table on her way to the restrooms. Kyle bends down and picks a small piece of a white napkin off the floor. He studies it then tosses it across the table at me. "It's her phone number."

"Her who?"

"The redhead. I think she tried to drop it on the table but her drunk ass missed."

I snort and throw it back at him. "You keep it. I'm not interested."

He folds it up and stuffs it in his wallet. "I'm going to. I'll get some fuckin' fake tattoos. She'll be all over me like flies on shit."

Yawning, I stretch my arms and crack my neck. "I should go. My back's killin' me."

"Go?" he repeats, leaning his arms on the table. "It's still early. Let's have a few shots and get some girls over here and have a belated bachelor party."

Standing, I pull on my leather jacket and straighten the collar. "Two drinks is my limit now. You gonna be okay to get home? I can give you a lift."

"I'm not that drunk. I'll be fine."

He's less wasted than he usually is. The crowd has thinned out and the college party seems to have moved on to a more exciting venue. I'm sure once I leave Kyle will get bored and go home.

I squeeze his shoulder. "I'll see ya Monday morning. Don't be hungover."

* * *

"This is your idea of late?" Skylar says, glancing at the clock on the living room wall when I get home. "It's barely midnight."

"I think riding in the heat all day made me tired."

Her eyes fixate on me. "What's on your face?"

"Where?"

"On your cheek."

I reach up and brush off the side of my face.

"The other side," she says, narrowing her eyes like an eagle. "Is that lipstick?"

Cringing, I wipe my hand across the other side of my face. "Yeah, some chick kissed me."

She squints at me curiously. "A girl just walked up to you and put her lips on you?"

"Basically, yeah."

She scratches her head. "Does that happen often?"

I flash her a smirk. "Not often enough."

"It's a tacky shade. No wonder you came home," she teases. "You want to watch some TV with me?"

"Are you still watching Highlander?"

"*Out*lander. It's soo tragically romantic and good. They're kind of in an arranged marriage, too."

I hope the show's not giving her crazy ideas. Our story isn't going to end tragically good, or romantic. It's just going to end—simply and anticlimactically.

She'll go her way.

I'll go mine.

Simple.

I try to ignore the fact that if it were simple, I wouldn't have turned down sex with a hot chick because I couldn't stop thinking about my eighteen-year-old fake wife.

Not good.

Not good at all.

"I think I'm just gonna head to bed," I answer.

Disappointment flashes across her face and disappears just as fast. "Okay. Goodnight, Lucky."

"'Night."

"Watch out for any random kisses on the way upstairs," she jokes.

The first thing I do when I get to my room is scrub the hell out of my face.

CHAPTER 19

SKYLAR

I'm doing Pilates in my room when my phone buzzes with a text.

Jude: Can you come down to the basement?

Me: That's not at all creepy, said no one ever. 👀

Jude: Just come down here. Wear shoes with rubber soles.

Me: Still creepy.

Jude: Stop being a bad wife 😬

Laughing at his little joke, I roll up my Pilates mat, slip on my sneakers and head downstairs.

The basement is unfinished and musty, with a cold concrete floor. I rarely come down here unless I need something out of the big wooden pantry or need to do laundry. Jude stores his tools down here, and lots of old boxes and furniture. One corner is set up as a gym, which he uses several times a week.

My sneakers squeak as I make my way toward him at the far end of the cellar, and I realize the floor is wet. By the time I reach him, we're standing in about two inches of water. He's frantically moving cardboard boxes off the floor, piling them up on an old workbench and on stacked wooden pallets.

"Yikes. What's going on?" I ask.

"The sump pump broke," he replies, not looking at me.

"What's a sump pump?"

"It's like a vacuum that keeps the basement from flooding when it rains a lot."

"Oh," I say, looking at the rising water on the floor. This can't be good.

"Help me move this stuff. I can't let it get ruined. Try to move the lighter ones, if you can."

Quickly, I grab an old dusty box that has *Erin* written on it in black marker, and move it to the other side of the room where it's still dry.

I carry two more Erin boxes, then help him push an old filing cabinet and a desk out of the water.

"Thanks," he says, wiping the back of his hand across his forehead. His long hair is sticking to his sweaty face.

"You're welcome," I reply. "Who's Erin? A former wife?" I counted six boxes with her name on them, and he was obviously in a rush to move those first.

Catching his breath, he leans back against the old desk. "My little sister."

"Oh. She used to live here, in my room?"

"Yeah."

I wonder why Erin didn't take her stuff with her when she moved out.

"How old is she?" I ask curiously.

He lifts the hem of his T-shirt and wipes his face with it, putting his abs on full display.

Holy moly.

My mouth has suddenly gone dryer than the Sahara. Swallowing, I drag my eyes from his chiseled eight-pack.

"Hopefully, she's twenty-six," he says.

"Hopefully?"

"It's a long, long story, Sparkles. I gotta run to the hardware store, get a new sump pump, and clean this mess up with the shop vac. My entire Saturday is fucked."

"I could go with you," I suggest tentatively. "You could tell me about her on the drive. I'll help you when we get back."

His attention shifts down to the growing puddle on the floor. I wonder if I've overstepped our roommate line in some way. We've been married four weeks today, and we've been pretty much keeping our distance from each other, except for dinner and a television show together.

"Or I could start shop-vacking the water while you're gone," I say, trying to fill the silence. "I'm not going to let you do all this by yourself. I live here, too."

He finally lifts his gaze. The thin lines around his eyes are deeper. His eyes a little red-rimmed with exhaustion and defeat.

"You can come, if you want," he says.

Silence sits between us for the first few minutes of the drive to the hardware store. I think back to the first day we met when he gave me a ride home.

I had no idea he'd change my entire life.

I'm just about to bring that up when he starts to talk in a low, haunting, voice, "Erin was my younger sister." He tells me all about how she simply disappeared one day. How he searched for her for weeks and how the police had finally assumed she was either a runaway, or dead.

Horrified, I listen. Erin was only sixteen. Two years younger than me. Vanished, without a trace or a clue other than a strange text message. Jude's voice cracks with emotion as he talks about her, and it's heartbreaking. He believes she's dead because she wasn't the type to run away. They were close—she'd never leave him without saying good-bye or being in touch, especially after all this time. The story doesn't end there, though. He goes on to tell me about his mother and her fight with cancer, her recovery, and the way she moved out—leaving him with a house full of memories and little more than the occasional phone call and a few birthday and holiday cards since. I knew Jude had a bad time with drugs and alcohol when he was younger, but I didn't realize it had anything to do with everything he just told me. It shifted my idea of his substance abuse from something reckless and rebellious to the thing that numbed his pain.

I reach across the truck and put my hand over his. "I'm so sorry," I say, my own voice strained. "It's just... horrible."

I can't believe a young girl could disappear like that. Where did she go? What happened to her? The unknowing and lack of closure would drive me insane. My dad basically disappeared from my life, but I know he's somewhere living a new life—just without me. But with a situation like Jude's, I'd *need* answers. I can't imagine how he feels.

Jude nods, and spreads his fingers apart, inviting mine to interlock with his. The way he squeezes my thin fingers between his sends a cozy warmth through my limbs. It's that subtle, unspoken connection—the hand hug.

We stay that way—hands locked together—until we get to the hardware store. While we're shopping, I can't stop thinking about his missing sister and the way my chest hurt hearing the pain in his voice. I like thinking that holding my hand was comforting to him. When I first met him, I wouldn't have pegged him as the affectionate, vulnerable type, but I'm slowly seeing that under his rough exterior, hides a totally different animal.

It takes us hours to dry up the basement. Using the shop vac to suck up the water is oddly satisfying, though. Jude has been in a state of frustration, venting about old houses and the dangers of mold spores.

"I'm going to mop with a little bleach," he says when we've dried up all the water. "Why don't you go upstairs? The smell will give you a headache."

"What about you?" I ask.

"I already have a headache. I have a mask to wear, it's not a big deal."

"If you're sure?"

He gives me a tired grin. "I'm sure. You were a big help. I'll be up in a bit."

Reluctantly, I go upstairs to feed the pets and take a hot shower. I've felt sweaty and sticky all day, and my feet have been wet and cold for hours. Wrapped in a soft terry-cloth robe, I sit on the bed and scrub at my hair with a towel. My stomach growls, reminding me I didn't eat today—something I'm still struggling with.

Earlier, Jude stopped at a fast-food restaurant on the way back from the hardware store, and I froze up when it was time to order. I wanted a roll. All the pictures of food on the glowing menu in the drive-through overwhelmed and nauseated me. So much stuff oozing on burgers and salads. A row of cars accumulated behind us, pressuring me to decide fast, with no time for me to analyze ingredients.

Jude was frustrated and rightfully so. He was having a shitty day and was stressing about the house. He took a chance and ordered me French fries, but they were soggy and felt icky on my tongue. I gagged and spit it out, then refused his offer of half his hamburger bun. Because I wanted him to enjoy his entire burger and not ruin it by giving part of it to me.

He actually offered to give me the top of his burger bun, just so I'd eat. How sweet is that? And now I feel like an epic bitch because I said no. He probably thinks I'm an ungrateful brat.

Today was what I call a bad food day. I note this in my journal app so I can discuss it with my therapist and dietician this coming week.

"Hey."

His voice startles me, and I almost drop my phone when I look up at my doorway. He's holding a plate of cinnamon toast in his hand with that damn grin on his face.

Toast is still bread, but it's what I think of as *enhanced* bread.

"I thought you might want something," he says, which is his polite way of saying *you should eat*.

He tries. He really does.

"Lucky… you don't have to feed me," I say, taking the plate from him.

"You worked your butt off today helping me."

"I live here. I should help when shit breaks. You don't have to thank me or make me dinner."

"It's toast, not surf n' turf."

I take a bite and chew slowly. He continues to linger in my doorway. He never comes all the way inside unless he asks first, or if I tell him to. I sneeze and rub my nose. "Damn. I can smell the bleach on you. You should change or shower and clear your head so you don't get sick."

"Yeah, I'm gonna go clean up." He rubs his hands together. "It's only eight o'clock; you want to Netflix and chill after I shower?"

I choke on my toast. "Um, I don't think that means what you think it means."

His face goes blank with confusion. "What? Watch a movie and unwind after a shitastic day?"

"That sounds great, but that's not what Netflix and chill means."

"Care to enlighten me?"

I lick butter off my fingertips. "It's basically slang for hang out and fuck."

He pales. "Seriously?"

"Yup."

He holds his hands up defensively. "I just want to watch a movie. No side of fucking involved."

A mild tinge of disappointment tugs my mouth into a frown that I quickly try to cover up by taking another bite of toast. How does he do this to me? I really just want us to be friends, but somehow, I keep tipping over into this weird, unfamiliar place of stomach butterflies, awkward conversations, and racing heartbeats.

"Don't worry," I say. "I didn't think you were trying to hook up with me."

"Good. If I was, I wouldn't be lame enough to lure you in with a movie."

I blink at him.

"Not that I'd be trying to lure you at all," he says quickly. "Or hooking up with you."

"Um, thanks?"

"Wait, only because I wouldn't be into you like that."

"You want a shovel, Lucky? You're digging yourself pretty deep."

"I'm just saying I wouldn't do that. I mean, you're pretty, but—"

"You're being a *really* bad husband," I interrupt, using our little inside joke. I can't remember how or when we started teasing each other about being a bad spouse, but at times like this, it breaks the awkwardness.

I smile at him as he shoves his hand through his messy hair. "I'll be in the living room in about an hour. If you want to watch a movie and impress me with your ability to not eat hot, buttery popcorn, that'd be great."

After he leaves, I pick up my cell phone and text Megan.

Me: Change of plans, I can't hang out tonight.

Megan: But Carson was going to stop by. I wanted you to hang with him.

Me: I'm sorry. I'm not feeling great. Maybe another time?

Megan: Sure! Feel better! Xo

Netflixing and not-chilling with Jude sounds way more fun than enduring a not-so-random setup. Anyway, I'm married now. Should I really be dating? Isn't that bad karma, even if it's not a *real* marriage?

CHAPTER 20

JUDE

I've just settled on the couch with a bowl of fresh popcorn in my lap and the dog at my feet when Skylar joins me, wearing a white sweatshirt and fleece footie pants with peace signs printed on them.

Laughing, I shake my head and shovel popcorn into my mouth.

"Don't you laugh at my pants," she says, sitting in her usual place—the recliner a few feet away from the couch. "My feet were freezing from standing in all that water."

"Your outfits never disappoint."

"You're just jealous because my feet are all warm and cozy."

"Not a lie," I say.

"Did you pick a movie yet?" she asks, twisting her hair up into a messy ponytail and tying it with the white band she had around her wrist.

"I was waiting to see if you were coming down."

"I felt like I had to after your badly misplaced pick-up line."

I grab the remote and bring the Netflix movie menu up on

the screen. "Obviously, I haven't tried to pick up a chick in a while."

"Obviously," she repeats. "Speaking of, Megan was trying to set me up with some dude named Carson tonight. She described him as *odd*. I bailed out of that fast."

"Why? It's Saturday night, you should be out having fun."

"Nah. Having awkward convos with some guy with a last name for a first name who's probably just going to try to get me drunk and have sex with him isn't my idea of fun."

I stifle a laugh. I was that dude when I was seventeen. "What's your idea of fun, then?"

"This," she says simply. "Sitting in comfy clothes, not dealing with any fake BS, curling up with my cat later in a nice, clean bed, and sleeping as late as I want tomorrow." She pauses and tilts her head playfully. "And hanging out with you isn't so bad."

Her answer surprises me. Most girls her age wouldn't be caught dead spending a Saturday night at home, especially with—

With *who*? What does she even think of me as? The older-dude roommate? The fake husband? I chew my popcorn as I flick through the movies on the screen. I probably don't want to know how she refers to me in her head and with her friends.

"Ooh, let's watch that!" she suddenly says, pointing excitedly to the screen. "*Almost Famous*."

"That movie's been out for years."

"Yeah... but it's one of my faves. I can watch it over and over and never get tired of it."

Grinning, I select the movie. "It's one of my favorites, too. It's got a kick-ass soundtrack."

"It *so* does!" she agrees.

As the movie starts, I put my feet up on the coffee table and stretch out. My back and neck ache from being bent over in the damp basement all day.

That's what she said, the voice of Erin says in my head.

"You can sit over here, ya know," I say a few minutes into the movie. "You'll be able to see better." The recliner sits at an awkward angle from the television, making her crane her head to see the screen. When I lived here with my mother, I hated sitting there. I bought new furniture a few years ago, but I ended up putting it all in the exact same place. No idea why, since my goal was to make the house look and feel different.

"You sure?" She asks it like sitting on the couch with me has been off-limits, and I've granted her VIP access.

"Yeah." I nod my chin toward the other end of the couch. "That spot is yours."

She crosses the room and plops down, wiggling her butt into the cushion with a big smile on her face.

I hold the bowl out to her. "Want to try some popcorn? It's still warm."

Her nose lifts up a bit. "I can't. I got a piece stuck in my throat when I was little."

Most of her food fears are confusing as hell to me, but I don't push her about it. All that matters is that she's doing better.

I don't remember the last time I've hung out and watched movies with someone. Especially a woman. But since Skylar moved in, we've done it a lot. I didn't realize how much I missed having another person around. Or having someone to talk to other than my dog.

I'm struggling with the fact that I like having Skylar around. Way more than I should. When she's laughing like she is now, my mind drifts back to the kiss.

Yeah—the kiss that never should've happened.

And the second kiss that never should've happened.

And, if I'm not careful, the third kiss that should never happen.

I can't, though. She's only eighteen. Not on the menu for me.

She's wearing footie pants, for fuck's sake. Too young, too innocent to get involved with someone like me. Women love me, until they hate me. I'm a dating wanderer. I stay for a while, then I move on. I've always been a "fun for the moment" type of guy. The problem is, I'm nice to them. I treat women well—I'm not a dick. I'm upfront with where we stand. I just don't want to *stay*. Somehow, that makes it worse. It's like they'd rather I was a total douche than be honest and nice.

Leaning back, I stretch my arms up over my head, and pain shoots from my neck down to the base of my spine. I groan and twist, grimacing from the discomfort

"Oh no… did you hurt your back?"

"I've got some messed-up discs in my back and neck. Sometimes they act up."

"Sucks getting old, huh?" she jabs playfully, but there's a flash of worry in her eyes.

"You have no idea."

I scavenge through the popcorn, trying to find an extra-buttery piece and one catches my eye that doesn't have any butter on it.

"Look at this." I hold it up. "It looks just like Cassie."

"Are you nuts?" She laughs. "It's a piece of popcorn."

"No really, look. These look like little floppy ears, and those are eyes, and a nose."

I hand it to her and she examines it until a big smile spreads across her lips. "Oh my God. It *does*. How funny is that?"

"You should eat it. Make it your first new popcorn trial."

"Hmm…"

"That piece doesn't even have any butter on it, so it's not soggy or weird."

"Okay. I'm going to try it," she says triumphantly, popping it into her mouth.

A few seconds later she coughs, covering her mouth with her

hand, and anxiously gripping the arm of the couch with the other.

"You okay?" I ask.

She shakes her head rapidly back and forth and turns to me with a look of terror in her eyes.

"It's stuck in my throat." She gags. "A piece of it."

Fuck. I put the bowl down and move closer to her. "It'll go down."

Her chest heaves up and down as she gulps air. "I can't breathe… I'm going to choke."

She's spiraling into a panic right in front of me, on the verge of hyperventilating.

"You're talking, so you can breathe. You're not choking. It's just tickling your throat." I grab my soda and hold it out to her. "Take a sip of this."

Her eyes grow even wider as she coughs and clutches at her throat. "I can't."

I forgot—she won't drink soda. It's on her bad list.

Helplessly, I watch her throat bob up and down as she swallows, trembling with fear as she gasps for breath.

She's not choking, I'm sure of it. The little piece stuck in her throat—probably one of those fucking kernel skin things—has launched her into a massive panic attack.

"Skylar, try to breathe slow," I say evenly. "You're not choking."

"I can't swallow it…" she cries, her cheeks reddening. "It's stuck."

"Lemme go get you some water."

I run to the kitchen to grab a bottle of water, but when I come back to the living room, she's gone.

"Skylar?"

Gagging sounds from the bathroom down the hall turn me in that direction. The door is ajar, so I cautiously poke my head in.

My heart sinks when I find her sitting on the floor, leaning against the bathtub. Tears are streaming down her cheeks, her body shaking uncontrollably as she wretches.

Kneeling in front of her, I twist the top off the water bottle.

She grabs on to my arm, her nails digging into my skin in desperation. "I'm dying… I can't breathe…" she begs, gasping for air. The raw fear in her voice tears my heart to shreds and sends a chill down my spine.

"Skylar… baby, you're fine. Look at me." She raises her tear-filled, frantic eyes to meet mine. "You can breathe. You're not dying, I promise. Drink this, okay? I promise it'll go down."

Gasping for breath, she says, "I can't, I can't…"

Mentally, she's in another place—not here with me at all. It's there in the terror in her eyes and the anguished trembling of her lips. She's been sucked back into time, gripped by a childhood memory that hasn't let go.

I had no idea how deep her fears ran, how strong of a hold they have on her. This isn't just an eating disorder. It's as if a monster is terrorizing her, threatening to kill her.

"You're okay. I promise." I hold the bottle to her lips. "Sip a tiny bit. The water'll make it soft and it'll go down."

Pushing the bottle away, she gags and sucks in a breath. "I'm gonna pass out… I'm gonna die…"

I shake my head. "You're fine. Trust me." I hold the bottle to her lips again. "Just sip it. I'm right here. I'm not going to let you die."

She's not even close to dying. But she believes she is. Her demons are real. She didn't leave them behind in that dump of a house. They're right here, inhabiting her damn soul, convincing her she's going to choke to death.

With shaking hands, she grasps the bottle and slowly swallows the water.

"It's still there…" she sobs hopelessly as more tears spill from her eyes. My heart is wrecked seeing her like this. Maybe I *should* take her to a hospital. I'm not equipped to take care of someone having a serious emotional breakdown.

"Keep drinking," I say, holding out hope that we can avoid a trip to the ER. "It'll take a sec."

I watch her take small sips of water, waiting for that fucker to dislodge out of her throat, and the moment it happens, I see it. Her eyes light up, her grip around the bottle loosens, and she gulps more water.

Finally, she lets out a deep, shuddering sigh. "I think it's gone," she whispers.

"See?" I rip off some toilet paper and hand it to her. "You're okay."

Sniffling, she wipes her face and blows her nose.

"Jude… I'm so sorry—"

"Hey," I interrupt. "Don't apologize."

"I'm so embarrassed." She hides her face in her hands. "I couldn't breathe… I choked when I was little… I was so scared."

"It's okay."

"It's not." She shakes her head and moves her hands to clutch the back of her neck. "I'm a mess. I thought I was getting better."

"You *are* getting better. It's not an overnight thing. I'm sure the doctor told you that."

She nods weakly. "Yeah…"

"So, it's normal to still go through stuff. You've been in therapy less than a month. Go easy on yourself."

Standing, I hold my hand out to her and help her up.

"Splash your face with some water, it'll make you feel better. We'll go finish the movie. No more popcorn." I chew the inside of my cheek and study her blotchy face—such a change from how happy and cute she looked earlier. "I fucked up. I shouldn't have asked you to eat it."

Guilt weighs heavy in my gut. This was my fault.

I'm an asshole.

"It's not your fault I choked on your popcorn dog." A faint smile tips her lips.

"It is. I'll own it. But hey," I touch her chin and lift her face up, "If I thought you were choking, or dying, there's no way in hell I'd just sit here. I'd have you at the hospital fast as fuckin' lightning. I wouldn't let anything happen to you."

"I know," she says softly. Her body is still shaking as if she's freezing. "I'll be out in a few minutes."

Giving her space, I take the dog for a walk in the yard and smoke a quick cigarette while staring up at the moon. Seeing Skylar so scared and upset was unsettling. But witnessing it only solidifies that I did the right thing marrying her. She needs help to get better. No one should have to go through life being so terrified of food.

She's waiting for me in the living room when I get back inside, and she looks incredibly young and vulnerable sitting in the middle of the couch.

I sit next to her. "Feel better?"

"A little. I still feel shaky and my heart is pounding."

I hold my arm out to her. "Come here," I say.

She eyes me hesitantly before slowly moving closer to me. When she leans against me and rests her head against my shoulder, I cover her with a light blanket from the back of the couch and gently put my arm around her.

"Does this make you feel better?" I ask softly.

She nods and snuggles up against me. "Yes," she says quietly. "Thank you."

Just because I avoid relationships doesn't mean I don't understand the power of a hug and feeling safe with someone. She's scared, abandoned by her family, and living with a stranger. Showing her some human affection isn't going to kill me.

As we watch the movie, I slowly rub my hand up and down

her arm, hoping to soothe her and chase away her fears. At least for a little while. I lightly caress the side of her neck with the backs of my fingers, feeling her pulse beneath my touch. Her breathing slows and her body relaxes. At some point in the middle of the movie, she reaches for my other hand and holds it tightly.

I don't understand why we feel so comfortable together. How we naturally just fit. Or how these little intimate touches feel totally normal and not wrong or awkward.

I've never felt like this.

I could close my eyes right here and fall asleep with her in my arms. And I think I'd actually like it. The usual impulse to run as far away as possible from any sort of intimacy doesn't come when I'm with her. I've been waiting for it. Maybe even tempting it by letting myself have these random moments of closeness. But it doesn't come. What *does* come is confusion about why my feelings are shifting out of the friend zone.

I'm about as good with confusion as I am with intimacy.

When the movie ends, she sits up and turns to look at me. Her blue eyes are red and puffy from crying, and her ponytail is more lopsided than it was earlier.

This look shouldn't be attractive, but on her, it is. Adorably so.

"You're a good guy, Jude," she says softly.

She smiles when I wink at her. "Sometimes."

"I know you didn't sign up for this, but thank you for taking care of me."

"I vaguely recall agreeing to something about sickness and health," I say with a grin.

"Yeah, but they weren't *real* vows."

No, they weren't.

But somehow, they're turning out to be.

CHAPTER 21

JUDE

I'm surprised to see Skylar in the kitchen the next morning at eight a.m., nibbling on a croissant while staring out the window. Looking over her shoulder, I see a chipmunk racing around on the old rock wall out back has captured her attention.

"What are you doing up so early?" I ask. "You said you wanted to sleep late today."

She turns away from the window. "I wanted to, but I couldn't sleep. I think last night shook me. I haven't freaked out like that in a while. My therapist said it might happen as I start to eat new foods. I guess I was hoping it wouldn't."

"I don't think it's a setback."

"I hope not. I don't like that feeling at all." She watches me as I sit in a chair and pull on my old work boots. "Are you working today? It's Sunday."

"No. I'm going to visit my aunt and uncle."

"I didn't know you had an aunt and uncle."

"They're older—in their seventies. Mostly out of their minds, but I check on them a few times a month to make sure they haven't burned the house down or sent half their money to an overseas prince on the internet."

She laughs. "They sound fun."

"You can come with me," I suggest casually. "If you want to."

Her chewing pauses for a beat. "Really? You want me to meet your family?"

I shrug. "Why not? It's no big deal. It'll be fun. I told them about our arrangement a few weeks ago."

Surprise flashes in her eyes. "I didn't think you wanted anyone to know we got married."

"I don't want *everyone* to know, but they're family. I don't think my aunt was fully grasping the gist of the situation when I told her."

"I guess I wouldn't mind getting out for a while," she says. "Will she try to feed me?"

"Probably. But she won't get offended if you don't eat. I wasn't planning on staying for lunch. Just a quick visit. You should be fine. I got your back, don't worry."

"Okay." She looks down at her jeans and white sweater. "Should I change?"

"No, you look great."

"I'll go get my shoes."

Ten minutes later she comes back downstairs with the addition of silver chain earrings with little stars dangling from them, a purple scarf with glittery stars, and dark-purple vintage leather boots with big metal buckles on the side.

"I'm ready now. I had to add some glitz."

Laughing, I reach for my keys on the counter, but she touches my arm.

"Let's take my car. You can drive."

I shake my head. My back and neck were hurting so much this morning I could barely get out of bed, so I'm not about to crawl in and out of a car that's a foot off the ground. "No can do.

My back's still hurting way too much to get in and out of that thing."

She frowns. "That sucks."

"Maybe next time."

On the way to my aunt and uncle's, I stop at a Dunkin Donut's drive-through to get a much-needed coffee for myself. Skylar agrees to one glazed munchkin.

Don't ask me how someone can eat *one* munchkin. It's unnatural.

"Hey, Jude," the young girl at the pay window sings in an overly friendly voice as she leans past the glass partition like she does every time I come here. As if I've never heard someone mimic the song of my name before. "You're here early today," she says.

I nod at her as I take my order and throw a tip in the jar.

"Oh, hey, Skylar," she continues, peering past me. "I didn't see you huddled way over there. Are you hitchhiking?"

"Yes," Skylar replies. "But now we've teamed up to look for airheads to murder. When's your shift over?"

"Shut up, bitch," the girl tosses back.

Before pulling away, I reach into the tip jar and take my dollar back.

"You know her?" I ask, shoving the dollar into my front pocket.

"Yeah, we go to school together."

Ah. Now I remember. She was one of the girls giving Skylar a hard time on the first day of school.

Nodding, I say, "She's usually here on the weekends."

"Seems like it. She knows your name. And the time you usually come," she grumbles.

Is that a hint of jealousy coming from my little fake wife?

"She usually fucks up my coffee."

"I'm not surprised." She picks at her munchkin, pulling tiny pieces off before eating them. "Paige is an idiot."

Not wanting to fuel the flame of high school drama, I flick on my Doors playlist, and we sing *People Are Strange* together.

"Morrison was one of the greats," Skylar comments when the song ends. "So deep and poetic. Not to mention, dammmn sexy."

"Not at the end he wasn't."

She bobs her head to the side. "True. But in his prime, he was everything."

I don't know if he was *everything*. He was known for being moody, stoned, and emotionally unstable most of the time.

"You have any INXS on your playlist?" she asks. "Michael Hutchence gives me Jim Morrison vibes."

Skylar obviously has a distinct fascination for damaged men. I see a broken heart in her future.

"As a matter of fact, I do." I pick up my phone, find the song I'm looking for, and hit play.

"Oh!" she squeals when she hears it. "*Don't Change* is sooo good. This and *Never Tear Us Apart* are my favorites. Have you heard the cover of *Never Tear Us Apart* that Ashes and Embers does? It's seriously *so* amazing."

"I have. It's wicked good."

"Asher Valentine has the most emotional voice ever. And that dude on violin?" She fans herself with her hand. "Epic on every level."

"Should I turn the AC on to cool you off over there, Sparkles?" I tease.

She smirks my way. "Be quiet, you. A girl's gotta have someone to lust over."

"Does she now?"

"Yes. Just like men do. I'm sure you get all stupid when girls like Paige with her mile-long eyelashes are flirting with you," she playfully accuses, and pokes me in the arm.

"I can assure you I have zero interest in a girl—no, make that a *woman* because I'm not into girls—like Paige."

"Why's that?" She narrows her eyes at me curiously. "She's pretty in that *I must look runway perfect at all times* way."

"That's what I *don't* like. I like natural women. Not with all that makeup. Someone who doesn't blatantly flirt to get my attention. I don't like when women are always 'on,' trying to look and act perfect 24/7. To me, they're much more attractive when they're sitting around in sweats with messy hair acting goofy."

"Like me?" Her voice rises with hope. "In my footie pajamas?"

"Actually, yeah. Cute can be sexy."

Shut up, Jude.

"Maybe older men are different then, because all the guys at school go after the gorgeous, popular girls. They don't even notice girls like me."

"Trust me, they notice you. My guess? They're intimidated by you because you don't act interested in them. The so-called pretty girls flirt with them, invite the guys to pay attention to them. But you? You're not trying to get their attention. You're confident and unique. That scares them."

In hindsight, I may have spent too much time watching Skylar walking to and from the high school parking lot every day.

She turns to me, her forehead creased with thought. "You really think so?"

"Yup."

"Meh," she says dismissively, and leans back in her seat to stare out the windshield. "I'm not interested in any of them, anyway."

"There aren't any brooding, emo, musician-types in your school? It was full of them when I was there."

"None that I've seen."

"Check under the bleachers," I say. "That's where they usually hang out."

She laughs. "I'll do that."

I have lots of memories of hanging out under the bleachers with friends, smoking cigarettes and joints, having random philosophical discussions.

"So, does that mean *you* think I'm cute and sexy?" she suddenly asks while playing with the seat control buttons. "Wait—will this one make my butt warm?"

"Yes."

"Yes, you think I'm cute and sexy, or yes, this heated seat thing will make my butt warm?"

I swerve past a car taking too long to make a turn. My brain is doing the same—trying to swerve away from the conversation. Sure, she's cute and sexy as hell, but that doesn't mean I want to verbally admit it.

"Yes, it'll make your ass warm."

Swerve.

"Why would someone want their ass warm? Why doesn't this headrest heat up? That's something I might like."

Closing my eyes briefly, I shake my head and stifle a laugh.

"Do I scare you, Lucky?" she asks in her playful voice. "With my confidence and messy hair?"

"Yes. I'm terrified," I tease back before taking a sip of my coffee.

"I think you are." Her voice lowers, and she side-eyes me with a crooked grin. A notification on her phone distracts her, and she pulls it out of her pocket to read a message.

Saved by the bell.

"Don't you want to know if I think *you're* cute and sexy?" she asks, laying her phone on her lap.

I glance in the rearview mirror and resist the urge to say yes. "Nope."

"Why not?"

"I mean, look at me. Of course you think I'm sexy." I flash her a sly grin. "There's nothing cute about me."

"You're hotter than this seat warmer is," she says, switching the button for the seat to *off*. "I hope you didn't pay extra for that feature. It's a fail."

"Agreed."

"And for the record, I think you're kinda cute. Especially when you smile. Not your signature slick, sexy smile, though. But this other little smile you do, when you're tired. It's super cute."

Ugh. Cute. When did that happen?

I glance at her and feign innocence. "What slick, sexy smile?"

She rolls her eyes. "Don't act dumb. You know the one I mean. And you know damn well it makes women all crazy."

"Really?" I say coyly, turning onto the street my aunt and uncle live on. "Tell me more."

I shouldn't flirt with her, but I can't stop myself. Banter is a wicked turn-on for me.

"You smiled that way at Rebecca. That day in the store."

I scoff. "I did not."

"Yes, you did."

"It musta been an accident. Do I smile that way at you?"

"What? You don't have control over your own face?" she asks with teasing sarcasm.

I shrug. "Depends on the day."

Laughing, she says affectionately, "You're an ass. And yeah, you've smiled at me with the slick smile a couple of times."

I pull into my aunt and uncle's driveway and kill the engine.

"Well, it wasn't intentional. I wouldn't want to make you *all crazy*, as you put it," I say, purposely flashing her the smile in question.

Her cheeks blush as she grins and shakes her head. "Don't worry. I don't mind being a little crazy," she says, opening her door and jumping out of the truck.

I chomp on that tidbit like a hungry dog, even though I know I shouldn't. In my mind she's got a huge, glowing, neon sign over her head flashing WARNING - KEEP BACK. But somehow, I keep edging closer.

CHAPTER 22

SKYLAR

"Should we have brought something?" I ask softly as we walk up the front steps of the brick ranch together. Why didn't I think of this earlier? I should have brought a cake, or flowers to meet his family in their home. I don't want them to think I'm rude.

"Nah." Jude takes one more drag off his cigarette before putting it out in a stone planter near the door. It appears to be serving as a huge ashtray with a fake flower arrangement stuck in the middle of it. "They might go into shock if I show up with gifts."

"But we're here *together*."

"Don't worry. It's just a quick visit to say hi, not Thanksgiving dinner."

"I know, but—"

The front door swings open, and an adorable, petite woman with shoulder-length gray hair and wire-rimmed glasses stands before us, her mouth hanging open in shock.

"Oh, my Lord," she says as a big smile spreads across her face. "It's true!" She turns her head to yell into the house. "Al!

Lucky and his wife are here! She's real! You owe me twenty bucks!"

Jude pushes past her, stopping for a second to kiss her cheek. "Yeah, yeah, yeah," he grumbles, even though he's smiling. "You two are a riot."

I follow him inside, and his aunt closes the door behind us. "Aren't you the cutest thing," she says, beaming at me. I can feel my cheeks reddening.

"She's not a thing," Jude says. "Aunt Suzy, this is Skylar. Skylar, this is my Aunt Suzy, and that over there," he nods behind us, where an older man is sitting in the living room, "is Uncle Al."

"It's so nice to meet you," I say, leaning in to kiss her cheek.

"Come in, come in. Make yourself comfortable. We're so glad you two stopped by. Lucky, you have to look at the washing machine for me," she says as we move into the living room. "It's making that clanking noise again and leaking sudsy water."

I blink to clear my vision, convinced there's no way I'm seeing everything I'm seeing. But it's all there, and my heart lurches with excitement.

We've stepped inside a time capsule. A house preserved from the 1960s.

I feel like I'm in heaven!

The carpet is a dizzying, orange-and-brown pattern. Orange curtains hang over the windows. Dark-wood paneling covers the walls. My trained eye from scouting flea markets and antique stores tells me all the furniture and decor is obviously authentic, not cheap copies. The awesome thing is, even though it's all old, it doesn't look worn, or dirty, like some old houses do when everything has been forgotten, ignored, and never upgraded. A slight floral scent fills the air. Everything here is clean—purposely preserved and taken care of. Like a museum.

I catch Jude watching me as I gape around the room. My heart flutters when he winks at me as our eyes meet.

He knew how much I'd love it here. It's one of the coolest houses I've ever been in.

"We thought Lucky was full of shit when he told us he had a wife," Uncle Al says from the orange chair in the corner. His voice is deep and gravelly, like he was a smoker for a long time. He reminds me of an old hippie—long white beard and hair, glasses similar to his wife's, faded tattoos on his arms. A green knitted beanie hat is perched on his head. Jude has his eyes and his bad-boy grin. I'm pretty sure back in the day, Uncle Al and Aunt Suzy were quite the attractive couple.

I smile at him, unsure what to say.

"A *fake* wife," Jude corrects, sitting on a matching orange couch and patting the space next to him. "It's not a real marriage. I told you guys that. We're just friends."

I maneuver around the glass, boomerang-shaped coffee table and join him on the couch.

"What kind of bullshit is that?" Uncle Al nods his bearded chin at me. "You okay with that, sweetheart?"

"Yes," I reply, nervous under his stare. "I'm totally okay with it. Jude was nice enough to marry me so I could have health insurance for a while." I hope I'm giving them the same story Jude did. I wish he had briefed me on the drive over.

Uncle Al points at us. "Well, you *do* like each other, right?"

Jude and I look at each other and laugh a little. "Sure," Jude says. "We're still getting to know each other, though."

Aunt Suzy flits across the room, stopping at the entry to the kitchen. "I don't understand why you young kids want to date forever and get to know each other before you get married. The only way to get to know someone *is* to marry them."

Uncle Al nods and tugs on his beard. "I married her a month after we met and we never looked back."

"That's fuckin' crazy," Jude comments.

"I think it's great," I say. "So romantic."

"Life's too short to wait around," Uncle Al says. "I liked her, I married her."

"He was a wild child, just like you, Lucky," Aunt Suzy calls out from the kitchen. I can't see her, since there's a wall between the rooms. Now I see why the new open-concept floorplans are so popular. "It took me years to tame him."

Uncle Al smirks and shakes his head. "She never tamed me. I just let her think she did."

"Your house is beautiful," I say when Aunt Suzy returns with a plate full of crackers and sliced cheese. She places it on the coffee table and sits in a retro, green chair across from us.

"Thank you. Our best years were in the sixties, so we thought, why not surround ourselves with it forever?"

"It's really cool," I comment, taking in all the details—statues, vases, lamps, old clocks. Even the TV and radio have that vintage look.

"Most of it is all our original stuff from when we first bought this house."

"It's all great 'til it starts to break," Jude snorts.

"Lucky told us you work in a store and take pictures?" Aunt Suzy asks, ignoring Jude's remark.

I nod, hoping they don't think I'm taking advantage of their nephew. "I'm in my last year of high school, but I work part-time at a boutique in town. I work the register, but recently, I got a promotion. Now I take pictures of the products and post them online to promote them and entice people to come to the store. It's a lot of fun."

"She's really talented at taking photos," Jude adds.

"Good for you. I love photography," Aunt Suzy remarks.

"You're how old?" Uncle Al asks me.

"Don't ask her age!" his wife exclaims. "Never ask a woman her age."

"She's eighteen," Jude answers, shoving a cracker in his mouth.

Bracing myself for shock and backlash, I pick up a cracker and nibble it gingerly. I don't want to appear rude by not eating some of the snacks Suzy put out for us.

"Just like me!" Aunt Suzy says instead. "I was eighteen when I married Al. I felt so old at the time, even though I was so young." She looks at her husband with wistful eyes. "I thought I knew everything."

"You *still* think you know everything," Uncle Al teases.

Suzy turns to us. "Age doesn't matter. You two will grow together and figure it all out. Just like we did."

"You guys, we're not really a couple," Jude says, shaking his head. "You understand that, right? She's only eighteen. And we're *just friends*. I don't want you two getting all excited thinking we'll be having babies."

"I love babies!" Aunt Suzy exclaims, grabbing on to that idea like a shopaholic on Black Friday. "It wouldn't hurt to just have *one*."

Jude and I laugh simultaneously. "No, Aunt Suze. No babies."

"I'll babysit for you. I have nothing to do all day."

"Still not happening," Jude says.

"Well, if she's going to babysit…" I tease, playfully nudging his arm.

He turns to me with a smile, leaning so close to me that, for a moment, I think he might kiss me. "Don't encourage them."

"You said you're living together?" Uncle Al asks, raising his eyebrows.

Jude nods. "Yeah, but—"

"Why not just be married for real, then?" Aunt Suzy interrupts.

"We don't *want* to be married," Jude answers.

Aunt Suzy waves her hand dismissively at him. "That's ridiculous. You already *are*."

With a sigh, Jude stands and playfully kicks his uncle's foot. "Okay, enough marriage and baby talk. You want to go look at the washing machine? See if we can find some missing socks in that thing?"

Uncle Al nods and stands up. "Maybe we can pull your head out of your ass while we're down there."

Jude chuckles and glances back at me before he and his uncle head down the basement stairs. "You'll be okay?" he asks.

I nod and reach for another cracker. "Yeah," I say happily. "I'm good."

Aunt Suzy claps her hands together when they're gone. "I was just about to chop vegetables for a soup I'm making. Want to join me in the kitchen and we can chat?"

I force a smile, but a little alarm bell goes off in my head at the mention of food and cooking. "Okay."

Taking a deep breath, I follow her to the kitchen. I'll be fine as long as she doesn't ask me to eat anything. I'm still a bit unsure about vegetables. They grow in the ground. With bugs. People and animals might have walked on them—or worse. Insects might be living *inside* them.

Shudder.

I finger the fuzzy edge of my scarf nervously as I follow her into the kitchen. It's a method my therapist taught me. Some textures are soothing to touch, and it distracts me from worrying or hyper-focusing on food.

"I'm so happy Jude finally has someone special in his life," Suzy says, pulling two cutting boards and a couple of huge, shiny knives out of a drawer and putting them up on the counter.

It takes me a moment to answer her because I'm captivated by the avocado-green kitchen appliances, and the white Formica countertop with the tiny boomerang design, just like I've seen in the older homes and in movies.

"Are these the original appliances?" I ask, touching the door of the refrigerator after she takes an armful of vegetables out of it.

"No, these are painted replicas. Lucky insisted we had to upgrade the appliances after the oven caught on fire." I can't help but laugh at the way she rolls her eyes, smiles, and begins chopping celery. "He bought the entire set for us last year. He does so much for us. He fixes things, helps us pay our bills. You got yourself a good husband, sweetheart. He's just like his Uncle Al." She leans closer to me and whispers, "A little rough on the outside but all love on the inside. You just gotta let them believe they're tough guys."

Picking up a knife and a carrot, I copy how she's chopping, feeling a bit sad that we might be disappointing her by not being married for real. She seems really excited about the idea of an extended family.

"He's a great guy," I agree. "But like he said, we're only legally married. We're not romantically involved. He's too old for me, but he's been a really good friend by helping me. There's medication I have to take. It's nothing life threatening, but I couldn't afford it without insurance. I can't tell you how grateful I am that he offered to help me for a while."

She pushes her glasses up her nose and looks at me with a knowing expression in her eyes as she waits for me to finish. "There must be more to it," she says in a low but friendly voice. "Even if you don't see it. People don't just get married."

I thought so, too.

"That's true," I say. "But we did. I know it's hard to understand and sounds crazy. But we really are just friends."

I'm starting to worry that we're going to spend this entire visit trying to explain how we're not really married. Even though they're older, his aunt and uncle don't appear to be suffering any mental impairment or confusion. They're just not buying into our marriage arrangement.

"Honey, if you were just friends, he wouldn't have brought you home to us. He's never brought a girl home before. Not once." She whacks a zucchini with her knife, as if to punctuate her statement. "And he talks about you all the time when he comes over or we talk on the phone."

My breath catches in my throat, and I almost chop the tip of my finger off.

"Really?" I comment, trying to sound casual and not overly excited.

She nods as she opens a cabinet and pulls out a bunch of tiny spice bottles. "Oh yes. Constantly. He sounds like he's crazy about you. Which is why I don't understand this fake marriage malarkey."

Tingles of excitement and nerves race up my spine at the thought of Jude talking about me, especially after he's been so adamant that there's absolutely nothing between us. It doesn't make sense.

Honestly, I thought Jude only invited me here so I could see all the cool sixties decor, but maybe I was wrong. Maybe he really did want me to meet his family.

I'm afraid to let my mind go to the next thought: Could he have feelings for me?

No, I tell myself. That would be crazy. Just because I've got a silly little crush on him doesn't mean he has one on me. But if he did? I honestly don't know if that'd be good or bad. Catching feelings could turn our situation into a mess.

"And age doesn't matter," Aunt Suzy continues, oblivious to my worries. "In fact, I think it's better. You deserve a man who knows what he wants and can take care of you after all you've been through."

So, Jude obviously *has* been talking to her about me, and not just about my job and my hobbies. Does she know about my mother? My eating disorder? She must think I'm a disaster.

I decide to change the subject before I go down a rabbit hole of over-thinking and end up passing out on her tile floor. "What kind of soup are you making?" I ask, pouring my sliced carrots into a big bowl just like she did with her celery.

"Vegetable and rice. It's my favorite. I hope you'll stay for lunch?"

"Oh, I'm sorry. I don't think we can. Jude mentioned something about having to be home."

"He works too much," she says with a mix of pride and sympathy. "You have to try to get him to relax. Have a little fun."

"I will," I promise, even though I have no idea how I'm supposed to accomplish that.

"Jude spent every weekend with us when he was a little boy. His mother is Al's sister."

"Oh, I didn't know that."

"They both worked a lot—his parents. So, we took the kids on the weekends. Jude kept us on our toes with his antics. He loved to make us laugh. He was always taking care of everything and everyone. I used to call him Little Mister Fixer."

That piques my interest. There's so much I don't know about him. "How do you mean?"

"He was always fixing things. If a toy was broken, he'd spend hours gluing it back together. He'd take my needle and thread and sew up ripped stuffed animals for Erin."

My heart melts. "That's so sweet."

"One day a baby squirrel fell out of the nest right there in the yard and broke its leg. Pretty sure it bounced on its head, too, because it wobbled all the time." I smile as she wobbles her own head back and forth to illustrate. "Anyway, Lucky nursed it back to health all by himself. He kept it in a big box and took it home with him and brought it back here on the weekends."

"Wow." I try to picture Jude as a little boy taking care of a tiny squirrel.

"Its leg healed, but it was never quite right in the head. It lived on our screened porch for almost six years. It was just like a cat, it'd sit on our laps and loved to be petted. It slept in a snuggly little bed. We loved him, but he was really Lucky's pet. He was heartbroken when it passed away."

"Aw," I say over the lump forming in my throat. "That's so sad. But it sounds like you guys gave him a good life."

"We did. Jude's much more sensitive than he lets on. He took his parents' divorce so hard. And then after Erin..." She exhales a deep sigh. "He was never the same. The drinking, then the drugs. All that self-destruction. We worry about him."

I don't know what to say about Erin. Do I offer condolences? Remark on how tragic it all is? Just not say anything?

"He's clean now. So, that's a good thing," I say optimistically. "He seems to be doing great."

"He is. But honey, forgive me for saying... I know you two keep saying your marriage isn't real. But if there's a chance for more, I think he'd make you very happy. He deserves to have someone love him. To take care of him like he tries to take care of everyone else. It's so hard for him to trust and let people in."

I nod and swallow back unexpected tears. "You're right. He *does* deserve that." I don't have the heart to tell her that will never be me. That's not what Jude signed up for.

And I feel awful that him marrying me might prevent him from finding the right woman.

"I've probably said too much," she says apologetically. "But I can't help myself. He's like a son to us."

"You didn't say too much. It's all very sweet. Do you have

any children?" I hope it's not rude to ask, but I'm too curious not to.

"No, that wasn't part of the plan for us. But we love Jude and Erin like our own."

"He's lucky to have such a loving family," I say, wishing I had relatives like this. I did, at one time. My grandparents were sweet and supportive. Like Jude, I also spent weekends and holidays with them to "give my mother a break," as my grandmother would say. It wasn't really to give my mother a break, though. It was to get me out of her house for a while so I could have some normalcy. Many times, my grandparents tried to convince my mom to let me live with them, but she refused and threatened to not let them see me at all. To her, I was one of the things that belonged in her pile of stuff.

"You're part of the family now, too," Aunt Suzy says, wiping her hands on a towel. "Actually, I have something for you."

"For me?" I ask in surprise.

"Yes, I'll be right back."

I wonder what she could possibly have for me as she darts from the kitchen and goes down the hall toward what I assume are the bedrooms.

"Okay," she says, when she returns a few moments later. "I think you'll love it."

She hands me a white, folded T-shirt. I slowly unfold it, dumbfounded as to why she'd be giving me a shirt. The fabric is soft, so threadbare that it's almost transparent. The neckline and hem are worn to a fray, and several tiny holes are scattered on the garment.

I stare at the light-blue guitar and dove logo on the front, trying to remember where I've seen it before.

And then it hits me.

"Oh my God." My words are slow. I'm overcome with shock. "Is this what I think it is?" My hands shake as I hold the shirt open and run my finger over the iconic Woodstock logo.

"It sure is. Jude told me how much you love old music and vintage clothes. I'd love for you to have it. I haven't worn it in years, but there was a time when I lived in it, as you can tell. I hate that it's sitting in a drawer."

"I can't take this," I say, trying to hand it back to her. "This is rare. And special. It must be worth money—"

She pushes it back to me. "Oh, sweetheart. I don't care about that. I'd love for you to have it. Please."

"A-are you sure?" I ask.

She smiles reassuringly. "I'm positive."

"I'm speechless." I hold the soft shirt against my chest. "I don't even know how to thank you for something so amazing. I love it." I gently hug her. "Thank you, Aunt Suzy."

I can't believe she just gave me a genuine, authentic Woodstock T-shirt. I have a lot of cool shirts, but none of them come close to the epic-ness of this one. And it means even more that it came from Jude's aunt.

We go back to chopping vegetables, and she tells me all about her Woodstock experience. She says the next time we come over, she'll show me photos of old concerts, Jude as a little boy, and the squirrel. She's excited to show me her record collection. I'm fascinated, but my mind is spinning with emotions.

She's an incredibly sweet woman, and it's clear she absolutely adores Jude. Guilt is eating away at my conscience—being in their home as a pretend wife, being treated like real family. A ball of sadness has crept up into my throat. If this were real, I think I would've grown to like this. I'd be looking forward to seeing Aunt Suzy and Uncle Al again and getting to know them.

But I don't know if I ever will.

CHAPTER 23

JUDE

"Do you know what you're doin', kiddo?" Uncle Al asks.

I peer at him from behind the washing machine. "It's just a washing machine, not a spaceship. I think the hose is loose."

"Not that, dummy. With the girl."

I flash him the shit-eatin' grin he's seen from me since I was five years old. "Do I ever know what I'm doing?"

"I figured as much."

I crawl out from behind the washing machine and rummage around on the shelves bolted to the wall until I find a big roll of duct tape.

"I'll tape it up for now until I can come by next weekend with a new hose."

He nods and sits on an old wooden bench. I worry because the older he gets, the harder it is for him to stand for long periods of time. "Good. Now tell me what in the hell you're doing."

I hold the roll of tape up in front of him before turning back to the washer. "Exactly what it looks like. I'm gonna tape this sucker up."

"With the girl, Lucky."

Damn. Why did I think they'd just accept the situation with Skylar and not ask me a million and one questions?

"I told ya. She's got some health issues and needed insurance. Her mom doesn't have insurance, and Skylar can't afford her own. It's only temporary until she graduates from school and can work full time. I'm just being nice. Doing a good deed and all that. That's it. No hidden motives. Nothing to get your panties in a twist about."

"I think you're playing with fire, kiddo."

I shake my head. "Nah. It's all good."

I wedge myself back behind the washing machine, yank a few inches of tape off the roll, and bite it off with my teeth before taping up the hose.

"So you're just gonna kick her out someday?"

When I finish taping the hose, I move out from behind the machine and shake my head. "No, I'm not gonna kick her out. We'll both just go our separate ways. Simple as that."

"It ain't gonna be that simple, Lucky. Trust me."

It will be. That was the deal. I don't understand why everyone's trying to make it more complicated than it is, or acting like I'm crazy for being nice to someone who needs help.

"I'll make sure it will be. Nobody's gonna get hurt. Don't worry 'bout it, okay?"

Upstairs, we find Aunt Suzy and Skylar in the kitchen, crawling around on the floor on their hands and knees.

"What the hell are you two doing?" I ask, bending to grab my aunt's shoulders, gently pulling her to her feet. "You're too old to be crawlin' around like that."

"I am *not* too old." She tries to pull away from me, and that's when I notice the tears in the corners of her eyes.

"Aunt Suze…" I look her up and down, still holding on to her arms, concern coursing through my veins. "Did you fall?" I shift my attention to Skylar, who's still kneeling on the floor. "What happened?"

"My ring…" My aunt holds out a trembling hand. "I was in the cupboard looking for my big soup pot, and I noticed my ring. The stone is gone."

"I've been looking for it," Skylar says. Her scarf is dragging on the floor as she searches, sliding her palms across the tile. "I'm sure it was there when we were chopping the vegetables. I remember thinking how pretty it was."

"We'll find it, love," Uncle Al says, grabbing on to one of the kitchen chairs in an attempt to lower himself down onto the floor.

"Whoa," I say, grabbing his arm. "Both of you, stay off the floor. We'll look for it."

"We have to find it," Aunt Suzy says tearfully. "It's my engagement ring."

"She never takes it off," Uncle Al adds. "I sold my car to buy that ring."

The heartbreaking look that passes between them almost kills me.

"You two sit. Me and Skylar will look for it. Are you sure it fell off in here?" I run my hand through my hair and scan the tile floor, wondering how the hell we're going to find a diamond in here.

"I'm sure."

"They'll find it," Uncle Al says, patting her hand.

Skylar smiles and nods at me as we search together. After checking every inch of the floor with her, I check over the countertops and sink, while Skylar pulls out all the pots and pans, one by one. If we don't find the stone, my aunt is going to have a meltdown. She's insanely sentimental, and her engagement ring has always been her most prized and loved possession.

"I found it!" Skylar suddenly exclaims, and I let out a sigh of relief as she holds the sparkling gem up.

"Oh, thank you!" Aunt Suzy cries. "I was so afraid it was gone forever." Skylar gently places it in her hand. "Special things like this can never, ever be replaced."

"Why don't you give it to me with your ring, and I'll take it to a jeweler and get it fixed."

"I don't know..." Aunt Suzy says, looking down at her stoneless ring. "I don't ever take it off."

"I know, but we gotta get it fixed. We can't crazy glue it back in. I promise I'll take care of it, and I'll get it back to you right away."

"Let him get it fixed, Suzy. You don't want to lose it again," Uncle Al says.

"There's a great jewelry store right down the street from where I work," Skylar adds. "We'll make sure they'll take extra good care of it. They can check all the prongs to make sure this doesn't happen again."

Reluctantly, my aunt pulls off her gold ring and hands it to me. I carefully place the ring and stone in a small Ziploc sandwich bag.

"I'll have it back soon, good as new," I promise.

My uncle leans over and presses a soft kiss to my aunt's forehead, whispering something that I can't hear. On the other side of the room, Skylar is watching them with a small, dreamy smile on her face, then shifts her gaze to meet mine.

There's a brief glimmer of longing in her eyes, chased away by a flash of sadness.

I quickly look away.

Nope. No way in hell am I gonna let myself think what my

aunt and uncle have is in the cards for me. They got lucky. Despite my nickname, I'm *not* that lucky.

Later, when we're home, we take Cassie in the backyard to run around, and Skylar puts Gus in a cat stroller and pushes her around the perimeter of the property. I stand on the back patio smoking, wondering how I ended up with a teen bride pushing a cat in a baby stroller across my yard.

And yet somehow, I can't imagine my life any other way right now.

"How 'bout I make us some grilled cheese sandwiches for dinner," I say when we get back inside.

"Like you made last time?" she asks. "With the same kind of white cheese and bread? And butter?"

"Exactly like last time."

She tugs on loose threads at the edge of her scarf. "And it's all new?"

"Yup. Got it at the grocery store yesterday." I open the refrigerator and pull out the new package of thin-sliced deli cheese. "See?" I say, holding it up.

"Okay. I'd like one."

As I start making the sandwiches, she opens one of the cabinets and takes out her bottle of digestive enzymes.

"How've you been feeling?" I ask. "Does all that stuff help?" She has a row of medication and supplements she takes several times a day.

"I think so. My stomach doesn't hurt like it used to, and my throat isn't sore anymore."

I flip the sandwiches over in the pan. "That's great."

Seeing her world slowly get better makes this odd

arrangement worth it. Sure, she's costing me a few hundred dollars a month, but it's nothing I can't handle.

Even though Skylar eats slower than a snail moves, I always sit at the table with her when we eat together and wait until she's done before I get up. This act is a double-edged sword. While she likes that I sit with her, it also makes her anxious, because she feels like I'm watching her eat. She's not wrong. At first, I did sit there and watch her cut her food up into tiny pieces, inspecting each bite before she put it in her mouth. A few times, she froze under the pressure, stopped chewing, and completely forgot how to swallow. She ran to the bathroom and spit her food out into the toilet, then came back to the kitchen, sniffling, hanging her head in shame.

These are things I don't ever want her to go through again.

So now I flip through a magazine while she eats. Keeping her company, but not watching her. It works.

"I can't believe your aunt gave me that shirt," she says between bites as she scratches off today's lottery ticket while she eats. "I legit had to hold back from freaking out and jumping up and down."

"She has a lot of old stuff. I wouldn't be surprised if she has five of those shirts lying around."

"I seriously love it." She frowns at her ticket. "I didn't win. Did you really tell her I like the older bands?"

"Yeah." I turn the page of my motorcycle magazine and lust over a picture of black-matte rims. Someday, I'll get a new set for my Harley.

"She said you talk about me a lot."

My aunt has a big mouth.

"I wouldn't say a *lot*. Just casually about everyday shit."

"I see," she says, with that teasing hint in her voice that tells me she's not buying a word I'm saying. "I think she really wants to ship us."

I look up from my magazine. "Ship us? Where?"

She rolls her eyes theatrically. "It means she wants us to get together."

"No. We're not *shipping*," I reply, grinning at her. "Who the hell makes up these fuckin' words?"

"Beats me. If you hung out on the 'gram or TikTok, you wouldn't be so lost."

"No thanks. I'm not getting sucked into all that internet fuckery."

Laughing, she picks up her plate and carries it over to the dishwasher. "You're being *old*, Jude."

"Don't care." I throw my magazine back on the pile at the edge of the table. "You want to watch some television with me?"

"I was thinking we could start a series. It'd give us something to watch every night."

Worry stops me from answering right away. *Every night* will morph into a habit. A standing sort of date-night thing.

Won't it?

"We could start *The Office*. Megan says it's funny," she says. "I like to watch lighter things before I go to sleep. Otherwise, I have disturbing dreams."

She waits for me to answer with an expectant, hopeful smile on her face.

I should say no. The word is waiting on the tip of my tongue. I should change my mind and watch TV alone in my room until I fall asleep. Continue to keep the walls up, the lines in place.

"Okay. But just one or two episodes. I gotta be up early."

I'll say no next time.

"Cool!" she says. "I'm gonna go change real quick."

Letting out a sigh, I look down at Cassie, who's sitting next to my chair, staring up at me with her little black, judgy eyes.

"You're right," I say. "I gotta learn how to say no."

CHAPTER 24

JUDE

"I was thinking about what your Aunt Suzy said," Skylar says as she pads into the living room. Her arms are crossed in front of her as if she's cold, but she's not wearing footie pants tonight. Tonight, it's pink, cotton pajama bottoms with angry cat-face illustrations printed on them and a white, long-sleeved top with the cuffs pulled down to her palms.

"We're not having a baby," I quip.

Kicking my feet up on the coffee table, I lean back into the couch cushion with a long sigh. I probably shouldn't have been crawling around behind the washing machine and on my aunt's kitchen floor earlier. My back is hurting worse today than it was yesterday.

I get a look from Skylar that says she thinks I'm crazy. "I will not ever want to have a baby. I was thinking about Aunt Suzy saying next time we visit, she'd show me her old record collection, and concert photos."

"And?"

She plops down on the other end of the couch and tucks her legs under her.

"Well, is there going to be a next time?" she asks.

I turn toward her. "What do you mean?"

"Will I ever see them again? Because I felt kinda bad spending the day with them, having them be so nice to me, and treating me like family. I feel guilty. She gave me a shirt that's worth a few thousand dollars. I wouldn't sell it in a million years, but I feel like I don't deserve to have it. I'm a nobody to them. I'm not family."

I blink at her and rub my tired eyes, not sure how to respond to this seriousness she's throwing at me out of nowhere.

"And then she was talking about next time and I didn't know what to say. I felt like an asshole, Jude. And the more I think about it, the more upset I feel. Because they're nice people. Like, *really* nice people."

Words like asshole and upset are like little red flags sprouting up between us and I'm still clueless as to what brought this on. "Skylar—"

She talks right over me. "They really love you. They want you to be happy. They think we're going to be *together*, together."

Pain radiates to my upper back as I sit up. "Where are you going with this?"

She puts her palms up in question. "I don't know. I'm just wondering why you brought me over there when you know I'm not a permanent fixture here."

"Because you're my friend, and I like being around you. I thought we'd have a nice time hanging out with them."

Confusion is contagious. Now she's blinking at me.

"Oh." Her shoulders sag a little.

"Why are you upset?"

"I'm not..." she says unconvincingly, pushing her hair behind her ear. "I just... I guess I just really liked them, and I was looking forward to seeing them again. I'd love to hang out with your aunt and see the photos, but—"

"Skylar," I interrupt, still baffled as to why she's so upset. "You can see them again. I go over there a few times a month. Come with me."

Her spine straightens and her shoulders perk up. "You're sure? Even though we're not married for real?"

I took her to my aunt and uncle's because I knew they'd treat her like family and make her feel right at home. I thought it would be good for her since she doesn't have a relationship with any of her own family.

And what I said is true—I like having Skylar around. She's fun and she makes me laugh.

But maybe it wasn't the best idea, given how upset it's made her. I wasn't thinking about her not being a "real" part of my life and family. I was just going with the flow and enjoying the day.

Uncle Al's words echo in my head. *You're playing with fire.*

"Of course," I assure her, shoving the warning aside. "We're friends. That's not gonna end, right?"

"You mean when we get divorced and I move out?"

The word *divorce* makes my stomach burn. I'd rather think of us as *parting ways* someday.

"Yeah," I say. "Don't you think we'll still be friends after? It shouldn't change that." I don't know what's going through *her* mind, but I assumed we'd stay friends.

Her mouth opens and she falters for a moment. "You're right. I guess I didn't know if you'd still want to be."

"And not get to see your funky outfits all the time?" I joke, hoping to make her smile. "How could I give that up?"

"True." There's the smile I needed to see. "And I'll have to keep you up-to-date on all the slang so you're not out in the world confused and unsupervised."

"Also true." I grin, relieved I put the fire out. "Can we watch the show now?"

She nods excitedly and swipes the remote from the cushion

between us to hit *play*. We spend the next half hour laughing more than I thought I would.

"Good choice," I say, standing. "I'll be right back and we can watch one or two more."

When I return from the kitchen with four Tylenol in my hand, she eyes me suspiciously as I carefully lower myself onto the couch.

"Is your back still hurting?" she asks.

I toss the pills into my mouth and chase them with a gulp of soda. "Yup."

"Can you do anything for it?"

"Just Tylenol. I can't take prescription pain killers or muscle relaxers."

"Why not?"

"Because I'll eat them like candy and prowl the streets for more."

"Oh!" The light bulb goes off in her head. "Right."

"Not worth it to tempt the demons, ya know? I'd rather be in pain."

Nodding, she turns to the television, then back to me, her lips pursed together.

"I could massage it for you. Your back."

My insides jolt with a massive battle of rights and wrongs.

"Nah, I'm okay," I grumble. "It'll pass."

"Jude," she says with slight impatience. "Would it be so bad to let me do something for you? You're always doing things for me."

"You helped me yesterday," I argue.

"I vacuumed water. You put in a new sump pump, moved furniture, moved the washer and dryer, crawled around with towels, mopped the floor with bleach. You even made me toast. And today you fixed a washing machine and crawled around your aunt's kitchen floor looking for a diamond. After working your ass off all week."

"It's life. I'm fine."

"Maybe I want to do something for you."

"Did Aunt Suzy put you up to this?"

"No." The vagueness in her voice is sketchy.

"Watch the show," I deflect, lifting my chin toward the screen.

She blows out a frustrated breath. "It's just a back rub, what are you scared of?"

So much.

So. Damn. Much.

"I'm not scared of shit," comes out of my mouth.

"People *pay* for massages. It's totally platonic. It's not like I'm asking you to Netflix and chill," she says with amusement.

I'm stuck. If I keep resisting, she's going to think there's something wrong with her. Or me. If I tell her she shouldn't be touching me, she's going to know there's a reason I don't want her to. Like it's inappropriate. Or that I'm attracted to her.

Which I am.

And I'm not sure how I feel about it.

"Okay," I finally say, ignoring the stare Cassie gives me from her plaid doggy bed in the corner. I know if the dog could talk, she'd be telling me I'm a dumbass.

Within seconds, Skylar's scooting across the couch and wedging herself behind me.

"Just relax and watch the show," she says, putting her hands on my shoulders. "I hardly ever see you just resting for more than an hour."

I take my feet off the table and lean forward, resting my elbows on my thighs. "I don't like to sit still. There's always something I should be doing."

"Yeah, but you should also rest. It's nice you're not a lazy bum, but it's okay to chillax. You're like my grandfather. He was *always* doing something. When he wasn't at work, he was working on the house, or on a car. Literally nonstop. I think that's why he had a heart attack. Too much stress."

I cringe. "Are you comparing me to your grandfather?"

"No, silly. I'm just worried about you."

"I'm not gonna have a heart attack. I promise."

"I just don't want anything to happen to you." Her fingers slowly move to the back of my neck, rolling in slow, careful circles, loosening the tension.

"Nothing's going to happen to me," I say softly. My eyes close, unable to resist the relaxing lull of her touch.

If I had half a brain, I'd be more careful of her getting attached to me. I can't let myself become all she has. When it's time to go, she has to be stronger. Able to take care of herself and never need anyone.

And I shouldn't get attached to her, either. If I do, it'll hurt when she's gone, and I've got nothing to numb the pain.

Inch by inch, her warm hands move down my spine, massaging my muscles with the perfect amount of pressure. Every press of her fingers escalates the conflict swirling up inside me.

This feels so good, it must be right.

This feels too good, it's totally wrong.

I lift my shoulders, stretching my muscles beneath her palms.

"Do you want to take your shirt off?" Her voice is so soft, her words innocent. But with my eyes closed, sitting between her parted thighs, alone in a dim room with her on a Sunday night, her words could be inviting. Sensual.

While my brain insists there's absolutely nothing sexual going on, my cock is devouring every word, every touch. It's hard as a rock, acting like it's never been near an attractive chick before.

Women coming on to me has never really done it for me. I

need more than that to get a rise. But this subtle, unexpected chemistry with Skylar is twisting me up like a pretzel.

Wordlessly, I pull my shirt off and toss it on the couch next to us. Her breath catches the first time her hands touch my flesh.

Or maybe that was my own breath.

"Is this okay?" Her voice wavers with a hint of nervousness as she pushes the heels of her palms into my tense muscles. "Am I hurting you?"

"No. It feels great." Hopefully she doesn't notice the sudden huskiness in my voice.

I focus on the TV to distract myself. *Detach* myself from her and her touch—like I would if this were a professional massage.

Of course, if it were, I'd be lying on a table, not sitting on the couch with a hard-on and her squished behind me.

The comedy we were watching drones on. What we're doing can't be wrong when we've got a happy, light backdrop of laughter and humor.

Right?

"Is this a real place?" she asks as her fingertips skim over the tattoo design that spans my entire back.

"Mostly."

It's a tattoo of a mountain cliff done in shades of gray, with a sunset in oranges, yellows and reds. There's a lone house in the mountains, way out in the distance. Trees run up the sides, framing the scene, and two birds fly across the sky. It's a vision of peace for me.

"Are these two people sitting here?" She touches a spot in the middle of my back.

"No, it's a rock."

"To me it looks like two people sitting together, looking out at the sunset. It's really pretty," she says. "I like it."

"Thanks."

"I don't see the point of getting a huge ass tattoo on your back, though. It had to cost a fortune, and you can't even see it."

"Doesn't matter. I know it's there."

"Yeah, but have you seen it? There's two people sitting there and you think it's a rock."

"It *is* a rock," I say.

"If you say so…"

I can feel her breath, hot on my back as she continues to move her hands up and down my spine, squeezing my shoulders, then roving lower over my ribs. My muscles might be relaxing, but my pulse is racing.

"Is this making you feel better?" she asks.

I wish she'd stop talking. Her soft voice is only making me want to turn around and kiss those pretty pink lips of hers.

"Yeah." I exhale slowly and stretch my neck back a little. "Maybe a little too much."

"There's no such thing as *too* much better."

Not true.

The episode on the screen ends and another starts, but we don't move to get up or say goodnight. Her touch becomes less of a massage and more of a slow, wandering caress up and down my back. It's not sexual, but it's intimate. Careful. Loving. Every few minutes she touches the back of my hair, winding a long lock around her finger. It sends thousands of tingles over my scalp and down my spine. At some point I wrap my hand around her leg, and I slowly match her touch, sliding my hand from her outer thigh, down to her calf, then back again. Her cotton pants with the funny cat faces under my palm is a confusing mix of comforting, innocent, and sexy.

My breathing has become shallow. She's lulled me into a stilled, dream-like state. I've never had a woman touch me in such a delicate, sensual way before. I'm used to the scratch of sharp, too-long nails. Impatient pushing and pulling. A rush of takes and demands.

But not this.

I don't even know what the hell *this* is. This breathless, aching, long-lost lover feeling.

How the hell can an eighteen-year-old girl wearing crazy pajamas make me feel like this?

But now that I've felt it, it's too much like that all-too-familiar euphoria in my veins that the addict inside me remembers vividly. It's the same kind of high—the kind I don't want to come down from. I want a little more. A little longer. I want to tease it and tempt it. Find out how good it can feel if I lose myself in it.

This is *not* cool.

When the end credits for the show start to roll, I quietly reach behind me and grab her hands in each of mine, pulling her arms around my waist. Clasping our hands together over my stomach, I gently lean back against her. Her small breasts press against my back as she breathes. Her heartbeat thumps against me like a ticking clock.

I struggle with all the lessons I've learned to make good choices. Like how *bad* is a master at wearing the mask of *good* and not to fall for it.

"I think this stopped being a back rub a while ago," I say softly, rubbing my thumb over her hand in mine.

"I think you're right," she whispers.

"It's late. I think we're over-tired."

"I think you're right," she repeats. Her breath is warm and wispy against my ear. "I should probably go to bed."

"Me too."

Neither one of us makes an effort to move. We stay there, quietly breathing together. Our entwined fingers slowly dance against each other. Hers long, soft and thin. Mine thick and calloused.

Resistance crumbles, and I turn toward her face, just inches from mine.

I don't know who kissed who. Maybe it was me. Maybe it was her.

Doesn't matter, because my mouth is on hers when it shouldn't be. But fuck, her lips are soft and sweet, and I can't resist one more taste of her.

And that's all this is. One more time.

The *last* time.

There's always a last time when quitting something. A final moment to savor.

Our lips touch softly, fading apart every few seconds and then meeting again for another quick kiss. And another. And another. Finally, I lift my hand to cup her cheek in my palm and the little moan that hums in her throat tells me she wants more just as much as I do. Tilting my mouth to cover hers, I edge my tongue past her teeth—subtly asking for permission. Her mouth opens to mine breathlessly. Our tongues touch, swirling together, and I swear to fuck I see fireworks. I move my hand to cup the back of her neck, pulling her closer, kissing her deeper. Her hand slowly inches up the middle of my bare chest to gently grasp the side of my throat, mimicking my own touch.

Her thighs tighten around me and I grab her leg with my free hand, bringing it higher around my waist.

Fuck, I want her.

And fuck, she wants me.

But I can't.

Reluctantly, I pull away, quietly disentangle myself from her, and stand up.

She blinks at me, her lips slightly parted, glistening with wetness from our kiss.

Way too tempting.

If I go any further, I won't stop.

Handing me my shirt, she watches as I put it on, then we silently go upstairs. We pause in front of her bedroom door, and she looks at me expectantly with her big eyes and her sweet lips.

"That's the last time that's gonna happen," I say. "I'm not going to kiss you anymore. It's not cool. We're friends and I don't want to wreck that."

"Okay, Lucky," she whispers, then goes up on her toes and presses her lips softly, briefly, against mine.

I don't pull away. I stand there, just inches away from her. Close enough to kiss her again. "What are you doing, Sparkles?"

"You didn't say *I* couldn't kiss *you* one last time."

Nope. I'm not going fall into the playful banter, which I usually love. I'm way too close to the flame. Not to mention, way too close to her bedroom.

I shake my head. "I'm saying it now. No more kissing each other. Or touching." My cock strains against my pants in protest. My chest tightens.

"Okay." She nods, her eyes still locked onto mine.

She says it like she doesn't quite believe me.

As I turn away from her to go to my own room, I don't believe me either.

CHAPTER 25

SKYLAR

"How was your weekend?" Megan asks as we head onto the high school track field. "I didn't hear from you after you jumped ship on our double date." Every Monday we spend our time in PE talking about our weekends. It doesn't matter if we saw each other or not—we still do a recap.

"I didn't jump ship. I never agreed to let you set me up with Carson." The cold bite in the air stings my face. Starting next week, we won't be outside for PE anymore and that can't come fast enough for me.

"If I don't try, you'll be single forever. Married, but single," she jokes. "Only you could be married and single at the same time."

"Right? Could my life be any more awkward?"

"I doubt it."

As we round the curve of the track, force of habit makes me glance over at the house where Jude recently built an addition. Butterflies used to flutter wildly in my chest every time I saw that house, or walked by it. But now, I feel a lonely void because he's not there anymore. He and his crew have moved on to a new job a few miles away. It was comforting having him work so close to the school, even though we refrained from talking to each other to avoid feeding the gossip hounds.

"Jude's basement flooded on Saturday, so we spent the entire day cleaning that up. I was standing in inches of water, sucking it up with a shop vac. My feet got so cold I couldn't feel my toes."

"Look at you, being all domestic!"

"Then, that night we were watching a movie, and I tried a piece of popcorn for the first time in years, and it got stuck in my throat. I had a major panic attack and turned into a gagging freakazoid, literally, on his bathroom floor."

"Oh my God, Skylar. Tell me you didn't."

"I did. It was awful. I was choking and crying and I legit thought I was going to die." I feel sick just thinking about it. How embarrassing.

"I'm not sure you can die on popcorn."

"You can die on anything."

"Okayyyy..." She's not convinced.

"Anyway, that was humiliating, but Jude was super sweet. The next day, he took me to visit his aunt and uncle with him."

"Dude, you are *so* living the married life."

I laugh and shove my hands into the front pocket of my hoodie. "I know, like what life is this?"

"No clue, but I hope there's some *good* stuff going on."

My pulse quickens just thinking about all the good stuff. "I'm getting to that."

"Well, talk faster, girl."

"His aunt and uncle are in their seventies and they were really cool. His aunt gave me a T-shirt she got at Woodstock. Like *the* Woodstock. No lie, Megs, I looked it up when I got home, and I saw someone selling the same exact one on eBay for six thousand dollars."

She turns to me with her eyes wide. "Shut up!"

"I'm serious."

"That's so insane. How'd she even know you'd be all batshit over a vintage T-shirt?"

"According to her, Jude talks about me *all the time*. That's exactly what she said. That he talks about me nonstop."

"Girllll... What is happening?"

"Wait, there's more."

"Ladies, it'll be spring by the time you complete one lap. Pick up the pace!" Mrs. Stephens yells at us.

We roll our eyes in unison.

Megan groans. "I can't walk any faster, I think I sprained my vag Saturday night." To demonstrate, she lifts her knees up abnormally high as she walks.

"Oh my God, *what*?" I'm not sure if I should be horrified, amused, or jealous.

She turns to me with a big Cheshire Cat smile on her face. "Erik decided to get his freak on. We had sex seven times."

"In one night?" Horrified. I'm horrified.

"Yes. He's slowly coming out of his shell and he does *not* disappoint."

"Okay that's not a good visual. Now I'm seeing like a dick coming out of a turtle shell, and it's not at all sexy."

"Don't be thinking about my man's dick, Skylar," she jokes. "I will cut you like a cheese slicer."

"Trust me, I've banished the vision already."

My pelvis hurts just thinking about having sex seven times in one day. I wonder if they spread it out over a span of twenty-four hours, or if they somehow crammed that into two or three hours.

I decide these are details I'd rather not know.

"I'm still waiting to hear what else happened over the weekend," she urges. "Your obsession with old clothes is great, but I hope there's more."

My kiss with Jude will probably seem lacking to Megan

compared to her and Erik's sexolympics. But for me, the kiss was earth shattering. I was up all night replaying the kiss in my head, reveling in how his lips felt on mine—how soft and full they were. His body, however, was anything but soft. He was all hard muscle and ink under my hands as I massaged his back. And hugging him from behind felt amazing. I didn't feel crushed or trapped—I felt safe. Then there's that thing he does with his hands—the way he moves his fingers in between mine all slow and soft…

But the look in his eyes before we said goodnight was *it* for me. The dark, intense longing, the way his sterling gaze slowly shifted to my lips. The way he licked his own lips before he walked away, leaving me standing there with a thundering heart and wobbly legs.

As dreamy as all that was, it also terrified me. I shouldn't be feeling that way about him, and what he said last night was true. We shouldn't be kissing and touching. We're friends. Roommates. Over a decade apart in age. Our arrangement doesn't come with a side of Friends with Benefits.

Crossing that line could get really, *really* complicated and messy, with my biggest fear being that he might divorce me before I'm able to get better and get my life on track.

I can't risk that.

"Skylar, hello?" Megan prompts impatiently.

I'm lost in my thoughts; not entirely sure I want to share my and Jude's private moments with Megan. I want to hold them inside, keep them as my very own, safe, near my heart.

"Nothing happened," I say casually. "We started watching *The Office*. You were right, it's really funny."

She stops walking and grabs on to my arm. "Seriously? That's not what you were going to tell me."

"Yes it—" We both jump as a shrill whistle pierces our ears.

"Ladies! If you don't move, you're looking at an hour of

detention, and you'll be required to sprint this track the entire time!"

Ugh.

"Don't lie to me, Skylar," Megan says as we begin a brisk walk under Mrs. Stephens' eagle eye. "What aren't you telling me?"

"Nothing…"

"I just told you my vajayjay is totally wrecked from having sex seven times. We're supposed to share everything with each other. The good, the bad, and the ugly."

Sighing, I say, "You're right. I'm just confused. I'm not sure I want to talk about it."

"Talking about it will *un*confuse you. I'm a great problem solver."

Trying to hold back a laugh-snort, I give in. She'll bug me nonstop if she thinks I'm keeping her in the dark.

Our walking picks up a bit as I spill everything to Megan. Everything Jude's aunt told me, the back massage, the sexy embrace, the kiss. I dial back my excitement about all of it. I'd rather Megan think I'm more curious about the situation than her knowing the myriad of emotions I'm feeling.

"Holy cannoli, Skylar. This is a whole situation playing out."

"Tell me about it. And like he can't be telling me we're not going to be kissing anymore when he's standing there with his smolder on."

"Agreed. Do you think he's a player? Maybe he likes this whole cat-and-mouse game."

She asks the question I've been asking myself.

"I've been thinking that," I say slowly. "And to be honest, I really don't think so. I haven't seen any hints that he's a player. I think he's in the same boat as me—surprised that there's…" I struggle to find the right word. "An attraction between us."

"Well, you're both beautiful people."

"Stop it," I say, looking down at my feet.

"It's true. He's hot as hell. You're adorable and beautiful. Ya'll would make the cutest babies."

I laugh, thinking of Aunt Suzy wanting us to have a baby, and a weird pain shoots through my jaw. I've felt it a few times over the past few weeks, and it's not going away.

"I'm not sure what to do or how to act," I reply, rubbing my cheek. "I wasn't expecting to be in this position."

"Do you feel safe?" she asks, her tone switching to serious. "Here you are, living in this older dude's house, legally married to him. He practically owns you. Maybe you should leave."

And go where? I want to ask, but I'm too embarrassed to admit that I'd probably end up living in my car.

"I don't feel uncomfortable or unsafe around him. There's nothing threatening or sketchy about him. And he doesn't *own* me. I've never felt any creeper vibes. I really just feel like we both went into this as friends, with totally platonic intentions, and now there's this unexpected connection between us. It's more than just physical attraction. It's hard to explain."

"Geez, Skylar. Don't tell me you're falling in love with him." The tinge of pity in her voice irks me. I'm not a little lovesick girl swooning over someone who's impossibly out of reach.

Am I?

"I'm not," I say quickly.

"Do you *want* something to happen with him? Like a friends with bennies situation? I mean, why not?" She shrugs. "You're both consenting adults. There's nothing wrong with it."

"I don't know… I guess I wouldn't be opposed to that if we were both on the same page." An add-on like that to our situation wouldn't exactly be horrible, but I'm still worried if things went wrong, he could boot me right out.

"If I were you, I'd stop analyzing. Just go with it. If he flirts with you, flirt back. Don't tease him, but test the waters. Think of it as a learning experience. He doesn't look like he'd be shy in the bedroom if you get my drift. It's your senior year; you should be having fun. Once we graduate, we have to start adulting."

"You're right."

"See?" she says, putting her arm around my shoulders. "I'm a fixer."

CHAPTER 26

SKYLAR

"After you posted the photos of those new cute, inspirational mugs, we got fifty new followers—just over the weekend," Rebecca says happily. "Great job."

"I saw," I say with a proud smile. "I kept checking stats. People love them."

"They do. Two customers came in today and bought a few for themselves and for gifts." She leans against the counter. "I've been thinking about something, and I think I'm ready to take the plunge."

"Oh?" My curiosity is piqued.

"Since you started posting the photos, I've been getting a lot of requests from non-locals for online ordering. It'll be a big change; I'll have to pack and ship the items out, but I think it'll open up a whole new avenue of sales."

"Wow. That's a great idea." I scan the displays. "You wouldn't even have to make *all* the products available online. Some might be hard to mail."

Her brows knit together. "True. I think we'd have to exclude some items. Like *that*." She points to a beautiful stained-glass lamp. "That would be a nightmare to mail."

"I think if you stay away from anything too big and fragile, you'll be okay. I'll help you as much as I can."

"You're a gem. I'll be doing more research this week, and I'm meeting with a new web designer on Wednesday. I made the appointment in the afternoon so you can sit in."

My first business meeting! I try to mask my excitement by straightening the business cards in their little holder next to the register.

"I'll be there," I reply.

She fixates on me for a moment, and I wonder if I said something wrong or didn't act interested enough.

"Is your cheek swollen?" she asks.

My hand comes up to touch the right side of my face. "Is it?" Worry instantly floods through my veins in a hot rush, obliterating the happiness I felt over the web-design meeting.

Squinting at me, she nods. "I think it is a little. Does it hurt?"

"Yeah, it started a few weeks ago, but today, it's much worse." I lightly touch the top of my jaw. "Right here."

"It could be your wisdom teeth. I was your age when mine came in."

My anxiety accelerates to a level eight.

"Oh no, I didn't think of that. What should I do?"

"You can take Tylenol, but you should probably go to the dentist."

Forcing a grateful smile, I say, "Okay. I'll try to find one."

"You don't have a regular dentist?"

My cheeks heat with embarrassment. "No, I haven't been since I was little."

"I see." She smiles sympathetically. "Actually, a good friend of mine is a dentist. I've been seeing her for years." Rebecca grabs a pen and writes a name and phone number on the back of one of her business cards. "Dr. Katz. Give her office a call now, tell the receptionist you work for me—she knows me. Maybe they can squeeze you in this afternoon."

"Today?" I repeat with surprise. "I was going to take new photos today."

"That can wait. You should have it looked at if you're in pain."

I call the dentist as soon as she goes back to her small office, and I'm surprised when the receptionist offers me a five o'clock appointment today.

Today… I have next to no time to mentally prepare myself.

After the call, I take a quick break in the restroom. Splashing cold water onto my face, I breathe in and out slowly, like the therapist taught me. When I go to the dentist, they'll put their fingers in my mouth. They'll put *things* in my mouth—like cotton and sharp tools.

Things that might taste weird.

Things I could swallow and choke on.

I stare at my cheeks in the mirror, examining my jawline. Stretching my mouth open as wide as I can, I lift my lip up. Nothing looks abnormal to me, but it's sore.

Calm down, I tell myself, but it does nothing to stop the churning of my stomach and the racing of my heart.

In my purse, my anti-anxiety pills are waiting in a tiny metal pillbox that has a hummingbird printed on the lid. The rationale was that taking meds would seem less scary if they weren't in a prescription bottle with warnings in itty-bitty text printed on the label next to my name.

I take one antidepressant and one anti-anxiety pill daily (among other pills). The doctor said I can take an extra dose of the anxiety medication when I'm feeling extra panicky and overwhelmed with all the thoughts in my head.

Now seems like one of those times, but if I take it, it'll make me drowsy. Within an hour, the brain fog will dull me down so much that I'll appear like a zombie to our customers, and to Rebecca.

And to Jude.

But if I don't take it, I'll spend the rest of the day hyper-focused on the pain in my jaw. The jittery feeling that springs from my anxiety will distract me to the point of making idiotic mistakes. My shaky hands will get me side-eyes from the customers. If I wait until I get home to take the pill, I'll crawl into bed before nine p.m. and wake up feeling groggy.

I want my mother. Maybe not *my* mother, but a real mom. I want someone to tell me what I should do. I want someone to tell me I'm going to be okay.

Even though my feet clomping down the basement stairs make quite a bit of noise, it isn't loud enough to be heard over the rock music blasting from the Bluetooth speakers mounted on the wall.

"Jude," I call out and stop short about six feet away from his gym area.

I debate turning around and going back upstairs before he sees me. I shouldn't be down here when he's working out. It feels like I'm invading his privacy—seeing him shirtless, on his back on the bench. Hearing his primal grunts as he presses the weighted bar up, then down, then up again. Sweat glistens over his body, beading up on his chiseled chest and abs, brightening the ink of his tattoos.

Standing by a stack of *Erin* boxes, I'm mesmerized by the bulge of his biceps when he pushes the bar up one more time, then rests it on the rack. Swallowing hard, I watch as he stands, grabs a towel, and wipes it across his face. This is the first time I've seen him with shorts on, and I'm not surprised to see tattoos on his thighs and calves. Nor am I surprised to see the muscles in his legs still pumped from whatever workout he was doing before I came down here.

Sweaty people usually turn me off, but he's incredibly sexy with his damp hair and shiny muscles. I have the urge to run my hand down the middle of his chest, trail my fingers through the tiny patch of damp hair there.

When he turns and catches me watching him, he takes a step back, almost knocking over the rack of free weights.

"What the fuck," he says, breaking me out of my trance. "You scared the shit out of me."

"I-I'm sorry," I stammer, startled by the deepness of his voice echoing in the cellar. "I wanted to talk to you and I—"

And I what? Got all distracted drooling over him?

"What's up?" he asks casually, as if he's not oozing all kinds of sexiness as he wipes the towel down his chest to his abs.

Regaining my composure, I take a few steps closer to him. "I went to the dentist today, but they told me dental procedures aren't covered under our insurance plan."

His brows pull together. "Your eyes look weird. Havin' a bad day?"

Jude *always* knows when I've taken the extra pill.

"Yes. A totally sucky day," I explain. "I've had this bad pain in my jaw that I thought I could ignore away, but it didn't go away. Rebecca sent me to a dentist friend of hers this afternoon."

He throws the towel over his shoulder and pins me with a concerned look. "What did she say? Are you okay?"

"I have two impacted wisdom teeth. I have to have them pulled, and I'm too scared to be awake while it's happening. I'm afraid I'll freak out. But the anesthesia is wicked expensive. The whole thing will cost around two thousand dollars."

"Fuck." He blows out a breath. "That sucks. We have a dental add-on. There's a different ID card, though, I'll have to get you one. I gotta warn you, it doesn't cover much. Mostly cleanings and x-rays, maybe a cavity."

Shit.

"Okay. I just wanted to check," I say, chewing my lip.

I'm totally screwed. How on earth am I going to pay for this? Dr. Katz made it sound like the surgery shouldn't be put off.

"I'll help you, ya know," he says, moving closer to me. His black sweat shorts have slipped dangerously low on his hips, revealing taut muscles not meant for my eyes. "If you need some money for the dentist."

"Jude, I can't let you do that." He's already lent me money to pay for my prescriptions and co-pays. I simply cannot let him keep giving me money. Especially now that I know he also helps his aunt and uncle with their bills.

"How come?" he asks.

"Because you've done enough for me already. You're not an ATM."

Smirking, he shoots an eyebrow up. "So… there's a limit to how much I'm allowed to do? Guess I missed the memo. You *are* my wife."

"On *paper*. But I'm not your *problem*. We have an arrangement, and I'm trying to stick to it. It wasn't supposed to include you totally supporting me."

It wasn't supposed to include random kissing and touching, either.

"You're my friend. Nothin' wrong with helping a friend. Why is it so weird that I want to do something nice? Everyone acts like I'm breaking some kind of fuckin' law."

"It's not weird that you want to help me. I'm not used to having—or accepting—help. It's humiliating and embarrassing for me. And it's just not normal for you to do so much for me."

His smirk disappears and his nostrils flare. "Lemme get this straight—you think I'm humiliating you by trying to help you get surgery? And you think I'm not normal? Thanks."

Scowling, he pushes past me, clearly done with the conversation. His bare arm—warm and wet with sweat—rubs against mine, and I resist the urge to touch the place where his flesh touched mine.

"Jude, wait." I sigh and follow him upstairs, where he goes directly to the kitchen sink to wash his hands. "I didn't mean it like that," I say to his back. "I appreciate everything you do for me. More than I could ever put into words. It just makes me feel bad, like I don't deserve it. It's too one-sided."

He turns, wiping his hands on his towel. "You should be more worried that you think you don't deserve it and less worried about me just being a nice guy."

The truth hurts. I don't believe I deserve his help.

"You're right," I admit.

"You want me to be an asshole, Sparkles? 'Cause I can be one if the nice me *humiliates* you too much. I can go back to the self-destructive, don't-give-a-fuck-about-anyone, selfish douche I was a few years ago."

"No." I shake my head back and forth, sickened by the thought of him being an asshole. "I wouldn't like you that way."

"Then don't make me feel like I was better off like that."

"Okay," I say, softening my voice. "I don't want you to feel like that. But I also don't want to feel like a charity case. I refuse to take any more money from you. It makes me feel like shit, like I'm using you. And it scares me when I feel like I can't take care of myself. It makes me feel like I'm drowning. I *need* to pay my own bills."

Easier said than done when my medical bills are exceeding my small paycheck. The initial tests I had at the hospital came with a lot of unexpected, out-of-pocket bills, totaling close to three thousand dollars. I'll be making payments forever. And now this sudden dental bill. It's never-ending.

Is someone my age really supposed to have all this financial stress?

"I totally get what you're saying, believe me. But how are you gonna pay for all this?" Jude asks, his voice softer.

"I don't know, obviously. I guess I'll figure something out."

Sighing, he looks down at his feet then back up again. "I guess you could sell your wedding band. I paid three grand for it."

My heart leaps up into my throat at that admission. I had my suspicions the ring had real gems in it, but hearing that he actually bought me something so beautiful and expensive is a total shock.

"Jude..." I swallow and try to ease the emotion out of my voice. "Why did you buy something so expensive? I don't—"

"What?" he interrupts, his gaze challenging mine. "You don't deserve it?"

"No," I say, close to tears. "I don't."

Disappointment darkens his eyes. "You're wrong. You do." His voice lowers. "Maybe I was trying to show you that."

My mouth has gone dry. I lick my lips. "I'm not going to sell my ring."

Even though I don't wear the ring in public, I wear it alone in my room at night. I sit on my bed and move my hand back and forth, marveling at how the diamonds sparkle in the light like itty-bitty stars. I fantasize that it's *real*—that the meaning and the vows behind it are real, and I have a person who loves me more than anything and wants to spend his life with me and only me. The daydream is so much better than the truth—which is that my life has turned into some kind of strange soap opera.

He glances at my bare ring finger, and I wonder if he wanted me to wear it every day, just like a crazy part of me was hoping he'd wear his.

"Why not?" The corners of his eyes narrow a fraction. "It's just a ring. Right?"

Clearly, it's not *just a ring* to either of us.

I jut my chin forward. "Because it means something to me, and I can count on one hand the number of things I own that have any value or special meaning to me."

He leans back against the counter. Looking down at his hands, he cracks his knuckles, then slowly raises his gaze back to me. He cocks his head to the side, as if he's gauging me. "How about this. I'll give you six grand for your car," he says evenly. "Cash."

I suck in a quick breath. His offer is like a punch straight in my gut. He knows how important the Corvette is to me. The extreme sentimental value it has. He knows I'd never give it up. But he also knows I'm in a financial bind with no options. I can't deny the awful truth—that kind of money would let me have the dental procedure, pay off my bills, and have a cushion in the bank—something I've never, ever had, and desperately need.

"You could pay off your bills free and clear," he adds. "You wouldn't owe anyone anything."

I swallow over the thick lump in my throat. "And how would I get to school and work?" My voice cracks and I swallow again. "I don't want to buy a piece-of-junk car. That'll end up costing me more."

"You can drive my Subaru. It's in great shape, low miles, it's only five years old. I never drive it since I have my truck. You can use it as long as you want to."

Leave it to Jude to have an extra car just sitting around.

Staring into his eyes, I can't believe I'm even *considering* selling him my beloved car. But as much as I hate it, I have to consider it because he's offering me a deal that's impossible for me to refuse. My mouth is throbbing more by the minute, and I can't imagine this pain continuing for days, weeks, or months. I'll lose my mind.

I wipe a rogue tear from the corner of my eye. "What would you do with it? Are you going to sell it?" I ask.

He gives me a soft smile. "Nope. I'll keep it in the garage and restore it someday. I'm not gonna get rid of it. It'll be smokin' when I'm done with it."

I should've kept my mouth shut. Let him lend me money to pay my bills. I could've just said thank you and been grateful, instead of letting my pride and need for independence get in the way.

Skylar, you're an idiot.

"Winter's coming. You'll never be able to drive the 'vette in the snow. The Subaru has four-wheel drive. It's a helluva lot safer."

Sniffling, I blink back hot tears. "You'll really take care of it?" I ask. "If I do this?"

"I promise," he says sincerely.

"And you won't sell it? I don't want anyone to have it. Ever. I don't mind so much if it's you, but no one else can have it."

"You have my word. Someday if you want to buy it back, then it's yours. I'd even sell it back to you for the six grand, no matter how much I put into it. But no one else will ever have it, okay?" He steps forward and touches my cheek, wiping my tears away. "I don't want you to cry," he says softly.

It takes me a moment to recover from the unexpected gentle touch. I take a deep breath to refocus. "And you can't ever let a girlfriend drive it."

He lets out a little laugh. "Really, Sparkles?"

"Yes, really. I'm not kidding. I don't want any rando chicks driving my car."

"Alright. That's not gonna be a problem. We got a deal, then?"

Those intense gray eyes bore into mine, daring me to accept. I'm sure there's a test here somewhere, but I'm not sure what the correct choice is. I just know there *is* one.

"I hope you have large bills," I answer defiantly.

"'Course I do. Wait right here."

My heart pounds and my throat aches as I wait in the kitchen. I kinda hate him right now for doing this, and I hate myself even more because I pushed him to do it.

Never look a gift horse in the mouth.

Moments later, he returns with a literal stack of hundreds and fifties in his hand. It's more money than I've ever seen, and it takes me a few moments to take it. Reluctantly, I hand him the keys. My heart feels like it's cracking into pieces. The memory of my grandfather happily jingling those same keys in front of me when he told me the car would be mine someday overwhelms me. My heart aches.

I'm so sorry, Papa.

I *won't* cry.

I *won't* have a meltdown.

"Don't get too attached, Lucky. I *will* be buying it back someday." I try to sound confident, maybe even a little flirty, but instead my voice quivers with emotion.

He tosses the keys in the air and catches them while flashing me his sexy, unforgettable smirk.

"Hope you like red interiors, Sparkles."

Ugh. That teasing voice. He's up to no good.

I glare at his muscular back as he leaves the room. As a matter of fact, red is perfect. It's the color my grandfather and I agreed on, way back when I was excited and dreamy—because it's the color of love.

CHAPTER 27

SKYLAR

People always tell us things will get better. And they do get better. But what people don't tell us is that things will get worse again.

There I was, sitting in the waiting room of Dr. Katz's office, trying not to freak out over the fact that at any moment, the nurse is going to come and take me to have my very first surgical procedure. I'm terrified of the needles and of being asleep while people do things to my body. I'm worried about how much pain I'll be in after.

All morning Jude has been swearing up and down that once this is over, I'll feel much better and I'll realize all this worry was for nothing.

I hope he's right, so I can finally rest my mind. My anxiety has been in overdrive all week.

But then Lisa Rottworth walks into the waiting room—Paige's ultimate BFF and right-hand mean girl. Don't ask me how Lisa got into the cool crowd with a last name like Rottworth, but somehow, she pulled it off.

Lisa glances at me with total disinterest as she and her mother take the seats across from me. I chose to be comfy today and wore black leggings, sneakers, and a white hoodie. I didn't bother putting makeup on. Lisa must not be here for surgery because she's decked out in full-glam makeup including fake eyelashes, high-heeled boots, skinny jeans, hoop earrings big enough to do acrobatics in, and a cashmere sweater. Being popular must be exhausting. Who wants to look perfect every moment of every day?

She's probably getting an Invisalign.

My eyes shift to Jude, who's at the reception desk checking me in because I felt too shaky to stand there and fill out paperwork and answer questions.

I am now greatly regretting that decision.

"You're the policy holder?" the receptionist asks loudly.

"Yes."

"And what is your relationship to the patient?"

Jude clears his throat. "I'm her spouse."

My breath is sucked out of me like a vacuum.

Shit.

Shit. Shit. Shit.

The woman's eyes dart to me, studying me from behind her bifocals as I offer her a weak smile. Pursing her lips, she gives Jude a judgy side-eye before she jams his insurance card through the reader.

My heart rate speeds to a thunderous gallop as I attempt to ignore Lisa's stare, which I can literally feel from across the room, drilling into me like a psychotic woodpecker.

This can't be happening.

At the front desk, Jude is paying my co-pay with the cash I gave him to do so, and the receptionist is going over the basic discharge instructions with him. Finally, she hands him written prescriptions for my antibiotics and painkillers.

I risk a peek at Lisa, and I was right. She's on high alert, spine straight, phone in hand, her attention laser-focused, shifting from me to Jude, gathering information.

Information I already know she's going to broadcast to Paige and the rest of their group.

"You're all set," Jude says, taking his seat next to me.

"Thanks," I whisper, swallowing hard. I feel like I'm going to be sick even though I haven't eaten since yesterday.

He grabs my hand, squeezes it in his reassuringly, and I love how naturally it comes to him to hold my hand, and that he's not afraid to be mushy in public. But now is the worst possible time and place.

"Relax," he says, his voice soft. "Once they put you out, you're not gonna feel a thing. You'll wake up thinking you blinked, and we'll go home and Netflix and chill."

He's trying to make me laugh—using our silly joke about Netflix and chilling.

But Lisa doesn't know that we don't Netflix and chill in the hooking-up sense, and her fingers are already flying furiously over her cell phone keyboard, no doubt detailing this juicy gossip.

My empty stomach rumbles with nausea, churning with waves of panic.

I'm going to be put to sleep and have my teeth cut out of my head.

The doctor is going to put all kinds of stuff in my mouth, while I'm *asleep*.

I might not ever wake up.

I might wake up in the middle of the surgery.

I might choke. And die.

Blood might drip down my throat, into my stomach.

Lisa Rottworth is going to ruin my life.

"You're shaking like a leaf," Jude says, leaning closer to me and brushing his lips across my hair, right over my ear. "Try to relax. You'll be okay."

Was that the click of Lisa's cell phone camera?

Resisting the urge to smack him, I pull my hand from his. Seriously, of all times for him to decide that *now* it's okay to be touchy-kissy, he has to do it right here in the middle of the waiting room in front of Lisa Fucking Rottworth?

In any other place on the planet, I would love the affection and the comfort. I'd be savoring it, tucking every detail into my mind to daydream about later.

But not here, in the damn waiting room in front of Lisa Freakin' Rottworth!

The door leading to the exam rooms swings open. "Skylar?" the young nurse calls in a cheery voice. "We're ready for you."

I stand on shaky legs and cross the room, glaring venomously at Lisa, who's whispering to her wide-eyed mother.

"We'll come back to get you when she's recovering, Mr. Lucketti. It'll be about two hours."

Damn it to hell. Just when I thought things couldn't get worse, now Lisa knows my husband's name.

Jude was right. Dr. Katz hooked me up to an IV and asked me to count backward from ten. I got to seven, and that's all I remember. I wake up with my mouth stuffed with cotton and the nurse smiling at me.

"How are you feeling?" she asks.

"Okay," I mumble, blinking. "It's over?"

She nods. "It sure is. You did great. I'll go get your husband. You can rest here for a few minutes, and then you can go home."

My husband.

It sounds so weird hearing someone refer to him that way.

I can't say I dislike it, because it makes my insides feel warm and fluttery.

Or maybe that's the anesthesia. I stare at a painting of flowers on the wall. One looks like it's smiling.

Smiling back, I let my heavy eyelids fall closed.

The next time I open my eyes, Jude is sitting in a chair in the corner of the recovery room with his leather jacket on his lap.

"Wakey wakey," he teases.

I blink at him and try to move my mouth. My entire head and face feel numb and oddly disconnected from the rest of me.

"You ready to go home, Sparkles?" he asks.

Nodding, I try to sit up, clutching the arms of the exam chair. Jude bolts over and helps me stand, keeping his arm around me as he walks me out of the office and to his truck. I'm too woozy to protest when he lifts me up into the passenger seat.

"I already got your prescriptions filled," he says when he gets behind the wheel. "This way we can go straight home."

I nod and mumble a thank-you.

"You're gonna feel messed up for a few days. Just take your meds and sleep it off."

I want to tell him that Lisa Rottworth saw us together, and thanks to the receptionist's big mouth, she knows we're married and has probably organized a group meeting to orchestrate the best way to circulate this scandalous development to the entire town and beyond.

But my mouth hurts, my head is floating like a balloon, and talking just seems impossible.

"We're married..." I whisper, leaning back against the headrest. "Lisa's a big bitch... You broke the rule..."

More unintelligible, nonsensical words spurt from my mouth, along with a bloody cotton ball that plops into my lap.

Yelping with horror, I pick it up and toss it out the window.

"Oh my God…" I moan, fighting to clear my vision. "Why am I dying?"

"You're not dying. You're just high as a kite. Don't try to talk. We can take the gauze out when we get home. Just bite down on it for now."

All this cotton in my mouth has me petrified. What's stopping me from swallowing it and choking on it? Especially when I can't even think straight?

How can this possibly be safe?

I am never, ever, ever having surgery again.

My cell phone vibrates in my pocket, but I ignore it. I'm sure it's just Megan checking in on me, but I feel too out of it to chat.

CHAPTER 28

SKYLAR

I'm a liar.

I've told myself, and anyone else who will listen, that I don't believe in love. Or marriage. Or soulmates. Or partners. Or happily ever afters.

But the truth is, I do believe in all of it. I just don't believe *I'll* ever have it.

Maybe I was wrong about everything.

Because Jude, who also seems to be lying to himself about all the same things, is turning all my beliefs upside down.

Earlier, he helped me up to my bedroom and gently removed the bloody gauze from my mouth without the slightest hesitation. He didn't act grossed out or annoyed at all.

As disgusting and embarrassing as it was, I was grateful because I don't think I could've done it myself without hurling.

It was then that I noticed he must've come back to the house while I was still in surgery, because he had my bedroom all ready for me. The comforter and sheets were turned down. The shades were drawn. A bottle of water, a new paperback book, an ice pack, and the TV remote were waiting on the nightstand. A white, greeting-card sized envelope with my name written across the front was leaning against my alarm clock.

Drowsy, I crawled into bed and must've fallen asleep immediately.

When I wake, my mouth throbs as I sit up in bed, but the pain isn't as bad as I thought it would be. I mostly feel sore and tired.

As I pad out to the hall, my eye catches the greeting card envelope again. I decide to open it later. My heart clenches when I get to the bathroom, and I see he's left a shaker of salt on the vanity so I can rinse with warm salt water as the dentist directed.

He thought of everything.

My breath hitches with a surge of emotion I can't even describe.

What *is* all this?

Up until now, I've always been on my own when I've been sick—alone in my room at my mom's, struggling to take care of myself during fevers, food poisoning, colds, and flus.

This care from him is foreign and overwhelming, and I'm not sure what to make of it. Is he just a nice guy doing me a favor? Did he take our fake vows to heart and is now embracing them?

Or is it possible that love doesn't let us choose if we believe in it or not? Does it just happen?

The voices in my head form a circle, surrounding me, and chant, *He'll never love you. You don't get love. He'll never love you.*

I'm not going to think about it. It's ridiculous. Being nice isn't love. It's just basic human decency. If anything, he feels sorry for me.

On my way out of the bathroom, I run right into him in the hall. I laugh a little when I notice we could almost be twins—both of us wearing gray sweatpants and white T-shirts.

"You're awake," he says. "I was just coming to check on you."

I smile groggily at him. "I just woke up." Even after a five-hour nap post- surgery, I still feel weak and foggy from the anesthesia.

"Good timing. I made you a protein shake." He holds up a tall glass and a spoon.

"Oh." My smile withers. "Thank you." I take it from him and he follows me to my room, where we sit on my bed together.

"I made it right—it's new almond milk, brand-new vanilla protein powder that I just opened today, and ice cubes."

I stare at it with trepidation. It's not just a shake. It's a twenty-ounce glass full of bad memories. When I was eight years old, I was so hungry I drank a milkshake that had been left in the fridge for over a week. It was lumpy and sour and it took over my body for three horrible days. I can still taste the thick vileness in my mouth.

I fight the urge to gag as I swirl the spoon though the shake, searching for lumps or bumps. There aren't any.

This isn't *that* shake.

This is safe and fresh. What I would label *clean*.

But still…

Jude watches me with a raised eyebrow and I feel like crying. He's trying so hard and I'm so fucked up inside. I wish I could have something different to eat or drink, but almost everything liquid or mushy scares me. It's all so *blended* and unidentifiable.

I want my bread and butter.

It never occurred to me that my go-to safe foods would be uneatable at a time like this. I feel betrayed.

Maybe I lied to myself about my eating habits just as much as I lied to myself about love. I thought I was keeping myself safe, but all I was doing was nurturing a bigger problem.

"You have to put something in your stomach," he says softly. "I promise it's safe to drink."

My jaw muscles ache as I smile at him. "I trust you," I say.

Slowly, I drink the shake while he distracts me by talking about the house and the rest of the renovations he wants to do. He asks me about paint colors and furniture as he brings up pictures on his cell phone for me to see and choose from.

It's sweet how excited he is about remodeling, and it works—having my mind engaged in something positive doesn't allow me to focus on food textures and bad memories.

"That was really good," I say when I take the last sip of the shake. I peek at him from behind the curtain of my hair. "Thank you for taking care of me."

He shrugs. "It's kinda my favorite hobby now."

My heart flip-flops when he winks at me after saying that.

"Do you want to stay and watch a movie with me?" I ask after I take my antibiotic and two Tylenol. I've decided not to take the pain killers because I'm afraid they'll make me sick. "I feel too wobbly to go downstairs."

The way his eyes shift uneasily from the television to the bed makes me regret asking and putting him on the spot. I'm sure hanging out with me again on a Saturday night isn't his idea of a good time.

"Um... sure." He rubs his hand across his chin. "Okay."

His less-than-enthusiastic reply tamps down the happiness I felt just moments ago.

"You don't have to, if you have plans," I say quickly. "I'm totally fine. Just sore and sleepy. Gus and Cassie will keep me company."

"No... I don't have any plans. I'll hang with you for a bit."

"I have to warn you, I'm planning on watching *The Notebook*. It's the ultimate chick flick," I tease. "If you want to change your mind, I'll let you out of it."

He groans. "Nah, I'll suffer through it just this one time 'cause you had a bad day."

I haven't told him about Lisa Rottworth yet. I'm hoping I imagined that she was texting Paige about me being married, and that she didn't hear Jude's conversation with the receptionist at all.

We get settled on my bed by piling a bunch of throw pillows up against the headboard. I turn off the ceiling light, switch on the small lamp next to my bed with the cool, blue bulb, then pull my fleece throw blanket up over both of us.

"All comfy now? Or do we need ten more pillows?" he asks with his thumb hovering over the play button on the remote.

I smile. "I'm good."

"The things I do for you," he jokes when the movie opens with its romantic, foreshadowing scenes.

"Shush," I say, secretly loving everything he does. "And it's okay if you cry at the end. I won't think less of your masculinity."

He scoffs, but grins. "I ain't gonna cry over a movie, Sparkles."

"We'll see."

Right around the middle of the movie, I slip into a sleepy, warm, relaxed state. I feel cozy and safe in my pretty room, under the soft blanket, with Jude and our two fur babies. I inch closer to him and rest my head on his shoulder, quietly inhaling the scent of his cologne. When we're close like this, everything in my world feels better, and I can't imagine ever wanting to be anywhere else.

"I like being close to you," I whisper.

"I like being close to you, too," he whispers back, gently putting his arm around me and pulling me closer.

"You always make me feel better. You're a good husband," I tease. But actually, it's true. If I ever wanted to get married for real, I'd want to be married to someone like him.

"You're a pretty good wife," he teases back.

I turn toward him slightly, tilting my face up toward his, and he kisses my cheek.

"I can't kiss you," he says, in a voice so low I can barely hear him over the movie.

My happiness wilts. "Why?"

He stares at the movie, where Noah and Allie are bickering adorably. The muscles in his jaw twitch. I wait for what seems like forever for him to turn his attention back to me.

"I don't want to hurt you," he finally says.

Avoiding my eyes, he brushes a few stray hairs from my forehead.

"Hurt me how?" I ask.

"Your mouth, baby," he says. "I don't want to hurt your mouth."

The tone of his voice hints at reasons that go much deeper than that.

I move my tongue over my lower lip, enticed by how his darkening eyes fixate on my mouth.

"Then kiss me somewhere else," I say softly, curling my fingers into the thin fabric of his shirt.

Inhaling deeply, he finally rests his eyes on mine, and he holds my gaze for a long time—maybe waiting for me to falter and look away.

I don't.

"Is that what you want?" His lips touch my nose, then wait, hovering just a breath away.

I nod as we breathe against each other. "Yes."

My answer is a subtle invitation. If he chooses to accept it, then any touching or kissing from this point forward won't be an oops or an accident.

It'll be a conscious choice. A decision we made together right here on my bed.

Fisting my hair, he gently pulls my head back, angling my

neck up toward him. My eyes fall closed as he presses his lips to my throat and holds them there, warm and soft, before lightly sucking. My breath catches when he slowly drags his mouth up to briefly touch mine—whisper soft and gentle—before lifting up and bringing his lips back down to the base of my throat. Open-mouthed, teeth grazing. Grabbing his shirt, I pull him closer. His grip tightens in my hair as we meld together under the blanket.

My body hums as he ravishes my neck then moves to my collarbone, breathing heavily against me. My head is spinning—either from the surgery or the fervor he's igniting in me—maybe both. All I know is I don't want it to ever stop.

Holding the back of his neck, I attempt to pull him up to my mouth, desperate to have his lips on mine. Screw the pain.

I don't care.

I want him.

"No," he says, pulling back and staring at me with mischief and lust in his eyes. "Behave or I'll stop."

His words only make me want him even more.

"Don't stop," I whisper.

He slowly lifts my T-shirt, his gaze still riveted on mine. My shallow breaths match his, as inch by inch, he pushes the material up until it's bunched under my neck. His eyes lower, lingering over my naked breasts. His fingers tighten around my waist, telling me he likes—*wants*—what he sees.

"I've been dying to kiss you again…to be close to you again." His ragged breath against my flesh sends goosebumps over my chest and arms. "It's all I fucking think about."

Slowly, he moves his lips over my breasts, trailing his tongue in lazy, taunting circles around one, then the other, back and forth, until I feel like I might scream. The scruff of his stubble grazes over my sensitive skin in the wake of his tongue. I had no idea the alternation of soft and coarse could be so crazy tantalizing.

A short gasp escapes me when his mouth finally sinks over my nipple and his teeth gently tug it to meet his flicking tongue.

Clutching the back of his neck, I run my hands through his long hair, weaving it through my fingers—something I've been wanting to do for a long time. I arch myself up to him, wanting more. He delivers by skimming a calloused hand across my lower body, caressing my rib cage before moving down farther. He pauses for a fraction of a second, just below my navel. His breath is hot and shallow against my breast. I can feel the internal debate coursing through his veins.

I don't want us to turn back.

Reaching down, I cover his hand with mine, gently push it beneath the waistband of my panties, then slip my hand away.

A groan rumbles deep in his throat, and it's the sexiest sound I've ever heard.

His fingertips brush over the soft hair. My body writhes with want as he sucks my breast hungrily into his mouth. My heart pulses faster. His hand feels so good, so incredibly warm. Comforting and electrifying at the same time. My stomach muscles flutter with a million butterflies in anticipation of his touch.

"Jude..." I breathe.

When he looks up at me, his hair falls into his face in the sexiest of ways. His lips are glistening from kissing me. I've daydreamed about being kissed by him again—a kiss that isn't just a quickie, or an oops. I need a kiss that makes me feel like he wants me. With no hesitation. A kiss that says *you're mine*.

I didn't know I wanted to be anyone's until we kissed on our wedding day. Maybe the kiss at the end of vows has magical powers. Because that one little oops changed everything.

"Do you want me to touch you?" he asks with his hand still pressed against me, unmoving.

"Hello?" I say, wincing from the pain of grinning. "Are you *kidding*?"

He doesn't laugh. "I need to hear you say it, Sparkles."

Oh. This isn't one of our teasing moments. This is serious. *As it should be.* I touch his cheek, and my heart melts when he turns to press a kiss to my palm.

How is it that he can look so rough and sexy, and still be so incredibly sweet?

"Yes," I whisper, all kidding gone. "I want you to touch me, Lucky."

"Good," he whispers, and dips his head down into my hair to kiss the sensitive spot just below my ear.

A warm shiver jets down my spine as his hand slides farther down beneath my panties. Wrapping my arms around him, I pull him closer and move my hands slowly up and down over the hard muscle of his back. The strength and solidity of him is so magnetic and grounding. I crave the safeness he makes me feel.

Actually, I crave *everything* he makes me feel.

Taking a breath, I part my legs, and he delves between my thighs. The moment his fingers touch my lips I let out a whimper and push myself up into his hand. He rains kisses from my neck to my chest while he works magic on me. His fingers strum the curve of my lower lips. His thumb presses against my clit and rubs it in slow, tantalizing circles. My breath quickens. My thighs squeeze around his hand. We moan simultaneously when he pushes two fingers inside me and fucks me slowly with his hand.

When I reach for his pants, he nudges my hand away.

"No," he whispers with his mouth against my ear and his fingers buried inside me. "Tonight, I just want to fuckin' devour you."

In a blink, he disappears under the blanket and quickly lowers my sweatpants. His mouth joins his hand between my thighs. His tongue laps at my throbbing clit, his lips cover me, so warm and wet.

I turn into a quivering, wet, orgasmic, lovesick mess.

Closing my eyes, I let go of everything, cling to him, and let myself get lost in *us*.

CHAPTER 29

JUDE

"I can't believe we're back here. These homeowners are a pain in the damn ass," Kyle says as we walk up the driveway of the house next to the high school.

"At least they pay on time. That's all that matters to me. It's a two-week job. In and out."

I was on the fence about coming back here when the homeowner called me about wanting a one-car detached garage built. Not just because they were difficult to deal with, but because I wasn't sure I wanted to be working so close to Skylar now that we're legally married and living together. I didn't trust myself to not constantly be looking over at the parking lot, or the school, hoping to see her and catch her smiling at me.

There's not much I look forward to, but her smile is definitely a highlight of my day.

Three weeks ago, I accepted the job because I had a break in my schedule while waiting on materials for a different project. At the time I was unaware how much would change between me and Skylar.

I had no fucking idea that I'd start to have real feelings for her, or that I'd end up in her bed, kissing and touching her while she was half-naked. Or that I wouldn't be able to stop thinking about her and wanting to be with her.

None of that was part of my plan.

Now, I don't know what the fuck I'm doing.

"I guess the little hottie lost her wheels," Kyle says.

"Huh?" I reply absently.

"That chick you took to the ER." He nods toward the school parking lot. "Now she's driving a mom car."

Thankfully, Kyle doesn't know that Skylar's *mom car* is actually my Subaru. Nor does he know that she's the one I married.

"She's still hot as fuck, though," he rambles on, staring at her. "I'll bet she's a lightweight. Get one beer in her, and she'll be drunk off her tight little ass, bouncing on my dick like a fucking pogo stick."

My blood boils like lava.

I give his shoulder a hard shove. "What the fuck, man?" I say.

He stumbles back and almost falls over his tools. "What's your problem?"

"What the hell is wrong with you? Saying sick shit like that. She's fucking eighteen years old."

And she's my wife.

Laughing, he shifts his gaze back to Skylar walking across the parking lot. "That's even better."

I glare at him. "No, Kyle. It isn't."

"You lose your dick somewhere, Lucky? She's a random hot chick, not your fucking sister."

When he moves to walk away, I grab the front of his shirt and slam him up against the back of the house. I get a sick satisfaction as the back of his skull bounces off the siding. "Don't you *ever* talk about my sister," I seethe.

His eyes widen, and he grabs on to my arm, trying to loosen my grip. "Dude, calm down. I didn't mean *your* sister. I'm just talking shit."

"Just keep your fucking mouth shut." I ram my fist into his chest once more before letting him go. "Get back to work."

"Whatever," he mumbles as he walks away, straightening his sweatshirt.

I light up a smoke and turn back toward the school. Skylar's walking with Megan, hefting her book bag onto her shoulder.

A slow smile spreads across my face. I think the book bag weighs more than she does. Every day she brings *all* of her textbooks home. Even if she doesn't have a test, she studies every night.

She's the most unique, beautiful, smart, and adorable woman I've ever met in my life. It enrages me that sick assholes like Kyle look at her like she's some kind of fuck toy.

At noon, I take a lunch break and drive downtown to the jewelers to pick up my aunt's diamond ring. She's been calling me every day asking when she'll have it back. While I wait for the manager to ring me up, I check out the glass cases filled with necklaces and bracelets. Everything is blinding and sparkling.

Speaking of sparkles…

I can see Skylar opening a pretty red velvet box on Christmas morning, squeaking with surprise, and smiling the biggest smile. Probably while wearing footie pajamas with freakin' red-nosed reindeers on them. Smiling at that mental image, I peer through the glass case at a heart-shaped necklace that would—

Ugh. I can't.

I bolt out of the store with Aunt Suzy's ring and nothing else.

Buying Skylar jewelry would send the wrong message. We're

not together. She's barely said a damn word to me since that night in her bed, and she's been holing up in her room every night with the door closed. In a way it's a relief. We got caught in a weak moment and weren't thinking. Us getting involved would lead to nothing but a mess.

When I get back to the job site, the homeowner is waiting for me, stalking around her backyard wearing workout gear.

"What color will the siding be?" she asks, nodding at the framed-out garage.

"The same color as the house, just like we talked about," I say, making sure I've plastered on my *customer is always right* smile.

"I don't know…" Mrs. Thompson says, studying the house, then the garage. "Maybe it should be a different color. Like a complimentary color. Maybe gray. Or light blue. Even dark blue. Or dark gray."

Here we go.

"It can be any color you want it to be, but you have to let me know by the end of the week so I can order it. I'll bring some color charts tomorrow."

She shakes her head and quirks her mouth to the side. "I'm just not sure. What color do *you* think it should be?"

"I'm colorblind," I lie. "So…"

"Oh. What a shame. Well, let me ask my neighbor what she thinks. She's an interior designer, so she knows all about these things."

"That sounds great."

She tucks her long, black hair behind her ear. "We love the work you did on the house. The new rooms are beautiful. Everyone says so when they visit."

This time I give her a genuine smile. "That's what I like to hear."

She stares at me for a few moments. "You have really nice hair. Do you use a hair mask?"

I let out a laugh. I don't even know what a hair mask is. "That'd be a no."

"It's so shiny, I just want to touch it," she says. I pray she doesn't try to pet me. "It's getting chilly out here. Are you cold?" She crosses her arms in front of her and shivers dramatically. "Do you want to come inside for a coffee, maybe?" Her brows rise suggestively.

Is a coffee offer the same as a Netflix and chill?

"Uh," I stammer awkwardly. I'll let my balls freeze off before I accept an offer like that. "I just had lunch and I gotta get back to work. Thanks, though."

Smiling, she nods and looks behind me at my four guys. I wonder if she's going to ask one of them next. "Okay, well, I'll be home all afternoon if you change your mind. I'll leave the back door unlocked."

Whoa.

I say nothing and head back to the work area. Was she just trying to pick me up in her own backyard on a Friday afternoon? I've met her husband and kids. And her dog, for fuck's sake. They seemed like the perfect family, and they spent over two hundred grand on this house to make it their forever dream home.

Unfuckingreal.

When four o'clock rolls around, we clean up for the day and I send the guys home. My plan is to get home early, shower, and head over to my aunt's to surprise her with her ring. I don't know if Skylar's working today, but I'll text her and ask her if she wants to come with me. Maybe it'll get her out of this weird slump she's been in all week.

On my way home, I'm stopped at a traffic light when, to my right, I see Skylar pumping gas into the car at the station on the corner. A man is standing close, leaning into her, with his arm on the top of the car. She's laughing at something he said. It takes me a few seconds to realize its Kyle.

Mother. Fucker.

As soon as the light changes, I peel into the gas station lot, park my truck off to the side, and get out, slamming my door behind me. I watch as Skylar finishes filling her tank and tries to move past Kyle, who grabs her waist and pulls her back.

"What the hell's going on?" I growl as I approach them.

Skylar looks up with surprise and relief. "Jude—"

"You followin' me?" Kyle asks, grinning. "Or her? I beat you to it, man. Just asking our little friend here if she wants to grab a bite to eat."

"Take your hand off her."

He scoffs. "Dude, don't be a cock blocker."

Skylar attempts to move away, but he grabs her arm. "C'mon, honey. Don't worry about him. We'll have a good time."

She wrenches her arm away. "If you touch me again, I'll cut your balls off."

Kyle's eyes rove over her like a dog eyeing a juicy steak. They travel over her denim skirt, black leggings, and fuzzy boots. He licks his lips when his gaze lands on her Woodstock shirt tied in a knot at the front, revealing a tiny glimpse of her belly beneath the faded denim jacket thrown over it.

My old denim jacket that she must've foraged from my closet.

"C'mon, sweetheart, you look like you *love* being touched," he says, and my vision goes blood red. Without warning, I slam my fist into his face.

"Fuck!" His head whips to the side. He stumbles, then lunges forward, slamming me into the gas pump behind me.

"Oh my God!" Skylar shrieks. "Stop it!"

Regaining my balance, I grab him and knee him hard in the gut. He lets out a groan, clutches his stomach, and falls to the ground. "Fuckin' asshole," he mutters under his breath.

"Stay the hell away from her," I warn, standing over him. We've been beating the shit out of each other since we were kids, but this will be the last time. He crossed a line I'll never let him come back from.

"Fuck you, Lucky." He spits out a mouthful of blood, and Skylar recoils. "Why you gettin' all bent over a piece of ass?"

"She's my wife," I say, my voice low. "And you're fucking fired. I don't want shit like you on my crew."

Skylar touches my arm. "Jude, you don't have to—"

I pull my arm out of her grasp. "We'll talk about this at home."

Kyle grabs the side of the Subaru and pulls himself up. Blood trickles from his nose.

"*She's* the one you married? What the fuck! You married a fucking *kid*? You're out of your damn mind," he says, wiping his hand across his face. "And you can shove your job up your ass."

"Hey, Skylar, maybe you'll get a spanking when you get home," a female voice says. I turn away from Kyle stumbling toward his car to see a small group of laughing teens hanging out at the gas station doors.

Fuck.

Skylar stares at me, her face ashen with shock and anger.

"What's wrong with you?" she demands through gritted teeth.

"He was touching you."

Her blue eyes narrow. "So what?"

My blood boils with jealousy—a feeling I've never battled

with before. "What do you mean *so what*?" I shove my hand through my hair and step closer to her, lowering my voice. "What—did you want him to? Were you actually gonna go with him?"

"Are you insane?"

I shrug. "I guess I'm gettin' there," I say sarcastically.

"I can take care of myself," she says, her voice shaking. "I don't need you going all fucking Hulk on people like an animal."

"My dad's a divorce lawyer, in case you need one, Skylar," one of the other girls yells across the lot. "Just sayin'."

Oh, shit.

Skylar throws the group a threatening glance, then turns back to me. The shimmer of tears and disappointment in her eyes pulverizes my heart. "Just great."

Shaking her head, she jumps into the car without looking back at me, and speeds away.

Fuck.

CHAPTER 30
JUDE

My mood is shot to hell. All I wanted to do was bring Skylar with me to go see my aunt and uncle and have a fun night. But instead, I'm pissed off, hungry, and confused.

I haven't randomly blown up on someone in a long time. But seeing Kyle's slimy hands on Skylar pushed me right over the edge. He's a douchebag.

His degrading sexual comments and his blatant flirting with Skylar made me sick. She's sweet and attractive, but she's only eighteen years old. Guys our age shouldn't be trying to pick up chicks still in high school. It's sick.

But aren't I worse?

I've kissed her. Touched her.

My dick is rock hard just thinking about the night we stopped holding back and let things go further.

It should've felt wrong, but it didn't. When we're together, she's not eighteen, and I'm not thirty-four. We're just two people who get along great, make each other laugh, take care of each other, and have insane chemistry. It's not about sex—I can get that anywhere. It's a magnetic pull to get closer. Emotionally.

Physically. Every time I'm with her I get this feeling of indescribable contentment that I can't even wrap my head around.

I don't know how all this snuck up on me.

I've never felt like this with other women. There's always been a disconnect with them—a wall that blocked any kind of real intimacy or happiness. And I was totally fine with that. In fact, I preferred it. It made things easy.

I wish that wall would sprout up between me and Skylar. Then I wouldn't have to deal with all this torment. Because even though age is just a number and all that bullshit, I can't just blow off the fact that she's eighteen. She's still in high school.

Too young to be tangling in my world of love 'em and leave 'em.

♥ ♡ ♥ ♥

Now I know how the dog feels when I don't come home on time. I've been pacing the floor, staring out the front window, listening for the front door to open.

Skylar hasn't come home. She never stays out after eight, and now the clock is creeping toward midnight.

I don't want to be that guy, but here I am, being that guy.

Earlier, she peeled out of the gas station in anger, and now I'm worried something happened to her.

Or who knows—maybe she decided to take Kyle up on his offer.

Unlikely, but still possible.

Gus meows in Skylar's bedroom until I fill her dish, and it makes me wonder if Skylar had dinner tonight.

Finally, I give in and send her a text:

Me: Hey you. Where are you?

Skylar: Been hangin' at Hampton Beach with friends.

A selfie of her and Megan comes through that they must have taken earlier, sitting on the beach together with the sunset blazing orange and pink in the background.

Me: It's after midnight and it's a school night. Come home.

Did I really just type that? Someone kill me now please.

Skylar: WTF. You're not my father, Jude. 😠 Go to bed.

Me: Last time I checked I was your husband. I want your ass home in an hour or I'm gonna come get you.

I'm not gonna play the stare-at-the-door-all-night game with Cassie.

Skylar: Chill out. I'll be home soon.

Soon turns out to be two a.m.

From upstairs, I hear the front door opening and closing. Then, her feet thumping on the stairs. I'm just climbing out of my bed and pulling on my sweats to go check on her when she shows up in my doorway—all legs in tiny cutoff denim shorts.

"What's wrong with you today?" she demands.

"Why don't we start by *you* telling *me* what's been wrong with you?"

Her face pulls into a frown. "Nothing's wrong with me."

"Bullshit," I say, taking a few steps closer to her. "Something's been bothering you. You've barely said a word to me since the night of your surgery."

The same night I had my lips all over her, feasting on her perfect body, falling harder and harder for her.

Focus, Jude.

"Oh, I don't know," she says flippantly. "I guess because I woke up the next morning with about a hundred notifications because that bitch Lisa Fucking Rottworth was in Dr. Katz's waiting room and heard you call yourself my spouse, and then she proceeded to tell the entire damn school." She reaches up and tugs the rubber band out of her ponytail, and her long hair falls around her shoulders. I remember how soft and silky it felt in my hands that night, and I wish I could run my fingers through it right now. "I guess I could've told you about it that morning, but you were gone before I woke up."

Old habits die hard. We fell asleep after I fingered and licked her into multiple orgasms, and I snuck out of her bed at five a.m. "Skylar, I—"

"It's been a really shitty week," she says angrily. "Everyone's been talking about me, and laughing at me, and posting dumb memes all over social media. Then when I finally think I've got it handled, you throw a tantrum at the gas station in front of half the school."

"I didn't throw a tantrum."

Her angry tone morphs to sarcasm. "Um, yeah ya did."

My defenses go up. "That asshole was touching you. You should hear the shit he was saying about you."

"Who cares? He's just a dick. And anyway, he's *your* friend."

I shake my head. "Nah. That guy's not my friend. Not anymore."

"You didn't have to fire him, Jude. I think breaking his nose was enough."

"Fuck that. I should've snapped his neck. I don't want a scumbag like that working for me."

"And what's *this*?" She waves her cell phone in the air between us. "*Get your ass home?* What the hell, Jude? I can stay out as late as I want, with whoever I want, whenever I want. You can't tell me what to do. I'm an adult."

"Then act like one."

"Oh, like you've been? Please." She rolls her eyes.

"Why are you being like this?"

"Why are *you*?" she shoots back.

"Because I care about you. And I don't like seeing men put their hands on you."

Her eyes narrow, then go wide, as if suddenly she had a lightbulb moment. "Are you *jealous,* Lucky?"

I crack my knuckles and put my hands up. "Look, I'm not doing this," I say. "This stupid fight shit? Nope."

"We already *are* doing it. You can't just say you don't do it when you're right in the middle of it."

"Yeah, I can. It's late. Go to bed." I point to the hallway.

"Don't tell me to go to bed. Why are you treating me like a little kid?"

I rub my eyes with my palms and blow out an exhausted sigh. "I don't know, Skylar. I'm tired. I gotta get up in three hours."

"I know why," she says matter-of-factly. "You're trying to convince yourself I'm young."

"You *are* young."

"You want to believe I'm *too* young."

"Too young for what?" I ask, even though I know exactly what she's talking about.

"Too young for us to be more than friends."

Damn. I can't believe she's going there, full force ahead. While I admire her rip-the-Band-Aid-off approach, I'm not ready to get into this right *now*.

Or maybe not ever.

"We really shouldn't be having this conversation," I say.

"Why not? I'm not afraid to say what's on my mind." She lifts her chin defiantly, and she looks sexy as hell. "I like you. You make me laugh and I love your sweet side. I like how I feel when I'm with you. And I think you're hot. I think you feel the same way about me. That's what put you in a jealous rage earlier."

"I don't get jealous, Sparkles."

And it was hardly a rage.

She slowly shakes her head back and forth with frustration. "I'm being honest with you, Jude. Because that's what *adults* do. You're the one who's acting like a teenager, not me."

Frustrated, I take a few steps back toward the bed, then change my mind and turn back to her. "Fine. You want honesty? Let's do it." I spread my arms out. "I like you, too. More than friends. More than I should, and more than I fucking want to. I think you're cute and sexy, and you make me laugh. You make me happy. I love your crazy-ass clothes and your cat with the fucked-up name. I just wish you weren't eighteen years old."

"Was that so hard?" she asks, stepping closer to me. She puts her hand on the middle of my bare chest, and fingers my necklace. That simple touch burns through me like a shot of whiskey. "Why does it bother you so much?"

The scent of beach sand and perfume drifts off her. Inhaling it, I struggle with the urge to pull her closer, bury my face in her hair, and roam her body for stray bits of sand clinging to her thighs and ass.

"Because I'm too old for you."

"I like old things, Lucky," she says softly. "You should know that by now."

Her words ignite a fire in my heart and sends a rush of heat through me.

"I'm serious, Skylar."

"So am I. If we both want more, why can't we have it? There are no rules here. No expectations. I'm old enough to make decisions about my life and my body. At least we know we won't hurt each other. Right?" She leans forward and presses her soft lips over my heart. It takes every molecule of self-control I have not to toss her onto my bed and tear her clothes off. "I don't expect you to date me or marry me." She lets out a little laugh. "Pun intended. But if I want you to kiss me, why not?"

I touch a lock of her hair hanging just past her breast. I wind it tight around my finger then release it. It falls back against her, still curled in the shape of my finger. "If I kiss you, I'm not going to stop."

She stares up at me. Her eyes are full of everything that draws me to her. Mischief. Fire. Desire. Honesty.

"Then don't stop," she says.

I grab her cheek in my hand and slowly drag my thumb across her bottom lip. She inhales slowly, and her eyes flutter closed in anticipation. The dark tattoos on my hand against her pale complexion are a wicked turn-on.

I feel like I've just pulled up to a traffic light, and *all* the lights are lit up.

Stop.

Wait.

Go.

They're all blurred together. I don't know which choice is right.

"Kiss me," she whispers, pulling on the chain of my necklace.

I can't resist anymore.

Grabbing her waist with my free hand, I pull her hard against my body and crush my lips down on hers. Her gasp of surprise fuels the fire she's already stoked with her inviting touches and perfect words. I move my hand over the curve of her ass and down to the back of her bare thigh, lifting her until she hops up and wraps her legs around my waist.

Kissing wildly, I kick the bedroom door shut with my foot, then push her back up against it. Breathless, she snakes her arms around my neck. Her nails graze over the back of my head as she shoves her fingers through my hair. Our tongues wrestle and caress hungrily.

I grab her hands in mine and pin them against the door above her head. Her thighs tighten around me and her eyes go wide as she meets my gaze. She's already breathless and I've barely touched her.

"Have you done this before?" I ask.

"Been kissed against a door by the hottest guy on the planet? No."

Smirking, I touch my lips quickly to hers. "I mean are you a virgin?"

If she says yes, I'm out. That's a place I won't go.

She swallows and raises her chin a little. "No," she says. "Is that a disappointment?"

I shake my head. "I want a woman, not a little girl."

A teasing smile dances across her lips. "Does that mean I'm getting more than a kiss?"

I kiss her again, long and hard, pushing my tongue past her teeth to meet hers. Tilting her head, she opens her mouth to mine, deepening the kiss. Her heels dig into me, pulling me in.

As her breath quickens, I pull away. I rub my thumbs along her hands, still captured in mine against the door, and grind my cock against her through our clothes.

When she moans, I kiss her throat, loving the vibration against my lips, then raise my head to look into her eyes.

"You tell me, Sparkles. Do you want more than a kiss?"

"Yes." Her tongue peeks out to lick her lower lip, and she nods. "Much more."

My heart thunders and my dick throbs in response as I slowly lower her to her feet, then touch her chin, angling her face up to mine. I plant a kiss on the tip of her nose.

"Get on that fucking bed," I whisper.

CHAPTER 31

SKYLAR

Get on that fucking bed.

My God, his voice is so incredibly sexy with that deep, raspy edge.

Are aural orgasms a thing?

Because I'm pretty sure I just had one.

He comes up behind me as I stand at the foot of his bed and puts his hands gently on my shoulders.

"Having second thoughts?" he asks.

I shake my head without turning to him. "No, just trying to decide which side is going to be mine."

He lets out a laugh. "Don't even think about it, sweetheart. Your bed is right down the hall. I have a no-staying-the-night rule."

"You stayed the night last week," I point out.

"Only because you had surgery and I didn't want you to be alone."

I'm glad he can't see the smirk on my face. He may have left my bed before I woke up, but I distinctly remember him holding me all night, and softly kissing my temple when he thought I was asleep.

More accurately, Jude has a no-getting-attached rule. I recognize all the signs because I also have that rule. However, it doesn't seem to be working for us. Our rules are breaking themselves. Although, a little voice inside tells me maybe they're breaking a little more for me than for him.

I just have to keep reminding myself that I'm here for the happily for *now* and not the happily ever after.

And right now, all I want is to get on that bed and let his touch banish the stress from all the bullying, my eating disorder, and all my various other worries about how my life is going. Jude is like a magic eraser. When I'm with him, it all fades away.

Turning around, I unknot my T-shirt and slowly lift it over my head. He steps back a bit and watches me with insatiable hunger. I'm definitely not ready to give a sultry, pole-worthy strip tease, but I refuse to let myself look nervous, shy, and awkward. All those things will throw up the *she's-too-young* red flags.

He looks insanely hot as he comes toward me, and I soak it all in. The messy hair. Those sterling eyes. Muscular arms and washboard abs; the sweatpants slipping down his hips, showing off a bulge big enough to have its own zip code.

Cupping my face in his hands, he kisses me long and slow. I think he's caught on to the power his touch has over me. I'm a rag doll—my insides turning to mush, my limbs weak. I lean my body into his and hold on to his huge biceps to keep from swaying. As we kiss, he moves his hands slowly down the sides of my neck, his thumbs grazing over my throat, then over my shoulders, to my back. He unclasps my bra, then slips it off and tosses it on the floor. Effortlessly, he lifts me up and lays me down on top of his puffy charcoal comforter. I lie back and watch him as he removes my shoes, then stands between my legs as he unzips my shorts and tugs them down, along with my panties.

"I think I just want to stand here and look at you all night," he says, inching his hand languidly up my thigh like he's got all the time in the world. His eyes sweep over me and he gives his head a little shake. "You're so fucking beautiful."

I peek at him through my lashes. "I could say the same about you."

He grins, and I sit up on the edge of his bed and grab the waistband of his pants. This time, he doesn't stop me. He lets me pull them down, and his stiff cock springs free.

"Commando?" I inquire. He's already hard as steel, pulsing with heat right next to my face.

"Only when I sleep." He touches the side of my head, gently weaving his fingers through my hair. "I thought I was going to bed, but someone was being a bad wife by staying out too late."

"You better not say you want to spank me," I warn, only half-joking. I'm not into the Daddy thing. If he is, I might just pack my bags and my cat and leave tonight.

"Hell no," he says, moving his hand down to caress the back of my neck. "I want to see your lips wrapped around me like a good little wife."

My pussy clenches, letting me know my body is totally on board with all these things, even if my mind has totally just hit a brick wall.

I can't put his cock in my mouth.

OhGodOhGodOhGod. I can't do this. It's too big. I can't even swallow vanilla pudding yet. There's no way I'm going to be able to swallow cum.

I was *so* close to being normal.

I'm totally defective. Abnormal. Damaged. Not good enough.

My hand trembles as I stroke his smooth shaft. He's long, hard and thick, throbbing with heat and desire in my hand. I can feel myself getting wet just touching him, thinking of him inside me. I want this man so bad, I just can't do *that*.

Above me, he sucks in a breath.

"Jude..." My voice wavers. I stare up at him and wait for him to open his eyes and look at me. "I can't..."

"What's wrong?" he asks softly.

"I can't do the blowjob thing," I whisper. "Because of my—"

"Shit... I'm sorry. My mind's like mush right now. I'm not thinking."

"It's not your fault. I'm sorry, I—" My voice catches in a tight ball of embarrassment and shame.

"Shhh..." He moves his hand from the back of my neck to my cheek, and with his thumb, brushes away the tear that spilled there. "It's okay."

His voice is soft, but there's a tinge of disappointment riding on it, and I don't blame him. I can only imagine what's running through his mind. Not only does he think I'm too young, but now I'm a tease who had a meltdown once his cock was in my face.

"I'm sorry," I say again, flushing with humiliation and releasing his still-hard dick from my hand. "I'm gonna go." I start to sit up, but he pushes me back down.

"You're out of your fuckin' mind if you think that's a deal breaker, babe."

Grabbing my hand in his, he wraps it around his cock and guides it along his length.

"Touch me," he says, his voice hoarse with desire.

I stroke him slowly, gripping him in my palm and caressing the hot, damp tip. His head bows down, his hair falls over his face, his eyes close. My heart swells with adoration and lust for him. Leaning forward, I put my lips against his flat stomach. His ab muscles flutter deliciously as I rain a slow trail of kisses from hip to hip. I feel like a little kid on Christmas morning, getting an amazing gift in the form of sexy tats and an incredible body all wrapped up with a big red bow of sweetness on top. He groans and grabs my shoulders, pulling me up to meet his lips, kissing me with such hunger I can't breathe. His hands travel roughly down my body, his fingers dig into my skin. He cups my ass in his hand, squeezing it hard, and slips his other hand between my thighs. I whimper against his mouth when his finger slides into the slickness of my slit and traces slow circles.

My knees weaken. *It feels so good.*

"Lay down," he whispers in that deep, rough voice that makes me clench tight around his finger.

I do as he asks, and my heart pounds as he crawls over me. The way his muscles flex as he moves is jaw-droppingly sexy. I can't believe I get to be with someone so beautiful.

I can't believe I'm *married* to someone so beautiful.

Wrapping my arms around him, I pull him down on me, so we're flesh-to-flesh. We kiss slower this time, savoring and tasting each other. Our bodies meld together, hot, hard and soft. I never knew being with someone could feel this way—so perfect and completely connected.

When we part for air, he gives me an adorably mischievous but sexy grin. "I have to find a condom," he says with a little laugh.

"Okay."

He kisses my forehead and holds his lips there for a few moments, inhaling slowly, as if he doesn't want to leave me. "I'll be right back," he finally says.

I'm breathless as I watch him get off the bed and rummage in his nightstand, then his top dresser drawer. Then his closet. My eyebrow rises when he starts fishing through his wallet.

I'm not sure if I should be glad he doesn't have an endless supply of condoms at his fingertips, or worried that he's sexually unprepared.

"Fuck," he mutters, throwing his wallet on the floor. "I don't believe this."

"I think I might have one," I say meekly.

"You do?" His tone is part relieved and part suspicious.

"I keep one in my purse just in case. I'd rather have one than *not* have one," I reply, swinging my legs over the edge of the bed. "Like now." I pull my shirt over my head and tug it down to my thighs.

"You don't have to get dressed..."

"I'll be right back," I say as he playfully smacks my ass.

When I get to my room and see the two stuffed animals on my bed—one my grandparents gave me when I was little, and the other the teddy bear Jude gave me the first time he came to my house, I suffer a moment of crushing anxiety.

Jude's friendship has become a lifeline for me.

What am I doing?

Is this going to wreck us forever?

What if he's disappointed in me as a lover? I've already denied the guy any kind of oral sex. Don't men live for that? What if he never wants to go near me again after this? What if it gets so awkward, he doesn't even want to spend time with me anymore?

If that happens, I'll miss our couch cuddles, our movie nights, our goofy talks, and our handholding. Those little intimate moments are everything to me, and I'll be devastated if it stops.

I take a few grounding breaths, then dig through my purse until I find the condom I threw in there a year ago. My therapist said I have to face my anxiety, so that's what I'm doing. I'm not going to let it get in the way.

"Thought you ran away," Jude says when I return to his room and shut the door behind me. He's sitting on the middle of the bed, still with an erection.

Impressive.

"Took me a minute to find it." I hold up the silver packet and climb up on the bed with him.

He immediately pulls me down on top of him and kisses me

like he hasn't seen me in a year, wrapping both his arms around me. "Are you still okay with this?" he asks when we come up for air, his eyes searching mine. "It's okay if you aren't."

"I don't want this to ruin us," I say, leaning up on my elbows to look at him. It surprises me how comfortable I feel lying in his arms, especially with him naked and his cock pressing into my thigh.

He nods slowly and brushes the back of his fingers across my cheek. Of course, I melt. "As long as we're honest with each other, that won't happen. I promise, Skylar. You mean too much to me."

"I promise, too."

Pulling me to him, he kisses me so softly and gently that my heart aches with the overwhelming feelings he stirs in me. He's total whiplash—sweet one moment, and raw and sexy the next.

He lifts my shirt off, rolls me over onto my back and kisses me from my lips down to my belly button, then back again, driving me wild with every nip and suck along the way. His teeth graze over my nipple and tug it into his mouth until I squeal his name. When he spreads my legs wide and lowers his head into the apex of my thighs, I thrust up against his face and thread my fingers through his long hair.

Spreading my folds open with his thumbs, he laves his tongue over me, tantalizingly slow, from my wet hole up to my clit, pausing to suck it between his full lips and lap it into a buzzing frenzy with the tip of his tongue. I dig my nails into his scalp when his thumbs push inside me, stretching me wider. My pussy pulses and clenches when he plunges his tongue deep inside, swirling it around my walls in slow, deliberate circles. My entire body trembles with desire as he fucks me with his tongue and fingers. Wetness drips down my inner thighs.

"Oh my God," I cry out as his tongue pushes me to the edge. I teeter there, fighting the urge to tumble into ecstasy so this heaven with him will last longer. He reaches up and cups both of my breasts in his huge hands, squeezing them possessively, then rolling my nipples between his fingers, tugging and teasing as he thrusts his tongue in and out of me, lapping me from my ass to my clit over and over again. I become delirious, pulling his hair and arching up to him—into his hands and into his mouth—wanting and needing more. When he growls against my pussy like an animal, I lose it. I can't hold back anymore.

I writhe beneath him, trembling uncontrollably with orgasm. He continues to lick and kiss my thighs, sliding his hands down to my hips, holding me until my shudders subside. Breathless, I lean up, desperately pulling him up to me and wrapping my arms and legs around him. I kiss his neck and chest, intoxicated by the sexy scent of him and the heat of his skin against mine.

He pulls away to look at me, and that wicked grin is all over his lips. "You. Are. Delicious," he groans before covering my mouth with his. My breathing calms as he slowly kisses me, but it doesn't last long. Within minutes our hands are all over each other, roving and caressing. I reach down between us and grasp his rock-hard cock, fisting his thick length into my palm.

"I want you," I whisper with my lips against his ear.

"You've got me," he whispers back.

The tear of the foil packet permeates the silence of the dim room, and a few seconds later his hands are on my outer thighs, his fingers digging roughly into my flesh. He pulls me closer and thrusts into me balls deep, stretching me to take his full length. I let out a gasp that's half-pain and half-pleasure. I don't even care that it hurts a little, because watching him lose himself inside me is like watching art come to life. The way his tattoos, shiny with sweat, flex with his muscles. The way his long hair flies around his head with every thrust. The rivulets of sweat dripping down the center of his chest. The bite of his teeth into his lower lip as he drives into me.

Pure. Hotness.

He slides his hands beneath me to cup my ass, pulling my body up hard into his. Wrapping my thighs around his sweat-slicked hips, I reach up and grab his shoulders, pulling him down to me. Our lips clash together, and when he sucks my tongue into his mouth, my entire body tingles. My nails rake into the plane of his back as the passion builds between us, our bodies slapping together, needing to be closer and deeper. My walls tighten around his thick cock like a vise. He feels incredible. Every part of him touches me, and it ignites wave after wave of ecstasy. I hold on to him tight as another orgasm ripples through me.

With a raw moan of my name, he collapses on top of me, breathing heavily. We kiss, foreheads touching, deep, slow and dreamy until we're too tired to kiss anymore.

"I'll be right back," he says, and disappears into the bathroom for a few minutes. He kisses me when he returns, tasting of mint-flavored toothpaste, and flops down on his pillow.

"By the way." He rolls over to face me and snakes his arm around my waist, nestling against my side. "You were right. I was jealous."

I smile in the dark. "I know," I reply softly.

When he drifts off, I watch him sleep for a few minutes, then slip out from under his embrace and tiptoe naked back to my own room. Even though I want to stay in his bed, I don't want to seem clingy or tread over his no-staying-the-night rule.

Before I go to sleep, I do what I do every night—I take my wedding band out of my nightstand and slip it onto my finger—wondering what it would be like if this was all real.

CHAPTER 32
SKYLAR

"I'm off to work," Jude says from my doorway, just like he does every morning before he leaves.

There's no good-morning kiss.

No *about last night*… talk.

"Okay," I reply, meeting his eyes, wondering if I'll see something different after what happened last night. "Have a good day."

There's nothing different in his eyes. Not a lingering look. Not a hint of regret.

"You too. See ya tonight."

When I hear the front door open and close, I move to the window and watch him walk down the walkway, get into his truck, and back out of the driveway.

A little ache burns in my heart and then spreads down to my stomach, then up to my throat. The familiar sting of tears wells behind my eyes.

Confusion settles over me like a dark cloud. I'm caught in a feeling of wanting to cry, but also wanting to sit here and replay last night in my mind and revel in how perfect it felt to be with him.

How he kissed me like he wanted to swallow me up.

How his hands gripped me like he couldn't get enough.

How it felt to have him stretching me open and pulsing inside me.

How I got lost in that look of hunger and desire swimming in his eyes.

How my heart melted when he kissed me so softly, so full of emotion.

My pussy clenches at the memories, like it wants to pull him back in and never let go.

Perhaps I should have stayed in his bed. He *did* put his arm around me as he started to fall asleep. Maybe he took my leaving as a sign that *I* wanted it to be a one-night stand.

I only left because I thought that's what *he* wanted, and I wanted to seem mature—like I'm on board with us just casually hooking up.

And, I thought I was okay with that. But now, with this awful longing for him nettling in my soul, I'm not so sure. He seemed so casual and normal this morning, not acting different at all. But, maybe he was expecting—or waiting for—*me* to act different?

Or are we just going to pretend we didn't have sex?

I sigh and turn away from the window because my phone notifications are going off like crazy. As soon as I pick my phone up, my stomach pitches. I've been tagged again on my social media accounts by Paige and her friends in a bunch of stupid graphics posted with my face Photoshopped into various wedding photos as the bride marrying a really old, wrinkly, gray-haired groom. I grind my teeth at the hashtags

#childbride #pedohubby #daddyjude #skylarthedirtyho

#mywifeisachild #oldhusband #youcantbringyourhus-bandtotheprom #skylarshoulddie

More posts and rude comments are posted as the morning goes on, and now I can hear the girls whispering and giggling about me at the table behind me in the cafeteria.

"Just ignore them," Megan says, pouring dressing onto her salad.

I meet her sympathetic eyes across the table and shake my head. Ignoring is easier said than done. I can't escape the constant teasing. Ever since Lisa saw me at the dentist, it's been going on all day at school, then continues online at night with the social media posts, hashtags, and group chats. Paige and Lisa are the ringleaders of the bullying circus, making sure the torment stays relevant for her minions to gossip about.

"I wonder if her parents sold her to him?" a female voice asks.

"Probably," Lisa answers. "I hear they were dirt poor, living in a camper in someone's driveway."

"Ew, that's gross," someone else says.

"How does that marriage even work? Does she go home after school and make him dinner every night? Does he help her with her homework? She'll probably be pregnant before we graduate. She better not bring him and a baby to the prom."

"Have you seen him? He's totally hot."

"Yeah, if you're into pedophiles."

A round of laughter ensues as I slowly chew my peanut butter and jelly sandwich. My blood is boiling with anger, my heart pounding with rage.

"They're just jealous bitches." Megan glares at the table of idiots behind me.

I continue to chew, but I can't get myself to swallow. Peanut butter and jelly sandwiches are one of my food choices to eat again as part of my therapy, to get over a traumatizing event attached to it. I loved PB&J as a little girl. Especially with grape jelly on super-soft white bread. When I was around six or seven, I was eating it for lunch and Daddy was saying goodbye. For some reason, I felt scared and started to cry. Mommy kept screaming at me to just shut up and eat, and I swallowed too much. It lodged in my throat, and I gagged and cried hysterically until Daddy smacked me on the back and I coughed it up. Mommy made me eat it again, and I threw up and got sent to my room.

I'm surprised I'm still alive with all the things I've had stuck in my throat.

"Skylar, don't listen to their stupid shit," Megan says. "They're just spoiled assholes with no lives."

Nodding, I grab my napkin and discretely spit my food into it. I fold it up and put it on the corner of my tray.

"Are you okay?" she asks. "I'm getting worried about you."

"Yeah. I just don't feel too great."

She cocks her head at me. "You've been doing so good, Sky. Please don't let them get to you. This will all blow over soon when they find a new target."

Paige rambles on at the next table, making sure she talks loud enough for me to hear. "Guys, did you know his little sister is that girl who went missing years ago? She went to school here."

"I heard he was the last one to see her alive. He was a *suspect*. Since he's into kids I bet he did something to her. Like, raped and killed her."

"Her body is probably hidden somewhere right in this town."

"Ew. Hopefully he'll kill Skylar next and put her out of her pathetic existence," Paige says.

I pick up my lunch tray, dumping my drink and sandwich onto the table. Standing, I turn and face the table of five girls who are giggling wildly.

My jaw clenches as I pin my stare on Paige. "What did you just say?"

She looks up at me with her snarky smile. "I said I hope your pedo husband puts you out of your misery."

"You don't know anything about him. Or me. Why don't you just leave me alone?"

She rolls her eyes at me. "What fun would that be? Run along, Mrs. Lucketti. Maybe ask your husband to buy you some new clothes."

They all go into a fit of hysterics again.

Gripping the blue plastic tray in both hands, I haul back and slam it into Paige's face.

Everything that happens after that is a blur. There's horrified screaming and scrambling. Chairs are upturned on to the floor. And blood. I definitely saw blood pouring down Paige's face, staining the front of her white sweater. I stand rooted there, watching it all happen but feeling absolutely nothing, until I'm grabbed from behind and dragged out of the cafeteria.

"Suspended?" Jude repeats, pacing the sunroom with a cigarette hanging out of his mouth. My recap of the drama at school has him all worked up, because he *never* smokes in the house.

"It's only for three days," I reply. I don't consider it a punishment to miss three days of school. It'll be a relief to get away from all the whispers, rumors, and hate.

"I already talked to Rebecca," I add. "I'm going to work for those three days. I won't be sitting around the house."

He shoves his hand through his hair and blows smoke up at the ceiling. "Still, Skylar. You can't go around breaking people's noses."

"She deserved it," I protest. "It's not even her real nose."

I place the lottery ticket he gave me earlier on top of a book and start scratching it with a penny.

He tries to stifle a laugh and fails miserably. "Look, no more violent outbursts, okay? Her parents might try to go after you for assault."

"Jennifer Dilly has the whole thing on video, and she showed the principal. It clearly shows how everyone was teasing me and saying horrible things. She also has a video of when Paige pushed me down the stairs the other day. I could've broken my neck. It was basically self-defense."

I'm not even really friends with Jennifer. She's just one of those girls who's always taking selfies and making videos of everything going on around her like she's in her own reality show.

Jude abruptly stops pacing the room and levels a tense gaze at me. "That little bitch pushed you?"

"Yes. They also put a bunch of those *just married* streamers all over my locker. They won't leave me alone, and I'm sick of it."

His eyes flash dark with anger and I catch the clench of his inked fist. "Why didn't you tell me any of this?"

I shrug. "I was just trying to deal with it." That's a lie. I didn't tell him because all of it is so incredibly juvenile, and it would be like plastering the fact that I'm eighteen and in high school on a billboard right in front of him.

And because I don't want him to regret marrying me.

He sucks a long drag off his cigarette, then puts it out in one of the potted plants. "This shit better stop or I'll be going down to the school my-fucking-self to make it stop."

I have to admit, his protectiveness is attractive. But it'll only make things worse if he shows up at my school like an outraged parent. "Jude, you can't do that. You're not my father. Even the principal said these are *very unusual circumstances*."

I go back to scratching my lottery ticket while he continues to pace the room.

"Fuck that. I don't let anyone hurt the people I lo—*care* about."

"I appreciate that, but I have to deal with it myself. The principal said the other girls are being suspended, too."

"Principal Dalton?" he snorts out her name. "She's a joke. She'd have a stroke if I walked into her office."

"Well, it's not helping matters that apparently you were a bit of a hellion when you went to school there, and now I'm legally married to you. The association with you isn't doing me any favors."

I can't bring myself to tell him about the two-hour-long meeting I had with my guidance counselor and the principal where they voiced their concerns about me being married to an older man with a *concerning past,* and how they're worried about *predatory behavior* and *unhealthy relationships,* and how men take advantage of young, vulnerable women. It was all beyond uncomfortable and embarrassing, but I was honest with them about the situation with my parents and my old home life and my reasons for getting married. I assured them I was in therapy with a great team of doctors. I left out the part about Jude and me having sex, for obvious reasons.

I'm just doing my best to live a happy life and reach my goal—to get out of this town and live a life free of stress, heartache, and drama. I want a new start. Have I made some bad decisions? Probably. But don't we all? I'm a work in progress, and I'm not going to beat myself—or Jude—up over any of it.

I scratch off the last square of my ticket and stare at the little images. *Oh my God!* I jump out of my chair.

"I won a hundred dollars!" I wave the card in front of him excitedly. "That's the most I've ever won. I'll give you half. That was the deal."

"Keep it. You might need it for bail if you keep it up, killer," he teases.

"I promise I won't hit anyone again. She just pushed the wrong buttons today." The things those girls said about Jude were disgusting and unforgivable, and honestly, I don't regret making Paige eat my lunch tray. Maybe she'll think twice from now on before being a bitch.

Jude hooks his finger in the belt loop of my jeans and pulls me up against him, wrapping his arm around my waist. I kiss his cheek, and he hugs me closer.

"If this shit at school continues, you tell me, okay?"

I nod. "I will."

"I kinda miss you," he says in a low voice that sends a tingle straight through my thighs.

"You saw quite a bit of me last night."

He laughs. "Yeah, I did. And that was fucking amazing. But I've missed hanging out and watching TV with you at night. It's the best part of my day."

"Oh," I say, surprised. I didn't realize he looked forward to our time together as much as I do.

"Look, I don't want you to think it's just sex between us, okay? It's a lot more. I'm not good at talking about my feelings or being gushy. All this is new for me."

I swallow and blink at him. "Okay. Me too."

"I have to run out and do an estimate, but I'd like to spend time with you when I get home."

My stomach instantly flutters with anticipation that he might want our relationship to be *more*.

"I'd like that, too."

♥♡♥♥

I've just stepped out of the shower when the front door opens and closes downstairs. I glance at my phone screen, surprised to see it's only six thirty. Jude's only been gone for an hour, but his estimates usually take him at least two hours.

I slip into my red silk robe and go downstairs to make sure everything's okay, but it's not him making noise in the kitchen—it's a young woman who appears to be raiding the refrigerator. My anxiety kicks into high alert. Not just because there's a stranger in the house, but also because she's in the fridge touching the food. I don't know what she's touching, or what she touched before I got here. Her hands could be covered in germs.

Now I'm going to have to throw all the food away and start over.

Disturbed, I pull my robe tighter around me as I move quietly across the kitchen.

My heart thumps faster. She's totally unaware that I'm in the room. I glance toward the front door, then to the knife set on the counter. I left my phone upstairs, and the landline handset is in the living room. What if she's dangerous? I'm not sure what to do or say, but I have to do *something*.

"Excuse me?" I clear my throat. "Are you lost?"

She peers at me from around the open refrigerator door.

"Maybe."

What the hell?

She definitely appears lost and unkempt. Her shoulder-length, light-brown hair is flat in the back and rumpled on the sides, as if she just got out of bed. Her makeup is smudged around her bloodshot eyes. The jeans she's wearing have red stains on them, which could be blood or hopefully ketchup. Her windbreaker is ripped at the hem, the zipper broken.

I wonder if she's homeless and hungry.

I scan the kitchen in confusion, wondering how she got in the house. Jude always locks the doors when he leaves.

"I'm sorry," I say, fighting to keep my voice calm. "What are you doing here? Do you need something?"

"What are *you* doing here?" she retorts in an obnoxious tone that raises my defenses even more.

My brain spins and my stomach burns. Is she an ex-girlfriend of Jude's? Or—even worse—a current girlfriend? Could it be someone Paige sent here to screw with me? I wouldn't put it past her to pay someone to terrorize me.

"I live here," I say stoically.

"Where's Jude?" she asks, cracking open a soda and chugging it.

My stomach practically lurches into my throat. She knows Jude, and she's acting like she has every right to be in the middle of his kitchen making herself at home. She has to be someone from his past, even though I can't imagine Jude being with a woman who looks so disheveled. The principal's words about Jude's *concerning past* echo in my head. I know Jude has a sketchy history with drug use, drug dealing, rehab and women, but I don't know the details of all those things or how bad any of it was. All that matters to me is the person he is now.

But maybe his past has shown up for a visit.

I swallow over the fear creeping through me. "He's at work. Can you please tell me who you are? How did you get in here?" I demand.

"I have a key."

The hairs on my arms stand up, and I quickly decide I don't want to be near this girl. I've had enough psychodrama for one day.

"Look, this is really weird," I say. "You can't just come into someone's house. I have no idea who you are or what you want, but I think you're going to have to just leave. Please. If you leave me your info, I'll tell Jude you stopped by."

She stares at me with a bemused look, and pulls a plate of

sliced honey-roasted chicken out of the fridge. My limbs buzz and tingle with anxiety as she eats it with her fingers.

I walk around the island and snatch the plate away from her. This isn't store-bought chicken. I cooked it for Jude myself to eat for lunch while he's at work. This bitch has no right to come into his home and stick her hands in his food. Especially food *I* made for him. Even though I'm going to throw it away now that she's touched it, I still don't want her to have it.

"You can't eat this," I say. "And I'd like you to please leave."

She doesn't budge. Instead, she just stares at me with her lips curled into a snarky smile. "He'd want me to wait here for him."

"I don't think so." I toss the plate of chicken in the sink. "He's with me now." Anger and jealousy are really getting the best of me today, and I see a long talk with my therapist in my future. I'm really not the jealous, violent type. "*I* live here with him."

Laughing, she reaches into the sink and grabs another slice of chicken, then makes a show of chewing it in my face.

What is wrong with this chick?

"I don't think Jude likes insecure women," she says matter-of-factly. "No man does."

"Get out or I'm going to call the police."

She puts her hand up. "Relax, blondie. I'm his sister. I'm not after your man."

Oh my God.

I blink at her and search her face for familiar features. "Wait... you're Erin?" My voice doesn't hide my disbelief.

She narrows her eyes at me. "How do you know my name?"

My heart jumps at her admission, and I'm speechless for a few moments. "Jude talked to me about you. He told me you've been missing for years..." I don't want to say that she's basically been assumed dead. I have no idea what's happened to her or where she's been all this time.

She lets out a laugh that sounds a bit maniacal. "I guess that's one way of putting it. But *ta-da*, here I am."

Where did she come from? And where has she been? "A-are you alright?" I ask awkwardly. What do you say to someone who's been missing for years and then suddenly resurfaces in your kitchen?

"I'm great. I just need to see my brother." She continues to eat the chicken, and I let her now that I know she's not some crazy ex-girlfriend touching my man's meat.

Something about her seems very off to me, though. The way she's sniffling and rubbing her arms is strange, and her attitude gives me the impression she's hiding something. She doesn't seem scared or overly happy, but she could be sick or suffering severe mental or physical trauma. Even though her eyes slightly resemble Jude's, I have no proof she's really his sister. This woman could've seen the missing posters that are still plastered around town and is now pretending to be Erin Lucketti. She could have dyed her hair to look like her.

I edge toward the doorway. "I'm going to go get my phone and call him. I'll be right back." Unease settles like a rock in my gut as I go upstairs to the bathroom where I left my phone.

I never call Jude when he's working, but I don't think I have a choice this time.

"What's up?" he says when he answers.

I peek down the hall to make sure she hasn't followed me. "I think you need to come home. There's a girl in the kitchen who says she's your sister."

The line goes totally silent.

"Jude?"

"I'll be there in fifteen minutes." The excitement in his voice makes my heart squeeze. "Don't let her leave."

CHAPTER 33

JUDE

I tell my prospective clients I have a family emergency and bolt out of their house like my ass is on fire.

Now I'm on my third cigarette as I fight traffic to get home. My mind is so blown my hands are shaking.

Erin is home.

She's not dead.

My little sister is back.

She's home.

Suddenly, it's like a curtain lifts, and my brain is a tsunami of plans. Since Skylar's in Erin's room and the other bedroom is being used for storage, I can convert the den into a bedroom suite and turn the hall closet into a bathroom so Erin will have her own space. It shouldn't take me long to do that, and when Skylar moves out, I'll let Erin decide if she wants her old room back, or she can stay in the new room. Until then, I'll let her have my room and I'll sleep on the couch. This weekend I'll have Uncle Al and Aunt Suzy over for a family dinner, just like we used to have when we were kids. Maybe Skylar and Erin will become friends. It would be good for Skylar to have a new friend in her life with all the shit she's been going through. I think Skylar would be great for Erin, too.

Finally, *finally,* I'll be able to sleep at night without worrying about all the unknowns of what happened to Erin. I can stop having nightmares that my little sister is rotting in a ditch somewhere or being tortured. I can't remember what it's like to sleep through the entire night and not wake up feeling lost and sick with questions.

I want to call Skylar back and tell her to put my sister on the phone. I need to hear her voice to know she's really alive, but I don't want to do that over a damn cell phone.

Just a few more minutes and I'll be there.

When I pull up to my house, there's a beat-up van in the driveway with Florida plates.

Has she been in Florida all this time?

I park my truck crookedly in the driveway and rush into the house, blindly yelling my sister's name. I find her in the kitchen with Skylar.

"Erin!" I pull her into a bear hug, squeezing her tight against me. I meet Skylar's eyes over Erin's shoulder, and I can't understand why she's not smiling, why she looks so sullen. This is the happiest day of my fucking life, and the person I'm closest to looks like someone just died.

As I hug my sister, I realize she's stiff; her arms hang at her sides, her head turned away.

It's too soon. I acted on crazy impulse. It's been a long time, and I'm sure she's not ready for hugs yet.

I let her go, and she backs up a step. "I can't believe you're really here. I feel like I'm dreaming." I take a deep breath. There's so much I want to know I can't even get my head together. "Are you okay?" I scan her from head to toe, looking for signs of trauma or a clue as to what happened to her. "Are you hurt?"

"I'm fine," she says simply, like it's no big deal that she's been gone for years without a word or a trace.

Her voice sounds the same— exactly like it does in my memories. But as I stare at her, a chill runs down my spine.

In my mind, Erin has always been alive and grew up to be a gorgeous woman. An older replica of her teen self with long, shiny hair, big, bright eyes, a year-round tan, and a beautiful smile.

But the woman in front of me doesn't resemble the image in my head at all. Her hair is greasy and stringy. Acne scars riddle her pale face. Angry red veins spider through her dull eyes.

Whatever she's been through, it's wreaked havoc on her.

"Where's Mom?" she asks.

I rub my fingers through my short beard. "She doesn't live here anymore. She lives in Paris with her new husband."

Her head pulls back in shock. "Paris, *France*?"

"Yup."

She makes a surprised face. "But you stayed here?"

"Yeah. I wanted you to know where to find me in case someday you needed me."

Frowning, she shuffles her feet back and forth and looks past me.

"Do you want to go sit in the living room?" I ask her. "Are you hungry?"

"She ate a whole plate of chicken," Skylar interjects.

"No, thanks." Erin avoids making eye contact with me. "I'm okay in here."

I can't take my eyes off her. I'm waiting for her to snap out of this subdued mode she's in and smile at me. Or break down in tears. *Something*.

"Erin, you gotta tell me what happened. Did someone take you? I searched for you for *months*. Everyone thought you were dead."

She leans back against the counter and scratches her head. "No one took me, Jude. I left. I told you that when I texted you. You put yourself in this denial. Not me."

Skylar covers her mouth with her hand and pours herself into one of the kitchen chairs.

"*What?*" I repeat.

Erin chews on a jagged fingernail. "I left, okay? Are you dense? I just didn't want to deal with shit anymore. So I just left."

"What shit?"

"Mom being a bitch all the time. This fucking dead-end town. Jimmy had some deals set up in Ocala and he asked me to go with him, so I went."

"Jimmy who?"

"Jimmy Vantz."

Hearing his name is like swallowing acid. "Wait a minute… You left town with Jimmy Vantz? He was a fucking drug dealer." I should know. I was one of his biggest customers for a long time. I never made the connection between Erin's disappearance and him leaving town.

How could I have been so fucking blind?

"Yeah. We were together."

"For fuck's sake, Erin. You were *sixteen* when you disappeared. He's older than *me*."

Her eyes sweep over to Skylar then back at me, with one brow arched up. "So?"

I want to grab her and shake some kind of emotion out of her. This detached, uninterested, cold demeanor is nothing like the Erin I remember. If I didn't recognize the hue of her eyes and the little scar on her chin from when she fell off her bike at five years old, I wouldn't believe this was my sister.

"So, you're telling me you just up and left town with Jimmy

Vantz and never wanted to talk to your family again?" I ask in disbelief.

"Pretty much."

I feel like I've been punched in the gut. My heart and my head are throbbing trying to make sense of this, because I can't believe my sister just took off and didn't give a flying fuck about any of us.

"Why? We were close. Do you have any fucking idea how worried I was about you? How devastated Mom was? We thought you got kidnapped. Fuck—we thought you were dead."

"I sent you a text. I told you to stop looking. I saw you on the news and I just wanted you to forget it and move on."

"*Move on*?" I repeat, leaning down to make her look at me. "You're my sister. How do I move on when you just disappeared into thin air?"

"Everyone moves on, Jude. It's what people do."

I grind my teeth until my temples hurt. "Not me, Erin. I actually care about people."

Skylar's been silent, but her mouth curves into a small, empathetic smile.

Erin lets out a noisy sigh that she directs at her bangs, blowing them up off her face.

"I thought you'd be glad to see me," she says. "Not be all heavy and shit."

"Of course I'm glad to see you. I don't get why you left and I don't understand why it took you this friggin' long to come back. You couldn't have sent me a text once in a while to let me know you were okay?"

"I just wanted to forget everything, and not deal with all this guilt-trip shit like you're doing right now."

"It's not a guilt trip, Erin. You don't just up and disappear when you're sixteen years old and let your family—hell, the entire town—go crazy worrying about you and looking for you."

"Sorry." Completely unfazed, she pulls out the cigarette that's been tucked behind her ear. "Can I smoke in here?"

"No," I say. "Where the hell have you been all this time?"

"Just hanging out with Jimmy in Florida. I worked as a waitress for a while. Jimmy went to prison for a few years, but we stuck together through it."

I wait for her to say more, but she doesn't. "That's it?" I finally say.

I can't believe I've been agonizing over her for years, and she's been serving burgers in Florida while living with a drug dealer.

I can't accept that. There's gotta be more. In my mind, there was a kidnapping. Duct tape over her mouth. Hands tied. Screaming and tears. Lying awake, crying at night, missing her family. Begging to go home.

"Erin, talk to me. Did something else happen? Did someone hurt you? Did he threaten you? You can tell me anything—you know that, right? That hasn't changed."

Her pale eyes lift to meet mine, and that's when I finally see the truth. The root of so many evils in my own life, and I'm damn sure hers, too.

She's high.

"Are you using, Erin?"

"Using what?" she asks with the attitude and annoyance of a teenager caught doing something they shouldn't be doing.

"Don't play games with me." I grab her arm and shove her sleeve up. My heart sinks like a boulder when I see the track marks.

Disappointment, fear, and that twisted tick of need course through my veins like venom. "Fuck, Erin. What are you doing to yourself?" I drop her arm like it just grew teeth, and she tugs her sleeve back down.

"Don't act high and mighty, Jude. I remember what you were

like back then. You partied constantly. How the hell do you think I met Jimmy?"

It's a hit I wasn't expecting, but it's deserved. She's right. Jimmy and I used to hang out in the basement, getting high and making deals. A few times, Erin wandered down there—even though I told her a hundred times to stay upstairs. Jimmy would tease and joke with her to make her giggle, and I thought he was just being cool to my little sister, not trying to pick her up.

My blood boils in my veins, and my heart feels like it's going to explode with rage and regret.

This is my fault, and it tops the list of shit I hate about myself.

"He's a fucking scumbag," I say.

"Show me a man who isn't."

"Right in front of you," Skylar pipes up. "Your brother's not a scumbag. Do you have any idea how much he cares about you?"

Erin whips around to face her. "Mind your own business, bitch. Who the hell are you, anyway?"

"Hey," I growl. "Don't talk to her like that."

"I don't need some basic bitch up in my face."

"I'm gonna go upstairs," Skylar says, standing. "Welcome home, Erin. I'd say it's nice to meet you, but I'm not a liar."

I watch Skylar leave the room, wishing I could go to her, but I've got bigger problems to deal with.

"Is she the best you can do, Jude?" Erin taunts when Skylar's gone.

"Actually, she's the best I've ever had, but we're not talking about her. I want to know what made you suddenly show up tonight. I'm gonna guess you ain't here for the holidays."

"I need some money, and a place to crash for a few days."

"Money for what?" I ask, even though I already know the answer.

"Just to get on my feet. Jimmy ran into some shit in Florida, so we got out of there."

I narrow my eyes at her. "What kind of shit?"

"A deal went bad, and he owes someone some money. You know how it goes."

Unfortunately, I do, and I don't want any part of it. My life is good now and I'm not going to let anyone fuck it up. Not even my little sister.

My next words come out of me like broken glass ripping through me and shredding my soul apart. "You can't stay here."

Surprise and resentment pass over her face. "This is my home, too."

"No." I shake my head, closing my eyes, so I don't have to see her face. "Not anymore. It's *my* home and I can't let a user stay here. I'm clean, and I'm staying that way."

"Come the fuck on, Jude. Don't be a dick." She glares at me with cold, hard eyes. "You wanted me to come home."

"I did. Always. But not like this." I hold my hand out. "I'm gonna need your house key back."

"Are you kidding me?"

"No. Give it to me."

She makes a noise and spit flies out of her mouth as she wrenches the key out of her pocket and throws it at me. "You're a fucking asshole. You said you stayed in this shithole so I'd know where to find you, in case I needed you. Well, I need you."

"Then let me help you. I'll take you to rehab. I'll pay for it. We'll get you clean, and *then* you can live here as long as you want. Look how nice this place is now. We'll find you a job, or you can go to college. Whatever you want."

"I'm not going to rehab, Jude. As long as I just do a little bit, I'm fine. I just need some money."

I've said those exact same words. For a long time I believed them—until I woke up half-dead in an alley.

"You're not fine, and I'm not giving you money to feed your habit."

She paces around the island, pulling at her hair. "I can't believe you're being like this. You think you're better than me? You're not. You're just like everyone else."

"I love you, kiddo, but I can't play this game with you. Been there, done that. If you want real help, then you've got it. A thousand percent."

She sets her eyes on me like a wild animal. "Just give me some cash, then, and we'll get the hell out of here."

"We?" I repeat. "Who the hell is *we*?"

"Jimmy's out in the van."

A disgusted laugh erupts out of me. "I should've guessed. I want that fucker off my property. Now."

Tears pool in her eyes, and I feel trapped in an impossible situation. This is a nightmare I never could've seen coming. I'd do anything for her. I've been down on my knees praying for her to be okay and to come home, but I never expected her to come back asking me for drug money, and I never expected her to look at me like she doesn't give one shit about me.

I pull my wallet out of my back pocket and take out two hundred-dollar bills. I toss it on the island between us.

"You can take that. Get a motel."

She snatches it up fast and shoves it down the front of her shirt, under her bra.

"Erin," I say softly, hoping it gets through to her. "Let me help you. I know how hard it is. I've fuckin' been there. Ditch that douchebag and let me help you get clean. You can start over. It's not too late."

As she shakes her head back and forth, she smiles weakly at me, and I catch a glimmer of the girl I remember—the one who still lives on in my memories. The one who had hopes and dreams and spent hours at the mall buying clothes. The one who used to wait up for me to come home, so she could tell me all about her day.

"I can't do that, Jude," she admits with the slightest tone of regret. "I can't leave Jimmy. We stick together. No matter what."

Defeated, I ask, "So what are you going to do?"

"I'm gonna take this and get a cheap motel, meet with Jimmy's hookup for a fix, and then we're going to Maine. Jimmy's got some friends there."

"Yeah," I bark out. "I bet he does."

We stare at each other for a few seconds, not saying a word. What is there to say? I can't believe this is where we are. I feel overwhelmingly powerless and guilty as all fuck. This entire situation is the product of my bad choices, and I'll never forgive myself for being the one who inadvertently put these wheels in motion.

I thought I had cleaned up my mess when I got my shit together. I had no idea it had spread to my sister.

All I want to do is go out to my driveway, haul Jimmy Vantz out of that ratty van and kill him with my bare fucking hands. I want to strangle him until his eyes pop out of his ugly head. But as tempting as that is, I've got Skylar to think about. *My Sparkle.* I can't—I won't—risk ending up in jail for assaulting or murdering a junkie and leave her by herself.

"Thanks for the cash," Erin says. "Sorry this wasn't the reunion you were hoping for."

The knife twists deeper into my heart.

"I don't want things to be like this," I say.

"Just go back to thinking I'm dead, Jude. We'll both be better off."

She doesn't hug me goodbye. She just leaves without so much as a glance back at me.

I sink into one of the chairs, completely fucked in the head.

CHAPTER 34

SKYLAR

Holy shit.

My heart is breaking for Jude.

From my bedroom window, I watched his sister leave. She stopped in front of the garage on her way to the driveway and peeked into the windows like she was casing the place. Then she climbed into the van, and I could see her and a guy, illuminated behind the windshield when she lit up a cigarette. Her hands waved frantically as she was, no doubt, giving the guy a recap about what just went down.

I'm proud of Jude for standing his ground. Turning Erin away had to be the hardest thing he's ever done. After all this time, she showed up alive and well (high, but well). Only she didn't come back to resume her life and integrate into her family. She came back to use him.

He has to be devastated.

A few moments ago, his bedroom door slammed so hard the walls shook and Gus ran, tail puffed out three times its size, to hide under my bed.

Worried, I sit on the floor and coax Gus into my lap. When she curls up on me, I pet her long, gray fur until she forgets about the big, bad noise and purrs with contentment. The house feels eerily empty and quiet, as if I'm the only one here, and the man down the hall is now nothing more than a ghost, void of breath and a soul.

I wait for an hour, but then I can't take the silence anymore. I pick up my phone and send him a text.

Me: Are you okay?

Fifteen minutes tick by before the three little dots show up on my screen.

Jude: No. I'm not.

My heart cracks.

Me: Can I come see you?

Earlier, before he left for his job estimate, he said he missed me and wanted to see me. Maybe he still does, and we can talk about all this and try to find some sort of closure for him.

Jude: Only if you want to end up on the receiving end of my rage.

I think I can deal with that.

I go down the hall to his room, hesitating for a second at his closed door, and then open it without knocking. I find him sitting on the edge of his bed in the dark with nothing but his jeans on and a bottle of whiskey in his hand.

Oh, shit.

From what I've put together, Jude's not an alcoholic. He used to drink a lot, but his real problem was with drugs. Now he'll occasionally have a beer when he's chilling out, but I've never seen him drink hard liquor.

Silently, I cross the room and kneel between his legs. He looks wrecked—his eyes are puffy and his face is blotchy, and his hair looks like he's run anguished hands through it a hundred times.

"What are you doing here?" he asks, slurring his words. "I'm in a really fucking bad mood."

I lay my hands gently on his knees. "I promised for better or for worse, remember?"

He scowls and tips the bottle against his lips. "That's all bullshit."

"It's not," I say softly. "I think we both know that."

"I don't know shit."

"I'm sorry about Erin. I know how much you love her."

He takes another gulp of whiskey and wipes the back of his hand across his mouth. "I don't love anyone."

My heart constricts. "You don't mean that."

He throws me a nasty look that chills my bones. "Yeah, I really fucking do mean it. You have no idea. I'm done with this bullshit. I'm sick of being treated like dirt and thrown away like trash. Fuck. It."

"I *do* have an idea. I know exactly what it feels like. For once I'd like to be the one worth staying for and not the one that's easy to leave and forget about."

"A-fucking-men." He raises his bottle to me. "I'll drink to that."

Shaking my head, I grab the bottle away from him and put it on his nightstand.

"I think you've had enough to drink."

"I think you're being a fuckin' bad wife."

Our little joke isn't funny when he says it with such anger and hatred dripping from his voice.

I let out a slow sigh. "Jude… tonight had to be really hard for you. Do you want to talk about it?"

He runs both his hands through his hair to clutch the back of his head. "No. I don't wanna talk about her. Ever." His eyes close for a long moment as he takes a few deep breathes. "I'm either gonna get drunk off my ass or have my brains fucked out. Give me the bottle back, or strip."

So, this is how it's going to be—self-destruction mode flipped on. Walls up and locked into place.

I'm not deterred.

Leaning back on my heels, I untie the sash of my robe then slowly let it slip down my arms and off my bare body. He watches the red silk pool on the floor beneath me, then drags his gaze up to my face.

"What the fuck are you doing?"

"Getting ready to fuck your brains out."

He sucks in a harsh breath. "We did that already," he says roughly.

"Oh?" I ask, determined to do whatever it takes to show him I'm here for him, no matter what. "Was it a one-time thing, then?"

Not taking his eyes from mine, he picks up the whiskey and takes another defiant swig. "Yup. This shit ain't happening between us, Sparkles. I've fucked up enough."

I snatch the bottle out of his hand again and put it back on the nightstand.

"We're doing this, not *that*." I cast my eyes over at the liquor.

"Don't mess with me, Skylar. You're not gonna like it if I put my hands on you like this."

I reach up and touch his cheek, running my finger over the dark stubble. He stares at me through half-closed, dark eyes.

"Try me," I whisper.

Without wavering, I hold his gaze. Whatever he needs right now—I'll do it. I'll *be* it. He's been my rock since the day we met—never wanting or expecting a thing in return. He's not drowning his feelings in the bottom of a bottle on my watch.

Suddenly, his hand flies up and grabs the back of my neck, pulling me hard to meet his lips. He kisses me ferociously, his tongue carrying the bite of whiskey. He palms my breast, twisting, pinching, and tugging my nipple between his fingers until I cry out.

He pulls his mouth from mine. "Touch yourself." His voice is low and raspy, and my clit quivers in response, like a dog to a whistle. "I want to watch you finger your sweet little cunt."

It takes me a beat to recover from the scintillating rush of heat that ripples from my breasts to my thighs. His voice is sinfully sexy, and I hold my breath, wanting to hear more.

Still kneeling before him, I arch my back and shift my hips in a slow, seductive, sway.

"Say please," I say, dead serious, holding on to my half of the control.

A wicked grin tips his lips as he reaches for the bottle once more, but I grab his hand and bring it to my lips, sucking his middle finger between my teeth, ignoring my germ and gag fears with every bit of control I can summon.

"Please," he drawls.

His gray eyes flash with lust when I slide my hand between my parted thighs and finger my wet slit.

My body pulses with desire—incredibly turned on by the darkness in his eyes and the mix of raw emotion emanating from him like heat from a blazing fire.

His chest heaves up and down with deep, even breaths as he watches me, shifting his gaze from my mouth to my hand pleasuring myself.

I swirl my tongue around his finger and his upper lip curls erotically. My stomach shudders with anticipation. I'm surprised that the excitement of turning him on far outweighs my anxiety over having things in my mouth. Every hitch of his breath and spark of desire in his eyes fuels my newfound feeling of power and confidence. It's addicting and intoxicating—just like him.

He pulls his finger from my mouth with a wet popping sound, and slowly trails it down between my breasts, past my belly button, and down between my legs. Moving my hand to the side, he pushes his wet finger deep inside me, pumping it in and out from tip to knuckle.

Grinding into his hand, I lean forward to kiss him, but he pulls away and rises from the bed, towering over me until he grabs my shoulders and pulls me up. He kisses the top of my head, then moves down to cover my ear with his mouth.

"I want you on the bed," he whispers. "I'm going to fuck you until I can't remember a goddamn thing."

Electric tingles race down my spine as I climb onto the bed then turn to watch him step out of his jeans. My thighs clench at the sight of his cock jutting from his inked-up body like a steel pipe.

Sauntering to the edge of the bed, he wraps his fingers around my ankle, and lifts my leg up high to rest my foot on his shoulder. Staring down at me, he lavishes kisses up and down my calf, then reaches down to grasp my other ankle, flipping me over, legs spread, in a mind-boggling, lightning-quick motion.

"I don't want you looking at me." The anguish and self-hatred in his voice and in his eyes rip my heart in two.

Turning on my side, I reach for him, wanting to kiss all the hurt away. "Lucky—"

"Do it or get the fuck out."

With a quiet nod, I flip back over onto my stomach, and he grabs my hips, pulling me up onto all fours and yanking me back to meet him at the edge of the bed. His hands grip my waist and he drives into me hard, fast, and unforgiving. Moaning his name, I clutch the comforter in my hands, head down, as he slams into me, his balls slapping against my wet pussy with each pounding descent. I've never had sex from behind, and it's painfully primal but so intensely erotic. I don't know if I should be ashamed or proud of myself for enjoying the raw, animalistic sensuality of it.

And him.

Breathing heavily, fingers digging into my flesh, relentlessly ramming into me, releasing all his pent-up anger, sadness, and guilt into every powerful thrust.

Is it toxic? Maybe it is. But that's all right. This is what he needs.

What *I* need, too.

Connecting with someone doesn't always have to be pretty and beautiful. It can be raw and ugly and infected with need. I want all of him—the good and the bad.

Driving into me, he skims his hands up my ribcage to my small breasts. His rough palms graze against my taut nipples, heightening my pleasure. When I arch my back, pushing to meet his thrusts, my walls clench around him again and again as wave after wave of orgasm rolls through me. As I'm reeling from the last of the lingering shudders, I cry out when he suddenly pulls his cock out and pushes me flat down, covering my entire body with his. The length of his stiff shaft wedges between my ass cheeks and spurts hot cum onto my lower back. He bows his head down into my neck and kisses my shoulder blade, biting my flesh and panting heavily, whispering words like *wet* and *tight* and *so fuckin' perfect*. A shiver of ecstasy cascades down my spine. He stays there for a long time, with his sweaty chest pressed against my back, and I revel in being entirely enveloped by him, trapped in his powerful embrace.

When our breathing calms, he lifts himself up and kneels

behind me, between my thighs. I inhale a sharp breath when his hands come down at the base of my spine and slowly rub his cum into my skin like a lascivious massage. Flutters stir deep in my stomach and radiate down to my pussy and thighs. I feel completely owned by the possessive sensuality of it.

I lie there, utterly still, until he flops next to me on his back with his arm thrown over his eyes. My mind and body feel like an explosion of jelly and I want to curl up into his warmth while the pieces of us fall back into place.

"You deserve better." His rough, soft-spoken words startle me in the dark, dead silence that's been swelling between us.

"Jude, I—"

He puts his hand up. "You should go now."

His words are sobering. My heart feels heavy in my chest, as if it might sever itself, fall away, and die.

"Jude…"

"Please," he says in a desperate, gravelly whisper. "Just go."

That's the last thing I want to do. I want to stay here with him. Show him I'm here for him, that he doesn't have to be alone, and not everyone leaves.

But that wouldn't be true, because someday, this charade will be over, and I, too, will also leave.

Blinking back hot tears, I pull on my robe, and silently walk away, hoping he'll call me back with each step I take.

He doesn't.

I take the near-empty bottle of whiskey with me, and dump it down the drain before going to bed, feeling very sticky, very sore, very confused, and very much like I left a big piece of my mangled heart in that room with him.

CHAPTER 35
SKYLAR

I'm glad I don't have to go to school today because I'm mentally and physically exhausted from last night. Jude must be, too, but I heard his truck pull out of the driveway at five a.m., half an hour earlier than he usually leaves.

He didn't peek in to say goodbye, which he always does.

He forgot to fill Cassie's bowl.

And I didn't get to make him a yummy chicken sandwich for his lunch to remind him that someone cares about him.

Routine is something I thrive on, and these little ripples upset me.

Jude is a pillar of stability for me, and I want life to calm down for both of us so things can be good again.

I'm due at the boutique at eleven a.m., so I have time to shower, feed the pets, and throw away any food that Erin's dirty fingers may have touched. Later, I'll stop at the grocery store and buy new groceries.

As I'm getting dressed, I send Megan a text:

Me: Have you ever had angry sex?

Megan: You've got my attention. Go on. 🤩

Me: Have you?

Megan: Maybe once or twice but it was lame. Why?

Me: I was just curious.

Megan: Lies. I know you, Sky. Did you and hubby have a fight?

Me: It's a long story, but we didn't have a fight. He was super pissed about something else.

I'm not going to tell Megan the details about Jude's personal life. At least not over text message.

Megan: And?

Me: And we had some wild sex. 😍

Megan: I'm here for these details.

Me: Is it bad if I enjoyed it? Like, I know I probably shouldn't because he was so pissed off and I offered myself up as sort of an outlet, but it was pretty hot.

Megan: I am very jealous and not at all ashamed to admit it.

Me: 😂

Megan: Erik is way too nice to have angry sex. He's all gentle and polite.

Me: That's nice, too. I wouldn't want my cervix rammed every day.

Megan: You lucky bitch. And no, it's not bad if you enjoyed it. Passion is passion. Some couples live for make-up sex.

I laugh and shake my head at the screen.

Me: I have to leave for work but I'll tell you more when I see you. How are things at school? Am I going to be stepping into a battleground when I come back?

Megan: I miss having you here. Everyone is gossiping, of course. Some are saying you punched Paige, someone said you were fucking her dad, some are saying you're a queen for giving that bitch what she deserves.

My stomach churns with anxiety. I don't want any more drama in my life, I just want it all to stop.

Me: Great 😢

Megan: Don't worry, I'm setting the record straight. I got your back.

Me: Thank you. I'll try to call you later.

Megan: Okay. Love ya.

Me: xo

"Good morning, naughty girl," Rebecca says when I arrive at the boutique. My heart jumps into my throat, and my brain scrambles to figure out how she knows I got rammed doggy style last night and then submitted to a cum massage by my angry, drunk, fake husband. "Even though it'll be nice having you here a few extra hours this week, let's try not to get suspended again, okay?"

I gulp in relief. "Agreed."

Smiling, she tosses a package at me. "This came for you this morning."

I hold the light-gray, padded envelope and look at it with curiosity. "For me?"

"Yup."

I take it to the break room and cut it open. There's a pretty card laying on top of something wrapped in purple tissue paper.

Dear Skylar,

We are very impressed with your photographs and captions for Belonging's Boutique. We have followed your personal account, @thatvettegirl, and we love your outlook and style. We would be honored if you'd accept this blouse, and if you love it, you can share photos of it with your followers and give them the special discount code below. You will receive 10% from each sale. If this is something you are interested in, we would love to work with you more in the future and increase your percentage.

There is no obligation if you are not interested in being an influencer, or if our products are not of interest to you, but please keep the blouse as a gift from us. We are a small, woman-owned company, and we appreciate young, fresh, and innovative women like yourself.

Keep up the amazing work - we see great things in your future!

Best wishes,

MaryAnn Rockport

CEO of BlueHueToo Fashions

• • •

Oh. My. God.

An influencer opportunity! I don't even have the coveted ten thousand followers yet! I run to Rebecca to show her the gorgeous white peasant blouse and the note.

"Wow!" she says. "This is amazing. I'm so proud of you!"

"Is it okay if I do it? On my personal profile?"

"Of course! Why wouldn't it be? I love seeing you succeed."

"I just don't want to create a conflict of interest."

She smiles warmly at me. "I'm totally fine with it. Who knows where this could lead for you? I think it's wonderful."

My mouth hurts from smiling so much. "Thank you."

"The blouse is to die for," she says, touching the soft material. "I'm going to be the first to buy one using your code."

I start to mentally plan my day—deciding which products I want to take photos of. The holiday items are starting to roll in, and Rebecca wants to run some sales since people will be buying gifts. I ordered rolls of fake snow, and I hope they make the pictures look cool and wintery and not like a tacky mess.

Out of habit, I reach into my back pocket for my phone, but it's not there.

Frowning, I grab my purse to see if I threw it in there. I want to send a quick text to Jude before I start taking photos, just to let him know he's on my mind.

I can't help wondering if he's been thinking about me today like I've been thinking about him.

After dumping the entire contents of my purse onto the floor, I realize I must have left it at home when I was texting with Megan.

"Crap," I mutter. I'm going to have to drive all the way back home to get it, then come back here.

Frustrated with myself, I tell Rebecca I'll be back and make the drive home. As I drive across town, my mood takes a dive. Not only do I not have my favorite playlist because it's on my phone, but I really miss my car. It might sound strange, but driving my Corvette always put me in a good mood and made me feel free. The car was a reminder of all the talks my grandfather and I had—like when he told me life will get better as long as I never give up hope. The car was symbolic of my life—a bit of a mess now, but with the potential to be beautiful with some patience, love, and care.

Someday, I *will* get my 'vette back from Jude.

When I get to the house, I realize I must've been more distracted than I thought I was this morning. Not only did I forget my phone, but the front door isn't shut all the way.

Worried, I run through the first floor like a lunatic, terrified that Cassie or Gus wandered outside and got lost, but I find them sitting in the sunroom together. I don't remember closing the door to this room when I left earlier, but I seem to be suffering some major scatterbrain moments today—probably because I keep thinking about Jude and how incredibly hot the sex was last night. If only it wasn't shrouded by his devastation over his sister and his attempt to drown himself in whiskey.

Relieved the pets are safe and sound, I give them each a kiss, then head upstairs. As soon as I walk into my room, I stop short and blink several times. My brain has been thrown into that confusing, surreal state of not quite processing what my eyes are seeing.

My room is completely trashed.

The closet is open—one of the doors hanging off the hinges—and my clothes and hangers are strewn all over the floor.

The dresser drawers are open, the contents dumped out in a big heap.

My nightstand is toppled on its side with the little drawer pulled out.

My heart leaps up into my throat as I whirl around, trying to take a mental inventory of my belongings and recalling what was where.

The little teddy bears are gone.

My laptop is gone.

My little cup of cash is gone.

Even my stack of losing lottery tickets that I've been saving just because Jude gave them to me is missing.

My small collection of jewelry—including my wedding band—is *gone*.

With my heart thundering and tears springing up in my eyes, I run down the hall to Jude's room to find the same exact mess.

Oh shit. Oh shit. Oh shit.

Someone broke in and robbed us!

As I stand in the middle of his room, overwhelmed with a wave of panic, the sound of breaking glass coming from the garage tears me out of the panic-induced haze.

I bolt downstairs, grabbing my cell phone from where I must've left it on the kitchen island, and then blast out the back door. I run toward the garage and push open the side door that's ajar—without even thinking about who I might encounter inside.

I gasp as a hooded figure comes around the side of the Corvette wielding a hammer and smashes it down on my beloved car's windshield.

"No!" I scream in horror.

The person turns to me, still holding the hammer above their head, ready to strike again.

My blood goes totally cold when our eyes connect.

"Erin?" I say in disbelief. "What the hell are you doing?"

"What the fuck does it look like, bitch? You think you can just move into my house? Into my room? And turn my brother against me? Fuck both of you!"

She brings the hammer down on the windshield again, and the glass cracks into a spider web.

I rush at her and grab her arm. "Stop it!" I scream. "Are you crazy?"

She stares at me with wild eyes, and that's all the answer I need. She *is* crazy. We wrestle for the hammer, both of our hands grasping the handle, screaming horrible obscenities at each other. Finally, I wrench the hammer from her grasp, and she falls back into one of Jude's metal tool chests. As she grapples to get up, my gaze lands on two pillowcases near the door. One from my bed, the other from Jude's—both stuffed with what I'm sure are our belongings. I run for the pillowcases with Erin on my heels, screaming at me like a rabid animal. I grasp the thin material of Jude's pillowcase, and it's heavier than I thought it would be. Erin catches me by my hair and whips me backward. Yelping in pain, I clutch Jude's things like my life depends on it and wrench my hair from her grip. Rolling onto my back, I kick my feet into her legs and gut just as she's about to spring on top of me.

"You fucking little bitch," she shrieks, clutching her stomach. "I'll kill you!"

Scrambling to my feet, I push my hair out of my face and try to catch my breath.

"Just get out of here!" I yell, not realizing she's picked up the hammer I dropped, and before I can duck, she smacks me in the head with it. Stunned, I fall into the fender of my car, and everything goes dark.

CHAPTER 36

SKYLAR

Thank God for nosey neighbors.

One of them heard the ruckus of me and Erin fighting and called the police. They found me lying on the garage floor bleeding from a blunt-force head wound, still clutching the pillowcase full of Jude's stuff.

I have no regrets. There was no way I was letting Erin take anything from Jude.

I had my first ambulance ride, my first stitches, my first concussion, and now I'm lying on a hospital gurney—with a headache bigger than Texas—waiting to be discharged.

What the hell is happening to my life?

I'm not sure how much time passes, but the next thing I know, Jude is barreling into the exam room.

He looks huge and primal in the tiny, sterile room, with his thick blue-and-black flannel shirt, dusty jeans, and heavy work boots. His hair is tied back, and he's got at least four days' worth of stubble. Despite my trauma, butterflies stir in my stomach as I recall how that stubble felt chafing against my thighs.

My heart literally aches when he stands next to the bed

staring down at me with tears in his eyes, and his hands clasped under his chin.

"I'm so fuckin' sorry," he says, slowly shaking his head.

"It's not your fault."

Choking up, he rubs his eyes with his palm, then pulls the guest chair close to the bed and sits. He takes my hand, holds it so tight in his it hurts, and presses it against his lips.

"It's fucking killing me to see you like this."

"I'm fine," I assure him with a weak smile. "It's just a mild concussion and a few stitches. They're discharging me soon."

"*Twenty* stitches." He reaches out and runs his finger lightly along my temple, right above the gash. "Every time I look at you, I'm going to be reminded that *I* did this to you." He pulls his hand away, and his jaw muscles twitch with anguish and anger that I can actually *feel* raging inside him.

A bolt of fear zaps through me, making my head throb even more. What if he can't stand to see me again, now that the two-inch scar on my face is going to be a constant reminder of his messed-up sister who completely screwed his head up?

Closing my eyes against the pain, I say, "Lucky, it's not your fault. Your sister did this because she's pissed off. I don't think her intention was to attack me. She wasn't expecting me to come home. I think she just wanted stuff to sell and she messed up the car to make some kind of a statement."

"I never thought she'd do something this fucking crazy. I already called a security company. New locks and surveillance cameras are going in fucking tomorrow."

I nod because that will actually make me feel a lot better. "I saved your stuff." I force myself to sound optimistic. "I think she took off with my things, though. My laptop, my wedding ring… she smashed my car." Thinking about the special things she stole from me and the image of my car windows bashed in makes me nauseated with despair. I furiously try to fight back the tears burning in my eyes, but they slip through and track down my cheek. I quickly wipe them away.

"Did the police get her?" I ask.

"No," he says gruffly. "I'm going to take care of it."

Fear prickles up my spine. "What does that mean?"

"It means I'm going to take care of it. I'm not going to let them get away with this. This has Jimmy written all over it. I don't even care if it was my sister doing the dirty work—she crossed a fucking line. You'll have your stuff back, and I'm gonna fix your car."

"Jude—"

He cuts me off. "Can Megan give you a ride home and stay with you tonight?"

I narrow my eyes at him as goosebumps sprinkle over my arms. "I'm sure she will. Why?"

"Give me your cell phone."

"What?" The throbbing in my head ramps up.

He lays his cell phone on the bed next to me. "You take mine so you'll have one, and give me yours for the night."

Nervously, I hand him my phone, which miraculously stayed in my pocket throughout the entire attack. "But why?"

"I'm gonna use it to track your laptop. Then I'm gonna find those motherfuckers and get your things back."

Oh, no.

No. No. No.

"Jude, please, just let it go. They're hopped up on drugs and dangerous. I don't care what they took. None of it is worth you getting hurt." If something happened to him, I'd be devastated. I can't even think about it.

"Yeah?" He stands. "You think *they're* dangerous? Well, so am I, and I'm not letting this fucking go. That scumbag took off with my sister when she was only sixteen years old. He took her from her family and turned her into a goddamn junkie, and I know he put her up to this shit today. It ends tonight. That fucker is gonna get everything he deserves."

The venom dripping from his voice and the intense rage blazing in his eyes is terrifying. It's hard for me to believe this is the same man who holds my hand, cuddles our pets, and brings me lottery tickets every night just to see me smile.

Though his face is hard, he leans down and presses his warm lips gently to my cheek. "I'm gonna make things right," he whispers. Straightening, he gives my hand a squeeze before he lets go. "You rest, and I'll see you when I get home."

I hold his gaze, wracked with fear that he's going to get hurt. *Or worse.* "Promise me you'll come home?"

He puts his hand over his heart. "Cross my heart."

"Look, Skylar, we need to burn some sage or something when we get you home. You got some bad mojo going on lately," Megan says when she arrives at the hospital to drive me home.

"You might be right." I sit on the edge of the gurney, feeling dizzy as we wait for an attendant to come with a wheelchair to take me downstairs for discharge. I can't wait to get home and put clean clothes on. The sticky blood on my shirt is making me feel sick to my stomach.

She grimaces as she studies my head. "She hit you with a *hammer*? What the ever-loving-hell?"

"She's obviously fucked up and probably high on something. Who knows?"

"I may as well tell you now, Jude texted me earlier. I met him outside the school, and he gave me his house key so I could go to the house and clean up your room for you."

"Oh my God, he did?"

She nods. "He didn't want you to feel traumatized when you

got home, and he didn't want you to have to clean up the mess. I did my best to put everything away for you. I straightened his room a little too, but I didn't go through his stuff."

I reach my arms out to her, and we hug. "Thank you for doing that," I say softly with my face buried in her silky hair. "You're the bestest."

"All this drama's gotta stop," she says, pulling away. "But, I *will* say this. I was feeling suspect about Jude at first, but he's a good guy. That dude loves you."

My head snaps up and a flash of pain stabs through my forehead like an ice pick. "What? Why would you say that?"

She arches her brows. "Hello? Are you blind? The guy is fierce over you… his eyes and voice totally change when he talks about you. It's crazy intense."

"You've got it wrong. Jude's not the love type. We're basically friends with bennies. It's all we both want. It works." Even as I say the words, I'm not so sure they're true anymore.

"You're both stupid and in denial."

We don't talk much on the way home, and I appreciate Megan's rare moment of quiet and calm driving. My head hurts. I'm stunned by everything that's happened. I'm heartbroken about my car and losing my personal possessions. I'm worried about what Jude's doing right now.

And I can't stop thinking about what Megan said—about Jude loving me. I know he cares about me, and he's obviously attracted to me, but *love*?

I doubt it.

To be honest, the more I think about love, the more it scares and confuses me. Sometimes I have these moments where I think, *oh my God, I might be falling in love with him and I might actually like it,* and I feel all happy inside. But then a huge wave of fear swallows that feeling up almost immediately.

Falling in love means I could get my heart shattered. Because, seriously, what are the chances of Jude falling in love with me and us actually staying together? Slim to none. He's thirty-four, and he's never had a serious relationship. I'm eighteen, and I haven't had one either. I'd rather stay friends forever than risk letting the L-word turn us into a mess. The road to falling in love can really only go one of two ways—toward forever or toward never speaking again. Both are terrifying.

"It feels weird going inside," I say to Megan as she unlocks the front door for us.

"How do you mean?"

"It's scary to find a stranger in your home. *Twice.*"

"I can't even imagine. I'm sure it won't happen again."

"I hope not. Jude says he's going to change all the locks and put in a security system."

Once we're in the foyer, I make sure the front door is locked behind us as Cassie and Gus come running down the hall to greet us. We both kneel down to pet them.

"I'm so glad that bitch didn't do anything to hurt Cassie or Gus," I say. "She had them both locked in the sunroom."

"Very true," she agrees. "I'm starving. Can we eat?"

My sore brain has a hard time following Megan's usual abrupt switches in conversation. "Um, sure. Of course."

She follows me into the kitchen, which thankfully, Erin didn't trash. "You can help yourself to whatever you want," I say.

She opens the refrigerator. "Aren't you hungry? I'll make us both something."

"I can't eat anything from in there."

She frowns at me. "Why? There's a lot of food in here."

"Because Erin was in there yesterday touching all of it."

"Okayyyyyy… everything is in containers, though. I don't

think she came in here, opened everything, and licked all your food."

That's true. I threw away the chicken Erin touched, but I don't know what else she could've had her hands on, and it's throwing up my triggers.

"I know, but I just can't."

She blinks at me. "Well, we have to eat."

"You can, I'm not hungry. I just want to go change."

"Sky, you have to eat. There must be something that's sealed and not opened yet in here." She rummages around in the fridge and pulls out a carton of eggs and a package of cheese.

"I can make us omelets," she announces triumphantly.

I almost gag. "Too squishy. I can't eat eggs like that."

"Okurrrr," she jokes, moving on to open the cabinets. "You are super high maintenance, girl. How about this?" She pulls out a box. "Instant mashed potatoes, never opened?"

"I eat that sometimes. I could have that, I guess."

"Good. I'm going to make an omelet for me, and potatoes for you." She studies my face, her smile slowly fading away. "Are you okay? Do you want me to come upstairs with you while you change? Then we'll eat?"

My voice catches in my throat, so I nod, relieved that I don't have to actually *say* I'm afraid to go up to my room alone.

Smiling sympathetically, she hooks her arm in mine. "Let's go do that. We'll put comfy clothes on, I'll make us dinner, and we'll chill out and watch a chick flick. We haven't had a sleepover in years!"

I think we were thirteen years old the last time I slept over at her house. It seems like a lifetime ago.

Upstairs, Megan gently cleans the blood off my face and out of my hair.

"That's a gnarly gash," she says, staring at it. "Do you think you'll need plastic surgery for the scar?"

"I'm not sure. The doctor said it was possible. I'll have to see how bad it is once it heals."

"Once the stitches are out, put vitamin E oil on it. I read that helps scarring."

I may opt for plastic surgery if I have a noticeable scar. I don't want to go through the rest of my life telling curious people that some girl hit me in the head with a hammer.

We eat dinner, then curl up on my bed together to watch movies. Megan texts with Erik almost nonstop. I don't mind though, because it's nice to see her so happy and smitten. I can't stop myself from glancing at Jude's phone to see if he's used mine to send me a text, but there's nothing. My brain is spinning with worry about him and conjuring up visions of every worst possible scenario. All I care about is that he comes home safe.

"So, he just gave you his phone, unlocked?" Megan asks when she catches me looking at.

I nod. "Yes. He has mine, too."

"And why aren't you snooping the hell out of it right now?"

"Why would I do that?"

She leans over me to look at the screen. "To see if he's talking to other women."

"That's none of my business."

"You're his *wife*. And you've been hooking up. You totally have the right."

I hold the phone in my hand, slightly tempted to look. Of course, I'm curious—who wouldn't be?

"No." I quickly put the phone down beside me before I change my mind. "I don't want to be that kind of person. It's an invasion of his privacy."

"Oh my God, Skylar. What planet are you from? Do you want me to look through it for you?"

I slap her hand away as she reaches for the phone. "Megan! No. It's wrong."

"I look at Erik's phone every time he goes to the bathroom. I know his passcode."

"Why? If you don't trust him why are you with him?" I don't ever want to be that way with a man.

"I trust him. I just want to see if other bitches are messaging him."

"Are they?"

She shrugs. "Just his mom."

I roll my eyes. "You're ridiculous. I'm pretty sure Jude isn't seeing anyone or having any booty calls. He's home every night." Since I moved in, Jude has never *not* come home at night. He never smells like perfume. He's never left the house looking like he's heading out for a date. I never catch him texting or leaving the room to have a private conversation on his phone. Everything about him screams *single*.

There was that lipstick stain on his face that one time, though.

"Hmm," Megan says, quirking her mouth to the side. "His phone could be riddled with porn, then. Maybe he jacks off every night."

"It's still none of my business what he does with his own hands and his dick. I have a vibrator, and I wouldn't want him creeping on me."

She looks surprised. "You do? Which one do you have?"

A knock on my bedroom door wakes me into a lurch of panic, and it takes me a few seconds to remember where I am. My brain is foggy and disoriented, my head still throbbing. I grab Megan, who's asleep next to me in my bed.

"What's happening?" she asks drowsily.

The knock sounds again.

"Skylar? It's me," Jude says through the door.

"He's home," I whisper. Relief floods through me but my heart is still pounding against my ribcage.

"Well, let him in, silly," Megan says.

I climb out of bed, and a quick wave of dizziness almost makes me fall back. Steadying myself, I carefully cross the room and unlock the door.

"Thank God," I say, choking on a sob and resisting the need to throw my arms around him and never let go. "I've been so worried about you. Why didn't you call or text me? I've been freaking out thinking something horrible happened. Like you were dead. Or in jail." I swallow hard. "I was afraid I'd never see you again."

"Didn't I promise you I'd come home?" His voice is deeper than usual, and it makes my insides vibrate.

I sniffle and my lower lip trembles. "Yeah, but I was still going crazy worrying."

He drops the pillowcase he's holding and pulls me into his arms. I press my cheek against his chest and he palms the back of my head. "Shhh..." he whispers, rubbing my back with his other hand. "I'm here. There's nothing to worry about anymore." I hug him tighter, clasping my hands behind his back. He smells of sweat and cigarettes, and his heart is pounding against my cheek. I close my eyes and let him blanket me in all his masculine heat. I feel safe and protected. *Finally*.

When we part, he hands me the ragged pillowcase of my things, and my phone. That's when I notice the knuckles of his right hand are cut open and bleeding.

Grabbing his hand, I ask in a hushed voice, "What happened?"

"I beat the living fuck out of Jimmy Vantz, that's what happened."

I stare up into his eyes in the dark hallway. "What about

Erin? You didn't hurt her, did you?" As crazy as Erin might be, she's still his sister and I wouldn't want him to hurt her over what she did to me. She's *family*, and I'm… I don't even know what I am to him.

"Of course I didn't hurt her. But she'll be too busy taking care of that brain-dead asshole to ever come back here."

I gulp, unsure if he's exaggerating or telling the truth. "You shouldn't have done this—just to get my stuff back. It wasn't worth it."

"Yeah," he says. "It was. Nobody gets away with hurting you, Skylar. *No one.* Not even me."

"What does that mean?" Has he hurt me? Does he think he might?

"Exactly what I said." He reaches out and cups the side of my head in his palm, and I think *oh wow, he's going to kiss me right here in front of Megan,* but he doesn't kiss me. Instead, he runs his thumb gently across my temple.

"Does it hurt?" His eyes, illuminated by the glow of the television in my room, are smoldering with a kaleidoscope of emotions.

Suddenly, I wish Megan weren't here.

I wish things were different, so I could fall asleep in his arms, in his bed, and feel safe here again. The feeling of security and safety I've always felt in this house has been rattled, and that's just as horrible as what Erin did to my car and to my face.

"It hurts a little."

He pulls me to him and touches his lips right over my stitches. I wince from the pain, but I don't care because I want every single kiss from him. The sweet ones, the angry ones, and even the ones that hurt.

"Maybe that'll make it better," he says all soft and sexy.

"It does," I say.

"Hey, Jude, you can sleep with us if you're afraid to be alone, too," Megan teases from the background, ruining the moment.

Jude grins and snickers. "Don't flirt with married men, Megan," he says, not taking his eyes from mine.

"Good answer!" she replies. "Unexpected and disappointing, but perfect."

"You're a good husband," I whisper.

He winks at me, then walks down the hall and disappears behind his closed door. I ache to follow him. He's been injured today, too—deep in his soul—and I wish I could kiss it better.

CHAPTER 37

JUDE

I've never dated.

This realization comes to me as I'm sitting in the sunroom with Gus purring on my lap, listening to Skylar talk to Megan on the phone in the living room.

"I'm fine, really. I've just been resting. Yes. It's so sweet you guys are doing that together. No, I've never eaten there. You know I don't like restaurants. You have to tell me all about it tomorrow."

I've never taken a woman out to eat, or to the movies. I've never vacationed with someone. My version of dating has consisted of drive-through dinners, hanging out in bars, motels or at her place, having sex, and then making a quick exit.

I'm not sure Skylar has ever had any real dates, either.

Suddenly, this is all bothering me.

A lot.

She took a hammer to the head trying to save my stuff. I've fucked her rough and raw; slow and sweet. I've laid awake at night thinking about her, worrying about her, wanting her, and missing her.

I've slowly fallen for her smile. *My favorite curve.*

Somehow, she's squirmed her way under my skin, and surprisingly enough, I don't want to dig her out.

I'm feeling like we should do something date-ish. Something to show her I'm not with her just to sit on the couch, watch movies, and have sex when one of us is fucked up.

I want—no, I *need*—to make her happy and show her that she's special to me and I want to be more than friends. She deserves that.

Dinner would be too much pressure for her, and a movie feels a little too cliché for us. I pet the cat, spinning date ideas in my head that I think she'll like *and* that I can pull off quickly.

When she's off the phone, I go to the living room, carrying Gus with me. She's lying on the couch, holding her phone above her face as she scrolls the screen.

"What are you doing tonight?" I ask her.

Her brows knit together as she stares at me, and my eyes are immediately drawn to the slash on her forehead. My stomach twists into an instant knot of anger and guilt.

"Why are you holding the cat?"

I pull my gaze away from the zig-zagged cut and look down at the cat, which I'm holding like a baby. "She was sitting on me and I wanted to get up." I shrug. "So, I just brought her with me."

She smiles. "Okayyyy..."

"Do you have plans?" I repeat.

"Tonight?"

"Yeah."

"Well, it's Friday night and my best friend is attached at the lip to her boyfriend, so... the answer is no."

"Good."

"Why is that good?"

"I want to take you out."

She sits up and pulls the throw blanket over her shoulders. "Out?" She eyes me suspiciously.

"Yeah, like a sort of date thing," I say awkwardly.

"Date thing?" she repeats. "I can't do—"

"It's not dinner," I interrupt, knowing exactly what she was going to say.

"Oh." She smiles crookedly. "Okay then."

"Someday, we *will* go out to dinner, though. Just not tonight."

She moves her wavy hair out of her face and looks at me with a puzzled expression.

"Did something happen?" she asks. "You're acting weird. Why are you still holding the cat?"

I put the cat on the couch next to her. "Everything's great. I just thought it'd be nice to go out of the house together."

Her smile grows. "What should I wear?"

"Something warm and comfortable," I say.

"And funky?"

I grin at her. "Of course."

"What time is this out-of-the house date thing happening?"

I didn't know having a date would come with so many questions. I feel like I need a nap.

"How's eight o'clock?"

"That works." She looks around the room. "Should we just meet out in the foyer, then? Or are you going to go outside and then knock on the door?"

"Cute," I say, walking away. "See ya at eight."

"Where are we going?" she asks when I come down the stairs. She's waiting in the foyer with her eyes all bright and animated.

Somehow, she managed to pick the perfect outfit. Dark,

skinny jeans, boots with faux-fur cuffs, a gray puffy coat with matching faux-fur hood, and a tight black sweater that hugs all her curves. She doesn't wear makeup often, but tonight her eyes are dusted with silver, glittery shadow and lined with black liner that make her eyes look crazy sexy.

"You look great." I lean down and kiss her, lingering on her lips, tempted to carry her upstairs. I fight it and stick to my date plan. "You ready to go?"

"You didn't tell me where we're going."

"You'll find out when we get in the truck."

I hold her hand as we leave the house and, continuing my date-ish theme, I open the passenger side door for her. When I get behind the wheel, I hand her a folded piece of paper.

"What's this?" she asks. "Instructions?"

I laugh. "Addresses of all the local houses that have cool holiday light displays."

Her mouth gapes open as she unfolds the paper. "Oh my God, is that what we're doing? Going to look at Christmas lights?"

"Yeah… unless you're not into it. If you're not, we can do something else. We could go to a movie."

"Are you kidding? I'm totally in to it."

Finally, I'm doing something right.

I tune the radio to a classic holiday music station and head toward the first house on the route of ten homes I mapped out from a list I found online.

With each house display we visit, Skylar gets more and more excited, claiming each one as better than the last. I'm too busy looking at her smile to even notice the lights. I haven't seen her this happy since before the attack.

I've missed her smile and her spark.

What Erin did to her changed her. She's been quieter,

withdrawn, more OCD, cautious. She suffered way more than just a nasty cut on her head.

Every time I look at her, I'm reminded of what happened, and I fucking hate myself because it's my fault. Maybe in some sick way the scar is meant to never let me forget all the shitty decisions I've made. I just wish it was in the middle of *my* forehead and not hers.

"We should put up a ton of lights on your house next year," she says as we drive past a house that has cool glowing icicles and lights bouncing across the yard. "You have that cool fir tree on the front lawn, we could put a big star on it, and lots of lights. And you could outline the house and windows like the other houses we saw. Maybe we could get the Santa with the sleigh and the reindeer and put it on the roof, and get one of those waving snowmen to put on the front porch."

As she babbles on, I reach across the console to hold her hand. Her happiness is contagious. Her hope is infectious.

Through her, I see *us*.

I see tomorrows and next years.

And I like it.

There was never supposed to be a next *anything*.

It's like our temporary arrangement has turned into a runaway train and we can either hang on for the ride, or jump off.

She grips my hand and bounces it up and down on her thigh, totally oblivious that I'm sitting next to her completely enamored with her smile, her eyes, her voice, the way she weaves her fingers through mine, her giggle—fuck, her *every*thing.

"This was the best date, Lucky." She leans across the front seat and plants a big kiss on my cheek. "You have no idea how much I've always loved to look at holiday lights. When I was little my grandparents used to drive me around on Christmas Eve and my gram would tell me if I looked out the car window, I might see Santa flying around. If I saw the lights of a plane fly over, I totally thought it was Santa and his reindeer." She glances over at me, her lips quirked in a shy smile. "Does that sound silly?"

I smile back at her, drawn to everything honest and innocent about her. "Not at all, babe."

"I miss them," she says, craning her head to look at the sky from the car window.

"I'm sure they're watching over you."

She smiles up at the dark sky. "I hope so."

"Can I take you to one of my favorite places?" I ask.

She nods happily. "I don't want to go home yet."

It's almost midnight by the time we get to the cliffs, and the temperature has dropped. I pull the truck off the desolate, mountain road and onto the dirt pathway that you wouldn't even know was there unless someone pointed it out. I've been here so many times I could find it with my eyes closed.

We zip up our coats and I dig a pair of my extra work gloves out of the console for her to wear. Her small hands are lost in them but I insist she keep them on so her fingers don't freeze.

"Wow, look at all the stars. It's gorgeous," she says after we step out of the truck in the small clearing that parts the woods. The sky is the perfect shade of royal blue-black, pebbled with millions of shining stars. There're no streetlights or houses nearby, but the moon is bright enough to give us enough light to see each other.

She lets out a little laugh when I lift her and perch her on the hood of my truck and then hop up next to her, hoping the heat of the engine will keep us warm enough to enjoy the view for a few minutes.

"This is so beautiful," she says dreamily, looking out over the downtown lights beneath us. "I had no idea this was even here."

"I've been coming here since I was about fourteen. The view

is cool during the day, too, but on a night like tonight, the stars are wild. And now, with all the holiday lights up, it's even better."

I watch her as she stares out over the cliff—her breath blowing out in frosty puffs, the lights reflecting in her eyes. She looks so beautiful that it hurts me to breathe. I don't deserve something as special and good as her. I know this, and she probably does, too. But, like with anything else that's beautiful and rare, I can't resist getting closer. Taking what I can while I can.

"Look," I whisper, brushing my lips across her silky hair and pointing to the right, where a stag and a doe have quietly stepped out of the woods just a few feet away. Like us, they stare out over the cliff for a few moments.

"So pretty..." she breathes as the deer walk across the clearing and disappear in the thick trees on the other side.

We huddle together, enjoying the view and the quiet stillness, waiting for the cold to force us to go back in the truck.

"What made you want to do this tonight?" she asks softly.

I reach for her hand, because it's always easier for me to talk when we're touching. I take a deep breath, and decide to tell her the whole truth. "I wanted you to know I *want* to be with you and I'm not just spending time with you because we're conveniently in the same house. And I wanted to share my favorite place with you."

"This is the place on your back, isn't it? Your tattoo?"

I nod, impressed she recognized it. "Yeah, it is. This place is like my zen. It always calms me."

"I can see why. So many wishes waiting to happen."

"What do you mean?"

"Any one of those stars could shoot at any second, and then you can wish on it."

That does it. I'm totally crazy about her.

"This is where I came up with the idea of marrying you. I

rode my bike up here and sat right there with my legs hanging over the edge."

Her lips press together as her gaze settles on the spot I pointed to. "Really? I can't believe you actually thought about me."

"I think about you a lot. Non-stop since our wedding kiss, if you wanna know the truth."

My admission puts her into a few moments of silence. "Do you regret it?" she finally asks. "Marrying me?"

Taking a deep breath, I weigh my answer. "I only regret the things that happened to you because of me. But I don't regret helping you."

"What about the other parts? Us being more than friends?"

I push my hair out of my eyes. "In some ways, I do."

Her gloved hand tenses in mine, and she tries to pull away. I don't let her. "Wait, don't do that," I say. "Let me finish. The only thing I regret is that I don't know how to treat you better. I don't know how to do… *this*. I've sucked you right into my dysfunction. You're only eighteen, you—"

She interrupts me, whipping her hair over her shoulder. "Jude, don't bring my age into this, please. We're so past that."

I sigh and soften my voice. "I just don't want to be the reason you get hurt any more than you already have. And I don't want to be the reason you make bad decisions."

She studies my face and shakes her head slowly "What happened with Erin isn't your fault. Not how she turned out, and not what she did when she came back."

"Actually, it is. I never should've been bringing drug dealers to my house—where my mother and my little sister lived. Erin never would've met Jimmy—"

"You don't know that, Jude. Maybe she would've met someone worse. Maybe she would've run away all on her own. She made her own decisions. I wanted to run away at sixteen, too. The only thing that stopped me was Gus. As crazy as it sounds, I couldn't bear the thought of hauling her around in a cat cage, making her live in strange places. Otherwise, I would've disappeared, too."

"You had a way worse life than her, Skylar," I say. "Erin was just a brat who didn't want to deal with her curfew. But she met Jimmy because of me. He's the one who got her into drugs and every-fucking-thing else."

"You have to stop blaming yourself. Who got *you* into drugs? Sometimes it's just in people's genes to turn to drugs and alcohol. I think she would've gone down that path whether she met Jimmy or not."

That might be true. There was no one person or incident that made me start to do drugs, it just happened.

"I dunno," I say sadly. "The whole thing's got my head fucked up. For years, all I did was think about her and miss her. I agonized over what happened to her. All I wanted was for her to come back. To find out she just left, and never even thought twice about maybe sending me a fucking text message to put my mind at ease, is doing my head in. She said she saw me on the news, she knew how fucking wrecked I was, and she just *let* me be that way. That fuckin' hurts."

"She was young and messed up," Skylar says softly. "Teenagers are selfish, Jude. I can admit that. We have our moments where we just don't care about anything but ourselves. I was a little bit like that when I was younger."

"Maybe that's what I'm afraid of. Not just that I might hurt you, but that *you* might hurt *me*. I'm sick of being forgotten and tossed aside. So fucking disposable."

She turns sharply to look at me. "So am I. I could *never* do that to you. You're so important to me, in so many different ways. I—" She sucks in a breath. "I can't picture my life without you. I don't want to. I know our marriage isn't real, but sometimes I wish maybe…"

She doesn't say the words. She lets the ghost of them hang between us to haunt us. And haunt me, they do.

I've had those wishes too and have snuffed them out fast because of her age.

But ever since Erin hurt her and I saw her lying in that hospital bed, my feelings for her have shifted. Friendship no longer feels like enough. A side of casual sex no longer feels like enough. I want the real deal with her.

It just scares the hell out of me.

"Neither one of us know how to be in a relationship, Skylar. We're both fucked up with abandonment issues. And the age thing *does* matter. It'll be a disaster."

Good move, Lucky. Talk her right out of wanting you.

"Or maybe it won't be." Her voice is laced with hope. "Maybe we're perfect for each other."

Her body trembles next to mine, and I'm not sure if it's because she's nervous for saying what she said, or if she's freezing.

"It's getting cold," I say abruptly, jumping off the hood. "Let's go back in the truck." Grabbing her waist, I lift her to the ground and pull her faux-fur-lined hood up over her head. I hold on to it and stare down into her eyes. Her cheeks are pink from the frigid air and the moon is shimmering off her glittery eye shadow.

She looks magical and beautiful and she's looking at me like she's making a thousand wishes and every single one of them includes me.

Her hope completely shatters me.

I'm so tired of putting walls up.

"Do you really believe that?" I say, moving my hands to cup her cheeks. "That we might be perfect for each other?"

A slow smile spreads across her face. "Yes," she whispers. "I do."

Her voice—her words—chase the chill from my veins.

"Do you think... maybe we should try to find out?"

"Lucky," she says softly, winding her arms around my neck. "Wasn't that the whole point of this date thing tonight?"

When we get home, we turn off all the lights and walk upstairs together, pausing every other step to kiss. We stop in front of her bedroom door and I unzip her coat, sliding it easily off her shoulders. She does the same with my leather jacket, then fixes her big eyes on mine. A sweet, yet slightly curious smile dances on her lips.

"I loved tonight," she says, leaning back against the wall just outside her door.

I hook my finger through the belt loop of her jeans. "I did, too. Next time you can pick what we do."

She unbuttons my shirt to the middle of my chest, and slowly walks two fingers—playfully but sensually—up to my shoulder. "When is next time?"

Pulling her to me by her belt loop, I lean my forehead against hers. "How's tomorrow night?" I whisper, closing my eyes and inhaling her. She smells of winter air and jasmine, and I want to drag her to the nearest bed and rip her clothes off.

I won't though.

I want her to know I can be happy with going slow.

With knowing there will be more days and nights together.

"Tomorrow is good," she says on a soft breath, and tilts her face up.

"Tomorrow is perfect."

"Maybe we can cook dinner together, light some candles and eat in the sunroom, in front of all the windows."

I stroke her hair and kiss her. "That sounds great. Maybe you have a cool skirt in that closet of yours?"

She smiles. "As a matter of fact, I do. Maybe you could wear that black sweater I like?"

"I can do that."

"I like how it makes your shoulders look so huge."

"You got a shoulder fetish?" I tease.

"I think I have a *you* fetish."

She makes my heart pound with how much she truly wants *me.*

I cover her mouth with mine, kissing her with a slow, burning hunger. And damn, her lips taste delicious with the flavor of hope, and the possibility of next year on them.

CHAPTER 38

JUDE

"You're coming for Christmas dinner, right?"

I hold the phone to my ear with my shoulder as I spread out the blueprints for this new residential job I'm right in the middle of.

"I don't know, Aunt Suze... I was thinking of staying home this year."

I spend Christmas with my aunt and uncle every year, but I've been mulling around the idea of staying home and spending it with Skylar.

The past few weeks have been up and down. While things have been great between me and Skylar, I'm still trying to wrap my head around everything that happened with my sister, and Skylar's been having a hard time mentally. She hasn't admitted it, but I see it. She walks around the house locking the doors, then checks them every few hours to make sure they're *still* locked. She's terrified to go in the garage, but that's actually working in my favor now because I've been working on a secret project in there.

She sees her therapist twice a week now, and I found out

she's upped her anxiety and depression meds. Lately she's been nibbling on bread again, which is a step back because she was doing great eating new foods and going to restaurants to eat things out of her comfort zone.

"It's Christmas, Lucky. A time for cheer! I'm sad about Erin, too. I cried myself to sleep every night for days after you told me what happened. But we have to keep going. Life is for living."

"I'm not feeling cheery."

"You will once you get here. I let you off the hook for not coming on Thanksgiving, but you have to come for Christmas. I'll make all your favorite things. And we have presents for you."

"I'm too old for presents," I grumble.

"You're never too old for presents. You're bringing Skylar, right? We have presents for her, too."

I walk across the demo'd second level and stare out the window. "I really don't know, I'll have to ask her. She might have plans of her own."

Actually, I'm pretty sure she doesn't have any plans. Other than me and Megan, who does she have? Does she spend her holidays with Megan and her family? I'd say probably not. If I had my guess, I'd say she sits home with Gus in fuzzy pajamas watching Christmas movies.

And now, with that visual stuck in my head, all I want to do is exactly that with her.

Pots bang on the other end of the phone. "She's your wife. Uncle Al and I would like her to come."

"I'll ask her tonight."

"Promise me you'll both come."

"I'll think about it," I say, knowing damn well I'll be there.

"This could be my last Christmas. I'm old, you know."

"Stop it. You are *not* dying. You've been pulling that since I was seventeen years old."

"Well, I'm definitely getting closer."

"Aren't we all?"

"Come by during the week and help your uncle drag the tree upstairs. You can tell me what Skylar likes to eat then. Oh, and I'd like an air fryer, and a parakeet for gifts."

I run the back of my hand across my forehead. "Please tell me you're not planning to air fry the parakeet."

"Of course not. I've always wanted one—they sing and chirp. I want a pale-blue one. Not green."

"Anything else?"

"No, just my favorite nephew and his beautiful wife. And a parakeet. And the air fryer. That's all," she says cheerfully.

"Okay," I say, too exhausted to argue with a determined seventy-something-year-old. She always wins.

After we hang up, I decide to go to the boutique to surprise Skylar with lunch. On Fridays she goes to school 'til eleven, then works the rest of the day, so the timing is perfect.

I tell the guys I'm heading out for a break and stop at the deli on my way to the boutique to get Skylar a cup of vegetable and white bean soup—perfect. Nothing too squishy, chewy, or chokey.

Her eyes light up with surprise when she sees me walk into the store, and I finally get a glimpse of that beautiful smile I've been missing all day.

"Lucky," she says, beaming. "What are you doing here?"

I put the small, white bag on the counter between us. "I brought you soup."

She takes the bag and gives me a teasing side-eye. "You want cookies, don't you? Is this a trade?"

Laughing, I shake my head. "Nope. I just wanted to see you. I heard you coughing this morning, and I thought, if you're getting a cold, soup is good."

"That's so sweet. Thank you." Her smile just about makes my

heart stop. "You can take some cookies," she adds. "I mean, since you're here."

I lean my elbows on the counter. "What are you doing on Christmas Day?"

Her eyebrows knit together. I try not to look at the pink scar on her forehead because it throws me into an instant inner rage when I do.

"Um… I don't know. I haven't really thought about it." She pushes her hair back. "Usually I'm just home."

I was right. She stays home with the cat.

Not that I'm any better. Every year after I have dinner with Aunt Suzy and Uncle Al, I go home and hang out with my dog.

"Aunt Suzy and Uncle Al want you to come for Christmas dinner. With me."

Her mouth opens, then closes, then opens again. She opens the bag and pulls out the small container of soup and plastic spoon. "Wow. That's really nice. Do *you* want me to go?"

"Yeah. I want you to come with me."

Her top teeth edge into her lower lip, as if she's trying to bite back a smile, but it slowly wins, tipping her mouth up. Big, bright-blue eyes steal a glance at me as she stirs the soup.

"Then I'd love to go," she says.

"I can't pass up the chance to see what kind of crazy Christmas sweater you're gonna wear."

"Oh, you mean like the one with Rudolph where the nose lights up?"

I let out a laugh. "Nothing would be better."

"I'll see what I can do."

No lie, this will be the first holiday I've ever spent with a woman.

Another first.

I used to enjoy being alone until Skylar came along. Now every minute that's spent without her feels lonely, like something is missing. But, my old friend *distrust* still comes to visit once in a while.

I was eighteen once. And when I was, I dated eighteen-year-old girls. They want to have fun. They want to date around. They change their minds every other day. And when they hit twenty-one, they want to party, go to bars and clubs, flirt with men. And hell yeah, I'm worried about giving my heart to someone who hasn't had a chance to really figure out who or what she wants yet. What am I supposed to do if Skylar wakes up one day and decides she doesn't want to be with an older, average-looking construction worker who doesn't want kids?

Life just had to fuck with me by throwing the perfect girl in my life and then twisting the knife by making her only eighteen years old.

Thanks for the ass fucking, karma.

"I better get back to work," I say. "I'll see ya at home."

"Thanks for the soup. I'm glad you surprised me."

Checking around the store to make sure no one's lingering nearby, I lean closer to her and brush my lips across hers. When I pull back, she grabs the collar of my shirt and tugs me back for another one. Groaning, I cup the back of her head and kiss her deeper.

"Skylar, I—" Rebecca stops short at the doorway at the other end of the room and eyes us suspiciously.

Skylar quickly pulls away from me and coughs. "Thanks for bringing me lunch," she says loudly.

"See ya later." I nod a bye at Rebecca, pick up a bag of cookies, and make a quick exit.

"Jude! Wait!"

I turn to face Rebecca, who's followed me out to the sidewalk.

"What's up?" I ask, biting into a cookie.

"Don't *what's up* me. What did I just see in there?"

I shrug. "I dunno, Rebecca. Your eyes aren't in my head."

Her lips press together into a thin line. "Don't be a dick. What the hell are you doing?"

"Going back to work. Maybe you should do the same."

She crosses her arms. "I warned her not to get too close to you. I don't trust you, Jude."

"You don't even know me, Rebecca. We're not in high school anymore."

"But *she* is. She's eighteen."

"I'm aware." *Way too aware.*

"And you think that's okay? It's ludicrous enough for a man your age to conjure up this ridiculous marriage idea with a teenager, but now you're getting physical with her? What the hell is wrong with you?"

"Nothing's wrong with me. What's wrong with *you*? Mind your own business."

"No, I won't. I care about her. She's way too young to be involved with you. She's very vulnerable."

"I care about her, too. We're friends. I just brought her soup because she needs to eat something besides bread."

I fucking hate lying to people. All it does is create a trail of messes that eventually, I'll have to clean up.

"I saw you kiss her. That's not something you do with friends. You need to take a big step back, Jude. She's just a kid. She's had a crappy life. Ever since she met you, it's been one crisis after the next. Your sister attacked her with a hammer for God's sake! She could've died! She's being bullied constantly at school. She got suspended—and she's a straight A student! You even took her car."

My gut is twisting into a knot with all the truths she's throwing at me. All these things have been gnawing at me, and I've been trying to shove them out of my mind, because the temptation to quiet all the demons with drugs and alcohol is always just one bad decision away.

I don't want to go there.

And I don't want to face the fact that I might be bad for Skylar.

I grind my jaw. "You don't know what you're talking about."

"Do the right thing." She jabs her finger into my chest. "If you're better than you were when we were kids, you wouldn't be crossing these lines. She's going to get hurt, and we both know it. She's a sweet girl with a hell of a lot of talent. Keep your distance, let this 'deal' run its course, but get back in the lane you belong in."

"Then do the fucking same. You're not her mother. She's an adult, and she's not stupid. She's capable of making decisions."

"*Someone* has to look out for her. She has no one to give her sound advice. *No one*."

I can feel Skylar's eyes on us as we argue on the sidewalk.

"I'd protect her with my fucking life."

"Well, you're not doing such a great job at that, are you?" she accuses.

"Fuck you. What happened to her was an accident. I had no idea my sister was even alive."

"You have sleazy connections, Jude. You always have. They follow you like rats."

"Not anymore."

She raises her brows questioningly. "I know all about falling in love with the wrong guy. Getting caught up in someone sexy and intriguing and totally losing yourself and any sense of right or wrong."

I stare her down. "Don't make this about you because you married an asshole."

"It's not about me. But I know a toxic relationship when I see one. She's a teenager. Let her be one. She should be out dating boys, going to movies, doing teenage-girl stuff, not shacking up in a house with an adult man living some farce of a marriage. It's disgusting and belittling to the real marriage she *will* have someday. I see the way she looks at you, Jude. You've got this magnetic thing about you and she's all caught up in it. She's going to get her heart broken and she'll never get over you. Do you want to be the one who helped her, or the one who destroyed her for all future relationships? Is that really what you want for her?"

If anything has ever made me feel like a low-life piece of scum, it's this verbal lashing right here.

"No," I reply. "I don't want that."

"I have a niece a few months younger than Skylar. I can't even imagine a guy your age trying to fuck her. I'd be in jail for his murder. If you don't get your act together, I might contact the school and talk to her guidance counselor."

"Hey," I say, stepping closer to her. "I'm not *fucking* her. I care about her."

"What if you had a daughter her age? Or a sister? How would you feel if she was in this arrangement?"

I think about my sister at sixteen, running off to Florida with Jimmy Vantz—a man old enough to be her father—and getting her life all sorts of fucked up.

"It would make me sick," I admit.

"Then keep your hands and your mouth off her. She's never even been in love. You're not playing on equal ground, and you're taking advantage of her innocence and her need to feel loved. It's *sick*. Do the right thing." She turns and stalks back toward the boutique. "And stop eating my cookies," she throws over her shoulder before opening the door.

I don't look through the window to see if Skylar's watching me. I can't bear the thought of looking into her eyes right now.

I'm afraid she's going to see the man Rebecca sees.

CHAPTER 39

SKYLAR

I spritz on perfume—something in a pretty glass bottle called *Design* that has a light, sweet scent that Jude loves, then slip into a light-pink, off-the-shoulder sweater that reaches the top of my thighs. Bending over, I pull on a pair of gray thigh-high socks and slouch them a bit. Under the sweater, I have on a pair of champagne-colored lace bikini panties, and no bra. One good thing about having small, perky boobs is not having to wear a bra all the time.

Especially when I want to look sexy.

My hope is that this little outfit will cheer Jude up. For the past few days, he's been distant and quiet. Out of nowhere, he's almost done a complete U-turn. One day things were amazing—lots of kissing, cuddling, and date nights, then suddenly he's either working late, or out in the garage, or going to bed early claiming his back hurts.

He's declined my numerous offers to give him a back massage.

Earlier, instead of greeting him at the front door like I usually do when he comes home, I waited in my room with the door closed to see if he'd come looking for me.

When he didn't, my worry started to morph into a panic attack consisting of racing thoughts, heart palpitations, sweaty palms, and that awful feeling like I have a blob in my throat.

Not wanting to waste the entire night curled up in a ball succumbing to worrying about things that I don't even know are valid, I took a hot shower. After that I sat in my favorite thick terry-cloth robe and patted Gus. Her little purrs always have a calming effect on me.

I heard his shower as I was blow-drying my hair, and thought he'd be knocking on my door any minute to ask me to make dinner with him, which has become a new thing for us.

But that was forty minutes ago.

Frustrated, I walk down to his room. His door is open a few inches, and I can see him sitting on the floor, leaning back against his bed.

"Jude?" I say. "Can I come in?"

It feels weird asking for permission to enter his room, but his stand-offish-ness isn't exactly welcoming.

He motions with his hand for me to come in, and his eyes languidly travel from my socked feet up to the bare skin of my thighs.

"What's up?" he asks, diverting his attention to his phone.

My heart plunges down into my stomach at his lack of reaction.

"I just wanted to say hi."

He throws me a quick glance and a grin. "Hi."

I clasp my hands nervously in front of me, feeling awkward and not at all sexy as I imagined in my head. Gus snakes around my feet, shedding fur onto my socks, and then jumps on the bed to get cozy.

Am I being ghosted? Dumped? Friend-zoned?

"How was your day?" I ask.

"Long."

I wish he'd tell me about annoying or crazy homeowners. Or how one of his guys shot himself in the foot with a nail gun. Or how he heard a song on the radio that reminded him of me.

"Is something wrong?" I force myself to ask.

His jaw muscle ticks and he tosses his phone onto his bed. "No, why?"

I can't pinpoint when it happened, but he's put an invisible wall up between us. And he did it so fast, so smooth. He told me all about his love 'em and leave 'em past, but to witness it being so skillfully executed is shocking.

If it wasn't happening to me, I'd be impressed.

But I'm not impressed. I'm dying inside with every passing second, wondering what the hell happened to our plan of trying to find out if we're perfect for each other.

Or did he come to the conclusion that we're not, and he doesn't want to tell me?

"I thought things were perfect."

He narrows his eyes at me. "Huh?"

I screw my eyes shut, trying to reverse the tears ready to spill. I didn't mean to actually *say* those words—they just came out.

"Nothing, I—" I run my tongue along the edge of my teeth. "Are you okay?"

"Just tired."

He certainly *looks* tired with shadows under his eyes, and slouched shoulders.

Kneeling down next to him, I reach out and comb his hair out of his face.

"I think you're doing too much since you got rid of Kyle. Have you had any luck hiring someone to replace him?"

"A new guy started on Monday. Bob. He's doing good."

I nod, wondering why he stopped talking to me about stuff that goes on at his job.

"Are you thinking about Erin?" I ask softly. "We can talk about it..."

"I'm just tired, Skylar," he says, not looking at me. "Stop digging."

Hurt, I lean back on my heels. My heart is racing with anxiety and anguish. He's never spoken to me so quick and cold.

"Okay."

I move to stand but he grabs my hand. "Wait..." he says, shaking his head. "I'm sorry."

"Jude, what's going on?" I ask. "And don't tell me you're tired or it's your back."

He lets go of my hand, and I guess that's the answer right there in that simple, yet glaring, action.

"I'm not lying about that stuff, but I think we need a little break."

My stomach pitches.

"A break?" My voice cracks in the middle of the word, and it comes out sounding like brrr-ache.

"Don't cry. Please," he says, closing his eyes and taking a deep breath.

I didn't realize tears were spilling down my cheeks until he brushes them off my face with his hand. And it's shattering, that the same touch—his palm over my cheek—has ignited love in me so many times, now feels like such a betrayal to my heart.

"I think we need to take a step back," he says hoarsely. "Think about things."

"What things?" I croak. "Why?"

When he doesn't answer I ask, "Is there someone else?"

"No," he says immediately. "Fuck no."

I've never been dumped before. Even when my father left, he

just disappeared. I've never experienced this agony of looking in the eye of the person I love and seeing good-bye there.

Suddenly all the sad love songs make so much sense.

"I don't understand," I whisper, sucking in a sniffly breath. "What did I do wrong?"

"Baby, you didn't do anything wrong. Not one thing."

"Then what the *fuck*?" Anger has surfaced like a best friend coming to defend me.

"I think the age thing might be a little too much. I think we need to kinda slow things down, maybe wait—"

"My age didn't matter when your dick was shoved up me."

His chest rises and falls in deep, controlled breaths. "Skylar, don't do that."

"Do what?"

"Say shitty things because you're upset. This was never about sex and you know it."

"Then what *is* it about? Because I don't understand."

"It's exactly what I said. I never should've let things go as far as they did. I'm sorry for that, I really am."

"You're sorry," I repeat. "That's just great."

His gray eyes lock on mine, and I can see the sorrow and the remorse there, mingling with the pain of whatever's going on inside him.

This is hurting him just as much as it's hurting me. I just don't understand why he's doing it.

"Skylar, I don't want to hurt you," he says in a low, tortured voice.

I cover his hand with mine and link our fingers, and his immediately squeeze mine. "Then why are you? We don't have to do this," I say tearfully. "We can just go back to how things were. Because it was perfect." I take a gulp of air. "Wasn't it?"

He smiles but it doesn't reach his eyes. "It was. More than you know. But it's still not right. Not right now."

"I don't care about our ages. It doesn't matter."

"I care. And so do other people."

Other people?

"Who—"

He cups my head in his hands and presses his lips to my forehead. "Please, Skylar. Go and do fun things. Graduate high school. I'll still be here."

"I don't want to do that. I want to be with you *now*."

Slowly pulling away, he leans back against the bed again with a look of utter defeat and exhaustion. "We can't do this. Not now. And I don't want you to worry, nothing else changes. I don't want you to leave. I promised to help you and that's not changing. I still want us to be friends, more than anything."

I try to put my arms around him but he grabs my wrists and gently steers me away. "Skylar, don't make this harder. Please. Just trust that I'm doing what's right for you."

I stand up and tug my sweater down.

"Is that the line you give women?" I spit out. "If it is, you should find a new one. Because it really sucks."

Not able to look at him, or hear any more of his shitty excuses, I pick up my cat and storm back out of his room.

As soon as I get behind my closed door, I wrangle myself out of the sweater dress, pull off the socks, and then crawl in bed and pull the covers over my head.

Surprisingly, tears don't come.

I'm completely numb and disconnected, as if I've drifted far away, up to the ceiling, and am looking down at myself. And I can see myself, lying in bed, as I have so many times.

Confused.

Broken.

Alone.

Tossed aside.

CHAPTER 40

SKYLAR

"Why did I let you talk me into this?" I say to Megan. The mall is hot as an oven and I feel like we've been in each store three times already while she tries to find the perfect *something*.

"Because we need to buy gifts. And clothes. I thought you said you still needed a fun holiday sweater?"

"I do, but haven't you ever heard of online shopping? It's so much easier than this." I hike three shopping bags up my arm. So far, I bought two gifts for her while she wasn't looking, a gift for Rebecca, a pair of boots for myself, and toys for Gus and Cassie. A few weeks ago, I had a gift custom-made for Jude, which I'm now second-guessing.

"Maybe your skinny ass has an easy time buying clothes online, but I need to try shit on to see if I can squeeze my tits into it."

I smile at her as two screaming toddlers run out from beneath a rack of blouses, each holding huge lollipops, and almost wipe us out.

"Where are the parents in this place?" I sigh. "They just let their kids run around like wild animals. Did you see the size of those lollipops? They could choke to death—"

"Let's go to the food court and get something cold to drink," she suggests.

Last year that suggestion would've caused me major anxiety, but this year, I'm totally fine with it.

We wade through the sea of people to get to the center of the mall, and I snag us a small table while she goes to get us two strawberry-and-banana smoothies.

"I got you a pretzel," she says when she finds me at the table twenty minutes later. "It's plain, just a little salt."

"Awesome."

"So, spill the tea, hon," she says after we've sipped our drinks for a few minutes and caught our breath.

I pull off a small piece of warm, soft pretzel and chew it before answering her.

"What tea?"

"With you and the hubby. How are things?"

My chest twinges at the mention of Jude. I was hoping we'd get through the day without talking about him. The wounds are still raw and aching and I've been working hard at healing them with the help of my therapist.

And Gus. Purrs and headbonks make all things better.

"Things are the same. We've gone back to being friends."

"That sucks. I was totally team Jude," she says, dipping her pretzel into a thick, bright orange cheese sauce. I'm not at a point where I could put something like that in my own mouth.

"I was too," I say sadly. "I've run the gamut of being totally devastated, to confused, to pissed off. I'm mentally exhausted. But I can't be mad at him for doing what he thinks is best for himself or for me."

"True. I just think you two were perfect for each other. The way he looked at you, and talked about you… that shit was *valid*."

Hearing that doesn't make me feel any better.

I lift my shoulder dismissively, trying not to look as upset as I still feel inside. I'm becoming an expert at masking my sorrow.

"Who knows," I say. "Maybe someday things will change again. When he put the brakes on, he kept sorta hinting at maybe in the future, when I'm older, we could try again."

She rolls her eyes. "That's stupid. You're eighteen, almost nineteen. I don't see what the big deal is. You're not breaking any laws."

Jude and I have had this argument quite a few times since he ended things, and I've lost every time.

"I know, but I guess it was bothering him."

"Maybe you should start bringing some guys over. Make him jealous. I bet he'd change his tune fast."

She's right—Jude would probably lose his shit if I started to date guys right in front of him. Especially in his own house. If he brought women over, I'd be devastated. No matter how upset I am, I can't do that to him.

"I'm not going to resort to games," I tell her. "He's been good to me. He's not a bad guy, I think he's just… conflicted."

"Most older guys would love to be nailing an eighteen-year-old. Leave it to you to find one with some morals." She picks up her phone, sends a quick text, then puts it back down in one huge robotic motion. "Are you sure you still want to live there? I don't think I could. It'd be awkward as fuck."

"It's not like I can move out, Meg. Not yet anyway. I can't let myself fall apart. At least things are civil and friendly between us. All I can do is try to get over it and reset back to our original arrangement. Which is two friends in a marriage of convenience that was meant to help me get my life together."

She shakes her head. "I just hate this for you. If we had extra room at our house, I'd be begging my parents to let you move in."

Living with her and her family would be equally as awkward, just in totally different ways.

"I know you would, and I love you for that. But I'm okay."

Her eyebrow arches at me skeptically. "Are you, though? Now it's like you're waiting to get divorced, but in the meantime, you have to live with your estranged husband. This is like a really bad movie. I don't think you're too young to date him, but I do think you're too young to be going through this crazy bullshit."

"I'm fine," I insist, trying to convince myself just as much as I'm trying to convince her. "Things just got complicated."

"That's an understatement, Sky. I could never deal with all the shit that's happened to you this year. My biggest struggle is totally trying to find the perfect outfit and a present for Erik."

I wish those were my biggest struggles.

"Do you want me to talk to him for you?" she asks, slurping the last of her drink noisily with her straw. "Maybe I can talk some sense into him?"

The hair prickles on my arms just thinking about how that conversation would go.

"No, that will only make things worse. Trust me, he's not a talker."

"The hot ones never are. I swear the better-looking Erik gets, the less he talks."

Megan has turned Erik into a total project. She convinced him to grow the front of his hair out, which now hangs just over his brows and has somehow made his puppy-dog eyes look sleepy and sexy. She's totally overhauled his wardrobe, she split up his unibrow, and he works out even more. He literally looks nothing like he did when they started dating.

"Your build-a-boyfriend skills have totally paid off."

She smiles smugly. "True. I just miss how he used to tell me how crazy he is about me all the time."

"How many times does he have to say it?" I snort. "If he says it every day, it won't seem special anymore."

Her smile falters. "I'm afraid maybe he doesn't feel that way anymore."

I pat her hand. "I'm sure he does. Go easy on him."

I've hung out with her and Erik together and she has nothing to worry about. He's totally into her. She's just a bit high maintenance when it comes to relationships.

She blows out a sigh. "Okay. I'm recharged. Let's go finish this shopping excursion. I still have to find Erik the perfect gift."

"I see you caved and went shopping with Megan," Jude says from the kitchen when I finally get home. I drop my shopping bags in the foyer as I take off my shoes.

"Never again," I reply, eyeing a huge box leaning up against the wall near the front door. "What's this?"

He shoves his hand through his hair. It's gotten longer since we first met and I can't deny I love the way it looks. "A Christmas tree. I thought maybe it'd be nice for us to have one."

"Oh," I say, surprised by his use of the word *us*.

He flashes me a grin as I wander into the kitchen then goes back to stirring something on the stove. "I actually ordered it a few weeks ago and it came today… so if you're not into it, I'll throw it in the basement."

Ah. So he bought it *before*. When we were experimenting with being perfect together.

The ache stirs in my heart again. We could've had a romantic Christmas together. He was doing so good being a boyfriend. Sweet. Fun. Caring. Sensual.

And then he quit.

Just. Like. That.

Trust is such a fragile gift. I'm not sure I'll ever give it again.

"You can do whatever you want with it," I say, and I can tell by the way his jaw tenses that my words come out a lot harsher than I meant them to.

Oh, well.

"Aunt Suzy sent me home with her homemade chicken, veggie, and rice soup, do you want some?"

"I had a smoothie and a pretzel at the mall."

"Pretzel is twisted bread."

"And?"

"And you're supposed to eat more than bread."

"I don't put meat in my mouth, remember?" I say, wondering if my aversion to blowjobs contributed to him not wanting to be together.

He turns to look at me, his lips set in a hard line. "Then just pick the chicken out."

"I can't eat something that meat's been bathing in."

"Okay… I'm only trying to help you eat new things."

"I know, but you don't have to worry about me."

I watch as he pours the soup into a bowl. "I'm not worried about you; I care about you."

Instinctively, I cross my arms over my chest, as if it can somehow protect my heart from getting hurt anymore. Him continuing to be nice to me *does* hurt. Not that I want him to be an asshole, but him outright saying he cares about me makes me want to smack him.

"Can we talk?" he asks, setting his bowl on the island and settling down on a stool.

Those three words make my heart jolt like it just got zapped with electric shock. My brain has already thrown up conversation possibilities.

Is he going to ask me to move out?

Is he sorry, and wants to try again?

Is he involved with someone else?

"Sure," I say.

"It's about Christmas. I told Aunt Suzy we'd be coming together. And then…" He stares down at his soup. "Well, you know," he says. "I still want you to come but I really don't want them to know what's going on between us. They'll just worry."

"There's nothing going on between us," I reply.

"You know what I mean."

"Yeah," I say. "I guess I do. Do you really think I should go with you, after *you know*?"

What's wrong with us that we can't even say that we were a couple for a little while, and now we're not?

"I think we're mature enough to spend a holiday together as friends. I mean, we *are* still friends." His eyes search mine, and I wonder what he's looking for. Forgiveness? A shadow of longing for him?

I look away, because what I see in his is that same glint of desire I've always seen. That same need, that same possessiveness. That same intense adoration that makes my heart flutter.

Does he even realize his own eyes betray him?

"We're still friends," I agree, resisting the urge to throw in his face that I'm also mature enough to be in a relationship. I don't want to be a bitter bitch, though.

He looks boyish and cute eating soup out of a big bowl, wearing a soft black sweater, with his hair hanging over his shoulders. He looks cozy and I miss having his strong arms around me, my hand in his. I yearn to nuzzle into his neck and breathe his cologne and hear his laugh.

"Do you want to watch a movie with me?" I ask softly. Just

sitting next to him on the couch will soothe the torment in my heart and make things feel normal again.

"I can't, Skylar." He clears his throat and pushes his bowl away. "I have plans."

Nodding, I smile weakly. "Okay."

An hour later, I hear his footsteps in the hall, then the front door opening and closing. I jump up and watch him get in his truck from my window, trying to decipher if he's dressed for a date. He's wearing his usual jeans, boots, and black shirt, which tells me nothing. Jude's not really a date-dresser.

Where is he going?

The only times I've ever seen Jude go out at night is to do a job estimate, or to do something with me.

He didn't knock on my door to say good-bye.

I can't remember the last time he called me Sparkles.

My stomach churns and burns, sending me to my nightstand to get some DGL tablets.

Everything hurts.

I light lavender-scented incense and put on my Pink Floyd playlist. I turn off my light and click on my galaxy projector night light that Jude surprised me with the day after we drove around and then went to the cliffs. He wanted me to be able to see all the stars at night whenever I wanted to. I almost smashed it the night he told me he didn't want to date me anymore, but now I'm glad I didn't.

I like having all these stars to make wishes on. Eventually, one will come true.

Dazed with emotion, I stare at the ceiling of stars and try to lose myself in them. I'm not sure how much time passes, or if I dozed off, but the chirping of my message app startles me back to consciousness, and I quickly grab my phone. Megan is with Erik, so it *has* to be Jude.

Unknown: Hi, sweetheart.

I frown at the glowing screen, knowing I'm not sweetheart, but wishing I were.

Me: I think you have the wrong number.

Unknown: Is this Skylar?

Me: Who is this?

Unknown: Your father. I want to say Merry Christmas. It took me forever to get your phone number from your mother. She wouldn't tell me where you were or how to get in touch with you. I was hoping we could talk?

Oh, shit.

CHAPTER 41

JUDE

I decide to go visit Uncle Al at his bar in Boston as a way to put space between me and Skylar.

My mood gets worse as I sit in traffic for over an hour with nothing to think about except that I wish I'd stayed home to watch a movie with her. When I finally get to the bar, I park my truck and walk down the street to a convenience store for some smokes and a pack of gum. Lighting up, I lean back against the brick wall of the side of the store and stare at my phone. I want to send her a text message. Something cute like we used to—but that will only make things worse.

Out of the corner of my eye, I notice a guy having a cigarette halfway down the alley. He tosses something into a nearby dumpster, and that's when I notice another dude behind him, in the shadows, slowly creeping up behind him with a bat in his hand, raised and ready to swing. It takes me a few seconds to figure out what's going on, but when I do, I act on pure adrenaline, run up behind him, and tackle him, causing his swing to go wild. When the bat glances the side of the smoking guy's head with a thud, I wrestle the attacker to the ground. His punches are pathetically sloppy, and he misses me every time I duck to the side. I decide to put him out of his misery and land a fist square to his jaw. He puts his hands up to shield himself from my next punch.

"Lemme go, man. I don't want any shit with you," he says, spitting blood onto the sidewalk.

"Get the fuck outta here, asshole," I say, "or I'm gonna kill you with your own bat."

He slowly rises and runs toward the other end of the alley, and I pick up the bat and hurl it at him. I let out a low whistle as it flies and spins through the air, heading straight at him like a torpedo until it nails him in the back of the head.

"Woohoo!" I yell. "Nailed you, you bastard!"

"Fuck!" the guy yells, and he falls hard, then stands a few seconds later and staggers toward the alley fencing—scaling it and then disappearing.

Pumping with adrenaline, I turn and help the guy up who was almost just mugged. He rubs the back of his head.

"You okay, man?" I ask.

"Think so," he says. "What the hell just happened?"

"That motherfucker tried to knock you out and mug you."

"Shit." He twists his neck from side to side and winces. "Thanks… for what you did."

"No problem."

"I was just standing here—"

I smirk. "You were standing in the wrong place. Not from around here, are ya?"

"Not really."

He runs his hand through long, dark, wavy hair, checking his head for damage. Something about him is familiar, but I can't place him.

"He didn't hit ya that hard, I grabbed the bat as it was coming down. I think it just stunned you for a few seconds."

"Good to know," he says, taking a deep breath. "Fuck this night."

I put a cigarette in my mouth and search my jacket for my Zippo. "You got a light?" I ask. "Think I lost my lighter."

Nodding, he tosses me a box of wooden matches.

"Thanks." My knuckles sting as I cup them around my mouth to light up my cigarette. I gotta stop punching people. "You need directions someplace? A ride? You look lost," I say as the guy stands there, bewildered, looking up and down the alley.

He shakes his head and laughs. "Just having a really shitty night. I'm not ready to go home yet."

Exhaling a cloud of smoke, I nod. "I'm in the same boat. I was just headin' to a bar my buddy owns down the street. Gonna have a drink, maybe shoot some pool or play darts to clear my fuckin' head. Want to join me? You stand here much longer you're probably gonna freeze to death or get mugged again."

He takes a phone out of his pocket and stares at it like he's waiting for it to ring. Minutes ago, I was doing the same thing. There's some bad mojo in the air tonight.

"Ya know what?" he says. "Why not. I owe you a few drinks."

Grinning, I wipe my hand on my jeans and hold it out to him. "Name's Jude Lucketti. My friends call me Lucky."

"Asher Valentine."

Motherfuck me. I just saved Asher Valentine—lead singer of one of my favorite rock bands, Ashes & Embers—from getting mugged. I *knew* he looked familiar. Skylar's gonna lose her mind when I tell her—she's crazy about this guy.

"The singer?" I say.

He shrugs. "On some days."

This dude looks tired. Like he wants to be anyone but himself right now, and that's a mood I can relate to.

"Not today," I say, leading him down the dark street. "Today you're just a guy going to have a drink."

Uncle Al's bar is old, dark and dingy. A real hole-in-the-wall—the kind of place you wouldn't even notice unless you were looking for it. And not many people are. Only the old regulars still come here to hang out and drink away their lives every day. Anyone else would be afraid to come in. But it's a damn good place to forget about the world for a while.

I nod at Uncle Al and two old guys when we walk inside the musty room. None of them look away from the tiny, dust-covered TV playing behind the bar.

"Hey, Lucky. What'll ya have tonight?" Uncle Al says.

"Give us two Long Islands!" I yell as we sit at my usual table in the back. "Good for you?" I ask Asher.

He nods. "I'm easy."

Uncle Al brings us our drinks and pats me on the back before he heads back to his station behind the bar.

"That hits the spot," I say after taking a sip. It burns going down, and I wish I'd had dinner.

The guy across from me looks like he's having an equally bad night and I wonder what's so bad that a rich, famous rock star wants to sit and have a drink with a stranger in a dive bar.

"So where's home?" I ask.

"Small town in New Hampshire."

"Really?" I'm surprised I never knew that. "Me too. Lived in Brookline my entire life."

"Small world," he says. "I got some friends in Brookline."

I tip my drink at him. "Now you got another one."

"Can't have too many friends." He shrugs off his jacket and leans back in the cracked leather booth. "You work here in the city?"

"Rarely. I'm in construction. Most of my jobs are local."

He glances over at my uncle skeptically. "And *he's* your buddy?"

I let out a laugh. "Nah, he's my Uncle Al. I wander in here a couple times a month. Check in on him. Play some pool or darts, get a few free drinks. It reminds me I don't want to end up like them." I cock my head toward the two old men at the bar. They're *always* here. "Lonely. Drinking all day. Nothing at home. Fuck that."

Despite my aversion to commitments and relationships, I don't want to grow old alone.

"I hear ya." I catch him eyeing the wedding band on my hand. "You married?"

I stare at my finger, surprised I forgot to take it off earlier. Sometimes, when I'm getting dressed and put my other rings on, I slip the ring on and think about Skylar and our wedding day. Testing what it would feel like to wear it. To forget all the bullshit and the judgement and just let the marriage be real. I don't know why I did it today. *Wishful thinking.*

"I guess you could say that. My life's a mess, man. And I don't know how the fuck it got that way."

"That's usually the way it happens."

I shake my head and swirl the ice cubes in my drink. "Ever just have a chick totally haunt you? Like no matter what, you just can't get her out of your head? Out of your veins?"

Closing his eyes, he nods like he knows exactly what I'm talking about. "Yup. Been living that since I was fifteen years old. I wouldn't change it, though."

Fifteen years old. Wow.

"This girl is doing my head in. I've never felt like this." I lean forward and whisper, "She's only eighteen. Eight-fucking-teen. What the fuck? I gotta be sick, right? To feel that way?"

I need validation. Someone to tell me what's right or wrong

because my brain's got it all muddled up. And who better to tell me than a fuckin' rock star?

He leans back and gives me a hard stare. Not judgmental, but thoughtful. "And how old are *you*?"

"Way older than eighteen, obviously."

He lets out a low laugh. "If you're just chasing after a piece of ass, then yeah, I'd say it's wrong. Really wrong in every way."

Shit, if I only wanted to get laid, that's easy. But that's not what I want anymore. "I'm not interested in a piece of ass. I mean yeah, she's cute as hell, but man, I think I'm in love with this girl." Damn. I finally said it out loud. And it didn't kill me. "We fuckin' click in all the right ways. I want to take care of her, spend my life with her. Like your songs, man," I say, remembering I'm talking to the king of rock ballads. "*You* get what I'm talkin' about. She makes me feel like I'm worth something."

He tugs on his beard. "Sounds like it could be love."

"Can a chick that young even know what love is? She'll probably break my heart and hand it to me on a platter while she's walking off with a younger guy." Like that ring pop dude she told me about. At least he saved her life without making a mess of it like I have.

"Lemme tell you a little story, Jude," Asher says. "About my best friend and my only daughter and how age doesn't always matter."

We go through another round of drinks and a bowl of pretzels as he tells me all about his best friend, who started dating his daughter, when she was just eighteen and the guy was thirty-two. Asher admits he was so furious when he found out that he beat the shit out of his friend and didn't talk to him for months.

"Once I cooled down?" he says. "I sat and took a good, hard look at all the years I watched them grow closer and closer. This dude is like my brother. I *know* him, in and out. He's a good guy. He doesn't fuck around—he doesn't play games. I couldn't deny what was right in front of me—they really loved each other. So, I got over it. Now they're married with a baby." He grins over the rim of his glass. "I'm more pissed off that he made me a grandfather than I am that he's fifteen years older than my daughter."

"I'd kill for that," I admit, after he proceeds to tell me his entire life story—how he fell in love when he was fifteen and how he waited eight fucking years for his wife while she was in a coma. "A love like you have, like your friend and your kid has. A best friend to go through life with. That's what it's all about. You don't just walk away from that, right?"

Only a dumbass would walk away from something good like that.

"No," he says with conviction. "You don't. You hang on to it, fight for it. No matter what. But you gotta believe in it yourself first."

I run my thumb over my wedding band, lost in thought, wondering if me and Skylar can have something real. If I let go of my fears of getting hurt, ignore the judgement, and finally just went all in one hundred percent in every way, could it work?

I think it could. I think it's what we both deserve—to be happy and have love.

"I'm gonna tell her how I feel," I finally say. "I'm gonna stop pushing her away."

"What about your wife?" he asks. "You better end that before you do or say anything to another woman. You seem like a good guy. Don't be a cheater. You'll get yourself in a bigger mess."

At first, I'm totally confused, then I realize he thinks I'm having an affair with a younger girl while being married to someone else.

I finish off my drink and plunk my glass on the table. "Trust me, it can't get any messier than it is. The girl? The eighteen-year-old? She *is* my wife."

His eyes widen with surprise, and he raises his hand to get Uncle Al's attention. "Can we get two coffees?" he asks. "We're gonna be here a while."

Turning back to me, he says, "Man, I did *not* see that coming."

"Yeah, me neither," I reply.

CHAPTER 42

JUDE

I spent the night with Asher Valentine.

Hold up—not like *that*.

Even though the guy's a famous, multi-millionaire rock star, he's the most down-to-earth person I've ever met. We stayed at the bar until two a.m. talking, and then we sat in my truck and talked for a few hours more about music, life, and relationships. By then I was too exhausted to drive. We fell asleep in my truck and I dropped him off at his house this morning.

Before he got out of my truck, he gave me one last piece of advice.

"Marriage has nothing to do with rings or vows or a fuckin' piece of paper. None of that shit binds people together," he said. "Marriage—being in love—is a choice to stay every day, and keep staying, no matter what. You don't lie, you don't cheat, you don't leave, and you don't give up. You *stay*."

I nodded at him, letting it sink in. If the dude managed to keep his marriage alive while his wife was in a coma for eight years, he's gotta be doing something right.

"And one other thing," he said, grabbing my shoulder. "Time

goes by fucking fast, man. Every day you sit on your ass, avoiding *living*, you're missing out. Take the chances, love the girl, before it's too late."

I left Asher feeling pumped and more clear-headed than I have in a long time. He struck a nerve—I'm sick of just *existing*. Working a job that doesn't do shit for me except pay my bills and kill my back. Avoiding relationships like they're poison just 'cause I'm afraid they'll go up in flames someday.

These walls I've put up haven't been doing me any favors. I'm just living in a cage.

When I get home, Skylar's coming down the stairs just as I walk through the front door and trip over the Christmas tree box. She's got on a sweatshirt with the letters STFU printed on it. It's so big on her it hangs to her knees.

"Oh, you came home," she says in a tone that makes it clear she thinks I spent the night with someone else.

I should've texted her last night instead of just not coming home.

It looks bad.

"Come talk to me," I say, walking into the kitchen. "If I don't get some coffee into me, I'm gonna fall flat on my face."

She follows me and perches on one of the stools at the island as I pour some milk into the reservoir of the fancy coffee maker Aunt Suzy gave me last year, stick a pod in, and press the brew button. "I'm sorry I didn't text you. I didn't think I'd be gone all night."

She's tight-lipped. "You don't have to check in with me."

The coffee maker whirrs and sputters its magical mix of water, espresso, and frothy milk.

"I know, but I still like to." I stir a heap of sugar into my foamy latte and sit on the stool across from her. "There's some things I want to tell you."

She leans her elbow on the granite countertop, her chin in her palm. "Good. I have some things I need to say, too."

I take that as a good sign.

"Okay… ladies first."

"I did a lot of thinking last night, and I finally realized that you're right. About us not being together."

I quickly swallow my coffee. "Skylar, wait—"

She mows right over my words. "Jude, you don't have to say anything. I did a lot of thinking, and I talked to someone who helped me understand that us being just friends is probably best."

I'm crushed. All I wanted to do was tell her I spent the night with Asher freakin' Valentine, and how his advice woke my ass up. I want to tell her I'm crazy about her and go put up our first Christmas tree.

I want to tell her I want us to *stay*.

Her chin lifts, and she sniffles back tears. "I'm not mad at you, and I don't blame you for the things that happened. Things between us just got complicated. I wasn't expecting it and…" She lets out a shuddering, heartbreaking sigh and looks past me, out the window to the backyard. "I wasn't ready for it. And you're right, I'm probably too young for this. For you."

"Skylar, I wasn't expecting it or ready for it either, but—"

She doesn't let me finish. "Too much shit has happened to me—and to you—in the past few weeks. We haven't been thinking clearly. I have to focus on getting my life together. I have to get healthy physically and mentally. *That* was the plan and the whole reason for this arrangement."

Anxiety waltzes up my spine and I nod as my hungover brain tries to figure out what I'm supposed to say to fix this. Do I agree and let things end? Is that what's right, after all?

I don't want to treat her like a ping-pong ball.

Oblivious to the hope that's dying a slow death inside me, she keeps talking. "I think the whole marriage thing kinda got to me." She puts her hands up and does air quotes when she says the word *marriage*. "Even though I don't believe in that stuff, a little part of me started to think it was going to turn into some kind of Disney fairytale." Her cheeks turn pink, and she lets out a short, sad laugh. "But, that stuff never happens in real life, and the first person I give my heart to can't be a thirty-four-year-old guy who's not into relationships and can't commit to save his life, right? I'll get destroyed, and that's a mess I can do without, thank you very much."

Fuckin' ouch.

My defenses fly up. I *can* commit. I just never *wanted* to before I met her.

The happiness I felt earlier deflates like a leaky balloon. I almost got caught up in the fairytale myself. Maybe guys like Asher Valentine and his best friend are lucky enough to have love stories like that, but not me—an ex-junkie hood rat. I've been paving the road to loneliness for a long time, and it looks like it's a dead end for me. The light at the end of the tunnel just got blown out.

I nod slowly and set my coffee mug back down a little too hard. "Right. And the first person I commit to can't be an eighteen-year-old girl who's never even *been* in a relationship. It'd be a total waste of my time," I add, just to be a dick and deliver the blow back at her.

I immediately regret it.

Blinking, she sucks her quivering lower lip into her mouth, and her top teeth edge into the pink flesh. The act makes me want to reach across the counter and drag her to me so I can suck that same lip into my own mouth and make her mine right here in the middle of the kitchen.

I run my hand across the stubble on my face. How do I manage to fuck shit up? I came home planning to follow the King of Rock's advice to *love the girl*. So, what do *I* do? *Insult* the girl.

Good move, Lucky.

Suddenly her eyes focus on my hand like laser beams. "You're wearing your wedding band."

"Yeah..." I glance at the ring on my hand that, until this moment, I forgot I was still wearing. "I stuck it on yesterday before I went out." Skylar's gaze hangs on to mine, her eyes doing that shimmery sparkle that always hypnotizes me. "I only put it on so women wouldn't hit on me while I was out."

Lies. Not even a good one.

"Oh." She straightens her spine and blinks away the emotion that was swimming in her eyes seconds ago. "Your turn. What did you want to talk about?"

I could tell her about my epiphany. Admit to her that I've been falling in love with her since the day I saw her cruising in her 'vette, blasting Meat Loaf. I could tell her I was a goner the second she blew that bubblegum bubble at me. I just didn't know that's what falling in love felt like. I could tell her she's the only girl who's ever made me happy, who's ever given me what I needed. I could tell her she's the only one who's ever been there for *me* and made me think, even for a minute, that maybe love isn't just a four-letter word.

I could tell her I don't give a shit about the age difference or what people think.

I could throw it all out there and tell her—for the first time in my life—I want to *stay*.

With her.

Indefinitely.

Try for forever together.

But, let's be real. She's clearly made up her mind. And she hit the nail on the head—I don't know anything about taking care of hearts. Skylar deserves so much more than I can give her.

I down the rest of my coffee in one big gulp. "Nothin'. I just wanted to tell you I was sorry about how everything went down."

She swallows hard, obviously choking on disappointment.

"I'm going to do what I can to get my life together. So we can move on." She lifts her gaze to meet mine, and I hate the sadness that's sucked all the brightness from her eyes. "I really do appreciate everything you've done for me, Lucky. More than I can ever say. Everything you've done for me… It's changed my life."

That was the plan—for her to eventually leave. But hearing her say it hurts like a bitch.

"I'm sorry for all the shit that's happened, Skylar. All I wanted to do was help you out, not fuck you up even more. No good deed goes unpunished, huh?"

A faint, sad smile touches her lips. "Yeah, I guess not."

Coughing into my hand, I rise to my feet, ready to end this demolition of hopes and dreams. "I meant what I said the other day—this is your home. I don't want you to leave. I can keep my distance. But nothing's going to change our friendship. That's something I *can* commit to."

She tilts her head with a sad, yet wistful look that just about crushes me. "You're a great friend. I don't ever want to lose that."

I go up to my room and yank the wedding band off, shoving it in my dresser drawer under the pile of lottery tickets I squirreled away to give her every day.

I'm never going to put it on again.

I never should've let myself think otherwise—a fake marriage is all I'm ever going to be good enough for.

CHAPTER 43

JUDE

"Maybe I should stay home," Skylar says when she meets me in the foyer. "It feels weird spending a holiday with your family when you and I aren't exactly in the best place."

"I promised Aunt Suzy we'd both be there. I think we can put on some fake smiles for one day."

"I guess you're right," she says, grabbing the bird cage off the floor. "Fake smiles should be a breeze compared to a fake marriage."

Ignoring her comment, I usher her out the front door and lock it behind us.

"Why exactly are we giving your aunt a parakeet? They say pets should never be given as a gift. Do you know how many pets end up in shelters less than three months after Christmas?" she asks when we're in my truck and on our way to Aunt Suzy and Uncle Al's. She holds the birdcage, wrapped with a big red bow, on her lap.

I glance at the small blue-and-white bird and turn the heat up a little. I don't want to show up with a dead gift. "It's what she wanted. A parakeet and an air fryer. Trust me, she's not going to get rid of either."

"He's cute. I've never seen one up close before."

"Birds are messy."

"So are people." She pokes her finger into the cage, and the bird eyes her warily. "Will it talk?"

"Maybe." I didn't read Birds 101; I just bought the one that had the most feathers. "I think they mostly make noise and shit."

"Lucky… don't be a grump."

"I'm not being a grump—just stating facts."

We've been giving each other the cold shoulder since our talk, and it's awkward as hell. I miss her.

I used to think that the feeling-so-connected thing that people talked about was pure Hallmark-card bullshit.

Until I met Skylar.

Until I had sex with Skylar.

Until I fell in love with her.

I've tried like hell not to think about it, but it's impossible to forget how she felt under my touch, how she tasted on my tongue, how her nails dug into my flesh. How she whispered my name when she came all over my cock.

How she knew I needed her.

It all could've been perfect.

"What are we giving Uncle Al for Christmas?" she asks, pulling me from memory lane.

"*We're* not giving him a gift. Every year he says he's got everything he wants, so I only give gifts to Aunt Suzy."

"Have you always spent Christmas with them?"

"Yup. Since I was a kid. They used to dress up as Santa and Mrs. Claus when I was little. They'd come downstairs with a big red sack full of gifts for me and Erin."

"That's so sweet. If I ever have kids, I'd love to do something cool like that for them. Keep the innocence and magic alive for as long as possible."

"I thought you said you didn't want kids?"

The bird sways back and forth on his perch in tune with *Lady* by Little River Band playing on the radio. Skylar watches him, lost in thought.

"I don't," she says. "But every now and then I think maybe, someday, with the right guy I might want to."

I've always been dead set against having kids until Skylar just went and planted an image in my head of us prancing around the living room dressed up as Santa and his wife for kids we don't even have.

But I don't want to think about that.

"Guess what," I say, flashing her a side-eye, hoping to keep the mood light as traffic slows to a near halt.

"What?" she asks, more interested in the bird than she is with hearing what I might say.

"I never got to tell you who I spent the night with that night I didn't come home."

Her face twists into a disgusted frown. "Seriously, Jude, why would I want to know that?"

Shit.

"No, it's not what you think. It was a guy."

"Wow." Her head moves back and forth and the bird mimics her. "It's like you *want* me to throw this bird cage at you."

"Skylar! What the fuck. I wasn't with a guy."

"It's totally okay if you were. I'm not going to judge you. If a man can be the one to finally make you happy and get you out of your head, I'm all for it."

"Will you stop? I'm trying to tell you I hung out with Asher Valentine at Uncle Al's bar."

She turns to look at me so fast I'm surprised she didn't give herself whiplash.

"Say what?" she says.

I snort out a laugh. "Yeah, I thought that'd get your attention."

"You expect me to believe you hung out with Asher Valentine, lead singer of one of my favorite bands—*ever*?"

"Yup."

"Get out," she says.

Her disbelief makes me grin. "It's true."

"How? He just wandered into your uncle's bar for a drink?" she asks skeptically.

"Not exactly. He was standing in an alley by the convenience store, and when I came out, I saw some guy coming up behind him with a bat. He was going to mug him."

Mouth open, she turns toward me, and the cage tilts. The bird jumps to a different perch and bobs his head at us. "Holy shit," Skylar says. "What happened?"

"I jumped the guy, and he ran off. We started talking, and he told me his name."

"Wait a minute. You didn't recognize him? The guy is a literal god."

"If he was singing, I would've recognized him but we were standing in a dark alley for fuck's sake."

"Well, what was he like?" she asks impatiently. "Was he nice? Please tell me he was nice. I will *die* if he wasn't nice."

"He was. We talked for hours like he was just a regular guy."

She beams. "What did you talk about?"

I shrug. "Work. His band. Relationships. Motorcycles. Love."

"You talked about *love* with Asher Valentine? Oh my God, I would freak *out*. Do you know he met his wife when they were only fifteen? And when she had that accident years ago, she was in a coma for eight years! I saw him do an interview and he said he stayed totally committed to her in every way the *entire* time."

I've missed seeing her excitement and hearing happiness in her voice. "Yup. He told me all about it."

"Wow. Now *that's* love. He's like the perfect man. Talented, romantic, a voice like sin, hot as hell." She sighs and smiles dreamily like she just had a daydream-gasm.

"Okay, fangirl, did you know his daughter fell in love with his best friend when she was eighteen and he was thirty-two?"

That snaps her out of her swoony haze. "Um, no. You better spill that tea right now, Lucky."

I laugh. "Ohh, so I've got some dirt you want?"

"Yes! Tell me more."

"I guess they kept it on the down low for a while, and when Asher found out, the shit hit the mother-fuckin' fan."

"Oh no! That sucks!"

"Yeah, but they worked it out. It's all good now."

"Are they still together? The daughter and the friend?"

"He said they're married with a baby."

Her big blue eyes nearly bulge out of her head. "Holy crap. Who knew Asher Valentine was a *grandfather*. That's insane—he's like *your* age. I follow him on social media. I think he's got even more tattoos than you do. He is sooo incredibly hot."

Jealousy starts to fester in my veins. "Yeah, I heard ya the first time," I say.

"The age difference between his daughter and his friend is close to ours," she says, not looking at me.

"I know; that's why we were talking about it."

"You really told him about us? About *me*? I can imagine how that conversation went," she says with a hint of sarcasm.

I'm starting to wish I hadn't brought up the topic of Asher Valentine now. I feel like a wild animal about to be cornered by an expert hunter.

"How's the bird doing?" I ask, straightening the bow on the cage.

"Jude, seriously? The bird is fine. Tell me what you told him. What did he say?"

"I told him everything."

"Everything?" she repeats. "What's everything?"

"Just that we got married. And why."

"That's everything?"

"Basically."

"Did you tell him we've kissed? And had sex?" she challenges. "That much everything?"

Memories of us having sex has been a major source of jerk-off material for me. I wish I could light up a smoke, but I can't with the stupid bird in the truck. "Not exactly like that, no. That's kinda private, don't ya think?"

She quirks her lips to the side. "I thought guys liked to talk about their sexual escapades."

"I don't consider you an escapade. At all."

"Good."

"You're here!" Aunt Suzy exclaims when she opens her front door.

I lean in and kiss her cheek as we move inside the living room. "I've been here on Christmas every year since I was born."

"Merry Christmas," Skylar says from behind the birdcage.

"Oh my God! A parakeet!" Aunt Suzy squeals.

"Why are you acting surprised? Every year I give you exactly what you ask for."

Ignoring me, she takes the cage and walks it over to Uncle Al, who's dozing off in his chair next to the Christmas tree.

"Look! We have a bird! Isn't he adorable?"

Jolting awake, he squints at it then throws me a glance. "I

thought we agreed years ago you can't give her anything that eats, barks, or shits."

"Leave him alone," Aunt Suzy says. "He always gives me the best presents."

"Because you tell him what to get you."

"Well, how else will I get what I want?"

Skylar shrugs off her coat and refuses to make eye contact with me when I take it from her.

"Aunt Suzy, your decorations are amazing," Skylar says.

My aunt and uncle deck out the entire house with vintage decorations every holiday. The mantel is covered with fake snow and hanging icicles, and there's a little fake frozen pond with tiny people that actually skate across it. Their tree is the same one they've had since they were first married, with an ornament for every year they've been together.

That's a lot of fuckin' ornaments.

I watch Skylar slowly walk around the room, oohing and ahhing over the animated elves and snowmen holding wrapped boxes. She catches me staring at her and then she quickly looks away.

I hate this.

"We love the holidays," Aunt Suzy says. "I've had these decorations forever. Some of them belonged to my mother and my grandmother. When I die, Lucky will get them all."

I'm probably not the best person to inherit sentimental ornaments. The tree I bought for me and Skylar is still sitting in a box in the hallway like the ugly elephant in the room.

I grab the shopping bag with the silver gift-wrapped air fryer and enough food and toys to keep the bird living a life of luxury for at least a year, and hand it to my aunt. "This is for you, too. And can we not talk about death on Christmas?"

Smiling, she puts a floppy red Santa hat on my head, just like she does every year. "Why? I'm not afraid to die. I'm afraid to not live."

As she busies herself getting the birdcage set up on a fake-snow-covered table in front of the window, me and Skylar sit on the couch together, and I finally get a good look at what she's wearing.

"I see you rose to the challenge." I nod my chin toward her ridiculous sweatshirt—the fox printed on it is all tangled up in a string of holiday lights that are actually lit and blinking. "Did that thing come with batteries?"

"It did. I scoured the internet to find something that would live up to your expectations."

"You succeeded."

She bats at the white puff hanging off my hat like a naughty kitten and then looks away from me.

"Let's open presents," Aunt Suzy says, pushing a pile of presents three feet high in front of us. "Just read the name tags on them. There's a bunch for both of you."

"Holy shit. Why did you get so much?" I ask. "Just get me a pair of socks and call it a day."

"You really didn't have to do all this," Skylar adds.

"What else do I have to do with myself? It makes me happy."

The bird squawks, once again waking Uncle Al from his nap. "What happened?" he mumbles.

"We're doing presents." My aunt tosses a box onto his lap.

Ten minutes later I've got a stack of new flannel shirts, socks, a scarf I'll never wear, a dog sweater for Cassie, a new Zippo lighter, chocolate coins, and a carbon fiber thermos.

"This is all so beautiful," Skylar says after she opens her stack. Aunt Suzy gave her everything she loves: an old Led Zeppelin shirt, crystal earrings, fuzzy socks, a catnip mouse for Gus, a flowery headband, and a hardcover book signed by one of her favorite authors. "I love everything. Thank you so much."

I get that heavy feeling in my heart when she gets up to hug my aunt and uncle.

It all looks so real.

It all *feels* real.

♡

After presents, we help Aunt Suzy put dinner on the dining room table, and Skylar's usual anxiety over anything food-related is visibly diminished when she sees that my aunt has made Skylar's "safe" foods in addition to our usual dishes.

Fresh bread with homemade honey butter.

Steamed carrots and cauliflower—something new Skylar has started eating after some recent therapy sessions.

Mashed potatoes.

And instead of putting the entire turkey on the table, Uncle Al sliced it—putting only the platter on the center of the table so Skylar wouldn't have to look at the turkey carcass as she was eating.

Trying to stay on my best behavior, I even refrain from making any eat-the-bird jokes in front of the parakeet.

"There's something I want to talk to you about." Uncle Al waves his fork at me as we're eating.

"Okay. I'm listening."

"The bar's not making much money. The same customers come in every day. Never anyone new."

"The place is old," I reply. "I've been tellin' you that for years. There's two inches of dust on everything. It's dark and musty."

"Lucky." Skylar kicks me under the table.

"It's okay, honey," Uncle Al says. "It's true, the place is a dump."

Aunt Suzy touches his hand. "I wouldn't call it a dump. It's just aged."

"I think it's time I sell it. I can't afford to give it everything it needs."

I lean back in my chair. "That bar's your life."

"We had a good run, but it's time. I'll miss it, but it's too much for me to handle now. I ain't getting any younger."

"So, what are you going to do?"

"Sell it. Thought maybe you'd want to buy it."

I choke on my turkey. "What? Me?"

"Yeah. I'll give you a good deal."

"What would I do with a bar?"

"Fix it up and make it successful. It's in a great location," Aunt Suzy says. "And it has parking. Most bars in the area don't."

"Did you two forget I have a business?"

Uncle Al shakes his head at me. "You think you're gonna be wanting to climb up on a roof with your back problems when you're in your fifties? Sixties?"

I don't even want to climb up on a roof *now*. "I can't afford to buy that place and fix it up."

"What about your settlement?"

I blow out a low breath and ignore Skylar's curious stare.

"There's not much of that left. Not enough to do everything that place would need."

A few years ago, a local, well-known entrepreneur rear-ended me at a stop sign late at night. My truck was basically totaled and it effed-up my already messed-up neck and back. The driver staggered out of the car, clearly having had one too many. He also had a barely dressed woman in the passenger seat he didn't seem to want anyone to find out about. In exchange for me not calling the cops or reporting it to my insurance, he bought me a new truck and gave me twenty-five thousand in cash on the spot. The dude literally pulled wads of cash right out of a bag in his trunk. In hindsight, I should've sued him.

Twenty-five K wasn't enough to put up with chronic back and neck pain.

Some of that cash went to new appliances for Al and Suzy, and some of it I used to buy Skylar's 'vette.

"It'd be really cool if you turned it into an era-themed bar. Like, all sixties or seventies themed decor," Skylar suggests, stabbing a baby carrot and nibbling half of it off her fork. "You could have that decade's music playing in the background. People love that stuff. They like things that are unique, so they can say, *hey, let's go to that sixties bar*."

"Yes," Aunt Suzy says excitedly. "I *love* that idea! She's right, people would love to go to a bar like that for a drink."

"It sounds great, but I don't know shit about running a bar."

My uncle's not swayed. "I could still work part time and help. And what are you talkin' about? You bartended there for years when you were younger. Hire someone to fill in when you're off so you don't get stuck there all day and night. It ain't that hard."

I'm tempted. I'd be lying if I said I wanted to run a small construction company for the rest of my life. I don't love it, and it's murder on my back. I can't see myself doing it forever, and the thought of working at some big-box hardware store when I'm fifty doesn't exactly excite me.

"It'd be cool, but there's no way I can afford it. It'd take up too much time and money. I'd never be able to get a bar off the ground *and* keep up with my own work in the meantime. I'm sorry."

"You're right, Lucky," Aunt Suzy says. "It'd be a lot for you to take on by yourself."

"Maybe I could help," Skylar suggests quietly.

I turn to my wife. "You're not even old enough to drink. What are you gonna do in a bar?"

She puts her fork down and glares at me. "Oh, I don't know, Jude. I guess just because I'm eighteen, I can't do *any*thing? Let's just forget that I came up with a great idea to make the place interesting, and I also happen to be really good at social marketing. But, whatever. If you want to swing a hammer for the rest of your life, have at it."

"Why would you say that to her?" my aunt asks.

"What?" I say. "You expect me to run a bar with a teenager?"

"Why does her age matter?" Suzy says. "You tell us all the time how smart and driven she is. And she's your wife. It'd be nice to run a new business together."

"She's not my wife," I shoot back. "She'll be gone in six months."

"Hey," Uncle Al warns. "That's no way to talk about a woman. Especially your wife."

I grind my teeth. "It's the truth. That was the deal. Why am I the bad guy? It's what she wants."

"Are you two really going to get a divorce?" Aunt Suzy asks.

"Yes," we answer simultaneously.

"Is that what you both want?"

Skylar and I stare at each other, waiting for the other to answer first. I want to say no. I want more time together. But if it's what *she* wants, then she should go and move on with her life.

"It's what we agreed on," Skylar answers. "It doesn't mean we don't care about each other."

"But you make such a cute couple."

"We can be cute friends." Skylar puts on her best convincing smile but I can see right through it. "We're okay with it, really. We both knew going into this it was just an arrangement. I'm very grateful for everything Lucky's done for me, and I'm so glad I got to meet you two."

Aunt Suzy's face falls as if her best friend just died. "I wish things were different. We really love having you as part of the family. Maybe things will change…"

Skylar forces a smile and pushes her food around her plate.

I jump in before things get worse. "We're still going to be friends, Aunt Suze. She can still visit." I turn to my uncle. "If I was in a better financial position, I'd buy the bar. I just can't take on something that needs so much work."

"There's a surprise," Skylar mutters under her breath.

"Skylar, are you going to be okay?" Aunt Suzy asks. "What about all your medical visits, and prescriptions? Where will you live?"

I feel like the world's biggest asshole as Skylar struggles to swallow the food in her mouth. Her thin fingers wrap around her glass of water, and she takes a few slow sips. "After I graduate, I can work full time. I'll get a small studio apartment. And once I have less stress in my life—" Her baby blues throw shade in my direction. "Then hopefully I can decrease my meds and see my therapist less. Jude's help has gotten me through the worst of it. This isn't on him. I'm not his responsibility. He did way more for me than anyone ever has. I'll be fine."

"He can't just kick you to the curb."

"Uncle Al, I'm not forcing her out. She can live in the house as long as she wants to. And once she moves out, we don't have to legally divorce ten minutes later. If she needs insurance for a few months after she leaves, I'm fine with that. No big deal. It's not like I'm gonna rush to go marry someone else."

One marriage is enough for me.

Aunt Suzy sighs sadly. "Well, it's your lives. I'm sure you two know what's best. It's just a shame you couldn't turn it into a real marriage. That would have been the perfect happy ending for both of you."

"I'm sure we'll both still get our happy endings, Aunt Suzy." Skylar's voice is full of sweetness and optimism, but I know better.

My little wife is full of crap. She doesn't believe in happy endings any more than I do.

CHAPTER 44

JUDE

I have a love-hate relationship with Christmas.

Santa one minute. Grinch the next.

Spending the day with Uncle Al and Aunt Suzy has always been a good time for me. But it always sucked to be surrounded by love and laughter all day and then go home alone to an empty, quiet house.

After we kissed Aunt Suzy and Uncle Al goodbye, that familiar empty feeling crept in on the drive home. Skylar and I barely said a word to each other.

She's slowly slipping away from me.

I don't know how everything got so discombobulated between us.

When we get home, snow is falling and there's a few inches accumulating on the ground already. I open her door and help her out of the truck to make sure she doesn't slip, and she hooks her arm through mine as we walk to the house.

"I've always loved watching the snow," she says, tilting her face up toward the sky. I laugh when she sticks her tongue out and catches a few snowflakes on her tongue. It's kind of a magical moment, to witness her playfully open up and let that tiny icy star into her mouth—free of fears and anxieties.

I don't even think she realized that she did it.

"I'll take her out real quick," I say when Cassie greets us at the door. I light up a cigarette as the dog darts out of the house and bounces playfully in the snow. When Cassie finally scoots inside, Skylar's still standing in the hallway next to the Christmas tree box.

"You forgot to give the Santa hat back," she says, eyeing the top of my head.

"Oh shit." I reach up and touch the fuzzy, red hat. "Aunt Suzy will yell at me."

She smiles crookedly. "Leave it on. Christmas isn't over yet."

"Is that right?"

"Yes. I have a gift for you."

That simple sentence shouldn't cause my heart and my dick to jump to attention, but it does.

"I have a gift for you, too."

Her brow arches up. "Good. But first," she taps the tree box with her foot. "I want to put this tree together."

"Now? It's nine o'clock."

"You need a nap, Grampa?"

"Shut up. I meant, what's the point? Christmas is over in three hours."

"That's bullshit. People leave their trees up 'til January."

"You really want to put it up now?"

"Yeah. I want a Christmas tree. I've been looking at this box with these stupid happy people on it every day since you brought it home. And I think you've been wanting to put it up, too."

"What makes you think that?"

"You never leave shit lying around, and yet you've left this six-foot box right where we both have to trip over it."

I lift my shoulder. "Maybe you're right."

She kicks off her shoes and smiles at me.

"C'mon, Santa."

"I'll make you a deal." I step out of my boots and line our shoes up together on the rubber mat by the door. "I'll put this monstrosity together if you have a hot cocoa with me."

Her lips purse into the pout that has quickly become my favorite expression of hers. "Lucky, that's not fair. I'm not sure—"

"It's just milk, chocolate, and marshmallows. And my secret add-on." I head to the kitchen, and she follows along with the cat and the dog.

"I'm not agreeing to any secret add-on until I see what it is."

I pull out a saucepan and the ingredients I need and start heating milk on the stove.

She watches me with fascination. "My mom used to make it in the microwave with water."

"This is better." I wink at her. "Trust me."

"Okay…"

I eye her playfully as I stir the milk and cocoa, hoping to make her smile. "What'd you get me for Christmas?"

It's been years since I've been given a gift from anyone other than my aunt and uncle, and now that I'm thinking about it, I can't remember the last time a woman gave me a gift.

It better not be socks.

"I'm not going to tell you, Lucky. You have to wait."

I pour the hot cocoa into two mugs and add some marshmallows. Skylar watches me skeptically as I pull a small, wrapped candy cane that I swiped from Aunt Suzy's house out of my pocket and throw it in a sandwich bag with a few graham crackers. After quickly crushing it up together, I sprinkle it over the marshmallow.

"It's good, you'll like it." I hand it to her in her favorite mug that has a picture of a sunglass-wearing cat on it. "Everything is safe, I promise. I made the crumbs really tiny for you. No choking hazards."

"This is what I have to do to get you to put a Christmas tree up?"

"Yup. It's my favorite holiday drink. When we were little, Aunt Suzy used to tell us that elves made it for us. Someday when you have kids, you should make it for them." I raise my mug to my lips. "This stuff is the shit."

Her eyes linger on mine, then she looks down at the mug she's cupping in her hands.

"This is the best Christmas I've had in a long time," she confesses quietly. "Do you know how sweet you can be sometimes?" She glances up at me with a flash of accusation. "Or are you just totally oblivious?"

"Oblivious." I sip my hot cocoa concoction. "Drink that before it melts too much."

Finally, she tries it, and a white marshmallow mustache clings to her upper lip. I'm dying to kiss her and taste my favorite drink on her mouth, but she quickly licks it away.

Probably for the best.

"Well?" I prod impatiently.

She moves her hair behind her shoulder and smiles. "It's actually really good. Very cozy and festive."

"Told ya."

She watches me drink my cocoa and laughs softly when I down the last gulp and lick the marshmallow from the rim of my mug.

"What?" I ask.

"Nothing…" Her cheeks blush. "I just like seeing this happy side of you. You don't smile enough."

"I guess I'll try to smile more, then. How's that saying go? You never know who's falling in love with your smile?"

"Ya never know… that just might be true." She brushes by

me to put her mug in the sink, then turns to look up at me. "Thank you for sharing your favorite cocoa with me."

"Thanks for drinking it and not spitting it out."

Laughing, she picks up Gus and pins me with a look of impatience and excitement.

"Can we put the tree up now?"

We drag the box into the living room and take out all the pieces of the fake tree and its stand. We laugh at Gus, who's having a blast diving into the box, peeking out at us, then doing it all over again.

"You know she's going to knock this tree over, right?" Skylar says.

"That's why we're not putting ornaments on it. Just lights. So if she knocks it over, no big deal."

She holds up a fake tree branch and frowns quizzically while bending it up and down. "It's like a big tree-puzzle."

"Maybe I should've gotten a real one. I thought this would be easier."

"It would've been dead by now if you left it in the hallway like you did with this one."

An hour later our tree is slightly lopsided, but finally together and strung with little white lights and garland.

"It's beautiful," she says, reaching up to fix some of the branches. "I love the simple white lights, don't you?"

Nodding, I pull the Santa hat off my head and gently put it on hers, fluffing her long hair around her shoulders.

"You make a cuter Santa than I do," I say.

She smiles up at me. "That's debatable. You've been rockin' the sinful Santa vibes all day."

As hard as it is, I don't take the flirting bait. The vibe is good right now and I don't want it ruined.

I change the subject. "Do you want your present now?"

She jumps up. "Yes! I'll go get yours."

"While you're up there, grab yours off the top of my dresser," I call after her as she runs upstairs.

Seconds later she comes back down carrying two small, gift-wrapped boxes. One red, one silver. She hands me the red one.

"Open yours first," I say as we move to the couch.

She holds the thin, silver box to her ear and gently shakes it. "Full disclosure," she says. "You're the first guy to ever give me a Christmas present. Other than my dad and my grandfather, I mean."

"Great. I'm glad there's no pressure."

She smiles, totally unaware that I'm drowning in regret. This gift-giving milestone should've been between her and a guy her age—one she's actually romantically involved with. It would've been cute and special like young firsts are supposed to be.

I wonder—for the millionth time—if I've ruined more for her than I've helped her.

Her fingers tremble a bit as she carefully unwraps the present like it's the crown jewel. I can't tell if she's excited or nervous.

I wonder if the gift is enough. Maybe it's not enough.

Maybe it's too much.

Gift shopping was a new level of confusing I wasn't prepared for. What do you buy for the woman you're married to, not involved with, but falling in love with? What kind of gift says, hey, I'm crazy about you, but I'm too much of a pussy to tell you?

You give her exactly what she's holding up in her hands right now—a small, glass tube topped with a vintage, sterling hinged cap hanging from a thin chain. Inside it are a bunch of miniscule letters jumbled together.

"Jude..." she breathes. "It's beautiful." She turns it carefully in her palm, examining the necklace as if it's the most fascinating thing she's ever seen. "Do the letters inside spell something?"

"They do. A short message."

Her eyes flit from the necklace to meet mine. "A message from you?"

"Yeah."

When she moves her fingertips to unclasp the lid of the tube, I grab her hand.

"I want you to wait. Save it for a day when you really want to know what it says."

Her brows pinch together. "I want to know what it says now, though."

"I think if you wait for a time when you really, *really* want to know what it says, it'll mean more."

She studies my face, and I can't tell if she's disappointed, mad, or intrigued. "Only you would give me a gift that can't say what it's really meant to say," she says.

"Fitting, huh?"

"Very." She smiles crookedly. "I love it." Leaning closer, she kisses my cheek. Her lips stay pressed against me, sticky from the marshmallow, and I want to turn, capture her mouth with mine, drag her onto the floor, and slowly undress her under the Christmas tree. I want to see the glow of the lights on her perfect skin, kiss her everywhere, taste the chocolate and peppermint on her lips.

"Will you put it on me?" she asks, turning away and lifting her long hair up, exposing the back of her neck, in a slow, sensual swoop. My large fingers fumble with the delicate clasp at the nape of her neck.

"There ya go," I say, struggling not to pull her back against my chest and put my lips on her.

"It's perfect." Facing me, she fingers the glass tube. "I promise I'll wait to put the little letters together. The mystery of it is very intriguing. I like it."

"I thought you would." I pull two lottery scratch tickets out of my pocket. "These are for you, too."

She plucks them from my hands with a big smile on her face. "Maybe one of these will be my coveted thousand-dollar win."

So far, she hasn't won more than a hundred dollars on a ticket, but her mission is to win a grand.

I wink at her. "Ya never know."

"I'll scratch them later. I want you to open your prezzie."

Wasting no time, I rip the wrapping paper off to find a small, gray box. Inside is a matte black custom lighter with an etched image of a gargoyle holding a red heart.

It's cool. Probably one of the coolest things I'll ever own.

"Wow." I slowly rub my thumb over it. "I dig this a lot."

"I had it made for you. Turn it over," she says.

I do, and engraved with our wedding date, are the words: *Thank you for being the best bad husband ever. Love always, Skylar* ✷ . There's a tiny sparkle at the end of her name like I put in our text messages.

"I thought I'd give you a souvenir of our fake marriage. It seemed a little more appropriate when I bought it, before..." She doesn't finish her thought.

Before things started to fall apart.

As if I'd need something to remind me of her. She's already embedded in my heart, branded there as the one and only woman I've ever had feelings for. And probably ever will.

I snap the lighter open, light it up, then close it—snuffing the flame.

"It's perfect." I smile at her, wishing I could show her how perfect it is with kisses instead of words. "This is much better than the 'I fake married someone and all I got is this T-shirt' shirt I was expecting at the end of this."

"Ha ha. Very funny." She pulls the Santa hat off and golden strands of her hair stick up from her head, electrified with static. "The gargoyle reminded me of you. So rough and hard on the outside, but fiercely protective of the heart he's holding." She touches the lighter in my hand, then runs her finger slowly over my thumb to the pulse of my wrist. The touch is so simple, and yet the warm, tingling sensation travels all the way up my arm to my chest. "I'm just not sure if he's protecting his own heart, or someone else's."

"Maybe he's protecting both," I say.

Her finger instantly halts its subtle caress on my wrist.

She slowly pulls away and gazes across the room, fixating on the Christmas tree. The lights reflect in her eyes like millions of tiny fireflies.

I'm enchanted with her. Always.

"Today was nice. And a little awkward," she says in a melancholy way. "But I'm glad I went and spent it with your family."

"I am, too."

She leans back against the couch and hugs her knees. "Can I tell you something?"

"Of course."

"I talked to my father."

My head snaps back with surprise. "Really? When?"

"The night you were out. He sent me a text. It showed up as an unknown number. I thought it was a random wrong number at first."

"Wow. How'd it go?"

Her chest heaves up with a sigh. "Good and bad, I guess. We talked for a while. It was weird at first, then it got better. We talked about my mom, and me, and him. We talked about you, too. He wants to talk more, maybe see me." She looks at me and shakes her head. "I'm just not sure how I feel."

I want to ask her what her father had to say about me, but I have a distinct feeling he's the one who gave her the advice she mentioned the morning we talked, when she suddenly agreed that we shouldn't be together.

I refuse to make this conversation about me, though. No matter what, he's her father and I'm sure whatever advice he gave her was right on point. It's important to me that she make her own choices. I don't want to do or say anything to sway her in any direction. I don't want her—or anyone else—to think I took advantage of her being young, and brainwashed her to marry me or have sex with me. The last thing I want is someone like Rebecca accusing me of grooming a teenager.

"What he did was wrong, but people change," I say. "He could be a different man today than he was back then. He could be living with a ton of regret. It can't hurt to hear him out. Lay into him if you want to—you have that right."

"I did go off on him a little. He took it well and apologized… for leaving me. Do you think I should let him back into my life?"

"I don't know, Skylar. That's only for you to decide. You're older now. You can have a real conversation with him about everything. Make him accountable. I'd hear him out and then decide if you want to tell him to go fuck off, or maybe try to start over. This time, the choice will be *yours*. At least then you'll have closure."

"I don't know what to do. But, I have to admit, it was nice to talk to him. He sounds much happier. Would you let *your* father back into your life? Or your sister?"

I rub my face, trying to put myself in that position.

"A few years ago, I wouldn't even think about talking to my father. But now? Yeah, I'd talk to him again. Everybody makes mistakes and goes through their own shit. As for Erin? That wound's way too fuckin' raw. If she ever got her shit together and got clean, I might. And that's a *big* fucking might. She'd have to show a massive amount of remorse and do a shit ton of groveling after what she did to you." I exhale a breath. "Me at eighteen would've said fuck everyone, but me *now* understands life and people a lot better."

She stares up at the ceiling, chewing on her lip. "I'm going to think about it. I'm feeling a little anxious with the idea of people coming and going from my life again."

Fuck. I wish I could be the one thing in her life that's rock fuckin' solid no matter what.

But I fucked that up.

"You're young," I say, hoping she doesn't take that wrong. "There's lots of time to mend fences. But I think, someday, you're going to wish you had some contact with your family."

She swipes her finger beneath her eyes, banishing tears from her cheeks. *Something I should be doing.*

"Will you watch a Christmas movie with me?" she asks, her eyes yearning for me to say yes. "I don't want to go to sleep yet. Who knows where I'll be next year for the holidays? I just want to enjoy being in a nice cozy house, and look at our pretty tree, and forget about reality for a little while."

My stomach burns. I guess next year I'll be back to spending holidays with Uncle Al and Aunt Suzy, and coming home alone to just my dog.

I nod. "Yeah," I answer. "Let's do that."

I'd like to forget about reality for a little while, too.

CHAPTER 45
SKYLAR

At the front of the class, my English teacher drones on and on. It's my first week back after the holiday break, and I try to pay attention, but my thoughts keep wandering back to Jude.

I focus on the hole in my jeans and scribble a heart on the revealed skin with my pen, then write Lucky's name next to it in little blocky letters.

Now I get why people get tattoos with the name of the person they love. I want his name etched into my body forever. With me always. 'Til death do us part. Just like the vows promised.

But we're not meant to be, after all.

Maybe the vows really were just lies we had to tell.

Jude has been spending most of his time in the garage after work and on weekends, working on his motorcycle. Apparently, he's rebuilding his engine, but I wonder if it's mostly to avoid being in the same space as me. He knows I won't wander into the garage after his sister accosted me in there. There's still a shadow of the blood stain on the garage floor, and it freaks me out.

I'm dying to open the necklace and put the letters together. It's killing me not knowing what the letters spell out. Still, I refrain from doing so, because it doesn't feel like the right time. I'm not even sure how I'll know when the right time is.

But, I'll wait for it to come.

"You're so pathetic," a voice to my right says. "Writing a pedophile's name on your leg. So trashy."

"Not nearly as pathetic as that makeup job trying to cover the bump on your nose," I shoot back.

I think Paige's dad ran out of money, because her perfect nose has yet to be resurrected by her plastic surgeon after I slammed it with my lunch tray.

I have no regrets.

She glares at me.

I smile back.

Technically, we're not supposed to be near each other after the cafeteria incident, but the people who run this school are a joke and don't even enforce their own rules. Therefore, I'm subjected to her endless torment every day.

"My older cousin went to school with your husband," Paige whispers from her seat. "She said he was a stoner and a drug dealer. She said he had girls lining up giving him blowjobs at parties in exchange for joints and pills. She said she saw him having a threesome in a hot tub once, too."

I grind my teeth together. I don't know if any of that crap is true, and I'm not sure I really want to know.

I continue to fill in the little heart on my leg. "Sounds like your cousin was a nosy bitch in high school, too. Must run in your family."

"You're such a loser, Skylar. Your own parents didn't want you, so you basically had to have some guy adopt you and raise you as a little wife-slave. Why don't you just kill yourself?"

I wonder if stabbing her with my pen would be considered assault.

No.

I won't do it.

This is my favorite gel pen.

My silence only eggs her on. "We've seen you going into that medical building downtown twice a week. We all know you're seeing a shrink. What's wrong with you? Are you depressed, little baby?"

"Leave her alone." Mark, the kid who sits behind me, has come to my defense. I have no idea why, since we've barely spoken two words to each other since school started months ago.

"Oh, please," Paige sneers. "You're not going to get your dick wet defending her, Mark. She's a married woman. By the way, Skylar, where's your wedding band? Or couldn't your drop-out, drug dealer husband afford one?"

"Just leave her alone. Stop being such a cunt."

"Are you cheating on your husband already, Skylar? Figures, you dirty slut."

"Excuse me," Mr. Gold says loudly. "Unless you want to get up here and teach the class, I suggest you all shut your mouths."

Shrinking back in my chair, I keep my eyes trained ahead as Paige and two of her friends continue to whisper and giggle.

By the time class is over, my insides are shaking with anger and humiliation, and there's a burning feeling radiating from my stomach up to my throat.

I fish the bottle of chewable DGL licorice tablets out of my bag and pop two into my mouth. They're supposed to help calm the acid bubbling in my throat, but I honestly don't even know if they do.

How am I ever supposed to get healthy if every time I start to feel better, these bitches start in on me and get my anxiety all ramped up again? My therapist tells me to ignore them, but how am I supposed to do that when they're right here in my space, and the teachers don't do anything about it? Paige and her friends are relentless with their nasty comments all day, every day. As luck would have it, they're in every one of my classes this semester, so there's no escape.

I leave school two hours early, biting back tears as I walk to the parking lot, and then sit in my car for twenty minutes, hoping the panic attack will subside before I drive home. My mind is spinning and dizzy with horrible thoughts, my heart is racing and pounding, my stomach is burning and rumbling.

Taking deep breaths, I rub my fingertips back and forth over my jeans.

He had girls lining up giving him blowjobs.

Your own parents didn't want you.

Are you depressed, little baby?

Some guy adopted you.

You dirty slut.

Nausea rises up to my throat in waves and I swallow it back down. I hate this so much—this shaky, overwhelming feeling of being stuck in my own head, feeling like I can't escape the terrible things people are saying about me and Jude. The more I think about it, the worse the acidic burn in my stomach and the throbbing in my head persists.

After a few minutes of internal debating, I pull my phone out of my purse and call Jude.

"Hey," he says when he answers. "You okay?"

The tone of his voice is immediately concerned, because he knows I should be in school right now, and he also knows I never call unless it's important.

"I-I'm having a panic attack."

"Oh, shit. Where are you?"

"Sitting in my car. In the parking lot."

"I'll be right th—"

"No," I say, quickly regretting calling him. "Just talk to me for a few minutes. You don't have to come."

"Skylar, I don't want you to be alone. I'm only two minutes away."

The last thing I need is anyone seeing him coming to my car during school hours. It will only fuel Paige and her posse.

"Please, Lucky, I just want to hear your voice. If we talk for a few minutes, it'll pass."

"Okay," he says, then I hear him talk to one of his crew. "I gotta take this. I'll be back in a few." A few seconds filled with the sound of footsteps go by, then a car door opening and closing. "I'm here, baby," he finally says. "Are you okay?"

Baby. A slip of the tongue that makes my heart jump around in a totally different way.

"I feel really dizzy and shaky. And my stomach is burning really bad."

"Take some deep breaths. What are you wearing?"

My fingers tighten around the phone. "Um, are we going there with this call?"

"I meant for your texture touching."

"Oh," I say, feeling stupid.

"But if you want to describe your outfit to me in detail, I'm not opposed," he jokes.

I let out a little laugh. "Are you in your truck?"

"Yeah, I wanted some privacy. Did something happen today?"

"Kind of…"

"Was it one of those asshole stuck-up bitches again?"

"Of course. They're so nasty. Usually I can ignore them, but some days…" I can't even finish my sentence because I can feel the tears coming on again.

"You want me to talk to the principal? And the parents of these little spoiled douchebags? I'll fix this shit right now."

"No… I don't want you to do that. We can't have you ending up in jail."

"I'll do it for you, Sparkles. As long as you promise to visit me and give me some conjunctival visits."

I burst out laughing. "It's *conjugal*."

I know he's trying to make me laugh, and it's working. I miss our playful teasing so much.

"Whatever it is, I'd have to have it." I hear the sound of his lighter snapping open, then closed. "Did you take your pills?"

"Just the ones for my stomach. I don't want to take the anxiety pills. They make me spacey."

"I hear ya." He exhales, and I can picture smoke blowing out his window. I wish he'd quit smoking. "Are you feeling better?"

"I am now. Talking to you helps. You always make me feel better. And you make me laugh."

"You always make me feel better, too."

"Really?" My mood brightens a little. "I never knew that."

"Now ya do," he says in his sexy, teasing voice. "Are you still in your car?"

"Yes," I answer, just as there's a soft tapping on my window.

"Open the door."

Turning toward the door, my mouth falls open and I quickly unlock it and push it open. "Jude! What are you doing?"

He kneels down next to my open car door and leans inside. "I had to make sure you're okay."

With tears in my eyes, I throw my arms around him, not caring who sees or what they think or say. Screw all that. None of that matters.

This is all that matters—this man who just dropped everything he was doing for *me* without the slightest hesitation.

We hug for several long minutes. I don't want to let him go. He feels like home, and it reminds me how much I've missed this closeness with him.

When we pull away, he cups my head in his palms and rubs his thumbs across my cheeks, wiping my tears.

"You didn't have to come," I say softly.

"Yeah, I did. You think I'd let you sit in a parking lot by yourself when you need me? I didn't let you do it the day we met, and I won't do it now. Or ever."

I grin at him and sniffle. "You're kind of amazing."

"I know. So are you," he says, winking at me. "Are you okay? I can drive you to work, or home."

I shake my head. "No, I feel a lot better now. I don't have to work today, so I can go home."

That's when I notice he's staring at my leg.

Oh, no.

"And what's this?" he asks, touching his name written on my leg through the hole just above my knee.

"Um… a fake tattoo?" I say lamely, feeling way too much like a teenage girl with a crush writing a boy's name with hearts all over her stuff.

He turns his gaze back to me with that damn smirk. "I'll take you to get a real one if ya want."

I push his hand away. "I was just scribbling."

"It's cute," he says. "I'm kinda flattered. I don't think anyone's ever written my name on them before."

I pull at the frayed threads in the hole and avert my eyes from his. "Is it true that you traded blowjobs for drugs?"

He chokes. *"What?"*

"Apparently Paige's cousin went to school with you. She said that's what you did at parties."

"What the fuck?" he says, shoving a hand through his hair. "Skylar, I was six-fucking-teen."

"So, it's true?" I ask, horrified, and hoping he'll deny it immediately.

His shoulders lift. "I think I did that once."

My mouth frowns in disgust and disappointment. "So gross, Lucky."

"C'mon, it was stupid kid shit."

"Okay." It's really none of my business, and I have no right to be feeling the jealousy boiling in my blood.

"I'm not gonna lie about it, Skylar. I have a scuzzy past. I can't change it."

"I know… you're right." I smile weakly at him. "Your past doesn't matter. I like who you are now."

He touches my hand. "I like you, too."

I remember he said those same words way back when we went to the park for the first time, and laughed on the swings together. I wonder if he remembers that day like I do. I wonder if he felt the same sparks when he helped me stand up, with my hand in his.

Our first hand hug.

"You're better now? he asks hoarsely.

"Yes." I nod. "Thank you for coming to sit with me."

He pulls his hand away slowly. Just as slow as he did that day. "I gotta go back to work. Text me when you get home. Drink some tea, cozy up with a book. I'll make us grilled cheese when I get home."

I nod and watch him walk casually back to his truck. How dare he look just as sexy from the back as he does from the front.

I wish I didn't want him, but I still do. So damn much it hurts.

I'm in such a daze on the drive home I don't even put any music on. I just want quiet so I can hear his voice in my head, saying those four words.

I like you, too.

I wonder if he misses me as much as I miss him.

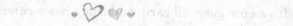

When I get home, I take Cassie out in the yard for a few minutes, hugging myself against the frigid breeze, then go upstairs. I text Megan on my way to my room.

Me: In case you're looking for me, I left school early. Paige was annoying the shit out of me.

Megan: She's such a witch!

Me: I know I'm so sick of her. Can I call you tonight? What time will you be home?

Megan: Try me at nine. Are you okay?

Me: Yes, just wanted to vent and stuff

Megan: Okay. Vent session scheduled at 9. xo

I change into yoga pants and an oversized sweater, and flop on my bed. Gus jumps up next to me and I kiss her head as she does happy paws across my stomach.

Reaching across my nightstand to pick up my book, I accidentally knock my phone onto the floor and it bounces under my bed.

"Crap," I mutter as I hang off the bed to pick it up. Something catches my eye as I'm down there, and I realize it's the card Jude left in my room the day I had oral surgery.

I was waiting to open it that night, but Gus must've knocked it and it fell behind the bed. I rip the envelope open and pull the card out. A smile spreads across my face when a twenty-five-dollar lottery scratch ticket falls out.

It's a cute get-well card, and Jude has written:

Don't worry, life gets better! No matter what, I'm here for you. Always. All my love, Jude

The smile slowly falls from my lips. I wish I had read these words sooner. Was he trying to tell me how he felt about me way back then? Did he think I read this and just ignored it?

All my love isn't exactly a platonic way to sign a card.

Is it?

"Why is everything so confusing, Gus?" I say, holding the lottery card. I don't know how many times I've told Jude not to waste his money on these expensive tickets. I'm totally happy with the one-dollar scratch-offs.

I scratch off all the little glittery squares and scrape the residue into my trash can before glancing at the rows of numbers and symbols.

Holy.

Shit.

Letting out a gasp, I stare at the numbers. My fingers tremble, jumbling the ticket in my hand.

I have all the numbers.

I blink and scan the card again, convinced my eyes are going screwy from crying and I'm not seeing clearly.

But they're all there.

Every. Single. One.

With my pulse racing, I read the instructions on the back of the ticket over and over—convinced I must be missing something—that there has to be a mistake.

Except I can't find any sort of mistake.

I won.

I just won *two hundred and fifty thousand dollars*.

"Oh my God!" I shriek.

I pick up Gus and dance around the room with her. "We won! We're rich! We can get our RV, blow this town and everyone in it and never look back, Gus."

I can't wait to tell Jude. And Megan.

Giddy, I twirl around and round the room until I'm dizzy and my vision blurs, and I swear I see a shadow in the doorway.

CHAPTER 46

SKYLAR

"Lucky..."

Startled, I put Gus down and stare at Jude, leaning against the doorframe like he's done a hundred times before, but I've never seen the look on his face that I do right now.

He looks like I just kicked him in the gut.

"Wh-what are you doing home?" I ask, trying to catch my breath.

"I was worried about you." His jaw muscles twitch and clench.

Spinning around, I grab the lottery ticket from the middle of my bed and hold it up with an excited smile.

"Holy shit, Jude... you're not going to believe this. I just won two hundred and fifty thousand dollars. Look!" I wave the ticket around like a lunatic. "I found the card you left me when I had surgery, the cat must have knocked it behind my bed that day. The ticket was inside... I didn't even know it was there."

"So, you're leaving? Never looking back." His voice is stone cold.

My stomach drops. "What? No, I—"

The fallen look on his face rips my heart apart. Every ounce of excitement I had goes up in flames and disintegrates with the realization of what my words must've sounded like to him.

"No," I say, shaking my head rapidly. "I didn't mean it like that. Not at all."

His eyes pin me from across the room, hard with a tragic resignation that stabs at my very soul. "Really?" he says. "Pretty sure you said *blow this town and everyone in it and never look back*."

"I wasn't even thinking. I was so shocked and excited," I say quickly. "And I thought you'd be, too. Half this money is *yours*. This is life changing for both of us!"

He shakes his head and his hair tumbles into his face. He flicks it out of his eyes with a quick jerk. "I don't want it. You can fuckin' keep all of it."

Turning, he storms to his room and shuts the door with such quiet finality, it sends a chill up my spine.

Undeterred, I march down the hall and open his door. Privacy and boundaries be damned. We're beyond that at this point.

I find him standing by the window, staring outside and playing with the lighter I gave him for Christmas. Lighting it, then slamming the cover over the flame. I can feel the depth of all the emotions coming off him like heat from a fire.

Anger.

Disappointment.

Heartache.

It's all right there, smoldering.

Slowly approaching him, I touch his arm. "Jude..." When he flinches away from my touch, a massive boulder of emotion rolls up into my throat, nearly suffocating me. "I don't want to leave *you*." I swallow hard as my voice crackles and trembles.

"That's not what you said."

"For God's sake. I was talking to my cat. I was completely

freaking out with shock. I just won the lottery! For years my ultimate goal has been to somehow get out of this town and away from all the shitty people who've hurt me. You know that."

He throws a quick glance at me. "I guess now you can do it."

I'm so confused.

I don't understand why he's acting upset. This is what he wanted. We're not together. We *both* decided that was best.

So why is he acting like I'm leaving him? And why do I *feel* like I'm leaving him?

"This isn't fair," I say. "Why are you upset? Even *your* plan was that I was supposed to leave once I got on my feet. Things have been up and down and back and forth between us. You've never said you wanted me to stay." Tears start tracking down my cheeks. "*Tell* me what you want."

"Maybe neither one of us knows what we want," he says quietly.

I don't know how to respond to that. Despite what's supposedly "right" for us, I still want to be with him.

"This is a turning point for both of us," I finally say. "Take your half of the money. Buy your uncle's bar. This could change your whole life. And mine. It's a huge fucking gift."

"And what are you going to do?"

I don't know. He's not saying the words I need to hear. I want to stay here. Stay married to him. Be part of his family and the bar and build a life with him. I want to take photography and photojournalism classes online. I want to see if I can be a social media influencer.

But I can do those things from anywhere. From here—or from the RV I've always dreamed of—or from anywhere. *He's* the only thing that would keep me in this town, and I'll happily stay. I can ignore the demons that lurk here if it means being with him.

If he would just say he wants me to stay!

"I don't know." My voice wavers with emotion. "I guess if I

won this money, there's no reason for us to be married anymore, and there's no reason for me to live here. I can pay you back everything you spent to help me, and I can leave."

Every word is like poison on my lips. Burning, making me sick. But I don't know what else to do to get a reaction out of him.

He continues to look out the window and rocks on his heels. "I guess you're right."

I stare at his back, hoping he'll turn around and look at me and tell me he wants me to stay. That our age difference doesn't matter and he wants us to take this money and make all our dreams come true together.

Where is the man who dropped everything when I needed him, flirted with me, and touched my hand earlier?

The silence between us becomes unbearably painful.

"Then you can have your lawyer draw up our divorce papers," I say, and I leave the room feeling totally abandoned.

Again.

My favorite Ashes & Embers song lyrics come to mind:

"Baby, I can only take you so far
and the rest… the rest is up to you
But I can't wait forever,
because every day takes me further away
And someday, it might be too late
for me to hear what you have to say"

CHAPTER 47

JUDE

"You dropped out?" I follow her up to her room. She tosses her book bag onto the bed like she never wants to touch it again.

She's wearing my favorite fringe suede jacket today, and I love the way the fringe swings as she turns to me with fire in her eyes. So much sass and beauty, just like the day we met.

"I didn't drop out. After being held back when I was younger, I was able to take some Advanced Placement courses when I started high school. You can test out of them and graduate early. I took the test, I passed, I graduated."

I'm surprised she did this without telling me. She usually talks to me about everything. Or at least she did, until everything crumbled.

"Isn't that a big decision? Why didn't you talk to me about this?"

She cocks her head at me. "Seriously? We've hardly said two words to each other this past week. *You* shut down, not me."

It's true.

My head's been a fucking mess.

Her winning the lottery was a blessing and a curse. She was

right—the money is life changing. My half is giving me the opportunity to buy Uncle Al's bar. I'm finishing up all my scheduled construction jobs and getting the hell out of that life. In less than three months, I'll be dissolving my business and starting an entirely new venture.

Her half of the money has given her exactly what she's always wanted. What I was trying to give her from the beginning.

Freedom.

A safe place to live.

Medical care.

She doesn't need my help anymore. She can have all that without me. But I'm still struggling big time. With the age difference. With not wanting her to go. With not knowing what to do or say. With being afraid of loving her—then losing her someday.

"So, you're done with school?" I ask.

She sits on her reading chair in the corner to pull off her shoes, and looks up at me. "Yes. Today was my last day."

I feel like this is my fault, too. I can see her grandfather looking down at us in disappointment, pointing a finger at me.

"I wish you'd talked to me before you went and did this."

She sighs. "Jude, it's done. I graduated. I get a diploma. It's no big deal, lots of kids do it. I just couldn't deal with the constant shit from Paige and her little yappy dogs bullying me all day long. You were cool and popular in high school; you have no idea what it's like. The anxiety of it all was making me physically sicker."

I've noticed her taking more of the antacids, supplements, and anxiety pills. There's been extra visits to her therapist and dietician. She spends more time alone in her room.

It's been ripping my heart out.

The whole "set the person you love free" thing has weighed heavily on my mind.

I don't want her to stay here—in this town, in this relationship—for me. I want her to stay because *everything* here is what she wants. It can't just be for me. I want her to feel fulfilled in every way—in love, in life, in whatever career she chooses.

I want her to have all the things a young girl should have, not just in life, but in a relationship. Magical dates, an engagement, a real wedding.

She didn't get any of that with me.

"What are you going to do?" I ask.

She throws her hands up. "Jump start my life, I guess? I'm going to take some online photography, marketing, and photojournalism classes. And I've decided to go visit my dad. I'm driving out to see him tomorrow. I'm not sure how long I'll be staying—a week, maybe a month. I'm taking Gus with me. Is it okay if I leave my things here until I get back? Then I'll look for a studio apartment and decide what I want to do next. I'm still thinking about my RV."

I feel like she just hit me with a freight train with all her plans.

And she's leaving *tomorrow*.

I nod, despite the fact that the moving out and moving on part is shredding my guts. "That all sounds great. I'm proud of you. You can leave your stuff here as long as you need to. There's no rush."

She huffs and pushes her hair out of her face, clearly taking my response as a sign I want her to go.

"I'd rather just get everything taken care of as soon as I can," she says.

I watch her pull two big suitcases out of her closet. She must have bought them in the past few days, because she didn't have them when she moved in.

"Where does your dad live?"

"He's in Connecticut."

I assumed he lived nearby, not almost three hours away.

"Are you okay with driving that far by yourself?"

She raises her chin with confidence I'm not really sure she feels. "It's not that far, I'll be fine. I'm renting a car so I don't put a bunch of miles on your car. When I get back to town, I want my Corvette back."

Uh oh.

"Are you staying in a hotel, or with him?"

She takes some shirts out of her dresser and lays them in the open suitcase. "I'm going to stay at his house. They have four bedrooms."

I swallow and try not to let my voice sound as worried as I feel. "Are you sure you want to do that?"

"He's my father, Jude. He's remarried. I did a video chat with him and his new wife. They both seem really nice and surprisingly normal, which is what I need right now."

I'm afraid she's running away. A few weeks ago, she was leery of her father, and unsure if she even wanted to talk to him again. Now she's going to stay with him for an indefinite amount of time, and she's acting all nonchalant about it—like it's no big deal—when I know damn well it is.

"Can Megan go with you? So you're not alone?"

"She can't, she has school. And I'm not afraid to go alone."

"I didn't say you were afraid, it's a long drive, and you haven't seen him in a long time. I want you to be careful."

"I will."

I look away as she bends over to empty out her bottom dresser drawer.

"You can leave Fupagus here until you come back if you want. She feels safe here. I'll take care of her."

She looks over at the cat curled up contently on the bed and ponders my offer. "I'd rather she come with me. I can't risk you changing your mind a week after I'm gone."

Stab. Stab. Stab.

Without her laughter, and without Cassie and Gus chasing each other from room to room, this house is going to feel like a fucking tomb again. I've missed eating dinner with her and watching movies together at night, but at least she was still here. I could still hear her, see her, catch the sweet scent of her perfume.

I chew the inside of my cheek as she goes to her nightstand, takes something out of the drawer, and then steps in front of me.

"Here," she says, holding her hand out to me. "You can have this back."

My eyes focus on the small, rose-gold ring in her hand, and my gut sinks with dread.

"No." I shake my head, refusing to take it from her. "That's yours. It was a gift."

She stares at me with her lower lip quivering. "It's a band of lies," she says. "I don't want it anymore."

I swear, I want to solder that ring onto her finger and just end all this craziness.

"Fuck, Skylar. Don't fucking do this."

"Do what?"

"Any of this." I throw my arms up. "Running to your father. Moving out. Giving me the ring back. Why are you doing this?"

Her cheeks flush red with anger. "Because it's what I should be doing."

"I think you're in shock or something from winning all that money. Why don't you take a week or two and just chill out before you make all these decisions."

"I don't want to chill out. I'll go crazy if I have to sit here trying to read your damn mind every day."

"What does that mean?"

"I can't do *this* with you anymore. I've had it. This back and forth and all the confusion. It's making me sick."

"Wow, jugular, much?"

Her eyes soften. "I don't mean *you* make me sick, I mean this whole situation."

My shoulders slump and I stare down at the floor before meeting her gaze. Everything she's saying is reinforcing every fear I have about us. *I* am bad for her. "Do what you gotta do, then."

She grabs my hand and shoves the ring into my palm.

"You should go," she says, whisper soft. "So I can finish doing what I have to do."

CHAPTER 48
SKYLAR

Seeing my father is surreal.

He looks better than I remember from the faded snapshots in my mind. He's lost weight, and now looks athletic and healthy. I realize I have his eyes. Lynn, his new wife, is even prettier in person than she was on the video chat. Her hair is long and chestnut brown with blonde highlights and she has deep-brown, wide-set eyes. She has a thirteen-year-old quiet son named Sam, who calls my father Dad. Lynn works as an accountant and my father is an electrical engineer, which I didn't know when I was younger.

It's obvious from their house on a cul-de-sac of identical houses that they're financially comfortable. The house is big and beautiful with a pool in the backyard and bright-green grass that looks too perfect to be real.

My first few hours here so far have been awkward but friendly.

I'm not sure how to feel about my father starting over with a new life while I was left behind, possibly forgotten. I wonder if he found an old picture of me in his wallet and suddenly remembered I existed, or if he's been thinking of me and missing me for the past almost twelve years.

When I arrived, we talked casually for a few minutes before Lynn showed me to the guestroom so I could unpack and get Gus settled before dinner. The cat immediately ran to hide under the bed, and I wished I had left her home with Jude, where she has all her favorite spots, and Cassie to snuggle with. My dad's house is way too big to let her just wander around loose. I'm afraid I'll never find her.

Lynn gave the cat carrier a big side-eye when I took it out of my rental car, and she mentioned that Sam might have allergies —especially to a longhaired cat. My father neglected to tell me that when we talked over the phone about my visiting.

Men.

Before I venture back downstairs, I send Jude the text he made me promise to send.

Me: Just letting you know I'm here, safe and sound.

Jude: Good. I hope you enjoy your visit. Text or call me if you need to talk.

As I'm fixing up my hair, another text comes through.

Jude: For what it's worth, I already miss you guys. 

His bittersweet words cause tears to burn in my eyes and my chest to tighten around my heart.

I wish we could both get on the same page. It's so ironic that we never wanted to get married for fear of the heartache it can cause, and now here we are, in a marriage that isn't even real, going through everything we were trying to avoid.

All broken hearts aside, Jude stepped up for me when no one

else did, and that has gained him a place in my heart, and in my life, forever.

Me: I miss you guys, too. 🩶

"Sam is staying at a friend's house tonight so we can talk," my father says when we convene in the formal dining room.

It's so strange to see my father in this setting after he slept in a rusty old RV in the driveway for years and lived on beer and Cheetos.

I guess people really can change their path if they want to badly enough.

"Skylar, I made steamed vegetables and mashed potatoes for you," Lynn informs me as she takes her seat next to my father. "The chicken is free range and antibiotic free, though. Maybe you can eat that?"

"Thank you, but I don't eat meat at all."

"It's not healthy to be so picky about your food," my father says, pointing his fork at me, which has a chunk of chicken at the end of it. "You need protein."

"I eat enough protein. And it's not being picky, I have an eating disorder and an unhealthy mental relationship with food."

His lips press together in a hard line. "This is something your crackpot mother did to you. I never should've left you there with that nut job."

So, we're going to start off by jumping right into the mess. Game on, then.

"Actually, my ARFID most likely stemmed from eating spoiled food as a child and having food poisoning several times. And choking. If I recall, you were still living there when all this was happening. She's not the only one to blame."

He cuts into his chicken aggressively, and the squeak of the knife against the plate makes me feel queasy. "I admit, I wasn't paying much attention back then. I thought your mother was taking care of you."

"I was taking care of myself."

Lynn smiles sympathetically at me, and I'm sure that behind her smile, she's glad she sent her son someplace else for the night so he didn't have to witness this drama. I wonder if she knew my father abandoned me as a child when she married him.

I suppose most skeletons escape the closet after marriage.

"You're right," my father says, holding my gaze with his. "And you deserved better. I'm sorry for all of it. For your mother, for not doing better, for leaving you there. I wish I could go back and change it."

"I do, too," I say sadly.

"I just hope you can try to forgive me and we can start over. I contacted your mother numerous times trying to get in touch with you. For years I sent money, but I never knew if it was given to you or used to care for you. She rarely answered my calls or messages. She finally gave me your phone number a few weeks ago, after I called her nonstop for months."

My mashed potatoes suddenly feel too thick in my mouth. I count to five and breathe through my nose and wait for my throat to relax so I can swallow. I know better than to have serious conversations when I'm eating or drinking—I just thought I could get through this one without an episode.

When the potatoes go down I take a sip of water and turn my attention back to my father, who's watching me with a distraught look.

"I had no idea you ever tried to contact me, or sent money."

A frown contorts his face. "I'm sure she took the money and used it to buy more crap."

I nod in agreement, thinking of the giraffe in the living room and the twenty-eight boxes of fabric softener piled in the hallway. "Either that, or she never opened the envelopes and just threw them onto a pile."

"I'm sorry, Skylar. I should've taken you with me, or checked in on you. Being married to her really took a toll on me, and at the end, I just wasn't myself, and I had to get away. I hate that I left the way I did."

I put my fork down and level my eyes at him. It's obvious he's sorry. I can see it in his eyes and hear it in the regret dripping from his voice. I want to try to forgive him, but I also want him to realize the severity of what his abandonment did to me, which goes way beyond a few missing checks.

"I can understand that," I say. "Unfortunately, *I* couldn't get away from her. Things got much worse after you left. The house was infested with bugs and mice. There was trash and rotting food everywhere. The kitchen and bathroom became unusable. I had to lock myself in my bedroom to keep her out. I had to climb through my bedroom window to get in and out of the house because the front door was barricaded. I had a tiny fridge in my room to keep fresh water and food in. I had to take showers at a truck stop and at school. And I had to put cat litter in a bucket in my closet to piss and shit."

My father and Lynn cringe at my words, but I don't care. If I had to live these horrible things, then they can hear them.

"Finally, I married a man in his thirties and moved in with him so I'd have a safe place to live and medical insurance to get on a treatment plan. I left high school early, missing the prom and graduation and things someone my age should enjoy, because I was bullied into a state of being unhealthy. That's the toll *you and mom* took on me, because you both forgot about me."

Lynn is sobbing quietly and my father's complexion has gone deathly pale. I don't feel one bit sorry for them.

"Skylar..." My father's voice catches and he coughs into his napkin. "No apology can ever be enough to make up for what you've been through. I know that. I understand if you want nothing to do with me. I deserve it. But if you can find it in your heart to try, I promise I won't let you down again. I want a second chance."

I push my plate away. "Part of my therapy is forgiveness, so I'd like to try."

He smiles weakly. "I'd like that very much."

"We truly are sorry for everything," Lynn says, even though she has nothing to do with any of it. I suppose she feels guilty by association. "We want you to know you can stay here for as long as you want. We have room. We'd love to have you."

"I think I'll stay for a little while, but then I plan to rent a studio apartment back home until I figure out what I want to do with my life."

"Have you put any thought into college?" Lynn asks. "We'd be more than happy to help you." She's under the assumption that I graduated early to focus on college.

They also don't know I've won the lottery.

"College isn't for me," I say politely. "I'm going to take some online classes, though."

"That's good," my father says optimistically. "And what about the man you're living with? Have you put up some boundaries like we talked about? Filed for divorce or an annulment?"

During my first phone call with my father a few weeks ago, I was lonely and upset, and probably word-vomited a little too much. I got caught up in having my father finally show concern and care for me. I told him things had gotten complicated with Jude, and feelings were involved, but I didn't tell him we've crossed more lines than a tic-tac-toe board. My father tried to give his best advice, and in that moment, I wanted to act on his advice, because I desperately ache to have love and acceptance from my parents.

But now, I'm not sure I need anyone's advice or acceptance.

"I'm thinking about all of it," I answer. "It's just a difficult, confusing situation with him."

Lynn is shaking her head and looking horrified. "Forgive me, but that situation sounds *very* inappropriate to me. It's sick for a grown man to be married to, and living with, a young girl. It sounds like he took advantage of you and could hurt you—"

"He didn't," I interrupt. "Jude is a good man. He cares about me. The only man who's ever hurt me is sitting next to you."

"Honey," my dad says, as if he's talking to a child. "We're sure he cares about you in his own way, but it's still a very questionable arrangement. It's not normal or healthy, and, as your father, I want you out of that house. We're both very worried about you."

I don't expect them to understand. They haven't been in my shoes, or Jude's, so it's impossible for them to truly grasp the depth of our feelings for each other.

"I respect your opinions, but the bottom line is, you don't know him. Or me. I'm working on figuring my life out, but I won't listen to you bad mouth him. He's been very good to me. None of us are perfect, we've all made mistakes, and we're all doing our best," I point out. "But I can assure you, he's not some kind of predator."

I can't deal with judgement and assumptions about my relationship with Jude anymore. I left high school to escape that behavior from others. I can't sort out my thoughts if others are constantly throwing in their two cents when they don't even know us or what we've been through.

"We just want what's best for you," my father says.

Everyone keeps saying that, but I don't know if anyone—not even myself—knows what's best for me.

CHAPTER 49

SKYLAR

I'm starting to feel homesick.

I miss watching the chipmunks run along the old rock wall in Jude's backyard.

I miss working at the boutique, taking photos, and talking to Rebecca.

I miss hanging out with Megan.

I miss my bed.

I miss Cassie and her wiggly butt when I walk through the door.

I miss my face-to-face appointments with my therapist.

I miss all things Jude—our movie nights, his damn sexy smirks, his gray eyes, having dinner together, listening to music, hearing about his day, his quiet intensity.

Ugh.

I've enjoyed spending time with my father, Lynn, and the ever-quiet Sam, but their house doesn't feel like home to me. It's too big, too cold, too motel-ish.

For almost a month, I've been at my dad's, and a little internal clock is telling me it's time to make a decision. I can stay here in

Connecticut and get my own place; start over in an entirely new atmosphere with my father and his family. Or, I can get an RV and trek across the country, leaving everything and everyone behind. But somewhere along the way, the appeal of doing that has faded. Being alone in a big box on wheels feels exactly like that now—being alone.

Alone doesn't seem exciting anymore.

Instead, I find myself thinking about staying in New Hampshire. Staying close to Megan. Taking on more responsibility at the boutique. And even though I know running into Jude from time to time would be the equivalent of getting stabbed in the heart over and over again, it's almost better than *not* being near him.

How odd it is that I have enough money to do basically anything I want, and all I want to do is go back home?

I thought being away from Jude and the constant emotional rollercoaster of our relationship would be helpful, but being away from him is even worse.

I'm contemplating all these options while sitting in the kitchen, watching my father prune his perfectly round shrubs in the backyard, when my cell phone rings.

"Hello?" I say.

"Skylar?" I instantly recognize Aunt Suzy's voice.

"Aunt Suzy," I say. "What a surprise. How are you?"

"Al and I are both doing well. How are you doing? How are things with your father?"

"It's good. I'm glad I came to reconnect with him. We've made some great progress."

"Honey that's wonderful," she says, and then pauses. "I absolutely hate to make phone calls like this, but I'm afraid I don't have a choice."

A chill courses through my veins. "Are you okay?"

"Yes, I'm fine, but Lucky is in bad shape."

I inhale a breath then slowly release it. Aunt Suzy is obviously still hell-bent on us getting together, even though she knows, from the last time we spoke, that me and Jude haven't been talking much other than to just say hi via text.

"I miss him, too, Aunt Suzy but this is for the best. Last time I talked to him, he was excited about taking over the bar. I think if we both just stay focused on the positives, we'll be okay."

Reciting advice from my therapist is easy.

Actually believing it is a different story.

"No sweetheart, it's not that. He was in an accident on the job site. I can't believe this was his last project and then *this* happens."

"Wait, what?" Every cell of my body has jumped into a panic. "Did you say he was hurt? Hurt how?"

"Apparently he fell through a floor. He hit his head and was out for almost five minutes according to that guy Bob who works for him. He has a severe concussion. When we got to the hospital, he kept saying where am I, where am I, where am I, repeatedly for hours after it happened. He was very disoriented. Al and I were terrified he had brain damage."

"Oh my God!" I say, running up to my room. "Is he alright? Is he home?"

"He's still in the hospital. He's doing better, but I thought you should know."

"When did this happen?" I grab my suitcases and start throwing my things into them.

"Yesterday morning. He was pretty bad all day, having difficulty remembering things and slurring his words. He was dizzy and vomiting off and on. But today he seems much better. Al and I just left the hospital so he could rest."

My heart is racing so fast I feel like I'm going to pass out. "Is he okay, though? Is he going to be okay?"

"The doctor said he'll be fine; he just needs to rest and take it easy for a few weeks. They said he can go home tomorrow or the day after. He also has a hairline skull fracture, a fractured tailbone, and his back is very bruised."

"Oh my God," I say again, wondering how he fell through a floor. "I'm leaving here as soon as I can. I have to be there with him."

"I don't mean to worry you, honey, and I know things aren't all rainbows with you two, but I thought you'd want to be there. And I'm sure he'd feel better if you were there."

"I wish you had called me sooner. I would've come right away."

"I know, we just weren't sure if it was serious. We didn't want to interrupt you when you're visiting your family."

"I don't care about that," I say. "I'm so worried about him. Is he talking now?"

"He was talking to us earlier. He's grumpy and tired, but he was making sense."

"That's good, right?"

"Yes, it's very good. Please be careful driving. You don't have to speed here, he's in good hands. Please call me when you get there, though, so I know you're both okay."

"I will," I promise.

"We'll be there in the morning. Uncle Al is keeping things moving for the bar, and that guy Bob is keeping the crew running, so there's nothing for Lucky to worry about except resting and letting himself heal. Oh—we've been stopping by the house to feed and walk the dog, but she's very lonely. We weren't sure if we should bring her home with us or…"

"No," I answer quickly. "I'll be there later today and I'll stay at the house. I'll take care of her. I think my poor cat misses her." I let out a little laugh and slam my suitcase shut.

"I'm sure Lucky and the dog will be very happy to see you," Aunt Suzy says.

"I hope so. Thank you so much for taking care of everything and for calling me. I'll be leaving within the hour."

"Okay, honey. Drive safe and try not to worry."

As soon as I end the call tears stream down my cheeks. I can't stand the thought of Jude being hurt, and lying in a hospital bed. I wish Aunt Suzy had called me right away. I could be there for him right now instead of being three hours away.

I wrangle the cat into her carrier and scan the guestroom for anything else of mine. Luckily, I didn't bring much with me. After I pack everything in my rental car, I find my father in the garage cleaning the inside of his Audi.

"What's wrong?" he asks as soon as he sees me approaching him. He puts down his rag and bottle of spray cleaner.

"I'm sorry, Dad, but I need to go back home. Right now."

"Now?" His eyes flash with concern. "Why? What happened?"

"Jude's aunt just called me. He was hurt on the job site and he's in the hospital. I need to go be with him."

"Oh, honey. I'm sorry to hear that. I really don't want you to leave, though. We love having you here. Maybe you should stay. You can call him, maybe do a video chat, put your mind at ease."

I glare at him with impatience. "Dad, I need to be there in person. His aunt says he has a bad concussion."

"I'm sure he'll be fine. I don't think it's a good idea for you to run to him."

"Yes, actually it *is* a good idea. In fact, it's the *only* idea."

"Skylar, I know you care about him but—"

I cut him off. "Dad, I have to be with him. He took care of me when I needed him. Many times. He's the only one who ever has."

His eyes darken at that. I don't mean for the comment to hurt him, we've made a lot of progress the past month. But it's the truth. "I just worry about you," he says apologetically. "I'm trying to be a good dad."

I smile softly. "I know you are, and I appreciate it. But I need to be there for him." I give him a quick hug. "I'm glad we had this time together."

"We are, too. Lynn is going to be upset when she comes home and you're not here."

"Can you please tell her goodbye for me? I'll be back. We'll talk on the phone. I'm going to figure out what I'm going to do. Soon."

I've been saying that for weeks and I still don't know what I want to do. My heart seems to be gravitating to everything back home in New Hampshire.

Everyone always says to follow your heart, but how are we ever supposed to know if it's leading us to the right place?

CHAPTER 50
SKYLAR

By some miracle, I don't hit any traffic on my drive back to New Hampshire. I return the rental car and take an Uber to Jude's house to drop off Gus and check on Cassie, who's so excited to see me she dances on her back legs with her little front paws waving in the air. Kneeling on the floor, I pet her and let her kiss my face before I drag my suitcases upstairs.

It feels odd being back in the house after being gone for a month. On one hand, I feel like I'm home. But on the other, I can't help but wonder if this *is* home anymore. Jude might not want me to live here again. For all I know, he could be involved with someone else by now. Our brief chats have been just that—brief, light. Not too flirty. Nothing serious. Total avoidance about *us*.

When I get to my room, I let out a sigh of relief when I see everything looks exactly the same. My things are all where I left them, untouched. Waiting.

Except my bed.

The comforter is curiously rumpled, the pillow dented as if someone has been laying on it. Slowly, I cross the room to sit on it. Jude's signature cologne is undeniably clinging to the pillow and the blanket, and it conjures up a flash of memories that almost bring me to tears. Hugging. Kissing. Touching.

He's been sleeping in my bed. Or, at the very least, lying on it.

My heart shimmies with hope that he misses me as much as I miss him.

He's sleeping when I arrive at his room in the hospital, and it's probably for the best because I need a moment to just look at him. To watch him breathe and give my heart time to calm down and believe that he's going to be okay.

His upper body is propped up on pillows. An IV line snakes into a vein in his arm. Beside the bed is a tray on wheels holding a small pitcher of water, a cup, and a plastic tray.

I'm caught off guard by how pale and vulnerable he looks. Jude has always exuded strength and masculinity. He's always the powerhouse in the room.

But not today.

Today he is bruised and weak.

I blink back tears, refusing to let them well up in my eyes.

I need to be strong today, because that's what marriage is sometimes. You take turns being the strong one.

Quietly, I move to stand next to his bed, and softly touch his hand. I fight the urge to bend down and kiss his stubbled and bruised cheek, not because I don't want to, but because I don't want to startle him awake and make his head hurt. My touch causes him to stir and open his eyes. Blinking, he stares at me with his forehead creased. For a brief second there's a blankness, a total lack of focus in his eyes that scares the hell out of me, but it passes quickly, and a slow smile curves his lips.

"Sparkles..." His voice is a rough whisper.

"Hi. I came as soon as I could."

He squeezes my hand, and my heart clenches like a vise when a tear slips from the corner of his eye. "Didn't think I'd ever see you again," he says hoarsely.

I can't resist any longer. I lean down and gently kiss his cheek.

"How do you feel?" I ask softly.

"Tired."

I suck my lower lip between my teeth as his eyelids twitch and then gradually close.

"Just rest," I say.

"Stay," he whispers, before he drifts off again.

"I'll be right here." Without letting go of his hand, I pull the guest chair close to the bed and settle in it. I stay just like that, watching the rise and fall of his chest as he sleeps.

I've missed him, and the life we inadvertently created together. I wish we could go back and untangle the threads that made a mess of things between us. I wish we could erase the doubts and fears that took hold of us and tore us away from each other. None of it seems to matter when reality such as this moment is staring me in the face. It wouldn't matter if I were a hundred, or five, or any age in between—I would still love and care about this man with my whole heart and soul.

"Excuse me." A soft voice and a hand on my arm wakes me. "I'm sorry, but visiting hours are ending in five minutes."

I rub my face and stare up at the nurse, then look over at Jude, who's still sleeping.

Sitting up, I stretch my stiff neck. "Can I stay a little longer?"

I ask in a hushed tone. "I'm his wife, but I was out of town when he got hurt. I don't want to leave him."

She smiles with sympathy. "I'm sorry, but it's hospital policy."

"I understand," I reply, quietly standing. "Is he okay? Is it normal for him to be so tired?"

"Yes, that's normal for a head injury like this. He's doing fine. He might be discharged tomorrow after the doctor does his rounds."

"That would be great. Thank you."

"I'll come back in a few minutes."

I push the chair back in the corner and pick up my purse before I stand by the edge of the bed. I don't want to leave him. I wish I could hear his voice, see his smile, before I leave.

I wish I could tell him I'm sorry for leaving the way I did.

I wish he could tell me why he didn't stop me.

"I'll be back in the morning," I whisper, and blow him a kiss before I leave.

I call Aunt Suzy, and then my father, on my drive back home to let them know that Jude seems to be doing okay. My dad attempts to start the *you need a new start in life* conversation but I cut him short. I'm too worried about Jude to think about divorce and moving to a new state for a fresh start.

None of that feels right to me.

While I'm glad to be back home, the house feels uncomfortably quiet and lonely without Jude here. Other than the time he stayed out all night talking to Asher Valentine, I've never slept in the house without him here.

I wander into his bedroom. Not to snoop exactly, but to see if there's any blatant signs that he's been with another woman. I feel like a sketchy bitch when I check his trash for condom wrappers, but I *have* to know.

I'm glad to see there aren't any.

Out of the corner of my eye, I see something on his

nightstand that I don't remember ever seeing before, and I cross the room to see what it is. At first, I think it's a postcard, but as I get closer, I realize it's a picture.

Of me.

My heart feels heavy when I pick it up. It's the first picture I texted him when we first met. My hair is a mess and I'm smiling like a goofball with Gus on my lap.

I smile at the memory.

I put the picture back, careful to make sure it's exactly where it was, and go to my own room. Gus and Cassie follow me and jump on the bed, seemingly happy to have their nightly routine back. Exhaustion has my head throbbing with a dull ache, but I know I won't be able to sleep when thoughts of Jude are running rampant in my mind. Him getting hurt is painfully eye-opening. What if it had been more serious? What if he'd died? I wish we had talked more over the phone while I was staying with my father instead of leaving things so unfinished.

Regardless, unless he outright asks me to leave, I'm staying here to take care of him until he's better, whether he likes it or not.

With a deep sigh, I flop down on the bed. My necklace falls to the side of my neck, and I bolt upright, reaching behind my head to unclasp it. I hold the small vial in my hand, staring at the tiny letters inside.

Now is when I need to know what the message says.

With shaky fingers, I unscrew the tiny silver cap and pour all the miniature letters onto my comforter. Frowning at them, I realize even my small fingers are still too big to easily rearrange the letters. I run to the bathroom to get my tweezers, then start to play around with words.

Never.

Love.

You.

Only.

Stay.

Holy moly. This is impossible.

Two hours later, I haven't made any understandable progress and I need a break. Venturing downstairs, I munch on some graham crackers and have a small glass of iced tea. I stare out the window at the moon and attempt to clear my head of jumbled words. Slightly renewed, I return to my room filled with determination to figure out the message.

At two thirty a.m., with my eyes blurry and my heart pounding with excitement, I finally have the letters arranged into what I'm positive is my message from Jude:

YOU'RE THE ONLY ONE I EVER WANT TO STAY.

A tiny squeak escapes from my throat.

My insides are fluttering wildly, wondering if he means these words literally—as in, does he never want me to go? Or am I just the only woman he'd ever *consider* staying with, if he actually wanted a relationship?

I take a picture of the assembled message with my phone so I can read it whenever I want, then gingerly put all the letters back in the vial and twist the cap back on.

The words are so subtly romantic, so powerful. If only he could actually *say* them.

CHAPTER 51

JUDE

"You're supposed to be resting."

"I *am* resting," I shoot back. It's not true, though. I can't sit still, or stop worrying about everything I should be doing. I've been home for a week and I'm going stir-crazy.

She reaches across the couch, pulls my phone out of my hand, and throws it onto the coffee table. "You're not resting. You've been on your phone nonstop since you came home from the hospital. You're not supposed to be staring at the screen that much. Are you trying to give yourself a seizure?"

Skylar's been amazing at playing nurse since I came home. The first few days, she helped me up and down the stairs, get in and out of bed, and on and off the couch. Every four hours she made sure I took my pills. She massaged my back with the gentleness of a butterfly. She held an ice pack on my head all night when I had a migraine, refusing to let herself sleep until I felt better. She cooked for me and did my laundry. She took care of Cassie. She read over all the emails going back and forth about the bar because the brain fog I had made me forget things ten minutes after I read them. She drove me to the doctor for my checkups. Anything I needed—she was right there with a smile.

We haven't kissed or touched, but the moments she's spent taking care of me, and me *letting* her take care of me, were intimate in a way that far surpassed sex.

I never thought I'd say that.

I never thought I'd *have* that.

"I'm not going to have a seizure. That would've happened right after the accident," I say, even though I'm still getting headaches. "I have to make sure everything is moving forward."

"Uncle Al is taking care of things with the bar."

"That's what I'm afraid of."

She frowns at me. "I'm sure everything is fine. The doctor said you have to rest—mentally and physically. You can't be stressed out."

Stressed out doesn't come close to describing how I feel. I've got a ton of money on the line with the relaunch of the bar, and I don't have the clear to start resuming my daily activities until next week.

Falling through the fucking floor wasn't exactly how I wanted to end my career. It's my own fault, though. I was exhausted and distracted and not paying attention when I should've been. My mind was on a certain little blonde who I was missing, madly.

Staring out the window at the snow falling, I drink the tea she made me, which tastes like dirt and honey, but I force it down, and eye her over the rim of my cup. She's sitting on the other end of the couch, engrossed in editing product photos on her iPad for the boutique. The way her blonde hair hangs over her face and down over her shoulder makes me want to push it back, nuzzle into her neck, and kiss her until she melts in my arms.

I resist.

I'm still fighting with the fact that just a few weeks ago, she dredged up all my fears.

Asking for a divorce.

Giving the ring back.

Leaving our home with half her stuff and a pet I grew to love.

Twice I brought my lawyer's number up on my phone to start the divorce papers while she was in Connecticut, and twice I couldn't get myself to do it.

I don't want a divorce.

Skylar hasn't just been playing nurse since I got hurt, she's been a wife.

My wife.

I've been falling deeper and deeper for her, and wrestling with decisions more and more.

And meanwhile, she's been looking at studio apartments and has plans to pick one soon.

"Are you tired?" she asks after I yawn.

"A little. I think I might take a hot bath before I go to bed. My back is sore."

Leaning her head back against the couch, she turns to me with a wistful smile. "It's a great night for a bath. Especially in *your* bathroom. Tell me you didn't put those skylights in for a night exactly like this so you could watch the snow."

I nudge my foot against her leg. "Aha. I knew you were in there fantasizing about my tub every time you went in there to get my pills."

"Guilty," she admits.

Last year I remodeled my ensuite with a big clawfoot bathtub perfectly positioned under two heated skylights. I added long windows along the wall overlooking the backyard—too high for anyone to see in, but giving me a great view of the sky and trees. It's the perfect place to relax.

"If you want to use my bathtub, be my guest. You earned it for taking care of me."

"Maybe we could together?" she asks in a soft, cautious tone like she would if she were attempting to lure a wild animal to go home with her.

I push my hair out of my eyes and stare at her, unsure I heard her correctly.

"*Together* together?"

She swallows and nods.

"I thought we weren't going down that road anymore."

She chews her lip and touches the necklace, gently moving it back and forth on the chain. The playful twinkle that was in her eyes seconds ago has been replaced with a vulnerable longing.

"Maybe we can make an exception for tonight?" Her words —her eyes—are infused with hope, and something else that makes my heart pound.

Love. It looks like love.

My defenses kick in to standby mode.

"We're not light switches, Skylar," I say softly. "We can't just flip on and off."

"I know," she whispers. "I'm sorry."

I inhale a low, steady breath. I haven't exactly been a pillar of consistency myself. "You don't have to be sorry. We *both* have things to figure out."

"We will… but for tonight maybe we can forget about all that? Please?" A hint of desperation laces her voice. "I want to have a fun, magical night. With *you*. I think we both need it."

The word *fun* is both sword and savior. It's sliced the thought of love right outta my head and saved me from all the emotions, expectations, and heartache that come with it.

Besides, the temptation of getting into a hot bath with her, skin against skin, enveloped in steam, is a whole lot of yum I can't resist.

Standing, I hold my hand out to her, and pull her body hard against mine.

"I can do fun and magical," I say.

I really should've said no.

But fuck it.

I finally feel stronger. We've been cooped up in the house for a week, dancing around each other, careful not to get too close, avoiding an end that we both know is coming.

She wants a fun night. That's my specialty.

CHAPTER 52

SKYLAR

I've been lusting after Jude's bathtub since the first time I saw it. It's just as sexy and masculine as he is. Sleek white with industrial fixtures. A cool mix of smooth and rough.

"Did you do all this?" I ask, turning in a circle in his bathroom. "The skylights, the double vanity, the tub…?

He nods. "Yup. Did it all myself. Even the tile shower."

"It's beautiful."

When I turn back to face him, he grabs my face in his hand and slowly backs me up against the wall.

"So are you," he says.

I stare up at him, instantly breathless from his touch.

I wish he was like this all the time—in control, taking what he wants, unleashing all his suppressed feelings.

Sex is where he feels confident and safe. I'm guilty of using it to get closer to him, just like I am right now. I'll probably regret it tomorrow, but I'm throwing in the towel for tonight. I want one more night with him before I decide to move out. One night to put everything else aside and just be close to him.

Leaning his arm on the wall above my head, he descends on

me and covers my mouth hungrily with his. His hand slowly moves from my cheek down to grasp the front of my throat. Fisting his shirt in my hand, I pull him closer and open my mouth to his, licking my tongue along his lips.

He inhales deeply through his nose and releases his hold on me. I catch the darkening of his eyes—a glimpse of the depth of emotions he tries so hard to hide. His gait is still slightly rigid from pain as he moves away to switch off the overhead light and then flick on a smaller, dimmer light above the vanity. We're bathed in a warm, golden-amber glow.

"Undress for me." He slowly leans over the tub and turns the faucet on, then sits on the edge with his long legs stretched out in front of him.

My pussy quivers in response to his soft, deep command. Grabbing the hem of my sweater, I slowly pull it over my head. His eyes cling to my every move as I reach behind me to unclasp my black silk bra. I let it fall at my feet along with my shirt, then unbutton my skinny jeans.

I'm glad to see his lips tip into an appreciative smile at the sight of the red hearts embroidered on the triangle of black fabric of my matching panties.

"I never knew your funky outfits continued under your clothes."

I kick my jeans off but leave the panties on for him to admire. "Surprise." Smiling, I hook my thumbs under the thin bikini straps.

"Wait," he says, stopping me. "Come here."

I slowly walk across the tile floor, drinking in the way his gaze wanders over every inch of me as if he wants to devour me—from my hard nipples, down to my toned calves, then up to my lips. I've always been confident in my body—despite having very small breasts and not a lot of curves. The lust in Jude's granite eyes stokes my confidence even more, banishing any doubts that my body might be too boyish for a man like him.

As I approach him, he grabs my waist. Stepping over him, I stand with my legs spread over his body.

His hands encircle my ankles, and he slowly trails his fingertips up my legs, all the way up to my hips. "These fuckin' legs in heels almost ruined me on our wedding day." He leans forward, pressing his forehead against my stomach, breathing me in. My body stirs with excited flutters beneath his touch.

His mouth moves along the thin waistband of my panties, his tongue dipping under the edge of the fabric. "I thought you wanted me to take the shoes off that day. You didn't like them," I point out.

His nostrils flare. "I wanted you to take everything *else* off."

The warmth of his breath and the rough stubble of his beard against my skin sends goosebumps over my flesh, and my heart pounds with the realization that he wanted me in secret even back then.

Grabbing my ass in both hands, he pulls me closer, and lowers his mouth to swipe his tongue over the thin silk, pressing it between my folds, wetting it more than my own juices already have.

I murmur a small moan and bow my head down to his, combing my hands through his long hair, gently tugging it in sync with the strokes of his tongue.

"Seeing you wet is so fucking sexy," he breathes, gliding his finger slowly over the damp silk clinging to my parted lips. Tugging the fabric aside, he drags his lips down tantalizingly slow. His tongue finds me wet, open and waiting, and he plunges it inside, eliciting a cry of pleasure from my throat.

Without leaving the haven of my thighs, he reaches behind him and turns off the flowing water. I let out a sharp gasp when he moves his lips away and palms my hips, pulling me down until

I'm flush against the hard bulge of him beneath his jeans with my breasts pressed against the stubble of his face.

There's no doubt in my mind he's finally feeling better.

I grip his wide shoulders for balance and grind myself over his hard cock, notching his length between the channel of my wetness. His fingers bite into my ass, coaxing me.

"God, you feel good," I murmur, closing my eyes and slowly riding him, embracing the inhibition he awakens in me.

"Get your sweet ass in that tub."

I lift my head to face him. "Are you coming with me?"

Mischief sparks in his eyes. "Fuck, yeah."

I swing my leg over him and push my panties down to the floor, then pause, captivated by the flex of his thick biceps and the ridges of his abs as he undresses. The sight of his pipe-hard cock extending from the apex of his muscular thighs quickens my pulse.

He's so sinfully beautiful. I could crumble and weep right here on the tile, knowing I will never touch him this way again, never feel his breath on my lips, never feel his body melt into mine.

Swallowing hard, I wet my lips. I can't think of what will never be. All I have is now, and I want to savor it.

I avert my eyes to the steam rising from the tub and dip my hand into the water. "It's still warm."

"It'll stay warm. The tub is heated."

I smile with surprise, not knowing such a thing existed. "Very cool," I say. "Do you have bubbles?"

He smirks. "Do I *look* like I have bubbles?"

I grab a bottle of shampoo from his shower. He watches with amusement as I turn the faucet back on and pour the shampoo into the water flow. Within seconds, bubbles cover the surface.

"You get in first," I say, and when he carefully lowers his powerhouse of a body into the water, my heart swoons and flutters all over again. The man looks simply delicious—all muscle and ink surrounded by glistening bubbles.

I kneel next to the tub and lean over the edge, feeling like a curious kitten.

He licks his lips, and a slow, devious smirk spreads across his face. It's obvious he loves the effect he has on me.

"I wish I could take your picture like this," I say. "You look so. Fucking. Hot."

"No pictures," he says. "You want to see me like this? Take my clothes off."

Laughing, I climb into the large tub, and the hot water sloshes as I settle between his legs. He snakes his arm around me, pulling me flush against his chest. I like that he wants me close—keeping his arm around me, pressed against my bare breasts, with his hand cupping my shoulder. The water is warm, just shy of being too hot, but is incredibly soothing. I tip my head up to watch the snow falling on the skylight, feeling a bit of sorrow as each perfect little snowflake melts the very moment it lands on the heated glass.

How sad to fall so far, only to disappear as soon as the destination is reached.

"This is so beautiful and relaxing," I say softly, almost afraid to break such perfect quiet. "I would be in here every night."

He nuzzles his face into the side of my neck, beneath my ear. "You can come in here any time you want," he whispers in a deep, seductive tone that makes my entire body quiver.

I lean into his soft touch. "I don't think I'll be doing that."

Resting my hands on his thighs under the soapy water, I close my eyes and breathe in the steam wafting up around us. Behind me, Jude leans his cheek against the top of my head, and everything just feels *right*.

Calm.

Safe.

Content.

These are feelings I've been chasing for what seems like my entire young life. I thought the only way to feel those things was to be alone, but I was wrong.

I didn't plan this sensual, romantic interlude tonight. For the past week I've been keeping things platonic between us because I thought it was the right thing to do. I've stayed focused solely on taking care of him, work, and my therapy. I've had to force myself to not touch him unless it was to help him when he was sore. I've resisted thinking about him or sending him cute text messages.

I've mentally scolded myself at least twenty times a day when I've almost given in to the impulse to touch his hand or kiss his cheek.

I've held back from snuggling up to him on the couch with Cassie and Gus.

I've caught him doing it too—leaning in as if he's going to kiss me, then suddenly backing away. I've felt his eyes on me as I've moved around the house.

We've forced a separation. But why?

Because of our age difference?

Because of our fears?

Because I felt intimidated by his past?

Because my father convinced me it's wrong?

None of it seems to matter anymore.

Since we met, every touch, every kiss, every talk between us has come naturally. Effortless in every way. Without motive or expectation.

Isn't that the way things are supposed to be?

Nothing has ever felt more unnatural and wrong than forcing myself to stay away from Jude.

At night, I lie in bed and ask myself what the hell I'm doing. What *we're* doing. The answers used to be so clear.

I'm afraid of getting hurt. I have a deep-seated need to feel free—to have an easy escape. I don't ever want to trust another person again who might let me down.

But distancing from Jude has unexpectedly fragmented my heart. The mere thought of not having him in my life terrifies me. Not because I'm afraid of being free—I've been free since I was eleven years old. But because being with Jude makes me feel complete and whole. Like I'm where I belong.

I believe what he said in the necklace message, and I think Jude is the one who will stay with me. I believe that in my soul and in my bones.

I no longer want to live on the verge of a quick escape plan. I want to go through the rough times *with* him, rather than running away.

And I especially want to go through the good times with him.

I want the wedding vows to be real. I want us to live them and honor them with our whole hearts, and see where life takes us together.

But I need him to want those things too. And I'm still not sure that he does.

"You okay?" he asks, stroking his damp thumb along my cheek.

I wonder how long I was lost in my thoughts.

"Yes... just enjoying being with you and watching the snow fall."

He takes a breath so deep I feel his chest press against my back. "I miss you," he says quietly.

I close my eyes, understanding his words. Being in the same place is not the same as being together.

"I've missed you, too."

Pushing my damp hair to the side, he kisses the back of my neck, open-mouthed, hungry, and possessive. His hands move in the water to cup my breasts, squeezing and pushing them together, pinching my nipples between his fingers until they burn and tingle. I arch my back, pushing my tits into his palms and my ass against his cock. He groans wildly in my ear as his hot shaft slides easily against my flesh in the soapy water.

My head falls back against his shoulder and I turn to kiss his neck, nipping at him with my teeth. Water splashes as his hand dives between my thighs like a shark. Two thick fingers zero in on my G-spot, curving upward with precision and rubbing rhythmically. Whimpering, I grip the sides of the tub to steady myself as I rock back and forth, thrusting up into his hand, then back against the ridge of his cock.

He grasps the side of my face and turns me to him. Our lips clash, breathless and needy. He crosses his legs over mine, pinning me down. My body is buzzing, my hips rolling up and down, back and forth. The tip of his thick cock pushes between my ass cheeks, nudging my pulsing entry. I suck his tongue into my mouth, crazy hungry to devour any part of him I can get. Inside me, his fingers swirl against my walls, his thumb perfectly positioned over my swollen clit, flicking and circling me into a trembling frenzy. I push my body harder against his hand and his cock, needing him to fill me and give me release from this sweet torture.

He pulls his mouth from mine. "You're begging me to fuck that ass, aren't you?" he growls.

Euphoria has taken over my mind and body like a drug. At this point he can climb into any hole he wants and live inside me forever. "I want you…" I murmur.

Clutching my hair in his fist, he pulls my head back to stare into my eyes. "I want you, too." He slowly drags his nose down the length of mine. "Put your legs over the sides of the tub," he whispers.

He untangles his legs from mine, grabs me beneath my knees, and bends each of my legs up over the edge of the tub, spreading me wide over him. I grasp the slippery sides of the porcelain as he lifts me by my hips, positions me over his cock, then lowers me down onto him.

"Holy shit," I gasp as he spears my pussy hard and deep.

Cupping my ass with one hand, he guides me up and down his shaft while his other hand reaches between my thighs, circling and lightly slapping my clit.

I feel his lips on my wet back, kissing a trail up my spine to the curve of my neck. His breath is ragged, matching mine, as we move faster and harder, splashing hot water around us in waves as my body plunges deliciously down onto his.

When he whispers my name in a deep, erotic groan, it vaults me into a shuddering orgasm. He suddenly pulls himself out of me, and I fall back onto him with a cry as his cock throbs and releases in thick, hot spurts against my ass.

Lingering in post-orgasmic haze, I pull my sore legs into the tub and turn over to straddle him. He looks incredibly sexy and sated, leaning back against the tub—eyes hooded, long hair clinging to his forehead, misted with sweat and steam.

His grin is all drowsy and satisfied. "I think I'm dead."

Still panting for breath, I cup his face in my hands and kiss him long and soft, not wanting the intimacy to end here.

"Are you okay?" I ask against his lips, worried that we've made his back worse.

He pushes my wet hair from my flushed face and kicks the tub stopper with his foot. "I'm fine. But bath time's over," he says. Taking the hint, I reluctantly start to climb out, but he pulls me back in for another kiss. "The night doesn't have to be, though."

I raise my eyebrow. "It doesn't?"

He shakes his head back and forth, flinging droplets of water from the tips of his hair. "Stay with me tonight."

My heart jumps. Since we live in the same house, that can only mean one thing. "Stay… in your bed? All night?"

"Yeah." He inhales a steady breath and slowly exhales, locking his steely eyes on mine. "I don't want you to leave."

I take a moment to answer. The swirl of the water draining from the tub is the only sound between us. It gurgles and sputters, just like my brain right now.

It's special—spending the night together. It's an epic level of intimate trust, to fall asleep next to someone in the dark, in his bed. Breathing next to him, asleep and vulnerable. At least, to me it is. And I know tomorrow night when I'm down the hall in my own room again, I'm going to be thinking about him, aching for him, wishing we weren't sleeping a hallway apart.

But despite that, I'd rather have our night together than never have it.

"Okay," I finally say. "I don't want me to leave, either."

Jude winces as he climbs out of the tub and wraps a towel around his hips. I follow him to the bedroom, also in a warm, fuzzy towel. The hot water and the even hotter sex has made my limbs feel wobbly. I sit at the foot of his bed and watch him lose the towel and pull on a pair of boxers.

Something about me puts a smile on his face as he takes a white T-shirt from his dresser and hands it to me.

"What?" I ask. "You're making a weird face."

He laughs. "You just look adorable sitting there, like you're not sure what to do with yourself."

"Accurate." I change into his shirt—which is thin and soft from years of wear, and I never want to give it back—and take our towels into the bathroom, so they're not sitting around wet.

When I come back, he's lying in bed, propped against a bunch of pillows.

"Should I turn off the light?" I ask, wondering how it's possible that I felt more comfortable spread-eagled in a bathtub riding his dick than I do getting into his bed with him.

His eyes narrow curiously at me. "Sure."

I switch off the light and join him on the bed, copying his pillow formation. I'm surprised when he turns on the television and puts on a streaming music channel.

He puts the remote on the night table, then pulls me to him. I turn slightly and lay my palm flat on his chest.

"You can come closer," he says, laughing a little as he pulls my hand so my arm is around his waist and my body is curved into his. He touches his bare foot to mine and rubs it slowly up and down the arch of my foot. "Why are you acting so nervous? Would you rather not be here?"

I really don't want to be anywhere else but here. Unfortunately, a case of insecurity has just suddenly taken over. Does being in bed with a man mean we're here to have sex? Do we talk first? Do we just go to sleep? What happens in the morning? Is it like eating dinner, where you don't leave the table until everyone is done eating?

Ugh.

Apparently, being eighteen with a thirty-four-year-old man actually does have its hiccups.

"I'm not sure what I'm supposed to do," I admit awkwardly.

"Just be you. You're not ever supposed to do—or be—anything else." He tightens his arm around me. "Except happy. Always be happy."

"I'm very happy." For now, at least.

"I am, too." His lips press against the pulse of my temple. "There aren't any rules or expectations—especially with me. I only want to be close to you."

I nod and move my fingertip over the tattoo on his rib cage.

"I just thought it'd be nice to sit and talk," he says.

"Okay. I'm sorry I'm acting strange."

"It's all right," he says.

Rolling onto his side, he pulls the blanket up over us, and leans his head on his arm to look down at me.

In the background *Wildfire* sung by Michael Martin Murphey is drifting from the TV. It reaches back into my memories and pulls out a mental snapshot of me as a little girl hearing this song while staying at my grandparents, feeling safe and loved.

I want that again.

Jude bows down and kisses my lips—soft, sweet, and long, taking his time, making love to my mouth in a dreamy way that completely steals my breath and sends my heart into flutters. Such a stark contrast to the hungry, demanding kisses we shared earlier in the tub.

I'm captivated by the hard and soft sides of him—rough in just the right moments, but so incredibly gentle in the perfect moments, too. Jude may not talk much, but his touch speaks a thousand words.

He pulls away a few inches and I look up at him with his hair falling down over his face, tickling my cheek.

"Thank you for taking care of me," he says softly. "Especially when things were rocky between us."

"None of that changes how much I care about you."

"I've been thinking a lot," he says. "About you, and me, and everything."

My heart shift gears and pounds with uncertainty and anxiety. He's finally going to open up about his feelings.

"I wish things weren't complicated, Skylar. I wish you hadn't gotten hurt so much in all of this. I wish people didn't look at me like I'm some kind of fucking predator. I wish you weren't bullied into leaving school. I wish I could feel the way I do about you, and touch you, without feeling like I'm doing something wrong and I'm gonna rot in hell someday. I don't blame you at all for wanting to leave and get away from all this."

He traces the tip of his finger over the two-inch scar on my forehead—delicately, as if he's afraid my head will split open—then softly presses his lips to it. Closing his eyes, he stays that way, inhaling and exhaling with slow deliberation. Finally, he pulls away. "I want you to have a life like a girl your age should, to have adventures, away from here. I don't want to hold you back. Sometimes I wonder why I couldn't have met you when you were older. It's fucking shredding me, trying to win this feud of rights and wrongs with you." The raw remorse and lost hope in his voice has a heartbreaking finality to it.

He hides his feelings so well that I was unaware how deeply everything has been affecting him. It's not fair, because all he wanted to do was help me. Things never should've gone the way they have, and I'm partly to blame for it.

I reach up and push his hair out of his face. There's so many things I want to say—and *should* say. But what can I possibly say that won't make him feel worse?

If I tell him I want to be with him, he'll feel even more guilty. And if I tell him I don't want to be with him, that'll hurt him, too.

The last thing I ever want to do is hurt him.

I force the brightest smile I can, and wrap my arms around his neck.

"Then I guess I'll be coming back for you when I'm older," I say, hoping to give us a doorway into the future.

"You better," he says with a growl, then rolls me onto my side and pulls my back up against his hard chest, molding our bodies and entwining our legs together under the blanket.

"Good night, Sparkles," he says, brushing his warm lips over my ear, then resting his cheek against the top of my head.

"Good night, Lucky."

My heart melts into a puddle. I thought I was here for a continued romp in the sheets. I never expected to be cocooned with him, kissed softly, cuddled to sleep. I blink in the dark, waiting for something to change, but it doesn't.

He's falling asleep, hugging me.

Exhaling softly, I settle in his arms, and grab his hand. I hold it against my chest, locking us together. After a few minutes, his breathing slows, and his grip around me loosens just a tiny bit. I force myself to stay awake for a while longer, just so I can memorize all the little details of falling asleep in my husband's embrace. The lingering scent of his cologne. The warmth of being enveloped in his muscular arms. The soft hiss of his breathing. The lulling beat of his heart against my back. The overwhelming feeling of sanctuary.

This is the thing I never believed in. What I feared the most.

And, sadly, what I can't have.

"I love you," I whisper because I need to put it out there into the universe that I'm crazy in love with this man. I don't care if it's right or wrong or complicated or that he doesn't even hear the words leave my lips.

I love him.

Enough to stay, enough to go, enough to wait.

CHAPTER 53

SKYLAR

Waking up in Jude's arms the next morning was what dreams are made of. We didn't roll away from each other in the middle of the night to seek out space. We hugged until the sun came up. If one of us shifted, we moved together, staying tangled up in each other. I awoke to kisses and his warm hands moving slowly over my body. We made love slowly, wordlessly, dare I say, gently. Every soft kiss and stroke nearly cracked my heart into pieces.

I never knew sex could feel so emotional and connecting, and yet so heartbreaking. I didn't want it to end, but at the same time, it didn't feel like a beginning, it felt very much like the end.

And, in a way, it was.

Because that was two weeks ago, and since then, I've felt off-kilter. Jude hasn't been home much, and I've been teetering on the fence, trying to decide what to do. My plan was to get my own place, but I keep hoping something will happen to stop me.

I wait until after dinner to approach him. He's sitting in the living room, going over the plans for the bar on his iPad with blueprints on the coffee table.

"Jude?"

"Mm?" He doesn't look up at me.

I toss a thick, white envelope on the coffee table next to his blueprints.

"I want my car back," I say. "That's the amount you paid for it."

He slowly looks up and blinks at me, his jaw tense. "You can't have it."

My heart skips with shock. "Excuse me?"

"You can't have the car back."

"We had a deal."

"I know, but the car's in pieces now."

"Pieces? Why?"

"I've been fixing it up. I told you that. But it's not done yet. I've been kind of busy, dealing with migraines, brain fog, and starting a new business." He waves his hand over the blueprints.

"Believe me, I've noticed how busy and distracted you are." My words come out more bitter than I wanted them to sound. I know it's not his fault. I've seen how much he's been struggling with everything since the concussion.

His eyes narrow. "What does that mean?"

I swallow and tilt my chin. "Ever since we spent the night together, it's like you forgot about me. You're hardly ever home, we haven't talked much at all."

Worry flashes in his eyes. "Skylar, I've been busy. I had a lot of catching up to do after I got hurt. I have to stay on track if I want the bar to be ready for the reopening."

"I know," I reply, feeling like a spoiled child.

"I'm not ignoring you. I thought we were okay."

"I read the necklace," I blurt out.

Surprise washes over his face. "You did? When?"

"The night I came back from Connecticut."

He runs his hand through his hair and leans back into the couch. "I meant it."

I wait for him to say more, but he sits in silence.

"Actions speak louder than words, Lucky. Otherwise, they're just words. And I love what the message said, but they're still just words."

"And what about *your* actions, Skylar? You left. You gave your ring back to me. You ran off to Connecticut."

"And I came back," I say defensively.

"Only because I fell on my fucking head," he says.

"That's not true. I wasn't going to stay there."

"No, you were going to come back and then move out."

"I'm still going to do that. Wasn't that always the plan? That I'm supposed to leave? I've been looking at studio apartments."

He rubs the back of his head "What's the rush? You don't have to move out. I've said it a hundred times."

"Yes, Jude, I do. This isn't healthy or good for either of us. This weird, roommate slash lovers slash friends slash spouse situation. You say you don't want me to move out, but you never really say stay, either. You just say I can live here, but as *what*? I mean, what the fuck is this?"

"I don't know," he says quietly.

"It's limbo," I say pointedly. "Both of us hanging here, afraid to make a move. Afraid to stay, afraid to go, afraid to talk. We're just hurting each other, aren't we?"

"I don't want to hurt you. Ever."

"I know that."

"I want you to be happy. I just need more time..."

I give him an exasperated look. "Time for what, Lucky?"

"To give you everything you deserve."

"I don't even know what that means."

"It means I love you, Skylar. And I just need some time to get my fucking head together to make things better."

I reel back from the shock of hearing the words I've been

dying for him to say. But not like this, not in the middle of an argument.

"*That's* how you're going to say that to me? What the hell?"

He snorts. "At least I didn't say it while I thought you were sleeping."

My insides freeze up. *Shit.* I had no idea he heard me that night when I whispered *I love you* to him.

"At least I actually said it!" I throw back tearfully.

He shoves the blueprints to the side. "This isn't how I wanted this to go. Everything is fucked up."

I've never been so confused in my life. What does he want? Why does this have to be such a struggle?

"Jude, please just talk to me. What's going on in your head?"

"Is this really what you want? You want me to just throw all my cards on the table right now? When my head's all twisted up and we're both in a bad mood?"

"Yes," I say with my heart palpitating. "I do."

He covers his face with his hands for a few seconds, pressing his fingers into his forehead.

"I'm afraid of everything," he finally says. "Saying too much, not saying enough. Holding you back from the life you're supposed to have. Us staying together and then you waking up in ten years filled with regret and animosity, wishing you hadn't strapped yourself to someone when you were so young. I'm afraid of losing everything at a time in my life when I finally want to keep everything."

"Strapped myself?" I repeat. "I don't think wanting to be with you is strapping myself. And don't you think I have fears, too? You don't think I worry that you'll want a woman who can actually give you a blowjob?"

He scoffs and flashes me an incredulous look. "Are you fuckin' serious? That's the lamest, shallowest thing I've ever heard."

Okay, that's true. But it's the first thing that sprung to my mind.

"Maybe you'll want someone more mature."

"Nope."

"Maybe you won't even want to be married to me."

"I never did, until you came along and kept falling in front of me, then into me, then *for* me."

I'm guilty of all the above, but maybe fate had a hand in my chronic clumsiness.

"I'm not going to hurt you, Jude. And I don't think you'll hurt me, either."

"I think you believe that now. But you're only eighteen. Do you know how much will change over the years? Your likes and dislikes? What you want in life? *Who* you want? When you're thirty, I'll be almost fifty. What's that gonna look like?"

"And that's not shallow? I'm pretty sure I'm never going to care about our age difference. I care about making each other happy and being there for each other. Growing together. Plus, you're going to be hot as hell when you're fifty. So, I'm all good, Jude."

He sighs and closes his eyes. I can tell he's in pain and mentally exhausted, and it makes my heart hurt that I'm the cause of it right now. "I don't know, Skylar. None of this was supposed to happen. I wanted to get married to help you, and you ended up getting attacked by my sister and getting bullied out of school. Even my best of intentions get all fucked up. I don't know how to protect you from what life is going to throw at us, and this age difference shit doesn't help. It's just another obstacle that could end up hurting you."

"You don't have to protect me. None of that was your fault. Now that I'm out of school, I don't care what people think about our ages. Do you think I want to be with a guy my age, who most likely has no idea what he wants to do with his life and can't handle a real commitment? I know that's what you're afraid of with me, but I'm afraid of that, too. We're the same, Jude. We're both afraid of being abandoned. We both crave trust and commitment. No matter what age I am, that will never change for me. You're the only one I'll ever trust."

He doesn't say anything, but I can see my words slowly sinking into him. His eyes are softening, but the rest of his body language screams his defensive walls are still up.

I force the rest of my thoughts out before I lose him. "We were both dead set against marriage and love when we went into this farce. But guess what? We've been married this whole time. Living a *real* marriage, loving and caring for each other, whether we knew it or not. You can't tell me that doesn't mean something."

He nods slowly. "You're right. It means everything. More than you know. But we've only known each other a few months."

"So? It feels like much longer."

"It does. I just feel like it's been a fuckin' whirlwind. Like maybe we're stuck in the honeymoon phase."

"Honeymoon phase usually means everything is perfect. We're far from that. And that's okay. We don't need perfect. Look at your aunt and uncle. They got together fast."

"Come here," he says softly.

I cross the room and sit next to him on the couch. He takes my hand in his, linking our fingers together.

He heaves in a breath and slowly exhales. "I'm sorry I've been distracted. I'm trying to do a lot of things in a really short amount of time." His eyes are gray pools of emotion, dark and turbulent. "I heard what you said that night," he says hoarsely. "And it woke me up in so many fucking ways. I meant what I said in the necklace. I don't want you to leave. Hold off on moving out, okay? Too much is going on all at once. Give me a little time, okay?"

He presses his lips softly against mine in a kiss that begs for patience.

"Are you alright?" I whisper, reaching up to touch his cheek. The anguish in his voice and in his eyes is worrying me.

"I've just got a lot on my mind. I need some time to think about everything with a clear mind."

"I'm sorry I've put doubts in your head," I say.

"I'm sorry I've put some in yours."

I lean my forehead against his, touch my nose against his. "We've been a bit of a rollercoaster, huh?"

He grins. "I like fast, crazy rides, but I think we've both had enough."

Holding on to his hand, I stand and pull him up. "Will you come do something with me?" I ask.

When he nods, I lead him upstairs to my bedroom. He waits in the doorway as I turn on the galaxy night light, and the ceiling lights up with stars.

"Since we can't get to your favorite place on the mountain, maybe we can look at the stars here and it'll make you feel better. Help you clear your head."

Smiling, he pulls me into his arms and whispers, "I think you're my favorite place now."

CHAPTER 54

SKYLAR

"Can you float me a loan for about five grand? I want to get my tits done," Megan says, as we choose a table in the corner of the cafe.

I can't tell if she's kidding or not.

"Is that how much new boobs cost?" I ask, taking the lid off my tea and stirring it with a straw.

"I'm not sure. I'm just teasing you. I think when I graduate, I'll ask my dad if he'll pay for it."

"You look perfect the way you are."

She juts her chest out for my inspection. "They could be bigger. And firmer."

I look down at my own small chest. "So could mine."

"Well, you can afford to get them done now. You'd look so sexy with bigger boobs. Especially with your tiny waist."

I shake my head and cut my corn muffin up into four pieces. "Nah, I'm good." Now that I've got financial security, I'm not going to waste a dime of that money. If there's one thing I've learned, it's that my life can change in a matter of seconds.

"How's Jude feeling?" Megan asks.

"He's better, still has some headaches. He's working out all the stuff for the bar. Licensing, upgrades... it's a lot. But, he's going with my seventies-themed decor idea. And guess what he's naming the bar?"

"Tell me."

"Fupagus!"

She laughs. "You're kidding. That's amazing."

"Right? Once things get moving and the inside is ready, I'm going to take pictures and manage social media accounts for the bar. I can do that from anywhere, I guess," I say. "It's overwhelming and stressful, but I really think it's going do great once it's all off the ground."

I wish I felt as excited as I tried to make myself seem. Things have been bittersweet. Me and Jude are both happy about the progress with the bar, but unfortunately, he's been distant. Nothing between us has changed or progressed yet. He's still suffering from fatigue, headaches, and mood swings from his head injury, and I've taken the position of giving him what he asked for—time.

Time for what exactly, I don't know.

Megan sips at her latte and leans forward. "I still can't believe you won the lottery!"

"Girl, me either. It still feels like a dream. The damn IRS took a huge chunk."

"Ew, taxes. Have you decided what you're going to do? Are you going to hang around here? Get a condo or something? Hit the road in an RV? You can totally do that now. It's like you manifested it!"

"I know," I reply, staring out the window. Rebecca's boutique is right across the street, and I can see the seasonal window display I put together from here. I'm still part-time since I've also been creating content and sharing for some other small businesses, but I love working with Rebecca.

If things don't change soon, I'm going to throw in the towel and move out of Jude's house. His silence is making me crazy. I've put off signing a lease on my own place. As much as I don't want to do that, I can't live in limbo forever. If I did leave, I'd miss Jude in a soul-crushing, heart-wrenching, I'll-never-get-over-him way. Every time I sit down and seriously try to decide what I should do, the thought of moving out makes my heart ache so much that I feel physically sick.

Fake marriages are no joke. This shit has fucked us up royally.

"What about you and Jude?" Megan asks, reading my mind. "Anything new going on there?"

"No. He really hasn't said anything more about us. He's either doing stuff for the bar, or holed up in the garage working on his motorcycle. We're basically still in limbo." I nibble on my muffin and try to push down the sadness that's creeping up my chest. The distance between me and Jude the past few days has been like a chasm. I've never felt so empty. So many times, I've wanted to tiptoe into his room in the middle of the night and crawl under the sheets with him, kiss him, and just stay there.

"I thought, since he said he loved me, that meant he wanted us to be together. But we're still in separate rooms. We haven't been intimate. Maybe I was wrong or misunderstood."

"I don't think you were wrong. Men are weird. And he *is* recovering from a head injury and dealing with a lot of stress. Give him time," she says, glancing at her watch. "You never know what could change at any moment."

"I've been giving him time, but I can't just wait around forever. I told him the other day I found a cute studio apartment that I love, and he looked like he was having a panic attack. I have to give the landlord an answer by next week."

"Can we switch seats?" she asks suddenly, popping up and almost sending our drinks flying.

Frowning, I grab my cup and say, "Um, okay. Why?"

"I don't like my back to the window."

"Since when?"

"I think I feel a draft. I'm getting a cold, so I don't want to get sicker. Erik and I have plans this weekend."

"Alright." I laugh at her as we get up and switch seats.

"That's better," she says, glancing at her watch once again, then out the window behind me.

"Are you okay?" I ask, starting to worry. "You're acting really sketchy right now."

She smiles and waves her hand in the air between us. "I'm fine. I have to meet Erik in a little while, that's all."

My phone vibrates on the table. I pick it up to see a text from Jude.

Jude: Hey you.

Me: Hi.

Jude: What are you up to today?

Me: Just having a tea with Megan at the café.

Jude: Can you meet me at the park in about half an hour?

My stomach flutters with nerves—both the scared and the excited kind.

Me: Sure. Is everything okay?

Jude: I just want to talk.

I almost drop the phone into my tea.

Me: Ok. I'll be there soon.

"Everything okay?" Megan asks, shifting her eyes to my phone.

"I think so. Jude wants me to meet him. To talk."

"That's good, right? Why do you look scared?"

I read the text messages over again.

"I don't know," I say. "Meeting somewhere public to talk sounds bad, doesn't it?"

She rolls her eyes. "Skylar, don't be so paranoid. You watch too many movies. Not everything is bad news. Your luck is on the upswing now, remember?"

Maybe so, but I have a bad feeling brewing.

"I guess I should go, then."

We gather our things and walk out front to the street where our cars are parked. I hug her good-bye and tell her I hope she feels better.

"Call me later," she says as she walks to her car.

I wave at her and climb in my car, but once I put the key in the ignition, it won't start.

Oh, crap.

I try again, but the engine won't turn over.

Not again! I should've bought a new car with my lottery money instead of continuing to use Jude's Subaru and waiting for my Corvette to be put back together.

Megan appears at my window. "Is your car broke?"

"Looks like it." I let out a big sigh and try to start it again, but I get the same result. "This sucks! What am I supposed to do now? Jude's probably on his way to the park already."

"I'll drive you. Let Jude deal with this later."

"I thought you had to meet Erik?"

"I'll call him and tell him I'm running late." She smiles and pulls my door open. "Come on, it won't take long. Jude will probably come look at the car later. I'm sure he'll get it to start."

"Okay..." I say reluctantly.

I'm so distracted on the way to the park, I'm barely bothered by Megan's bad driving, which seems to have gotten worse, if that's possible.

"Can you try not to kill us?" I say as she swerves past a car making a left turn and almost drives us into a ditch.

"I've got this," she says over the car horns blaring angrily behind us.

My thoughts shift back to wondering why Jude wants to meet at the park out of the blue.

Why there?

Shouldn't he be working at the bar?

Why can't he talk to me tonight at the house?

Megan attempts to distract me by babbling about a movie she and Erik watched last night, but I'm only half-listening.

I feel like a bad friend.

And most likely, Jude's going to tell me I'm a bad wife and serve me with divorce papers in the middle of the park surrounded by trees and giggling toddlers.

The other *real* wives in the park will watch and whisper. Somehow, they'll know I've just been dumped. They'll gawk at his tattoos, and his hair, and his sexy ass, wishing they were single again.

Maybe I'm destined to be laughed at and tormented by others.

I'll have to watch him walk away, and I'll be left alone on a park bench with a broken heart and no car.

And even though I've got a ton of money in the bank right now, it can't buy me the things I want most.

Sniffling, I rub my forehead, trying to quell the throbbing pain from all the emotions clashing inside me in a war of sadness, anger, fear, and disappointment. Why am I always the disposable one, and never the choice?

"Skylar, please stop thinking bad thoughts. I had no idea you'd be upset like this."

"What do you mean?"

"I mean just in general because a man wants to talk to you. You're getting yourself all worked up and you have no reason to."

I cough back tears. "I'm worried he's going to have the divorce papers. It feels so final."

"Are you nuts? Do you really think he'd do that to you? In a park? Or at all? The guy loves you and protects you like a rabid Doberman. Handle your shit, Sky."

"My shit is handled."

"It's soooo not handled."

Megan is right, I'm an emotional mess, and I don't even know why.

We pull into the park's parking lot on screeching wheels, and she idles in a parking spot.

I sigh with relief that we made it here alive, and unbuckle my seatbelt.

"I have to go." Her fingers tap over her cell phone. "Call me tonight."

I scan the parking lot. "Jude's not even here yet."

"I'm sure he'll be here any minute."

"You're just going to leave me here?"

"I don't want to be even later meeting Erik. Just wait over by the picnic tables. You're not going to get dismembered. There's a bunch of parents and kids right over there."

I stare out the windshield, feeling even more abandoned. "How am I supposed to get home?"

"Jude's going to drive you home, wackadoo. Will you relax?"

"Fine," I huff. "I'll relax."

She leans across the car and kisses my cheek. "Please smile, chickie. You're very loved. Have some faith, okay?"

Nodding, I force myself to smile at her, feeling very disconnected and not very loved at all. I feel like those dogs we see videos of on the internet, where their owners push them out of the car and drive off, and the dog sits on the side of the road—confused and hopeful—wondering when the hell they're coming back.

After she drives away, I walk to the picnic tables and watch the little kids chase each other while their mothers chitchat.

The minutes tick by.

I chip at my nail polish, and a quick jolt of panic brings up a new worry: maybe he's not coming.

I'm just about to text him to make sure he's actually on his way when suddenly Cheap Trick's *I Want You to Want Me* starts blasting from the parking lot. I turn my head to see a shiny, old silver Corvette pull into a spot. The engine rumbles so loud the ground vibrates.

Putting my hand up to block the sun, I squint at the car, and my chest clenches with grief.

It looks just like mine, only without the rust and dents. The chrome rims glint in the sun, the metallic paint sparkles like millions of tiny diamonds.

It's absolutely beautiful—my dream car.

I watch with envy as a tall guy wearing sunglasses steps out of it. His muscular arms are sleeved with tats and his hair is tied back in a low ponytail, and *oh my God,* there's no denying that familiar smirk as he leans back against the hood of the car and looks in my direction.

"Lucky?" I say to myself, swirling with confusion as I slowly walk across the park to him as if I'm in a dream.

"Sorry I'm late," he says, holding up a spark plug. "I had to pull this out of your car while you were in the cafe so Megan could drive you here."

What the what?

They planned this?

My mouth falls open as my gaze roves over the car. The curve of the fenders. The sleek hood.

"Jude... is this—" I stammer, circling the car in disbelief. I run my hand across the smooth paint.

"Your car? You bet your sweet ass it is." He holds the keys out to me. My hand shakes like a leaf as I take them. "I bought it for *you*, Skylar. It was the only way I could get you to take my fucking money."

Tears start to stream down my cheeks. "You did?" I choke and cover my mouth with my hand. "You did this for me?"

"Yup. Do you really think I've been working on my bike in the garage all this time? I've been going crazy trying to get this done. It was in the shop for two weeks, and you didn't even realize it wasn't in the garage. The whole lottery ticket thing, and then my accident, and then you getting all impatient, kinda threw a monkey wrench in my plans though, and I had to speed things up."

"What do you mean?"

He smiles that adorable, boyish smile I haven't seen in weeks. "Don't you want to check out the inside?"

"Yes" I wipe at my eyes. "I think I'm in shock... I can't believe you did this—" I climb into the driver's seat and touch the new bright-red upholstery. It smells so new and clean. Everything's been restored—the steering wheel, the pedals, the stereo, the floorboards. And from the sound of it, the engine and pipes and things I don't even know the proper names of. It's like it's a brand-new car again.

Bittersweet happiness lodges in my throat. *Oh, Papa. Look at our car.*

Jude gets in the passenger seat and pushes his sunglasses up onto his head.

"Do you like it?" he asks.

Bursting into full-blown tears, I throw my arms around him and hug him as hard as I can. "I love it. It's exactly how me and Papa dreamed it would look someday." I suck in a shuddering breath. "I don't know how to thank you for this. This means so much to me. You're the best person in the whole world."

"You can thank me by saying yes," he says, untangling from me.

"Say yes?" I repeat, furrowing my brows at him. "To wh—"

I follow his gaze to a thin chain hanging from the rearview mirror. Something silvery and dazzling is dangling from it.

My hands fly up to cover my mouth and my eyes bulge. "Oh my God, Jude. What is that?"

Completely stunned into silence, I watch him take the chain off the mirror and then undo the clasp to pull the rings off it.

Holding the diamond ring in front of me, he leans forward, splays his hand across my cheek, and kisses me like he wants to swallow me up.

When we finally part, I'm breathless and swaying in the seat.

"You better breathe, Sparkles, or I'm gonna have to give you CPR."

"Jude… is that…" My voice catches in my throat.

"A vintage engagement ring? Yup. And your wedding band. I know you were getting upset, but I needed time to do this right." He lifts his eyes to meet mine. "I love you, Skylar. I'm not afraid to say it or feel it anymore. I love you so fucking much. I don't want you to leave. Ever. I promise I'll never hold you back from what you want. I want you to have everything you dream of. I want us to build a life together. We can travel, like you always wanted. We can run the bar together, and you can still do photography and social media. We're perfect together, and I don't give a fuck what anyone thinks. I'm not letting my fears get in the way of what we both want anymore."

I gasp when he slips both rings onto my finger.

"Will you be my wife? For real this time?"

"Yes," I whisper, staring at the rings. "Yes! That's all I've been dreaming of." New tears roll down my cheeks, and I grab his face and kiss him. "I love you," I say breathlessly. "I really love you so much."

"I love you, too." He brings my hand to his lips and kisses it. "I really love saying that. Promise me it'll be forever," he says. "No matter what, promise me we'll always work it out. I'd never get through losing you."

"I promise." I squeeze his hand. "But you really have to talk to me. I get you're the sexy, strong, silent type, but maybe dial back on the silent, okay?" I say playfully.

He grins and my heart swoons. "I'm tryin'. I said a lot today."

"You did. And I can't believe you did all this." I kiss him again.

He pulls me into his arms from across the console. I don't want to let him go. I'm afraid I'm dreaming, and I'll wake up and this will all be gone.

I nuzzle my face into his neck and inhale his cozy scent. "Is this real?" I whisper. "I'm so scared this isn't real."

Cupping the back of my head, he holds me to him. "It's real, baby." He hugs me for a long time, then touches my chin, lifting my face to his. "I've messed up a lot. I should've told you how I felt sooner. I just wanted to do things right."

"Lucky, it's okay…"

"It's not. I let all this age shit and my fears of getting hurt mess with my head. From now on, I'm listening to my heart and my gut. We'll learn to trust and love and grow *together*. I want us to have a real wedding and a honeymoon. And I've been thinking I want to sell the house."

"Sell your house?" I repeat. "Why?" He's done so much work on that house.

"Because it's not *our* home, and it has too many bad memories for both of us. It's bad juju. I found a piece of land for sale, not too far from Aunt Suzy and Uncle Al. We can build a house there. Make it our dream home."

My heartbeats speed up with happiness. *My own home. With my husband.* "Can we have a big bathtub? And a porch, and a window seat in the bedroom?"

He laughs and kisses my nose. "You can have whatever you want."

I wet my lips. "Okay, but I have one condition."

"Name it."

"You have to let me put some of my money toward it. I need to feel like I contributed to our home." I refuse to take any more free rides from him. I want us to be equal and fair, two adults.

"Skylar—"

"I mean it, Jude. This is important to me."

He nods and gives me a quick, soft kiss. "Okay, babe. I get it. And I'm having the lawyer get rid of the pre-nup. What's mine is yours."

"And what's mine is yours." Closing my eyes, I lean my head against his and whisper, "I love you," before pulling away.

"I love you. Now start up your car and drive us home like you stole it. We're moving your stuff into the right bedroom tonight, Mrs. Lucketti. No more guest room. I'm gonna kiss my bride all night, every night."

CHAPTER 55

JUDE

When I pull into the driveway, I kill the engine, stare at the front door, and exhale a massive breath.

I feel like a huge weight has been lifted off me.

Today I officially closed my construction business, and if all goes well with the bar, my time of sweating and freezing my ass off outside every day and coming home with my back killing me is over.

Well, except for me and Skylar's new house, which we start building next month. That's a project I don't mind killing myself over, though. That'll be a total labor of love.

Once inside, I find her sitting on the couch in the living room with Cassie and Gus—one on each side of her feet like furry bookends.

She's engrossed in her laptop, probably taking one of her online classes or saving decor ideas on one of our many wish-list boards.

I take a few moments to just look at her and fall in love with her all over again from across the room. *My wife*. She's seriously the most beautiful thing I've ever seen, with her long hair flowing over her shoulders—one bared by the pink sweater slouched halfway down her arm. I smile at the small four-leaf clover tattoo with *Lucky* in tiny print on her shoulder.

So. Fucking. Sexy.

All mine.

Smiling, I walk up behind the couch and touch her shoulders, and she bends her head backward, all smiles and blue eyes looking up at me, extending her arms up to pull me down for a kiss.

I kiss her hungrily and slowly move my hands from her shoulders to embrace her neck. She murmurs my name and the vibration of her throat against my fingertips drives me wild.

"I'm gonna go take a shower. I want you naked in our bed when I get out," I growl against her lips.

When I move to pull away, she grabs the back of my head, clutching my hair.

"Forget the shower," she says in a sultry voice. "I want you dirty. Right here. Right now."

"Fuck," I whisper-groan. My cock is already rock hard, straining against my zipper.

I cover her mouth with mine and slide my hands down the front of her sweater and suck in a breath when my palms find her bare-breasted. I move my lips down to her neck, then her collarbone, sucking the delicate flesh between my lips. Her nails dig into my scalp, her head tilts to the side. Leaning over her, I skim my hand down between her thighs to cup her pussy through her jeans. I can feel her warm, wet heat through the fabric.

She grabs her laptop, slams it closed, and tosses it on the cushion next to her.

In a quick motion, I scoop her up in my arms and sit her on the back of the couch, facing me. I stand between her legs, and with a smile, she pulls off my dusty sweatshirt, then reaches to undo my jeans. Going in for another long kiss, I kick off my boots. Her bare foot pushes my jeans down, and I hurriedly step out of them and yank her sweater up over her head. She grips my arms as I grab the waistband of her jeans and pull them off without bothering to unzip them.

I glance down to see kitten-faced panties equipped with little fuzzy fabric ears sticking up from the waistband.

"Did you wear these for me, you little imp?" I hook my fingers in the thin straps and pull them off her.

She giggles. "Of course."

"I'm keeping them."

She wraps her long, toned legs around me and pulls me in, reaching down to cup her hand around my cock. Grabbing the back of my neck with her other hand, she tugs me back to her lips.

"You're so fucking hard," she whispers, making my dick twitch in her hand.

I stroke her pussy, and she all but purrs and writhes against my hand. "And you're so fuckin' wet." I bite her lip, and she lets out a little sexy yelp.

Hooking her heels into my ass, she guides my cock into her pussy and arches back, gripping my shoulders as I sink my shaft deep into her. I bow my head to feast on her uplifted breasts, flicking my tongue over her perfect nipples.

She breathes my name as she moves her hips up and down to meet my thrusts. Her tight walls pull me in, my balls slap against her pink flesh, the sound of rhythmic, wet suction an erotic chorus between us.

Grabbing her throat, I pull her up to me and kiss her deep, delving my tongue into her mouth until I own her every breath. She pants against my mouth with her small hands splayed across my hips.

I pull out almost completely, and she gasps in frustration.

Resting the tip of my cock against her entry, I cup her face in my hands and kiss her lips softly, then pull away, hovering just millimeters from her mouth. Slowly, I push into her just a fraction. Her wet lips envelope me, deliciously tight and hot.

"Give it to me," she begs.

"Look at me," I whisper. She opens her eyes and stares into mine, and I watch her eyelids flutter half-closed when I feed my cock into her inch by inch. She looks so fucking beautiful and sensual, it takes all my self-control not to cum instantly. She lets out a satisfied moan when my cock is finally completely buried in her, and I rock myself against her, slowly stoking the building passion.

Reaching up, she winds her arms around my neck and clasps her hands together. "I love you," she murmurs breathlessly.

"I love you, Sparkles."

When I feel her tighten and tremble around me, I capture her lips and kiss her through it, spilling myself into her for the first time, so fuckin' glad we don't have to stop or pull away or have latex between us anymore.

Moments later, she rests against my chest and I stroke my hands up and down her spine as we catch our breath.

"I missed you today," she says softly.

"I see that." I tip her chin up and touch my lips to hers. "I missed you, too."

Silently, I pick her up and carry her upstairs for round two in a nice, hot shower.

Later, we're lying in bed watching a movie in matching white tees and gray sweats, looking at the digital floor plans of our new house. A vanilla-cookie-scented candle burns from the top of the dresser. Gus and Cassie are sleeping at the foot of our bed.

I've never felt so domestic.

I've never been so happy.

"I've been thinking..." she says softly, closing the space between us to cuddle up into my side.

I put my arm around her. "Okay..."

"I don't want a wedding."

Worry whips through me. Did she change her mind about me, after all?

I clear my throat and brace myself. "You don't?"

"No. I loved our wedding day. I don't want another one."

I'm surprised. And relieved as hell. I thought all women wanted a wedding with the white dress with the veil and the long train with lots of guests and food and music.

"Babe, are you sure?" I ask. "I thought you wanted a real wedding?"

"Actually, I never wanted one until the day I was standing in front of you in the backyard. That became my dream wedding." She cranes her head up to look at me. "That *was* our real wedding. It's the only memory I want of marrying you."

She melts me.

"Ya know what? I feel the same way. That's my favorite day."

I put my iPad on the nightstand and turn back to her.

"I've been thinking about something, too."

Her eyebrow arches up inquisitively.

"I was thinking... if you want a baby someday, I'd be happy with that. If you don't, I'm okay with that, too. But if you want a baby, I promise you, I'll be a really good father. And I'll be there with you in the delivery room, all that stuff. I'll be there a thousand percent."

She swallows hard and blinks up at me. "Lucky, I—"

"And if you decide you never want a baby, I'll get a vasectomy. I don't want you to have to take birth control for half your life. But I'm leaving the choice up to you."

Leaning up, she touches her fingertip to my lips. "Shh... don't say anymore. We'll decide together someday. Right now, I just want us to focus on us." She smiles gently. "But thank you for letting me know that it's something we *can* do."

"I just want you to have a happy life. With no regrets."

She rolls over on top of me and smiles dreamily.

"You're a really good husband, Jude," she says.

I flash her my infamous smirk. "You're a fuckin' kick-ass wife."

Bringing her lips to mine, we kiss softly, and entwine our fingers. Our wedding bands clink together, and it's my favorite sound in the world.

EPILOGUE
SKYLAR

Two Years Later

Sipping a cup of tea, I sit cross-legged on the Sherpa chair in the corner of our master bedroom and watch snow flurries begin to fall from the sky. Gus jumps up to sit on the back of the chair and joins me in watching.

"There you are," Jude says, coming into the room. He pulls off his sweatshirt and throws it into the hamper.

"Were you looking to give me a strip show?" I ask with a smile as my eyes rove over his muscular arms and chest appreciatively

Grinning back, he pushes his long hair out of his face and leans down to kiss me. "You wish," he teases. "I'm putting something clean on because I'm taking you somewhere for a special surprise."

Intrigued, I watch him disappear into the walk-in closet and reappear a few seconds later wearing a black, long-sleeved shirt that hugs his wide shoulders.

My heart thumps faster just looking at him. Jude is one of

those men who gets better-looking with age, and I consider myself extremely lucky.

"Where are we going?" I ask. "Can you give me a hint?"

He takes my hand and pulls me up to my feet, wrapping his arm around my waist and drawing me in close. I go up on my toes and press my lips to his.

"You'll see when we get there," he says.

"Why do I have to wear a blindfold?" I ask after being in the car for ten minutes. "Do you not want me to see the speedometer so I can't see how fast you're driving my car?" I tease.

"I don't want you to see where we're going. It'll ruin the surprise." He reaches across the Corvette console and holds my hand. "Don't worry, we'll be there soon."

"Is it still snowing?" I ask, worried about my car, which doesn't drive well in rain or snow.

"No, it was just flurries."

"Will we be back in time to have dinner with Aunt Suzy and Uncle Al?"

"Yup."

I have no idea where he's taking me, but I'm excited and bursting with questions. The last time my husband surprised me, it was with a beautiful engagement ring and a Corvette. I have no idea how he can top that.

With a puppy, maybe.

Or a lovebird.

"Is it a puppy?" I ask excitedly.

I hear him scoff. "It's not a puppy."

"Is it a lovebird?"

"It's not a lovebird. I told you if you want a bird, go hang out with Aunt Suzy. I don't want a bird squawking and shitting sideways on the walls. Besides, Gus will eat it. Then you'll cry, and I'll feel horrible, then I'll buy you another bird, and the circle will continue. I'll go broke buying birds."

"Gus wouldn't do that," I protest. "She's a very gentle creature."

"I'd rather not take any chances."

"Are Megan and Erik involved in this surprise?" I ask, remembering how Megan helped Jude orchestrate his proposal.

"No."

I feel the car pause and then turn.

"Are we there yet?"

"Almost."

I raise his hand to my lips for a quick kiss and catch the faint scent of the Ernest Hemingway cologne I bought him for his last birthday. It instantly brings my mind back to making love with him in the tub last night, how the sexy aroma clung to his damp body. How his lips tasted like cinnamon-flavored toothpaste—his favorite. How he woke me in the middle of the night with kisses just to tell me he loves me, then we snuggled each other back to sleep.

I'm the luckiest woman in the world.

The car slows down, turns, then stops.

"We're here," he announces.

"Yay!"

I wait for him to come around and help me out of the car, then he puts his arm around me and walks us across what feels like gravel.

"I hope you're not taking me into the woods."

"No woods, I promise."

"Are we at the park?" I question.

"You're an annoying surprise recipient," he teases.

"I'm just excited to see what it is."

He stops walking and moves to stand behind me. His hands

brush across my cheeks. "I'm gonna take the blindfold off now," he says, then whispers close to my ear, "but I think I'll save it for the bedroom tonight."

"Promises, promises," I sing.

The blindfold is whisked away and suddenly I'm staring at a big gray and black—

My heart leaps wildly and I grab his arm.

"An RV?!" I squeal, looking back and forth from the huge vehicle to him. We're in the middle of what appears to be an RV parking area. "Are you *serious*?"

"I figured since we never got to take a honeymoon, and you never got your dream of taking off in an RV, it'd be cool if we hopped in this and drove off for a month? Just me and you. And the pets can come, too."

I stare at him with my mouth open, a hundred happy and nervous thoughts running through my mind. "C-can we leave the bar for a month?"

"Don't worry about that. Uncle Al's going to take care of it. Remember we promised we wouldn't let the business run our lives?"

I nod. We vowed to always make time for each other. "You're right." The bar has been successful beyond anything we could have imagined, but it's hard to disengage from working seven days a week.

My eyes are drawn back to the sleek beauty of the motor home.

"It's so pretty!" I throw my arms around him and he picks me up and spins me around. "I love it! Where will we go?"

He puts me gently back on my feet. "Anywhere you want. Or we can just drive aimlessly until we find places with the brightest stars in the sky."

That sounds like the best honeymoon ever.

"When do you think we can go? Soon?"

He winks at me. "How about two weeks from today?"

I go up on my tiptoes and wind my arms around his neck. "You're amazing," I say, staring up into his gray eyes. "I love you so much. What did I do to deserve you?"

He bows down and kisses me softly, reaching around to cup my ass in his hands and pull me close. "You vowed to love me, Sparkles. For better, for worse, for richer, for poorer, in sickness and in health. Forever. *That's* what you did."

about carian cole

Carian Cole has a passion for the bad boys, those covered in tattoos, sexy smirks, ripped jeans, fast cars, motorcycles and of course, the sweet girls who try to tame them and win their hearts.

Born and raised a Jersey girl, Carian now resides in beautiful New Hampshire with her husband and their multitude of furry pets. She spends most of her time writing, reading, and vacuuming. Carian loves to hear from readers and interacts daily on her social media accounts.

connect with carian cole

Visit Carian's Web Site:

www.cariancolewrites.com

Join Carian's Facebook Reader Group:

https://www.facebook.com/groups/CarianColeGroupies

books by carian cole

StandAlone Romance

No Tomorrow

The Lovely Return

Don't Kiss the Bride

All Torn Up Series

Torn - Book One

Tied - Book Two

Ashes & Embers Rock Star Series

Storm - Book One

Vandal - Book Two

Lukas - Book Three

Talon - Book Four

Loving Storm - Book Five

Asher - Book Six

newsletter

Sign up to receive info on upcoming books, plus fun random stuff like Carian's favorite things and a peek into her writing life.

Subscribe to Carian's Newsletter:

https://www.cariancolewrites.com/signup